Other Avon Books by
Douglas W. Clark

ALCHEMY UNLIMITED
REHEARSAL FOR A RENAISSANCE

Whirlwind Alchemy

DOUGLAS W. CLARK

AVON BOOKS • NEW YORK

WHIRLWIND ALCHEMY is an original publication of Avon Books. This work has never before appeared in book form. This work is a novel. Any similarity to actual persons or events is purely coincidental.

AVON BOOKS
A division of
The Hearst Corporation
1350 Avenue of the Americas
New York, New York 10019

First AvoNova Printing: July 1993

AVONOVA TRADEMARK REG. U.S. PAT. OFF. AND IN OTHER COUNTRIES, MARCA REGISTRADA, HECHO EN U.S.A.

Printed in the U.S.A.

RA 10 9 8 7 6 5 4 3 2 1

To Miguel de Cervantes,
one of the greatest alchemists of all time.
He took the base material of his own suffering
and transmuted it into literary gold.

Among those who contributed to the evolution of this book, I particularly want to thank the following: my wife, Sharon—friend, companion, and inspiration on the greatest of journeys; Nancy V. Berberick, writer and fellow spirit, for her encouragement throughout the writing; the members of my critique group, George Anderson, Melvin Eisenstadt, V.A.L. Lewis, and Doris Stremel, for their many insights and helpful suggestions; my editor, Chris Miller, whose keen perception and subtle touch have invariably improved my writing; my agent, Maria Carvainis, for her invaluable help in the business of writing; the Southwest Writers Workshop, for its continuing help to struggling writers; the staff and facilities of the University of New Mexico General Libraries; and finally, special thanks to Codependents Anonymous, which gave me the faith to embark upon my own quest for the Holy Grail.

Prologue

IN A VILLAGE IN LA MANCHA—THE DRIEST, MOST desolate region in Spain—there lived an aging gentleman named Corwyn who devoted his considerable idle time to reading books of alchemy, and with such ardor that he entirely abandoned the management of his rightful affairs. To such a pitch did his infatuations go that he sold his belongings to buy yet more alchemical texts, seeking out all of them he could find.

Eventually, he became so absorbed in his books that he spent his nights from sunset to sunrise poring over them, and his days from dawn to dark performing the experiments they described; and what with little sleep and much reading and the breathing of so many noxious fumes, his brain shriveled up and he lost his wits. His imagination was stuffed with all he read about calcinations, fermentations, distillations, and similar sorts of nonsense. The idea became so firmly planted in his mind that the fancies he read about and attempted to perform were true, that to him no study in the world was better substantiated.

In a word, his wits being quite gone, this Corwyn hit upon the strangest notion that ever a madman in this world conceived. Being from so arid a region, he decided that the noblest of all elements was not gold,

1

but water, and that the highest goal to which he as an alchemist could dedicate himself was to restoring that element from any taint of corruption. He furthermore determined that it was right and proper, no less for his own renown than in the service of greater financial reward, that he should make an alchemist-errant of himself, proclaiming himself a "don" and roaming the world in full alchemical apparel, hiring himself out for the transformation of polluted waters everywhere. He would put into practice all that he had read of as being the usual pursuits of alchemists: purifying that which was corrupt, turning base things into noble, and reaping eternal fame and glory (not to mention profit) for his efforts.

And so, carried away by the anticipation he found in these fantasies, he began at once to put his scheme into execution. . . .

—Cid Hamete Benengeli,
  El Ingenioso Alquimista
  Don Corwyn de La Mancha, Part I

THE
FIRST SALLY

Chapter 1

Which deals with the pleasant conversation Corwyn the alchemist had with his apprentice upon discovering he'd been made the subject of a book.

NINETY LEAGUES FROM LA MANCHA, IN FRANCE rather than Spain, Corwyn was returning to the town of Pomme de Terre where he really lived, unaware of the fame that had descended upon him.

His donkey, *Roche-naissante* (so named because in color as well as temperament she was one with the bones of the earth, as drab and enduring as any stone), plodded wearily under its double burden of plump alchemist and full sample bottles. Corwyn regretted adding his own weight to the bottles the donkey already carried, but the day's trek up from the plains into the foothills of the Pyrenees had left him too tired to walk. He sweated under the great cloak he'd worn against the anticipated chill of the mountains, for the summer had turned unusually hot, even for southern France. Corwyn wiped his bushy white eyebrows and told himself he was too old for this kind of work. He could feel the weight of every one of his eleven hundred years. This work called for a younger man.

And he had just the man in mind, he added to himself, thinking of his apprentice, Sebastian.

Of course, Corwyn had been accompanied on this journey by Oliver, his assistant and longtime companion, but Oliver didn't count. The two of them together couldn't make up for one strong back and vigorous body.

For the past two weeks, Corwyn and Oliver had traveled an extended circuit, sampling the waters of the region. Their journey had started in the watershed high amid the peaks overlooking the town, then had gone northeast in the direction of Toulouse. Once well out on the plains, they had turned west, ending a couple of days ago at Lourdes, where reports about the local waters had been particularly intriguing. Now, returning to Pomme de Terre, Oliver rode at Corwyn's back, too light to matter and dressed like a monk to hide his true form.

The church bells began to ring as if in greeting when the alchemist entered the town. To Corwyn's surprise, his fellow citizens spilled into the streets to welcome him, apparently having awaited his arrival. People cheered and laughed and called him by name. Oliver, ever shy of strangers, clung to Corwyn with thin, rigid fingers. Several boys, usually known for their mischief, strewed fresh pine boughs in the path of *Roche-naissante*. Corwyn smiled, pleased that the bishop's influence against him was finally waning. "Here he is, *Don* Corwyn—the prophet of alchemy!" one boy shouted, and this hosanna was quickly taken up by others.

The use of the Spanish honorific *don* puzzled Corwyn, and something about the boy's cry sounded like a jeer rather than acclamation. The laughter of the crowd, too, was a trifle disturbing. Still, Corwyn told himself, the important thing was the renown he was receiving at last as a result of his alchemy. Even as fire can't be hidden, so true virtue couldn't go forever unrecognized. And the virtue of alchemy surpassed all others.

"Master Corwyn!" one voice called suddenly above the noise. "The devil take you and this idle crowd. Silence them and send them home, for you're nothing but a madman who makes fools of us all."

For a moment, the townspeople fell silent. In the void, the stones of the mountains threw back the echoes of their cries. "Get along with you," a nobleman from the duchess's court answered after a moment. "We're no fools. Go away and don't meddle where you're not wanted."

Growls of agreement sounded from the throng.

The man threw up his hands. "*Pardieu*! To advise this poor madman is to swim against the current. I only say that it distresses me to see good effort wasted on his alchemy. But bad luck be mine if I ever offer advice to any man again, even if he asks me for it."

He turned away, shaking his head, and Corwyn rode on, *Roche-naissante* picking her way slowly through the press of the shouting crowd. Despite the enthusiasm around him, it troubled Corwyn to hear that there were still doubters living in the darkness of their disbelief, when he wanted only to bring enlightenment into the world.

There was another factor weighing on Corwyn's thoughts and dampening his spirits, though he wasn't yet aware of it. For here on the eve of that great renewal which would eventually be called the Renaissance, the old alchemist had just entered a much more personal time of trial known as a Middle Ages crisis.

When he reached his shop and the dim, silent interior of his laboratory, shielded from the outer world by ancient walls several feet thick, new concerns soon occupied Corwyn's mind. The water samples he'd collected needed to be made ready for alchemical analysis right away, and Corwyn was anxious to turn them over to Sebastian for this tedious task. But the laboratory was in disarray. Dirty glassware littered the room, the fire in the analytical furnace had gone out, reagents lay untended on the tables, and that lazy, worthless, incompetent son of a nobleman, Sebastian, was nowhere to be found. Here the citizens of Pomme de Terre had finally welcomed Corwyn in proper style, and Corwyn's own apprentice wasn't there to witness it. To make matters worse, Oliver had scampered off as soon as he and Corwyn reached the laboratory, leaving Corwyn to do all the work.

Muttering angrily, Corwyn set up the breath of demons test—one of the procedures he'd developed for determining whether a body of water had become corrupted. He filled matching pairs of bottles with water taken from each sample location, then placed a couple of minnows in one bottle from each pair. Then he sealed both sets of bottles.

At first, the minnows swam vigorously in their respective vessels. Eventually, however, they began to languish, flopping spasmodically as the air in the samples ran out. Corwyn watched how long it took for each set of minnows to die and wrote the times down in a large book. This done, he took the matching set of bottles to the incubatorium, where they would be immersed for five days in flowing water. At the end of that time, the seals would be broken and the part of the test with the minnows would be repeated using this second set of bottles.

The results would tell Corwyn whether the water sources from which the samples had been taken had become contaminated by malevolent demons, making the waters unfit for ordinary use.

Setting up the breath of demons test went smoothly, except for one sample. Corwyn wasn't sure afterward whether fatigue caused him to doze off during the procedure so that he was unaware of the passing time, or whether a pair of minnows actually died immediately after being placed in one of the bottles. He shook his head to clear the fog that had descended upon him and checked his notes for the source of the sample in that particular bottle. The hairs on the nape of his neck rose as he realized it was the only sample he hadn't collected himself. Instead, it had been given to him by a crazed hermit who lived in the mountains above Pomme de Terre.

Once upon a time, the hermit had been the duchess's physician and personal advisor, Dr. Tox, before greed entangled him in a plot against the duchy. When Dr. Tox double-crossed his new master and got caught, the penalty had been demonic possession. Although the demons had since been exorcised by the Inquisition, the experience had left him permanently deranged. Now he thought himself some kind of prophet, living in the wilderness on grubs and berries and warning anyone who would listen of a terrible doom about to befall the duchy. Corwyn had accepted the sample from Dr. Tox merely to placate him, for the madman smelled unmercifully and wouldn't leave the area until Corwyn took the sample.

Yet if the minnows introduced into Dr. Tox's sample had indeed died immediately, this suggested contamination of the most virulent sort. Corwyn ran a hand over his face, trying to think. He considered opening the second bottle of this sample and putting another pair of minnows in it right away, instead of incubating the bottle for five days first. But if he used the second bottle now, there wouldn't be enough sample left for a third and he wouldn't be able to complete the test at the end of that time. At last, Corwyn concluded it was more likely that he had erred than that the sample actually contained malevolent demons, and he decided to complete the test as planned. He would estimate times of death for the initial pair of minnows based on the results from the other samples. If there was a problem with Dr. Tox's sample, it would show up after incubation. Besides, he told himself as he placed the bottle in question into the incubation trough with the others, a sample collected by an untrained person was of questionable validity at best, and cast doubt on the results determined by any test.

Sebastian still hadn't returned, so Corwyn headed wearily back to the main laboratory. There he lighted a candle and began adding oil of vitriol to a small amount of sample in a retort, preparing to heat the mixture for an alchemical destruction test. He held the retort in one hand and carefully poured the thick, caustic reagent from a flask with the other, trying to keep his hands from trembling with fatigue.

The alchemical destruction test would provide further

evidence of any contamination in the water. Although it didn't take into account the interplay among the various creatures present, it was quicker than the breath of demons test, and the results from the two procedures were complementary.

Suddenly, something outside thudded against the laboratory door, and the alchemist glanced up, anticipating Sebastian's arrival. But the door remained closed, leaving Corwyn still without an outlet for his anger.

During this lapse in his attention, something dribbled onto Corwyn's hand. He looked down to find he was spilling oil of vitriol over the sides of the retort. The acid burned him, and he jerked his hand away in surprise, dropping the retort. The glass vessel hit the table and shattered. The contents spread across the surface, the liquid bubbling as it flowed, scorching everything in its path.

Corwyn set the flask with the remaining oil of vitriol aside and quickly wiped his hand with a rag. Then he began daubing at the spill. There was another sound at the door, as if someone whose hands were full was trying to kick it open. But Corwyn was too busy to investigate, especially when his elbow bumped the lighted candle. The candle, still burning, slowly toppled onto a stack of ancient parchment sheets, the text of which described the procedure Corwyn had been following. Melted wax dripped onto the sheets, quickly followed by a tongue of flame. Corwyn gasped and snatched the burning pages. He beat out the fire, then moved the sheets to safety at the far end of the table.

He was returning to the spill and the upended candle when Sebastian finally flung the door open and stumbled into the room, carrying a large, squarish object. A breeze off the Pyrenees hurried in with him, stirring up the laboratory air and blowing the parchment sheets from the table. With a cry, Corwyn lunged under the table after the pages as they drifted toward a puddle where the oil of vitriol was dripping onto the floor.

From beneath the table, he heard Sebastian scurrying over to help, his footsteps heavier than usual. Just as

Corwyn grabbed the sheets, rescuing them from certain destruction, Sebastian's foot crunched down on the broken neck of the retort. Sebastian yelped and slammed the object he was carrying onto the tabletop above Corwyn. The alchemist jumped at the noise, hitting his head on the underside of the table and knocking off his black, conical hat. The parchment sheets slipped from his stunned grasp and settled to the floor directly in the path of the dripping acid.

"Bon dieu! Sebastian, what do you mean by bursting in here like that?" Corwyn demanded, clutching his hat before it, too, landed in the puddle. He scowled at the floor, where the parchment pages were blackening from contact with the fluid. A wisp of acrid smoke rose from the charred, sodden mass. Then he looked at his apprentice, who was hopping on one foot and holding the other with both hands. "Haven't you any manners? And where were you when I got back from Lourdes? It looks like you haven't done any work around here for days."

"Master, thank god you're back," Sebastian gasped. "You've got to see this." He approached the table, stepping gingerly on his injured foot, and tapped a massive, leather-bound volume—evidently the object he'd been carrying. Even in his hunched position, Sebastian towered over Corwyn. But then, the alchemist added to himself, so did just about everyone.

"This book's been the talk of the town for almost a fortnight," Sebastian went on. "I finally managed to get a copy of this new deluxe edition. The smaller, cheaper editions are all sold out. You won't believe it, master— some Spaniard's written about you and everything that happened two years ago, when I first came to be your apprentice."

"Vraiment?" Corwyn smiled, the debris around him fading into insignificance as he read the title on the gold-embossed, lacquered cover. *El Ingenioso Alquimista Don Corwyn de La Mancha.* He touched the book reverently, then hefted it, pleased by its weight. Obviously the author had seen fit to treat his subject in depth. The vague concerns which had begun to trouble him

in recent days quickly disappeared. "Well, well, what do you know? And about time, I must say!"

"That's not all you'll say, once you read it," Sebastian muttered darkly. "Master, apparently the author mentions things in this book that happened in private. How could he have learned of them? And so quickly, too!"

"What do you mean, 'apparently'? Don't you know what he says?" When Sebastian didn't answer, Corwyn felt his eyebrows rise. "Are you telling me the whole town's talking about this book, that it's been written about me, and you haven't read it yet?"

Sebastian reddened. "You know I can't read Spanish. I have enough trouble with French."

"Oh, of course. I'm sorry, Sebastian. I forgot."

Although born in the duchy, Sebastian had been raised in the traditions of his Saxon grandfather, who had arrived in France under Edward the Black Prince and had been awarded a title and lands here for his service. Sebastian had become Corwyn's apprentice only after his family had lost this inheritance and been stricken from the rolls of the nobility.

Corwyn quickly changed the subject. "I suppose the author must be some sage enchanter, to have divined whatever it is he's written about me."

"I don't know about his being an enchanter," Sebastian grumbled, "but his name's on the title page, if that's any help."

Corwyn opened the book to the first page, noting with disappointment that the text had been printed on ordinary paper with the new, movable type, rather than having been hand-copied onto more expensive parchment. In the short time since its introduction in Germany, movable type had already revolutionized the nature of the books that were being published, leading to a sharp increase in the number of cheap, preposterous romances. It annoyed Corwyn that his history might be mistaken for one of those.

"Hmmm, Cid Hamete Benengeli," he read, scanning the page. "A Moorish name. 'Cid' means 'Lord' in Arabic. I suppose that explains the honorific 'don' he added to my name. Arabic writing tends to be rather flowery." He smiled to himself, realizing that was why the crowd outside had been calling him *"Don* Corwyn." Then he frowned. "I wonder why he claims I'm from La Mancha? Maybe he's trying to honor his own region by linking it with me."

Sebastian hesitated before answering. "Maybe. Although it's more likely he was just protecting the reputation of Pomme de Terre."

Corwyn had closed the book again to admire its tooled leather cover rather than look at the relatively inferior quality of its printed pages. Now he forced his gaze away from the book and up to the face of his apprentice, wondering at the latter's grudging response. He realized with surprise that Sebastian must be jealous of the honor Corwyn was receiving, which bothered the alchemist, for he'd thought his apprentice above such pettiness.

As for himself, Corwyn could hardly believe such a book existed—and so soon after the exploits related in it had occurred, too. But he had no doubt that since the book was about himself and aquatic alchemy, it must be grandiloquent and lofty. "Sebastian, nothing could grant me as much pleasure as this," he explained, giving the book an affectionate pat. "It's the ultimate reward of my career to find myself in print within my own lifetime, my achievements and good name made familiar to people everywhere."

"Peut-être," Sebastian said, peering at the soot-stained arches overhead. "But you know how it is when someone publishes a book, master. No matter how many people like it, the author can't please everyone." At that, he stared down at Corwyn.

Feeling flustered, Corwyn glanced away and realized his fingers had been idly tracing the embossed letters of his name. He pulled his hand away with a stern, disapproving frown. "Yet this one, which is about me, has evidently pleased quite a few."

"Oh, that it has. In fact, I think you could safely say this Sid Helmet Vermicelli has produced a work sure to entertain all mankind."

"You really think so?" Corwyn asked, awed despite himself.

"*Oui!* Why, there must be at least twelve hundred copies of the Spanish version in print alone, with reports that it is soon to be published in France, England, and Italy as well. I doubt there's a single nation into whose tongue it won't be translated. The copies here in town are already dog-eared with use, and those most eager to read it are your own students. A person can't set a copy down anywhere within the walls of the Academy of Alchemical and Renaissance Arts without several students rushing over to grab it, while others beg to read it next. There are even hints in the first book that the author is planning a second, although no one seems to know for certain. Some people say there shouldn't be another one, that sequels are never as good as the first volume, and that besides, one book about 'Don Corwyn' is too much already. Others, however, cry out for more. For myself, I'll wager the author turns out another volume as quickly as he can, more eager for the profit than for any kind of praise."

"Profit?" Corwyn mumbled, realizing for the first time that someone else might be making money from his life story. He shook his head to dispel a wave of envy, assuring himself that fame would bring its own reward in time. "As long as he doesn't hurry too quickly. Work that's done in haste is never as good as it ought to be."

"If you're afraid he might leave something out, don't worry. This Sid fellow is very thorough, leaving nothing in the inkwell unsaid. Why, he even tells about the time I fought the Black Knight's empty suit of armor and lost."

"You mean he included you in this history as well?" Corwyn asked, disgruntled.

"Oh, yes, I'm mentioned too. And by my own name, more's the pity. I'm said to be the second most important person in it. Some readers even seem to think my parts are the best in the book."

"Well, all true histories contain both ups and downs," Corwyn said, comforting himself with the thought that at least Sebastian's role that summer had consisted mostly of the latter. "They can't be full of only fortunate incidents."

Sebastian looked at Corwyn strangely. "Some readers say they'd have preferred for the author not to have dwelt so much on the many times when your attempts at alchemy failed. But I suppose you're right. That's where the truth of the story comes in."

"Humph! Cid Hamete might in all fairness have kept quiet about those," Corwyn grumbled. "He could have written more as a poet and less as a historian without affecting the essential truth of the matter." He stirred uncomfortably. "But tell me, Sebastian, what are people in town saying about me now that they've all heard about this?"

"Promise you won't get angry?"

"Of course I won't get angry," Corwyn snapped. "Quit beating about the bush and tell me."

"Very well . . . They say you're a madman and I'm a fool."

"Huh? Why would they think me mad?"

Sebastian was staring at the table, again avoiding his master's eyes. Corwyn followed the direction of his gaze and became aware for the first time of the extent of the mess he'd made of the table and floor. With a sweep of his arm, he tried to clear the top of the table, but succeeded only in jabbing himself with a piece of broken glass and smearing debris over a wider area. The sleeve of his robe smoked and shriveled where it touched the acid. Corwyn frowned at it, feeling that the cloth had let him down. He resumed talking, his words muffled as he sucked his punctured finger. "I admit, a few of my efforts that summer went astray, but what about my successes? Which of my exploits are most highly praised in this history?"

"Praised?" Again Sebastian eyed him with a guarded look. "I guess I'd have to say that opinion on this varies. Some prefer your battle with the windmills."

"My battle with the windmills? What batt—"

"Others prefer the part where you tried to domesticate

demons by breeding them in bottles of water," Sebastian continued as if he hadn't heard.

"Domesticate demons?" Corwyn cried. "Preposterous! It makes it sound like I was raising pets!"

"And then there are those who claim the best part is where you tried to manufacture dragon farts, making the mines outside town uninhabitable and putting the poor miners out of work."

"Sebastian, what are you talking about? I never put any miners out of work. And as for the so-called dragon . . . er, flatulence, you know what that was about." He squinted at his apprentice. "Are you telling me that the author of my history wasn't any sage, but some idle chatterer who couldn't get his facts straight?"

Sebastian slowly shook his head. "Master, I don't think you've grasped the full significance of what's happened yet. The greatest fault with this 'history' isn't that the author got a few details wrong here and there, but that most of the book has nothing to do with events as they really happened. That Sid son of a bitch mixed up everything."

Corwyn's eyebrows rose. "As bad as that?"

Sebastian nodded, then reached over and flipped open the book at random. "Look for yourself."

Reluctantly, Corwyn began reading the words before him, his eyes widening as he proceeded down the page.

So addled had Don Corwyn's brains become that he fancied himself extremely old, or perhaps imagined the world younger than it was, so that he believed he had formerly lived in a golden age, now lost to antiquity. At any rate, in a village near his own, so the story goes, there lived a very pretty farm-girl named Aldonza Lorenzo. In his madness, Don Corwyn decided that this village was really the famed city of Alexandria, and that the farm-girl was actually Hypatia, the last head of that city's great library. He had seen this Aldonza once or twice, or perhaps had only heard of her, and he praised her sweetness and gentle disposition so

constantly that the epithet dulce *seemed perma-*
nently affixed to her name. So extravagantly did he
speak of her that she became known as La Dulce
Mia del Toboso by her fellow citizens (for their
village was called El Toboso), and she was the
object of much scorn and derision among them.
Don Corwyn, however, heedless of the distress his
misplaced affections caused the unfortunate girl,
sighed her name frequently and thought her his
beloved Hypatia, commending himself to her in
moments of adversity. . . .

Corwyn grabbed up the book and shook it, too blinded
with fury to read any further. The sense of ennui which
had begun to infect him recently now returned in greater force. Who did this author think he was, to treat
with contempt what Corwyn felt for Hypatia, one of
the greatest women ever to have graced the world? "Of
all the . . . the . . ." At last, unable to find words scornful
enough, he raised the book, intending to slam it down
on the laboratory table.

"Master, watch out!" Sebastian cried, just as Corwyn
realized he'd been about to fling the book into the shattered remains of the alchemical destruction test. At the
last instant, Corwyn swung toward his apprentice, arms
outstretched as if offering him the volume. Sebastian, in
the midst of a desperate leap to save the book, collided
with it and knocked it from Corwyn's grasp. The book
crashed to the table, smashing the flask with the remaining oil of vitriol and making the shards of broken retort
tremble.

For a moment, Corwyn and Sebastian watched in
silence as the back cover began to hiss and char from
the acid. "*Quelle salaud!*" Sebastian murmured at last,
breaking the spell.

Corwyn spun on him. "What do you mean, calling me
a dirty louse?"

"Huh? What are you talking about? All I said was,
'what a mess.' "

Corwyn sighed, turning back to the book. "*Quelle*

salade, Sebastian. Not *quelle salaud*."

"If you start correcting my vocabulary," Sebastian grumbled, "we won't be through in this life."

Corwyn let the matter drop and wrinkled his nose against the stink of wet, burning leather. He felt anguished at seeing the book—any book—destroyed. Then he thought about the lies this particular work contained. "Good riddance!" he muttered. "Nothing but fabrications, anyway."

Sebastian nodded. "The author couldn't have done your reputation more harm if he'd set out to destroy it. He changes one thing into another, mingling a thousand lies with a single truth, and alters the order of events so that nothing remains faithful to history. These aren't exploits he's relating, but misfortunes. Why, according to him, you had to be carried home from the mines laid across the back of your donkey, having been beaten senseless by angry miners after attempting to battle a host of imaginary demons. I tell you, he's nothing but a spineless coward, with the blood of a cabbage in his veins."

Corwyn thumped the table with the back of his hand, then winced. "Why, the scheming liar!" He scowled at the smoking book, hoping the acid would consume the entire wretched volume. "And it's 'the blood of a turnip,' Sebastian, not 'cabbage.' "

"Master, there's something else I think you should know," Sebastian said slowly, ignoring the correction.

"What?"

"As a result of this book, several students have been withdrawn from your school by their parents."

"What!"

"And the two Italian schoolmasters quit this morning," Sebastian added in a rush.

"The Italians!" Corwyn exploded. "But they were the school's only other faculty!" He cursed Cid Hamete's forebears back several generations, then threw in a few imprecations against book printers and sellers in general. "Let's find Oliver and get him started cleaning up this mess while you and I go over to the academy and see just how bad things there are," he said after he'd calmed down a bit. "After which, I have half a mind to cross over into Spain myself and petition the king of Aragon to stop publication of this nonsense."

He cast a final glance at the table, gratified to see that the book was continuing to disintegrate, then led the way from the room to look for Oliver.

Entremés

DESIRING AS HE DID TO MIMIC EVERY DETAIL OF THE stories about famous alchemists he had read, Don Corwyn decided he must provide himself with an enchanted staff or scepter. He found an old, discarded broom with a branched pole, then spent many fruitless nights in a vain effort to charge or enchant it with magic. Satisfied at last by only partial success, Don Corwyn resolved to name this misshapen implement, for he had read that it was traditional among the great alchemists to always christen their equipment. In the end, he settled upon either Al-Aver *or* El Aver *as a name, although the archives of Argamasilla are not altogether clear on this point. The resulting ambiguity as to the exact article he used creates a regrettable lapse in the otherwise unblemished authority of the archives, for the correct term is a matter of some significance. If the name actually was* Al-Aver, *as some contend, the Arabic article* al *would suggest that the name derived from the Moorish word* 'awāriyah, *meaning "damaged merchandise," which in turn gave rise to the Spanish word* averia, *for "breakdown" or "failure." Such an Arabic origin would thus indicate that Don Corwyn was aware of the faulty nature of his enchanted staff and his own failure properly to direct the thaumaturgical flux used in its creation. If, however,* El Aver *is the correct name, as others argue, and the article is the Spanish* el, *then a possible Latin origin is suggested in the form of* avere, *"to covet," which led to the Spanish root form* avar- *for words having to do with avariciousness. Such a Latin derivation would therefore indicate that Don Corwyn was aware of his staff's acquisitive nature, which will be more fully revealed in an upcoming account of the ingenious alchemist's Italian adventures. It is to be hoped that the matter of the correct article—and thus the true origin of the name—will eventually be resolved through continued scholarship and research on the part of the members of the illustrious Academy of Argamasilla. . . .*

   —Cid Hamete Benengeli,
     *El Ingenioso Alquimista
     Don Corwyn de La Mancha,* Part I

Chapter 2

**In which we meet the real *Al-Aver,* and learn
of the restful way in which Corwyn passed the
night.**

CORWYN, HIS COMPOSURE TAXED, LED SEBASTIAN FROM
room to room through the rambling structure which
housed the laboratory, growing more irritable at every
step. They finally found Oliver in the stable, holding
court over the animals from an old feed trough.

It was, Corwyn reflected, where they should have
looked for the little creature first, knowing he would be
drawn there as surely as if his polestar hung overhead,
marking the spot.

Oliver had abandoned his monk disguise as soon as
he'd reached the safety of the alchemist's shop, and he
now reclined with regal dignity on a makeshift bed of
straw, his spindly form revealed. Originally a common
broom, his straw base parted into two tufts which formed
his legs. The pole, handle, or was both body and head,
while a pair of branching arms sprouted from where
shoulders would have been on an ordinary person. The
branches ended in the clusters of thin twigs that were
his fingers.

The animals pressed around their erstwhile manger, waiting patiently while Oliver petted and fussed over each in turn.

For a moment, the two mages—master and apprentice—hesitated at the entrance to the stable, reluctant to intrude. Then Corwyn bustled in, told Oliver about the mess in the laboratory, and sent the broom to clean it up.

Oliver scuttled off to do as he was told, his straw tufts swirling up dust in his wake. When he'd gone, Corwyn turned to Sebastian. "I suppose we should go over to the school now," he said reluctantly. He thought of his arrival in town a couple of hours earlier, seeing it in a new light, realizing that he'd been greeted like some favored fool. He might as well have worn a placard on his back to proclaim his idiocy. Then he shuddered at the thought of having to face the young hellions in his school without the two Italian schoolmasters to administer discipline.

"It would be best to get on over there," Sebastian agreed, sounding more certain than his master. "At the rate things there are going, we'll soon be broke—without a cabbage, as they say."

"Without a radish," Corwyn corrected with a sigh.

Having previously tasted the bitter aftertaste of the *chou*, or cabbage, which was standard fare in many French expressions, Sebastian now thought himself that vegetable's master. But although the cabbage formed a staple of the French verbal diet, it wasn't the only food for which they showed a fondness, and Sebastian often transplanted the lowly *chou* into many another crop's furrow.

Sebastian scowled at his master. "I've asked you before not to correct my words, but to simply tell me when you don't understand what I mean. Otherwise, please occupy yourself with your own cabbages."

"I don't understand you, Sebastian," Corwyn replied. "What do you mean, 'occupy myself with my own cabbages'?"

"You know—mind your own business. It's a common expression."

"Ah, now I understand. Occupy myself with my own onions!"

"Oh, all right, onions," Sebastian muttered. "*C'est chou comme.*"

"You mean *c'est tout comme*—'it's all the same.' Except it isn't, not the way you say things." He paused, then added, "Honestly, if I were a cobbler, you'd soon put me out of work. You're the biggest *chou*-maker around."

Sebastian's scowl deepened. "You understood what I meant from the beginning, didn't you? You just wanted to confuse me so you could hear me make more blunders."

Corwyn shrugged noncommittally, suppressing a smile.

"Sometimes I think you enjoy making me look as stupid as a cabbage. And this time I know I have the right expression!"

"For once, Sebastian, I must agree." Before Sebastian could respond, Corwyn went to check on *Roche-naissante* as a pretext for further delaying his visit to the school. But Oliver had fed and curried the donkey as soon as they'd returned from the sampling expedition. The other animals—a pig, a milk goat, and a handful of chickens—had also been cared for. There was nothing here to detain the alchemist any longer.

"Let's make sure Oliver's doing what I told him to," Corwyn suggested, this new excuse sounding thin in his own ears. Sebastian's eyebrows lifted, but if he found his master's reluctance odd, he was prudent enough to avoid mentioning it.

When they reached the laboratory, they discovered Oliver perched on a stool at the table, the debris around him forgotten as he sat with his tuft legs tucked under him and his stalk body leaning over Cid Hamete's book. At Corwyn's arrival, Oliver looked up and pointed to the book, then at Corwyn.

"*Oui*," Corwyn snorted. "It's about me. At least, it purports to be."

Shyly, the broom turned his twig finger to point to himself.

Corwyn nodded, his manner softening. "Yes, Oliver, you're in there too."

The broom brushed dry fingertips reverently over the book, then hopped off the stool and began strutting about the room. Corwyn snorted again, seeing a reflection of himself in the broom's behavior. He strode to a side door which had been added to the laboratory the year before, then paused, his arm reaching for the handle. "I don't see how you could let the faculty quit without even giving notice," he complained to Sebastian. "That doesn't sound like the proper way to run my school in my absence."

"You didn't actually put me in charge when you left," Sebastian snapped.

There was an awkward silence. Corwyn pursed his lips, aware that Sebastian wanted an explanation, perhaps even an apology. And maybe he deserved to know the reason why he hadn't been placed in charge, although Corwyn felt in no mood to argue about Sebastian's ability to administer the school. The boy simply wasn't ready to handle that kind of responsibility. Corwyn opened the door a crack and peered into the bright afternoon sunshine that filled the small courtyard separating the school from the main laboratory. "Well, it's getting late," he said. "I don't suppose there's really much we can do until tomorrow."

"Late?" Sebastian didn't sound convinced. "Well, perhaps." After a moment, he added, "I should tell you, the cook and the housemaster also left this morning."

Corwyn took advantage of this to slam the door shut before turning. "*Dites donc*! Is there anything else you haven't told me?"

Sebastian frowned as he considered this. "I don't think so. But don't worry, everything's taken care of. Gwen's doing the cooking until we find a replacement, so the remaining students won't go hungry. And she and I'll stay at the school tonight so they won't be without supervision."

"Hrmph!" Corwyn grunted. "Keeping an eye on that bunch is a lot for a man to ask of his wife, especially when she's seven months pregnant. Still," he went on quickly, "I suppose you were doing the best you could, under the circumstances. Right now, however, you'd better get back over there." He opened the door again and pushed his apprentice into the courtyard between the two buildings. "Gwen shouldn't be left alone to deal with those delinquents. Not in her condition."

Sebastian peered over his shoulder with bewilderment as Corwyn started to close the door from the inside. "But, master, aren't you coming?"

"You go ahead," Corwyn said, shuddering again at the thought. The students undoubtedly knew of his reception by the townsfolk earlier in the day, and had probably participated in his humiliation. Corwyn couldn't endure the thought of facing them now. "I'll be over first thing in the morning." Anxious to be alone while he sorted out the tangled skein of his thoughts, he shut the door and latched it before Sebastian could object.

Oliver was cleaning up the wreckage from the ruined experiment, so Corwyn, arming himself with an oil lamp, padded down the corridor in search of solitude. Out of habit, he wandered to the incubatorium, where he often went to think. It was cool and damp inside the tiny room, and the lamp cast flickering shadows on the walls. Corwyn set the lamp on a small worktable and crossed to a stone trough at the far end of the chamber. He sat on the edge of the trough and studied the water that gurgled and sighed as it swept by, dark and secret in the uncertain light. The water came from a nearby tributary of the River Ale, rechanneled to flow through the room. Corwyn reached under the surface, felt around for the smooth, hard form of one of the bottles he had deposited there, and fished it out.

The wet glass glinted feebly, giving little hint of the great mystery taking place inside. Yet this bottle, unimportant though it seemed, represented the crowning achievement of a lifetime devoted to alchemy. Inside, invisible forces carried out the endless struggle between darkness and light, good and evil, life and death, for this bottle was one of the vessels which housed Corwyn's breath of demons test.

Long ago, Corwyn had concluded that all waters contain relatively harmless, invisible sprites and nymphs which, along with the fishes and other creatures that could be seen, consumed the life breath or *pneuma* infused in the water. Because these sprites and nymphs— these lesser demons—didn't consume large quantities of *pneuma*, they and other living creatures could inhabit a given body of water at the same time. Some demons, however, were more powerful and greedy, devouring any *pneuma* present at the expense of other life. Eventually, such powerful demons would befoul any water in which they occurred and render it unsuitable for normal use. But Corwyn's breath of demons test enabled him to detect their presence before that happened.

The difference between the time it took a pair of minnows to asphyxiate and die in a sample of water on the first day of the test, and the time it took them to do so on the fifth, told him how much of the *pneuma* originally present in the water had been consumed during incubation. From this, he could determine how potent the demons in the sample were. If they were too powerful, he could have the body of water they'd come from exorcised to restore it to its rightful state.

Ordinarily, the subtleties of this test—the unseen complexity of its interactions, which appeared simple only to the uninitiated—brought great satisfaction to Corwyn. He could stare into the depths of one of these bottles during incubation and feel he was peering into the very soul of aquatic alchemy.

Today, however, the bottle in his hand seemed only a cold glass container, dripping wet on the outside and holding nothing but more water within. He recalled what (according to Sebastian) Cid Hamete had said about the test.

Breeding domesticated demons, indeed!

Corwyn replaced the bottle in the trough, groaned, and got to his feet. Feeling at a loss, he ambled to the library he had established in conjunction with the school. Here, he had assembled more than a thousand volumes, ranging from works by contemporary authors such as Dante and Chaucer, to almost forgotten works from antiquity, some of them exceedingly rare. Corwyn took pride in the fact that his was a very eclectic library, including religious and popular books as well as technical treatises on alchemy. He even had a shelf of books just for his students, with pages missing or rearranged on purpose to challenge them. By modern standards, the library was an impressive collection, although in Corwyn's mind it always paled in comparison to the library of Alexandria, in which he had first been introduced to the search for knowledge.

Normally, Corwyn felt a profound sense of peace simply from being in the presence of so much learning. Books had been among his few close companions throughout long centuries of wandering. Today, however, a new thought poisoned his contentment, for according to what Sebastian claimed, more copies of *El Ingenioso Alquimista Don Corwyn de La Mancha* had already been published than there were books in this room, with no sign that the demand for Cid Hamete's book had waned. Far from it, for *Don Corwyn* was even now being translated into other languages. In time, production of this one foolish book could rival in number all the texts originally held in the entire library of Alexandria.

It was, Corwyn thought, a sad commentary on the decline of learning in the modern world.

Thoroughly discouraged, Corwyn headed back to the main laboratory, where Oliver had finished cleaning up the mess. The broom had left Cid Hamete's book on the table, however, where the oil of vitriol it had soaked up earlier continued eating away its pages. In time, the entire text would be destroyed.

With a sense of foreboding, Corwyn drew up a stool and began to read, pausing once in a while to storm around the room, swearing at the book's absent author. At one point, he slammed the volume shut in disgust, determined to have nothing more to do with it. Cid Hamete made Corwyn sound like an addle-brained Parcival, searching for an alchemical version of the Holy Grail.

To his surprise, Corwyn discovered that daylight had given way to night hours ago. He was exhausted and famished. He fixed a little dinner for himself, some bread and sausage, cutting off the moldier parts of each. Then he took down the earthenware pot that contained his most valued possession—dark, aromatic beans smuggled from Arabia, where the penalty for selling them to foreigners was death. As he measured out a portion and began grinding them with mortar and pestle, Corwyn thought wryly that these beans perhaps came closest of anything he'd found to embodying the elusive Philosopher's Stone—the *lapis philosophorum*—of alchemy. Not that they could turn lead into gold, or polluted water into pure. Nor did they cure any disease. But as for offering eternal youth—well, they certainly made Corwyn feel younger and more energetic again, especially when like tonight, he suffered from fatigue.

He poured boiling water through the crushed beans, supporting the powder in a cloth filter over a crude pottery cup. Then he added a dollop of honey to the resulting elixir, having developed a taste for drinking it this way since Sebastian's arrival. Unfortunately, there wasn't any fresh cream in the shop.

Corwyn held the hot cup as gently as if it really were the Holy Grail, filled (as Cid Hamete claimed) with the ultimate alchemical elixir. He sipped the sweet, black liquid and grimaced at its strength. After a lifetime devoted to alchemy, he wondered, would these be the only accomplishments to show for his work—*kawphy*, a library, and the breath of demons test? He chuckled humorlessly. The obscure herb wasn't even his own discovery, for he'd learned of its properties long ago from a nomad, in return for saving the old man's life. And the library was but a dim reflection of the one in

Alexandria that Corwyn had known in his youth.

Was the breath of demons test by itself, then, enough to justify his life?

After finishing the elixir, Corwyn took off his outer robes, readying himself for bed. Instead, however, he returned to Cid Hamete's book, having known he would when he first prepared the draught. Now that he had drunk it, there would be no sleep for him tonight. This time he read almost to the end of the book, where the pages were blackened and crumbling from the absorbed reagent and he couldn't read any farther.

The book was a hideous tentacled thing, a literary chimera made up of multitudinous limbs lacking in proportion and disconnected from the unifying body of a central plot. The style of the writing was brittle, the adventures were preposterous, the dialogue absurd, and the alchemy ludicrous. The best parts of the book were Cid Hamete's tedious digressions, where at least he wasn't distorting alchemical reality or humiliating his character, Don Corwyn.

Nevertheless, Corwyn had to admit that the book displayed a disturbing congruence between fact and fiction, for although this imbecile, Cid Hamete Benengeli, altered real events, he hadn't altogether ignored them. In the book were detailed such incidents, for example, as Corwyn's imprisonment by the duchess for the demonic possession of her husband, and the alchemist's subsequent escape from Pomme de Terre after Sebastian rescued him. The very similarities between events as they had actually occurred and those related by Cid Hamete made the book all the more insidious, for undiscerning minds might fail to distinguish between truth and invention. The book even cast doubt on the veracity of the demonic plague which figured so centrally in later portions of the story, attributing the entire outbreak to Corwyn's demented imagination.

He closed the book at last on a scene describing his final confrontation with the demons—a scene cut short by the absorbed acid. Corwyn knew, of course, how the true version of his exploits had turned out, but he

couldn't help wondering how Cid Hamete had miscon-
strued them. Certainly the final incidents described in
the book would show scant resemblance to their real-life
counterparts.

By the time he finished reading, night had begun
to wane. But Corwyn couldn't think of sleeping, so
distraught was he over what he'd read. Besides, the
kawphy still pulsed in his veins. He remembered his
comment to Sebastian, made half in jest, of taking his
case to the king of Aragon to have publication of the
book suppressed. Now he considered the idea again more
seriously and decided on a journey to Zaragoza.

No sooner did Corwyn settle on this than he heard
Roche-naissante braying in the stable. Taking this as a
good omen, he resolved to set forth that very hour. He
wrote a brief note to Sebastian explaining his decision,
then promoted Sebastian from apprentice to journeyman
and placed him in charge of the school. Almost immediately, Corwyn began to experience doubts over that last
point, so he followed this with several pages of advice on
how Sebastian should conduct himself in his new position, covering everything from deportment to discipline.
At the end, he remembered to add a postscript about the
samples being incubated for the breath of demons test,
and particularly about the sample obtained from Dr. Tox.
Finally, Corwyn stuck the now-voluminous letter in Cid
Hamete's book where it was sure to be found, gathered
up the remaining bread and sausage from dinner and
a few alchemical supplies, and scurried off to restock
Roche-naissante's saddlebags.

As he headed down the corridor toward the stable, Corwyn chuckled to himself, thinking how much
Sebastian's rise to journeyman status and his appointment
to temporary head of the school would mean to him.

Chapter 3

Which treats of Corwyn's peculiar encounter with some Spanish windmills, and his subsequent adventures at an inn which used to be a castle.

HIS PREPARATIONS MADE, CORWYN DECIDED NOT TO wait any longer before setting out, for he was troubled by how much his good name and the reputation of aquatic alchemy would suffer through further delay. Many were the wrongs against him that had to be righted, the slanders to be redressed, the misconceptions corrected, and damages awarded.

Cid Hamete Benengeli had much to answer for.

So, before dawn on a day which promised to be the hottest yet that summer, Corwyn put on his pointed alchemist's hat and black robes, mounted *Roche-naissante*, and hoisted Oliver up behind him. Leaving only the note to inform Sebastian of his intentions, he managed to depart from Pomme de Terre without being seen, traveling by back streets until he was out of town and into the fastnesses of the mountains. His initial feeling was one of relief at how easily he had made his escape.

Scarcely had he begun to climb when the sun rose, spreading its rays over the earth and awakening several thrushes and a wood lark to announce the dawn. Corwyn paused to cast a last look back at the gates of Pomme de Terre and the turrets and balconies of the duke's castle, warmed by the rosy light. Outside the great hall of the castle, sunbeams played on the sails of three windmills, which lifted water in stages from the River Ale to the top of a turret high above the hall. From there, the water was distributed by a series of brass conduits to all parts of the castle.

Once Corwyn had regarded the water system as one of his greatest achievements, but now the sight of it failed to warm his soul. In Cid Hamete's book, the three windmills had become the first step along the path to "Don" Corwyn's downfall, a personal Calvary of slowly revolving crosses upon which the alchemist-errant had crucified his insane career.

The recollection of that incident, as told by the Moor, fueled the doubt that had already begun nibbling again at Corwyn, eroding his resolve so that he almost abandoned his purpose at the outset. Secretly, he worried that Cid Hamete might be right, and that his beloved alchemy might be nothing more than the ravings of a madman who had spent too many years in solitary study. He had, after all, never discovered that Philosopher's Stone which was the proper pursuit of alchemists everywhere—even an aquatic alchemist such as himself. Only possession of the true stone could grant unassailable proof of the veracity of alchemy, aquatic or otherwise. Lacking that, knowing how to make *kawphy* was but a poor substitute.

So Corwyn slipped again into that quicksand of introspection common to many at this point in their lives, during which even petty concerns appear suffocating.

Oliver, however, unfamiliar with a crisis of this nature and therefore impatient with it, grew tired of waiting while Corwyn stared morosely at the sunrise, and he squirmed to show his annoyance. Corwyn prodded *Roche-naissante* into a jolting walk, letting the animal choose its path over the mountains while he sank back into his thoughts with a deep and self-pitying sigh.

They crossed the watershed a little before midday, while the ice and snow underfoot were still solid enough for safe passage. By afternoon, the route would become slushy and treacherous, and any travelers would be forced to wait until morning to venture through the pass, when the ground had again frozen.

Once in Spain, rivulets of meltwater trickled from snow fields and glaciers, feeding the relatively few rivers which flowed down the southern side of the mountains. Seeing this stirred distant memories for Corwyn of a time when he'd brought melting ice to the deserts of Arabia, creating oases where caravans stopped and watered their camels even today. It was strange, he thought, how unreal that accomplishment had become, as if he'd only heard tales of what another person had done. Of course, Corwyn had long been aware of a certain selectivity in his recollections of the preceding centuries. His failures and shortcomings remained with him always, ever fresh in his mind, whereas his successes tended to dim with passing time until eventually he saw them as indistinct shadows of events which might have happened to some-one else altogether. The discrepancy in this troubled him, for he suspected the fault was of his own devising, rather than being an inherent flaw in the workings of human memory.

Thus he entertained himself with a sense of tragedy all the way over the Pyrenees and into the first leg of his descent on the more arid Spanish side. The higher reach-es of his journey took him through a barren landscape of scree and scrub, where snow finches and ptarmigan nested on the stony ground and eagles wheeled overhead in the clear sky. Once, Corwyn saw a group of chamois scamper up a seemingly vertical crag. Then his route dropped lower into a region of tortured canyons and rugged defiles, the steep walls revealing folded layers of gray and ocher limestone. Dwarf mountain pines clung to thin patches of soil, their contorted trunks testifying to the harshness of life in this place. A lammergeier, or "bonebreaker," soared high above a pile of boulders and dropped the clean-picked tibia of some animal onto the rocks below; the bone bounced several times before coming to rest, cracked along its length to expose its precious marrow.

The eerie terrain matched the bleakness in Corwyn's soul—which, of course, can be very satisfying to one who has given in to excess and is afflicted by the pangs of inconvenience.

Farther on, granite replaced limestone, rising to form the Posets and Maladeta massifs. Between them nestled the Valle de Benasque, into which Corwyn descended, the narrow valley overshadowed by neighboring peaks. The upper end of the valley was austere and uninhabited, but farther down it became a sanctuary of relative abundance, lush with pines, larches, and firs despite the altitude, the meadows along the valley floor carpeted with laurel, sweetbrier, heather, and broom. The Rio Esera rushed in a clear torrent at Corwyn's side.

Corwyn spent the night in a hay barn at the edge of Benasque, a tiny mountain community of narrow, cobbled streets and winding alleys, its rough stone-walled and slate-roofed houses, some two- and three-stories tall, huddled together for protection from the elements and invaders alike. Forced to burrow deep into the hay to escape the cold nighttime air, Corwyn waited out the long hours until daybreak in restlessness, feeling old and tired, dwelling on uncertainty and anxious to reach Zaragoza.

Corwyn's only consolation during this time came from the realization of how distressed Sebastian would be at his master's unexpected absence, and how anxiously he would await the alchemist's return.

At this point, growing weary ourselves of Corwyn's self-absorption, it is time to leave him (hoping no doubt that he'll prove more amiable in the morning) while we return for a brief visit with Sebastian. The journeyman alchemist had finally managed to slip away from the demands of playing nursemaid to the school's remaining students and was off to see what had become of his master.

He reached the alchemist's shop to find everything oddly dark and quiet. At first, he wandered through the rambling structure, calling for Corwyn and Oliver. When that failed, he checked the stable, where he learned *Roche-naissante* was also missing.

Perplexed, Sebastian ambled back to the laboratory and sat on a stool at the main worktable to think matters through. He couldn't conceive of any reason for his master's sudden departure, especially so soon after returning from a lengthy sampling expedition.

While Sebastian endured the strain of contemplation—an activity contrary to his nature—he took to thumbing the pages of Cid Hamete's book as a means of occupying his otherwise idle fingers. Thus he stumbled upon Corwyn's message, stuck between the pages at the back of the book. Portions of the note were scorched from oil of vitriol, for the paper on which the book was printed had absorbed the reagent much faster than would pages made from parchment. As a result, Sebastian could make out little of his master's advice and none of his purpose for leaving, the sheets containing these parts having burned clear through. Sebastian was, however, able to make out that Corwyn was going to Zaragoza. And with effort, he deciphered the part announcing his promotion to journeyman and his appointment as head of the school during his master's absence, together with the merest fragment about a breath of demons test Corwyn had set up the day before.

Sebastian's chest—and perhaps his head—swelled with pride, and he determined to use this occasion to prove himself a capable leader, dispensing firmness and justice in a manner worthy of someone who was rising in life and about to become a father. Corwyn's problem in running the school, Sebastian had long ago decided, stemmed from an unwillingness to discipline the rowdy boys whose parents sent them here to be educated. (Although Corwyn had tried to recruit girls for the school as well, parents in Gardenia had proved unreceptive to so momentous a break with convention.) As a result, the boys at the school tended to be an opportunistic lot, Sebastian had discovered, looking for ways to turn lead into gold and thus become rich quickly, without effort on their part or any true understanding of alchemy. Unable to see beneath surface appearances to underlying reality, they were quick to judge everything as beneath them, failing to recognize the distortions caused by their noble backgrounds. In short, Sebastian found them, by and large, to be the snobbish, impudent, lazy by-products of an outmoded aristocracy, ill suited to any truly productive calling in a changing world.

Having started his own alchemical career with exactly that outlook, Sebastian now felt uniquely qualified to deal with such students. So he was elated by the news that he would have an opportunity to rectify his master's shortcomings by exercising a much-needed authority over the school, demonstrating to Corwyn what such an institution could amount to under stricter management.

Only when he was hurrying back through the courtyard between the school and Corwyn's laboratory to tell Gwen the good news did it occur to Sebastian to wonder why his master was going to Zaragoza. Then he remembered the alchemist's having mentioned something the previous evening about petitioning the king of Aragon to stop publication of Cid Hamete's book. At the time, Sebastian had thought it an idle threat, more of a joke than a statement to be taken seriously. Corwyn, however, had apparently meant it, and now was carrying out that intention. Sebastian knew (as did almost everyone in Christendom and at least half of the heathen kingdoms) that the king of Aragon held an annual tournament later in the summer, and would, therefore, be at his court in Zaragoza, overseeing arrangements. This, then, would be Corwyn's destination.

Sebastian smiled to himself, pleased at having so easily solved the problem posed by the missing portions of the note. He only hoped that his master remained away long enough for him to transform the would-be charlatans attending the school into true and proficient alchemists before Corwyn returned.

*   *   *

Early the next morning, Corwyn was still pondering his self-doubts when he resumed his journey, heading south from Benasque to Barbastro, where he would angle west to Zaragoza. After leaving the Valle de Benasque, Corwyn still came across scattered pockets of luxuriance—woodlands of beech and birch; meadows ablaze with buttercups and gentians, irises and forget-me-nots; and glacier-fed tarns and lakes. Yet these pockets grew smaller and more scarce as Corwyn continued south, and an overarching harshness devoured much of the land. Mountains gave way to foothills, which yielded in turn to that vast, inhospitable *meseta*, or high, barren plain, that dominates the Spanish interior. The clear, tumbling streams of the Pyrenees flowed into a few widely spaced and lethargic rivers, their channels cutting thin ribbons of fertility across an otherwise rocky and arid land. By day, the sunshine was fierce; by night, the air was brittle with cold.

During that second day, Corwyn had the sensation that someone else was descending by the same path from the mountains, for occasionally he caught glimpses of a figure behind him, the features indistinguishable in the distance.

Corwyn spent the second night of his journey in a deserted shepherd's hut, where he made a simple meal of what little food remained in *Roche-naissante's* saddlebags, then continued on the following day. In this realm of broken rocks and little water, he rode for hours without seeing anyone, except for the speck far behind that was his mysterious fellow traveler. At first, Corwyn thought it might be Dr. Tox trying to catch up with him, bringing more of his strange warnings and foul smell. But the figure maintained a constant distance, despite Corwyn's quickened pace.

The alchemist dismissed the matter as insignificant, more concerned with his own worries than with a stranger who remained so far behind.

The concerns inhabiting Corwyn's soul, on the other hand, plagued him fiercely. So fatigued did he become from the difficult mental and physical terrains he was traversing that even the appearance on the third afternoon of what looked to be a line of partially constructed windmills against the southern horizon failed to rouse him from his despondency. In fact, after reading Cid Hamete's book, the sight of them—unusual though grain mills were in this part of Spain—appeared as ominous in his eyes as a line of gibbets, waiting like eager executioners to hang a condemned man's reputation. With a shudder, Corwyn reined *Roche-naissante* to a halt. He couldn't continue toward Barbastro, and hence to Zaragoza, without approaching the mills, and something about the structures drew him, like a moth to a flame. Yet so reluctant was he to venture any closer that he remained there, indecisive, until Oliver and *Roche-naissante* both began to fidget at the delay.

Finally, Corwyn was struck by a solution. Instead of traveling to Zaragoza and seeking an audience with the king of Aragon (the outcome of which had begun to seem doubtful in any case), he would proceed directly to Barcelona and take the matter up with the printer who had published Cid Hamete's absurdities. The printer was a fellow businessman; he would listen to reason.

So Corwyn averted his gaze from the dreaded windmills and forced *Roche-naissante* (who seemed even more reluctant than usual to alter her course) southeast toward Lérida, midway on the route between Zaragoza and Barcelona, never pausing to wonder what purpose windmills might serve on so barren a plain, far from any town or farm.

Sometime during the remainder of that afternoon, an unexpected change took place in Corwyn's thinking, for which we may all be thankful. Perhaps it was having decided upon this new destination, or perhaps it was just the heat, which seemed enough to melt his brains and unhinge his senses, but Corwyn's despair began to lift and he found his faith in alchemy gradually restored as if by a miracle. The *ars magna*—or Great Art, as it was called by its practitioners—might never have been proved true beyond all doubt, he reasoned, but neither had it been shown conclusively to be otherwise, and within this gap between opposing certainties Corwyn found soil fertile enough to cultivate his renewed belief. Alchemy, particularly aquatic alchemy, was true because it produced verifiable results, he told himself, and not because it could be proved absolutely. So long as it yielded workable solutions to practical problems, allowing him to purify corrupted waters and perform other such acts, he could afford to believe in its authenticity.

His doubts settled, at least for the time, he went on in better spirits, content to let *Roche-naissante* set the pace. Nevertheless, the windmills he had encountered earlier remained in the back of his mind, their afterimage burned into his awareness as if he had stared too long at the sun.

Evening found Corwyn and the donkey dead tired and hungry, with Oliver squirming at the alchemist's back from having been confined for so long to a saddle. Corwyn wondered how far they were from Lérida. He looked around for shelter and perceived not far off an inn, built upon the ruins of a small castle. Once a border outpost when the wars between Moslems and Christians had swept across this part of Spain centuries earlier, little remained of the castelet now except a tumbled-down wall and three piles of rubble that marked the turrets at its corners. Only a single dilapidated turret still stood, and that just barely, in the fourth corner of the square. The inn, built of stone scavenged from the ruins, huddled in the corner farthest from the remaining tower, as if afraid that ancient structure might collapse and crush the newer building. Surrounding the castle was a dry moat, half-filled with rocks and drifted sand, and crossed by a decrepit drawbridge. Two women lounged in the portal that was now the entrance to the inn, the purpose suggested by their casual stance casting doubt upon their maidenhood.

Corwyn hesitated, wary of entering such a disreputable-looking place regardless of how tired he was. For a moment, he considered pushing on to Lérida. But fear of the bandits and marauders who roamed Spain unchecked, preying on travelers and villagers alike in these lawless days when the peninsula was divided into warring kingdoms, finally drove the alchemist to a decision. Besides, he couldn't remember whether he had seen the mysterious traveler of the previous day following him again today. Night was falling, and Corwyn determined to regard the first star, which twinkled faintly above the castle gate, as a favorable omen guiding him to safety.

He was about to urge the donkey onto the drawbridge when a swineherd somewhere nearby blew a blast on his horn to bring his herd together. The sound, like a trumpet announcing Corwyn's presence in the heyday of the castle, caused the two women to look up and notice him. They must have recognized his hesitancy, for the older of the two arched her back, straining her breasts against her blouse. "Have no fear, *señor*," she purred. "It's not the way of our profession to harm anyone, especially a highborn gentleman such as you appear to be."

Whatever seductiveness she might have intended, however, was offset by the lavish endowments of her figure. She was broad-faced, flat-nosed, and her head appeared to be squashed in back. Blind in one eye, she squinted at Corwyn with the other, hampered by its tendency to wander. Not more than four and a half feet tall, she had large, rounded shoulders that dragged at her alluring frame and drew her attention to the ground in front of her, except when she tipped her head back in an effort to see farther.

Corwyn struggled for composure. "Ladies," he replied, bowing and prodding *Roche-naissante* into a walk, "forgive me if I offended you. I am at your service."

"And service us you may," the first woman promised, waggling her bountiful hips. "For a fee."

"I'm afraid you mistake my meaning," Corwyn said hastily. "I'm trying to be courteous, not to engage your professional services."

The first woman frowned at her companion. "What's he talking about?"

"I think he wants us to give it to him for free," replied the younger—but no less attractive—woman.

The first snorted. "Generous about granting himself what's ours to give, isn't he? Ah, well, he's just a miserly old fool on an ass, anyway. Probably can't even get it up, let alone remember how to use it."

The second woman laughed. "I don't see an old fool, Maritornes. I see only the ass, mounted on a donkey."

For a moment, Corwyn's resolve wavered like the flickering of the star overhead. Then he prodded *Roche-naissante* into a trot, anxious to escape their derision. The animal's hoofbeats reverberated on the aging timbers of the drawbridge, seemingly amplified in the waning light. "Laughter without cause is a sure sign of folly," Corwyn growled as he reached the women.

They guffawed all the harder, then stopped abruptly as he passed, staring at his back. "What's that?" the one called Maritornes asked.

"It's the staff, *El Aver*, that my father has read to us about," her companion hissed. "The old fool must be Don Corwyn."

Corwyn groaned softly, realizing that he had forgotten to dress Oliver to disguise him, having allowed the broom to travel through the mountains unhindered by clothes. He hoped the two women would doubt what they had seen in the growing dark.

He entered the inn yard, pursued by the whisperings that had replaced their chortles, and guided *Roche-naissante* to the stable. The large number of animals quartered there gave evidence to the inn's popularity, a fact which Corwyn found strange for so remote a location. Most of the animals, however, appeared to be mules from a pack train of the kind frequently used for freighting goods throughout Spain. Indeed, as Corwyn searched for an empty stall in which to stable *Roche-naissante*, he noticed the load the animals had carried—a large shipment of bulging wineskins— carefully stowed for the night in the dim recesses of the building. For a moment, the wineskins seemed to shimmer, giving Corwyn a start. He rubbed his knuckles into his eyes, realizing again how exhausted he was.

Corwyn quickly dressed Oliver to look again like a little monk and left the broom to feed and curry *Rochenaissante*. By the time Corwyn left the stable, eager to escape the acrid stench of animal dung and urine, the women at the gate had disappeared inside the inn. With a grimace, the old alchemist followed.

The innkeeper, a huge man with wild hair and beard and a pair of great, unruly mustaches greeted Corwyn. "If your worship is looking for lodging, you'll find we have plenty of everything," he said amiably. "Except for a bed, that is, for there are none left in the inn. Yet to one so skilled as you (for your reputation precedes you, *señor*), perhaps even such hard comfort as we can provide can be quickly transmuted into the softest mattresses and bedding of the finest silks."

Behind him, the two women from the drawbridge and several other people snickered, but the innkeeper gave no sign of having heard. Corwyn, faced with such apparent humility, assured the innkeeper that whatever he could provide would be sufficient. "But I'd like something to eat," Corwyn added, "for in truth, I'm famished."

The day happened to be Friday, and the innkeeper responded that there was no food in the inn, either, except some portions of a fish that is called pollack in Castile, and cod in Andalusia, and in some parts ling and in others troutlet. Asked if he would like some troutlet then, as there was nothing else to eat, Corwyn (who was unfamiliar with the term) replied eagerly that several pieces of troutlet might suffice for one whole trout.

A table was set for him at the open inn door, where the air was freshest. With a flourish, the innkeeper brought out a portion of badly soaked and worse-cooked salt cod and some bread as black and gritty as a desert night.

Corwyn bent over the cod, only to draw back quickly, wrinkling his nose. "I thought you said this was trout."

"And so it will be," the innkeeper said equably, "as soon as you free its spirit from the base matter in which it's housed, transmuting it into nobler form."

Again there were titters at the innkeeper's back, but he remained impassive. Corwyn, too exhausted to press the subject, pushed the cod away, wishing he still had some bread and sausage left in *Roche-naissante's* saddlebags. "Perhaps I'll just go to bed," he said, "if you'll see to it at once."

"Immediately, *señor*." The innkeeper motioned to the two women who had greeted Corwyn on the drawbridge and they led the alchemist to an attic which had evidently served as a hayloft for many years. Here they prepared him a miserable bed from four badly planed boards laid across a pair of uneven trestles. Over these they placed a thin mattress full of lumps that felt like stones (but which appeared through rents in the cover to be wool), a pair of sheets which seemed to be of rawhide, and a coverlet so threadbare Corwyn could have counted every strand. On this execrable bed, Corwyn lay down, accompanying himself with considerable groaning. Maritornes and the innkeeper's daughter (for so the second woman had proved to be) returned to the common room, taking the oil lamp with them and plunging Corwyn in darkness.

But though he was eager for sleep, the discomfort caused by his poor excuse for a bed wouldn't allow him that refuge, and so Corwyn tossed restlessly for what seemed like hours. Then, just when he finally succeeded in drifting off to sleep, a great disturbance outside the inn together with a light shining full upon his face brought Corwyn awake with a violent start—

What happened next, however, deserves to be told in a separate chapter.

Entremés

MEANWHILE, DON CORWYN WAS MAKING OVERTURES
*to a peasant, a young man with very few brains who
thought himself a squire of noble birth, and so affected
foolish airs. Finally, Don Corwyn convinced him with
such promises of material gain that the poor rustic made
up his mind to sally forth with him and serve as his
apprentice. Don Corwyn, among other things, told him
that he ought to go with him gladly, because at any
moment he might reveal to him one of the greatest
secrets of alchemy: the "Philosopher's Stone," which
all alchemists sought.*

*"What is that?" asked Sebastian (for so the peasant
was called).*

*"It is the elixir contained in the Holy Grail," answered
Don Corwyn, "a flask of which I always carry in my
robes, and with which one need have no fear of poverty
or death or any illness. And so when I give it to you,
all you have to do—should one of us come down with
the plague, as happens so frequently in these times—
is to administer two drops as swiftly as you can,
and whoever has been afflicted will become sounder
than an apple. Or, if in our adventures we should
find ourselves without money, simply add a drop of
this elixir to a piece of lead and it will instantly be
transmuted into gold. And the same for any corrupted
or impure waters that we might encounter, such as a
sacred spring which has been polluted by foul and*

treacherous activities, for this elixir turns all base things into noble."

"Sinner that I am!" said Sebastian. "Then why do you put off giving it to me? All I desire in payment for my many and faithful services is that you give me the flask or teach me the formula for this priceless elixir."

"Be calm, boy," answered Don Corwyn. "Other secrets do I also mean to teach you, and greater favors will I bestow upon you even than this."

On these and the like promises, Sebastian abandoned the religious studies in which he had been properly engaged and became apprenticed to Don Corwyn, longing to see himself soon risen in status and made the lord of some estate or castle, as promised by his new master.

Thus equipped with his apprentice and his enchanted staff (the latter of which Don Corwyn used as a walking stick when afoot or strapped to his back when riding), the alchemist set forth in search of adventure, straddling a donkey named Rociandante *because of its tendency to urinate all over the road in protest whenever it was prodded into moving....*

—Cid Hamete Benengeli,
  El Ingenioso Alquimista
  Don Corwyn de La Mancha, Part I

Chapter 4

Which briefly portrays the tranquillity of Sebastian's life before continuing Corwyn's adventures at the inn.

ABOUT THE TIME CORWYN AWOKE AT THE INN, SEbastian too was jolted from sleep in his bed in Pomme de Terre. He sat upright and listened, trying to hear over the hammering of his heart.

Next to him, Gwen was also sitting up in bed, so deeply immersed in whatever new book she was reading that she appeared unaware of the hideous noise that had awakened him. Sebastian glowered and checked the candle by her bedside. New when they had gone to bed, it was now little more than a flickering stump. Gwen held the book close to the flame to capture as much of its light as possible, chuckling occasionally as she read.

"What's so funny?" Sebastian demanded irritably.

Gwen slammed the book shut and turned to him, one hand dangling the book out of sight over the edge of the bed, a guilty look adding to the strain of sleeplessness on her face. The candleflame wavered in the air currents she created by moving. "Nothing, I was just . . . What are you doing awake?"

Sebastian smiled grimly, well aware of her effort to

hide the book and distract him from the subject. Yet he couldn't stay angry with her for still being awake or for reading to pass the long hours, even though she read little other than the chivalric romances that had become popular lately. He glanced at her grotesquely bulging belly, realizing again how graceless she had become, yet somehow also feeling completely awed by her splendor. Gwen's nights had grown fitful as she neared the end of her term, and comfort eluded her, awake or asleep. Sebastian couldn't begrudge her anything that brought her a measure of relief, even if it was just those silly books.

Suddenly, a sharp skirling noise rent the night. Sebastian, having slumped back down in hope of returning to sleep, jerked upright again, clenching his teeth against the sound. It seemed to be coming from directly overhead, where the students had their rooms on the upper floors of the school. "What was that?" he gasped when the noise faded away.

"Hmmm?" Gwen murmured sleepily. She seemed to be either daydreaming or thinking about the book she was still trying to hide over the edge of the bed. "Oh, that. It's just Henri, practicing his bagpipes."

"Bagpipes!" Sebastian ground his teeth. "I hate bagpipes. They remind me of when my uncle tried to teach me to play, when I was sent to stay with him as a boy." He shuddered, recalling the many humiliations and disappointments of the time when he had trained—unsuccessfully—for knighthood in England, never managing to measure up to the expectations of his uncle or the achievements of his older and more experienced cousins.

"Really?" Gwen replied. "I think they're rather nice." She let the book fall to the floor with a thud and snuggled down in bed. "Ready for me to put the candle out?"

Sebastian nodded and she snuffed the wick. Soon he could hear her snoring softly beside him. But for Sebastian, sleep was a long time coming, for every time he started to drift off, Henri produced another bone-jarring blast, finally working his way up to two or three sustained notes in succession—a musical accomplishment Sebastian could have done without. After what seemed like hours of this, Sebastian forced himself out of bed and trudged up the three flights of stairs to the boys' quarters, where he ordered Henri to stop.

Even as he said this and started back downstairs to bed, Sebastian had the uneasy feeling that all of the boys were snickering behind his back, as if he had committed some grave tactical error in his constant struggle for control over the students.

Well, he'd learn the consequences of this latest skirmish in time, he thought. But at least he wouldn't be bothered anymore by those wretched bagpipes!

Meanwhile, no sooner had Corwyn fallen asleep than he was disturbed, as has been said, by a sudden light in his face and someone's prodding him none too gently and calling his name. Outside the inn, a clamor had arisen with the din of horns and pipes and the banging of pots and pans. Above it all rose the shrill *Lelilili* of a Moorish battle cry.

Corwyn, who'd been having a nightmare in which Cid Hamete was tormenting him, thought this uproar was caused by his persecutor, and immediately grappled with the person standing by his bed, pulling the figure down on top of him. Whoever it was landed with a grunt, stunning them both. The bed, being rather weak, collapsed beneath the added weight, spilling Corwyn and his assailant onto the floor and putting out the light. For a while the two figures scuffled in the darkness, each shouting above the noise outside for help in subduing the other. Hard, calloused hands rained blows on Corwyn, and a foul breath blew in his face. Then the intruder hit Corwyn on the head with something that smashed, and he felt blood flow over his face from the wound.

"Help, help!" Corwyn roared. "I'm being murdered."

At last the innkeeper came running to the room, where that worthy man quickly stopped the fight. In the glow of the innkeeper's lamp, Corwyn discovered he'd been struggling with his host's daughter, one of the two wom-

en who'd greeted him at the entrance to the inn on his
arrival. Her hair, coarse as a horse's mane, straggled
from beneath the fustian kerchief with which it had been
bound. As for Corwyn's wound, the "blood" turned out
to be nothing more than oil from the lamp the girl had
carried, which she'd used to bash him on the head in an
effort to escape his clutches. Much chagrined, Corwyn
helped her up and began brushing off the front of her
shift, then stopped abruptly as he realized what parts of
her he was touching.

The innkeeper (whose name Corwyn had learned earlier was Juan Palomeque, for he was left-handed) stared
at them both with evident displeasure. "You were sent
to waken him, not crawl into his bed," he chided the
girl, speaking loudly to be heard above the noise outside. "You've been listening to that worthless Maritornes
again!"

"I didn't do anything," the vision of injured loveliness
before him protested in a martyred tone. "He grabbed
me and pulled me down before I could stop him. You
saw him fondling my shift just now."

"It was a mistake," Corwyn explained. "I didn't
know—"

"As for you," the innkeeper said, interrupting Corwyn,
"I'd have thought you too old for this kind of thing. In the
future, let me know when you require such service so I can
send Maritornes to you, not my daughter. Just don't pay
that miserable Asturian wench anything; I'll see that the
charge for her services is included in your bill." He glared
again at his daughter. "And don't let this one try to con-
vince you that she's going into business for herself!"

The girl pouted as if offended at having her innocence
questioned.

"But you don't understand," Corwyn tried again to
explain. "I thought—"

Again, the innkeeper cut him off. "Never mind that
now. We're privileged to have you as our guest, Don
Corwyn de La Mancha, and are eager for you to witness
the alchemical vigil we're about to perform in your
honor down in the inn yard."

Before Corwyn could ask what manner of event an alchemical vigil might be, his host hustled him from the room, not even allowing the alchemist time to put on his clothes.

A crowd of guests and servants had assembled outside the inn, with several people carrying torches while others played instruments or made noise in a horrible cacophony of sound. Between the firelight and the glow of a full moon, the yard was brightly illuminated, and the torches cast fiendish, overlapping shadows against the remnants of the castle walls. With a firm grip and pompous ceremony, the innkeeper escorted Corwyn through the crowd to a well in the center of the yard, next to a large, stone water trough.

Corwyn, dressed only in his oil-splattered undergown, shivered in the night air. He saw the well had been crudely boarded up, and wondered why he hadn't noticed earlier, and where the inn got its water.

As if anticipating the alchemist's questions, Juan Palomeque pointed to the boarded up well with a discarded old broom. "We've followed the account of your exploits with great interest, *señor*, as you soon will see for yourself," he said when the crowd fell silent. "For here we have duplicated your breath of demons test as closely as our humble circumstances would allow, and tonight we conclude the test."

Corwyn gritted his teeth but said nothing, realizing that the well hadn't been covered earlier after all. This hoax had been prepared since his arrival.

Juan Palomeque waved the broom over the well and motioned to two of the revelers, a pair of hog-gelders who appeared to have partaken liberally of the elixirs offered by their host's wine cellar. The two hurried to the well, where they began pulling off the boards.

"*Un momento*," one of the bystanders—a needlemaker from Cordoba—cried. He pointed to Juan Palomeque. "I've read the book, too, and you have to strip off all your clothes except your undergown and dance around like a madman, revealing such parts of yourself as are better kept hidden. That's what the book says."

Juan Palomeque scowled. "I'm not taking off my clothes and dancing around for anyone."

"But that's how it's done in the book," the needlemaker persisted.

The innkeeper glanced around, his eyes alighting on Corwyn. "He's already in his undergown, so I don't need to be."

"I don't know," the needlemaker said. "That isn't the way it's done in the boo—"

"And as for revealing parts of myself that would be better left covered . . ." Smirking, Juan Palomeque let his words trail off and spun around, lifting his leather apron with one hand and pulling down his breeches with the other, revealing a second moon that rivaled the full one overhead. Then he yanked his breeches up and turned back around, grinning at the laughter his antics drew from the crowd. The needlemaker shook his head doubtfully, but the innkeeper ignored him as he motioned to the two hog-gelders again. They pulled the rest of the boards loose from the well and began working at the crank as if drawing water, puffing and laboring strenuously.

While the pair worked, Corwyn's attention was interrupted by a tug on his sleeve. Looking around, he discovered Oliver, fortunately dressed in his robes again. The creature had made his way through the crowd to stand beside the alchemist, hanging onto the latter's sleeve for security. Corwyn started to turn away, then spun back when he realized that Oliver was holding a worn leather bag in his hand. In the past, the broom's conceptual abilities hadn't included ownership of property, and Corwyn was afraid he'd helped himself to someone else's purse again.

"Oliver," he whispered, "what is that?"

Shyly, the broom opened the bag and displayed a handful of ordinary rocks, which the little creature held as if they were treasures.

Corwyn sighed. "All right. But take them back to the stable."

Oliver rotated his stick body back and forth in the

way he had of motioning "no" and pressed closer to the alchemist.

"Oliver, you can't stay here with me," Corwyn hissed. "Not now, it's dangerous. Do as I say and go back to the stable."

Oliver's handle tipped forward so that he peered at the ground. Slowly, his twig fingers let go of Corwyn's sleeve and the little creature slipped back through the crowd.

Just then, the well rope snapped, sending the two men at the crank sprawling in the dirt. A shriek emerged from the well, followed by a splash. Juan Palomeque shouted at the two hog-gelders, who were lying in a daze on the ground, then he leaped to the well. Quickly, he unwound the broken rope and dropped the frayed end down to where the sounds of thrashing and cursing rose from the depths. Hindered by the two hog-gelders, who tried drunkenly to assist, the innkeeper soon raised a strange, bedraggled figure into view. Dressed in sack-cloth, the figure's face was blackened with ashes and soot and adorned with a long, pointed nose made from a parchment cone, which immersion in water had caused to droop toward the ground. A pair of oxhorns had been affixed atop the figure's head as if they'd grown there, although the sinister effect of this was diminished by the fact that one horn now dangled loosely from its leather bindings.

Once the individual had been safely brought out of the well and deposited onto firm ground, Juan Palomeque motioned the hog-gelders away and stepped back in exaggerated horror. The hog-gelders stumbled off toward the stable with the air of fellow conspirators, snickering and tripping one another in their eagerness. Juan Palomeque shook his head after the retreating pair, then addressed the apparition from the well. "Oh, fiend, who are you? For what purpose have you come?"

"You know who I am," the dripping figure from the well responded in a voice like Maritornes's. The fiend shook water from her hair, loosening the other oxhorn. "You and your stupid ideas!"

"Ah, it's just as Cid Hamete's book foretold," Juan Palomeque said, stepping forward to straighten the dangling horns. "This demon is indeed much annoyed by its captivity. Now it will do as we command."

These last words he uttered with an emphasis which suggested that the fiend would be well-advised to heed him if she wished to remain employed at the inn.

"Oh, very well," she said, her voice dropping into a hoarse croak that might have passed for demonic. "I am the devil and have come in search of Don Corwyn de La Mancha, whose dread alchemy has confined me, lo, these many days, and whose commands I must now obey." Her good eye came to rest briefly on the alchemist, then drifted off again.

Before Corwyn could respond, the innkeeper pointed his broom at the water trough beside the well. "Your new master, Don Corwyn, commands you to transmute this ordinary water into wine." He winked to those around him and added, "After which we shall celebrate the alchemist's victory by drinking it."

This announcement was greeted by a hearty cheer from the other revelers.

The devil that looked and sounded like Maritornes lifted her hands to silence the crowd. "It shall be as Don Corwyn commands. But first I need that magic liquor known as the Philosopher's Stone." She scrunched up her face (handsome by any equine standards) and added in an aside, "Although how anyone could be fool enough to mistake liquor for a stone is beyond me."

"Elixir," Juan Palomeque corrected softly. "Not liquor."

The devil shrugged her stooped shoulders. "Liquor, elixir—what's it matter? At least I know the difference between something to drink and a rock. But never mind. Whatever you call it, it'll taste like wine to me." She ran her tongue over her lips.

"But where'll we get this elixir?" somebody shouted from the crowd.

"As luck will have it, we happen to have just such an elixir on hand," Juan Palomeque called out for all to

hear. He indicated the two hog-gelders who were now
returning from the stable, dragging one of the large wineskins Corwyn had seen earlier. Again, Corwyn found
himself oddly unsettled by the skin, which seemed to
pulsate with a life of its own.

The alchemist wasn't the only person to react strangely at the sight of the wineskin, for one of the two mule
skinners staying at the inn cried out and crossed himself,
then ran off into the night. His companion also started,
but remained where he stood.

Then Corwyn caught sight of something that made
the wineskin fade into insignificance, for instead of
returning to the stable as ordered, Oliver was wandering
through the crowd. So far, the little creature hadn't been
noticed, dressed as he was, and Corwyn could only hope
he remained that way.

The hog-gelders, meanwhile, lugged the skin over
and prepared to replace the water in the trough with
the confiscated wine.

"Wait!" the remaining mule skinner cried. "That
wine is intended for the holy brothers stationed outside
Zaragoza."

"Ah, you'll be well paid for the loss," the innkeeper
assured him. "You can collect it from Don Corwyn."

One of the hog-gelders grabbed the side of the trough,
ready to dump out the water, while the other held a knife
to the wineskin to slit it open.

"Go ahead, then," the mule skinner said, his eyes
never veering from the bulging, shimmering skin. "I'm
sure the thirsty Dominicans will understand that you
need this wine more than they, despite how hard they
work in furthering the Inquisition."

An uneasy stir passed through the crowd. The innkeeper shifted his weight and considered the skin, apparently too busy pursing his lips to notice the little monk
who stood beside him, within easy reach of a different
purse. Corwyn rolled his eyes and uttered prayers to half
a dozen different deities in the hope that at least one of
them would respond.

"So this wine is intended for the Dominicans," the

Maritornes-demon said. "What of it? Shipments come
through here for that station of theirs all the time. The
good friars must all be drunkards to consume so much.
They'll never notice one skin missing."

The mule skinner caught Juan Palomeque's gaze and
hooked an eyebrow up, while Oliver hooked thin fingers
around Juan Palomeque's purse. Corwyn stood rooted
in terror while the innkeeper tried to stare the mule
skinner down. "Ah, take it back," the innkeeper said
at last, motioning the hog-gelders back to the stable.
The hog-gelders scowled, but did as they were told.
The mule skinner let out his breath and slumped in
obvious relief.

Corwyn, too, felt easier when the wineskin was gone,
although he was at a loss to understand his reaction.
He was even more relieved, however, when he saw
Oliver withdraw from Juan Palomeque's side, leaving
that man's purse still hanging heavily from the leather
girdle at his waist. Apparently Corwyn's prayers had
been heard and for once the broom had passed up a
full purse without emptying it.

Maritornes, having wandered off when Juan Palomeque issued his verdict, now returned, still dripping
water and shuffling more than usual under the burden
of a large rock.

"What's that?" Juan Palomeque demanded.

"It's a Philosopher's Stone," she snarled. "If we can't
have the wine, I say we devise some alchemy of our
own. We'll conduct a breath of alchemist test by tying
this stone to Don Corwyn's feet and dropping him in
the well. Then we'll time how long he lasts before he
drowns."

"And then where would I get water for the inn?" Juan
Palomeque responded. "People don't like to drink from
wells that have dead bodies in them. It ruins the taste
of the water."

"That's what they get for drinking such stuff in the
first place," Maritornes muttered, stalking away. "Serves
them right for not sticking to wine."

"Maritornes, wait," a barber called from the crowd.

"You're supposed to be the devil. How can we do any alchemy if you leave?"

"Do it with yourself," Maritornes snapped. "You practice doing enough other things that way—which is why I get so much competition from your neglected wife."

Juan Palomeque grabbed the barber and restrained him. "I think I know why our experiment failed," he said over an angry murmur from the crowd. He gave Corwyn a piercing stare. "This man must not be a true alchemist after all, or things would have gone as planned. Therefore, we must grant him the courtesy of a boon and turn him into an alchemist this very night."

The barber, once released, picked up a stave and hefted it. "A man may be dubbed a knight, but I say this one should be *drubbed* into alchemisthood, and very soundly at that."

"Hold your peace," Juan Palomeque said. "You don't drub a man to turn him into an alchemist. You transmute him. And here again, I have the perfect elixir, and the right vessel in which to hold it." He eyed Corwyn once more, the corner of his mouth lifting in a sneer. Then he glanced around at the crowd and frowned. "Why aren't those hog-gelders back from the stable? They should have returned by now."

"Maybe they stayed to sample the mule skinner's wares," the barber suggested.

As if to confirm this, an eerie sound drifted from the stable, a ghastly duet that might have been a pair of drunken singers, but sounded like souls in pain. The cry sent chills up Corwyn's spine.

"*Sangre de cristo*," the mule skinner hissed, crossing himself and backing away. "What have they done?"

"Gotten even drunker than they were, I'd say." The innkeeper dismissed the mule skinner with a wave. "Never mind. I'll get someone else." He called to his daughter and whispered in her ear, whereupon she giggled and ran inside, demonstrating the virtuousness with which she performed all her duties at the inn. Juan Palomeque, meanwhile, had regained his diffident, sardonic manner, and was quietly issuing orders to various members of the crowd, casting occasional malicious glances at Corwyn.

Before the alchemist had time to wonder what the innkeeper had in mind, there was another tug on his sleeve. He turned to find Oliver beside him, trying to show him his bag of rocks again.

"Not now," Corwyn whispered. "Oliver, you must saddle *Roche-naissante* and bring her out here. But don't let anyone see you. I think we're going to have to make a hurried escape." He stopped the broom once more from displaying his rocks and gave him a nudge to send him on his way.

Suddenly, men on each side of Corwyn grabbed his arms and held him. The man on Corwyn's left—the barber who had threatened him with the stave—grinned down at him with evident satisfaction. Corwyn swallowed hard and hoped Oliver remembered to hurry.

But the innkeeper's daughter arrived before Oliver, carefully balancing a cracked, aging chamber pot to keep it from spilling. She handed it to Juan Palomeque, who accepted it ceremoniously and nodded to the men holding Corwyn. "Make way for the alchemist-to-be," he told the crowd. "Bring him straight before me, and prepare him to receive the elixir of this Holy Grail."

From the corner of his eye, Corwyn saw Oliver emerge from the stable with *Roche-naissante*, just as the men at his sides hustled him over to the trough. Just as Corwyn was wondering how they would "prepare" him for whatever was to follow, the men grabbed him by his arms and legs and flung him into the water. When he surfaced, Juan Palomeque anointed him with the contents of the chamber pot, all the while mumbling words from an account book he used for keeping track of hay and feed. Then the innkeeper proclaimed, "With this water— and in the spirit of the elixir from this Grail—I transmute you." He used his broom to push Corwyn's head under again and held him for a moment before releasing him. Corwyn came up sputtering and choking and smelling like a sewer (for he remembered a time when the Roman Empire had had such things).

"Juan Palomeque mistakes himself for another Juan," someone chuckled. "The saint, Juan Bautista!"

"*Sí*, but this trough isn't the River Jordan, and San Juan never baptized anyone with the contents of a chamber pot!" a second voice replied.

Just then a dove, disturbed by the noise and perhaps attracted by the torchlight, swooped down as if to land on Corwyn, veering at the last instant and flapping away. As it flew by, however, it excreted a token of its passing, which landed with a splat on Corwyn's head. "Son of mine or not, I'm satisfied," the innkeeper roared, bursting into laughter.

Corwyn was wondering gloomily what further games might follow, when a scream from Maritornes split the night. "*¡Madre de diablos!*" came her voice from over by the stable. "So that's what one of them really looks like!"

The innkeeper, appearing perplexed, moved in that direction, drawing the crowd with him. Corwyn didn't wait for a more formal conclusion to the festivities, but hauled himself out of the trough and hurried over to Oliver and the donkey, who were waiting by the gate. *Roche-naissante* shied away, snorting through her nostrils as if offended by his smell. Corwyn grabbed the reins and clambered into the saddle, kicking the donkey into a trot even before he was firmly seated. Oliver clung to the alchemist to keep from being dislodged. Behind them, the commotion increased as the innkeeper and the rest of the crowd reached the stable. Unhindered and virtually unnoticed, Corwyn and Oliver sped across the rotting drawbridge and headed east toward Barcelona.

As far as Corwyn knew, only one other person saw him leave—the second mule skinner, whom Corwyn passed on his way through the gate and who also seemed to be fleeing from the inn. Glancing back in the moonlight, Corwyn saw the man turn northwest at the end of the drawbridge and disappear into the dark.

Corwyn paused from cursing Cid Hamete and his wretched book, and wondered briefly at the mule skinner's behavior. After all, what did he have to fear? It was

Corwyn who'd been the butt of the innkeeper's joke!

Then Corwyn shivered, realizing the mule skinner's route would take him toward Barbastro, and the windmills on the nearby plain. Since the publication of Cid Hamete's book, Corwyn wanted nothing more to do with windmills. Besides, something about those mills in particular disturbed him. It was with considerable relief, therefore, that he set out on a path which took him safely in the opposite direction.

In his eagerness to leave, however, Corwyn didn't see a third figure who left the inn a short time later. After hesitating a moment at the end of the drawbridge and checking the ground for prints, the figure reined his mount to the east, heading after Corwyn.

Chapter 5

In which Corwyn, much distressed, begins wandering in the wilderness for four days and four nights, tempted by self-doubt, while Sebastian is tormented at home by students.

FOR THE REMAINDER OF THE NIGHT, CORWYN GAVE *Roche-naissante* free rein, too lost in reliving the indignities at the inn to be concerned about where the animal took him. The ass, as constant as her name, continued in the easterly direction their flight had initially taken, gradually leaving the plain and rising into the mountains that girded Barcelona on the landward side.

Several times, Oliver tried to interest Corwyn in his little bag of stones, but the alchemist ignored the broom as firmly as he did his surroundings.

At last the sun rose before them, assaulting Corwyn with its blaze. He averted his face, only to be confronted by the sun's rays striking a granite ridge off to his left. Like the hand of an angry god, the rays seemed to proclaim Corwyn's professional downfall in letters of fire inscribed on a massive wall. Corwyn could almost read the words they formed, words that brought his lifetime pursuit of alchemy to an end. His career had been

measured and found wanting, his reputation handed over
to the lies of his detractor, Cid Hamete.

An alchemist-errant indeed! Cid Hamete made Corwyn
sound like a parody of an Arthurian knight, gallivanting
off on ridiculous quests for some alchemical version of
the Holy Grail.

Shortly after dawn, *Roche-naissante* straggled to a
stop. Corwyn grunted and swung his leg over to dis-
mount. Perhaps fate, eager to help Corwyn justify his
annoyance, placed the sharp stone beneath his heel, or
perhaps mere chance and the broken, rocky ground had
left it there. At any rate, Corwyn's bare foot came down
atop an especially jagged edge. He jumped and howled,
clutching his injured heel. Oliver leaped down from
Roche-naissante and hopped about, following Corwyn's
example in hopes that this was some new game the
alchemist was playing.

Corwyn stopped jumping when the uneven ground
hurt his other foot. The howling went on a little longer.
Finally, he shivered and rubbed his arms against the
morning breeze, distressed at finding himself alone in
the wilderness, wearing nothing but an undergown. The
rest of his clothes were still at the inn, along with his
money and supplies.

He'd done it again, Corwyn realized. He'd blundered
off on another ill-conceived quest, lacking clear purpose or adequate preparation—doing exactly what Cid
Hamete accused him of.

He sat down, then stood again abruptly and looked for
a more level spot. Broken rocks lay everywhere. After
a while, he made do with squatting miserably in the
scant shelter of a crumbled outcropping, wallowing in
the unfairness of his situation.

Back in Pomme de Terre, Sebastian was lying motionless next to Gwen, feigning sleep. He didn't want to
disturb her now that she was finally getting some rest.

Besides, he should have been up hours ago.

Gwen rolled over heavily, smacking him with an
outflung arm. Her hand returned to feel his face more

gently, as if checking to make sure it was he she had touched. She half opened her eyes and squinted in his direction. "Are you still here? Sebastian, wake up. You're supposed to be upstairs, overseeing the students."

Sebastian didn't move. "I can't do it, Gwen. Don't make me go. I can't teach them anything—nobody can. They won't listen."

"Oh, they're just boys." She squeezed her eyes shut again. "It can't be as bad as that."

"You don't know." Sebastian shuddered, recalling the interminable night just past. "They're horrible!"

Every time he had started to fall back asleep, he'd been awakened again by the harsh screech of Henri's bagpipes—each time being played (or so Henri kept assuring him) by some other student. By the time Sebastian put a stop to the whole business, he was beginning to suspect that all the boys had suddenly decided to take up the bagpipes.

Gwen responded to his complaint with a sleepy murmur.

Sebastian winced at the sounds of a muffled commotion overhead. "There's one boy in particular," he grumbled, glaring up at the ceiling. "Jean-Claude. He's the worst. Probably to blame for everything that went on last night. He comes from a noble family with nothing left for him to inherit, so they sent him here to learn a trade. But all he wants is to join one of the brigand 'free companies' that terrorize the countryside. He does everything he can to get thrown out of school."

"Sounds like when you first arrived," Gwen said. "You didn't want to be an apprentice, either. You and Jean-Claude should have a lot in common."

"That's the problem." The words hissed through Sebastian's clenched teeth. "Jean-Claude's just like I was. How can I deal with someone as difficult as me?"

"I'm sure you'll manage." She put her foot in the small of his back and pushed. "Now go on. They need you."

Sebastian stood reluctantly. "All right," he groaned, "I'll go. But they don't need me—except as a victim for their latest pranks."

But Gwen had fallen back asleep and didn't hear. Sebastian sighed and dressed slowly, postponing his fate. Seeking to stall a little longer, he circled the bed and retrieved the book Gwen had dropped on the floor during the night. He started to set it on the wooden chest she used for a table, then grimaced as he read the title: *El Ingenioso Alquimista Don Corwyn de La Mancha*. No wonder Gwen had acted so guilty when Sebastian caught her reading last night. She'd actually been enjoying the book!

Well, she could afford to laugh at its foolishness, he told himself; Cid Hamete hadn't included her in the story. For a moment, Sebastian almost wished he had— see if she still liked the book then.

At last he headed for the stairs, a condemned man being led to the executioner's block. How he envied Corwyn, off roaming around Spain, undoubtedly having the time of his life!

Midday found Corwyn still huddled under the outcropping. Now, however, it was to escape the burning sun. Oliver, having taken *Roche-naissante* to find water and grass, hadn't yet returned.

Corwyn was reflecting on his nearness to Montserrat, where for centuries men weary of the world had withdrawn into caves, living as hermits. That life appealed to Corwyn at the moment, and he considered escaping his problems by finding a cave there of his own. Gardenia and the rest of the world could struggle along without him.

But if Montserrat was a refuge for hermits, it had also become a popular destination for pilgrims, and Corwyn had no intention of being gawked at by hordes of idlers who came to stare at the inhabitants and their wild surroundings under the pretext of religious piety. Nor did he desire any contact with the Benedictine monastery which had taken root in Montserrat, growing more lush in that hostile place than any native plant, to the point that it now had its own mitered abbot. Corwyn had enough ecclesiastical problems dealing with the bishop of Pomme de Terre.

Besides, the Benedictines had also amassed a considerable library in Montserrat, and the last thing Corwyn wanted to see at the moment was another book!

As if all that weren't enough, there was yet another tradition surrounding Montserrat which deterred Corwyn from seeking refuge as one of its hermits, for at least one legend held that this was the final resting place of the Holy Grail. Other stories placed the Grail in a forgotten cave in the nearby Pyrenees, while yet other versions of the tale maintained that the mysterious castle said to house the Grail was located somewhere in Spain.

As if there really were such a thing as the Grail!

It was this Grail nonsense that irritated Corwyn as much as anything else in Cid Hamete's book. The Moor had taken two aspects of Corwyn's life—the wandering, episodic nature of his profession together with his continual search for the Philosopher's Stone—and, by casting them as parodies of the chivalric romances, had made a mockery of both. Worse, Cid Hamete had used not just the chivalric romances in general, but the Grail quest stories popularized by such writers as Chrétien de Troyes, Wolfram von Eschenbach, and Robert de Boron, equating Corwyn with Arthur's wandering knights, and the Philosopher's Stone with the Holy Grail.

What Cid Hamete didn't know was that Corwyn himself had first forged the Grail myth some nine hundred years before in an attempt to infuse new vigor into an ailing Camelot and breathe renewed life into a brooding, disenchanted king. Corwyn had alloyed his own search for the Philosopher's Stone with ores from a number of other sources, smelting bits of Greek and Egyptian legends together with lumps of Celtic belief and tempering the whole to a Christian luster that was more appealing to the newly established religion of the realm. The resulting metal he hammered into the story of the Holy Grail. With the lure of its retrieval as a goal, Corwyn was able to entice many of Arthur's knights away from court where they had grown lazy and fat, and lead them back into the countryside where they could do some good rescuing maidens and fighting ogres. Of course, eventually these quests had resulted in wars that undermined the whole of Camelot—but those hadn't been Corwyn's fault!

Corwyn had first cast the Grail legend for the most manipulative and calculating of purposes, however noble his intentions. But in so doing, he'd inadvertently forged a vessel that had since acquired a life of its own, and now his ruse had returned nine hundred years later, catching him in a cup of his own shaping.

To think there actually was a Holy Grail was nonsense, as foolish as Maritornes's mistaking an ordinary rock for the real Philosopher's Stone—the "stone that's not a stone" (as it was called), that ultimate goal of alchemy.

A rustling noise caught Corwyn's attention. He looked up, expecting Oliver, but it must have been a lizard slithering over the rocks nearby. Still, the alchemist was surprised to discover how late the day had grown. Soon it would be night again. How he envied Sebastian and the easy time he must be having in Pomme de Terre!

Corwyn hunched farther into himself, trying to delay the chill that darkness would bring by denying the passage of time, returning to the solitude of his interrupted thoughts.

"The stone that's not a stone"—what did this age-old conundrum mean for him, he wondered, as an aquatic alchemist? Mightn't the Philosopher's Stone of aquatic alchemy be different from that of ordinary alchemy? A liquid, perhaps, in keeping with the element in which Corwyn had specialized?

But if so, the particular Philosopher's Stone he sought should properly be called "the water that's not a water." And if that were the case, then he might as well give this paradoxical substance the dignity of a Latin name. He could call it *aqua mysterium*. Not that this alone made it any more substantial. The term itself held no more legitimacy than a bastard heir proclaiming the right to a contested throne. In the end, Corwyn concluded dismally, aquatic alchemy might be as fruitless an endeavor as the search for the Grail—an effort founded on fallacy and perpetuated by error, its goal given the appearance of truth by virtue of a name.

Damn that wretched Grail! How he regretted the day he'd invented it!

Throughout all of these thoughts, one in particular kept haunting him: Why, when he had already outlived so many other adversaries over the centuries, did Cid Hamete trouble him? In another hundred years or so, what would it matter?

Although Corwyn had often retreated into his own longevity in the past in order to avoid dealing with people who irritated him, he knew this distanced him from companionship as well. Surrounded by those who were granted only fleeting, ephemeral lives, Corwyn already felt the dislocation of his uniqueness. A near-immortal, he alone survived while the multitudes around him inevitably slipped away. Thinking in time spans sufficient to erase the problems of the present moment would simply accentuate his isolation, pushing his friends from this century into early graves in his eagerness to be done with Cid Hamete.

Besides, it was more satisfying to avenge one's self upon an enemy who was still alive—and who would therefore know he had been bested—than simply to stand aside and wait until he died.

Corwyn tried to swallow, wishing for a cup or vessel of some kind from which to wet his parched throat. His tongue felt thick, his mouth dry. He forced himself to his feet. He had to collect wood for a fire and find a better place to sleep. But even after he'd gathered a pile of sticks and taken them to the sandy floor of a dry wash he found, the fuel did him no good. Corwyn, an alchemist specializing in water, couldn't control that element's antagonist well enough to strike a spark.

Nor, for that matter, could his arts produce any water for him to drink.

"Isn't there even the lowliest rock sprite or tree nymph who can help me?" Corwyn cried theatrically into the gathering gloom. But only silence answered. Trembling with cold, weak with hunger and thirst, he huddled into a ball on the sand and tried to sleep.

Corwyn awoke on his second morning in the wilderness—the fifth day since he'd left Pomme de Terre—to the warmth of a crackling fire. The fragrance of roasting fish wafted upon the air, carried by the smell of woodsmoke. Corwyn licked his parched lips hungrily, grateful to Oliver, whose gifts these must be. Like a guardian spirit inhabiting this place, Oliver had apparently overheard Corwyn's plea the previous night. These offerings were his response. Corwyn felt only the slightest irritation that a mere broom had accomplished things which he, a master alchemist, could not.

He yawned and stretched, almost knocking over a stone bowl full of fresh springwater sitting next to him. The bowl had been made by breaking open a geode— a dull, unpromising nodule of rock on the outside, but inside a crystalline womb delivered up from the depths of the earth: in this case, a delicate, amethyst-lined cavity in varying shades of violet. The interior of the geode had been nourished for aeons by the mineralized amniotic waters needed to create this secret splendor, resulting in a vessel more exquisite than the costliest goblet ever served to lord or king.

Corwyn picked up the geode eagerly, his tongue awkward with thirst. But as he put the vessel to his lips, anxious for the first deep draught, he froze. This stone cup—so simple yet so rare, filled with life-sustaining fluid—was very like the Holy Grail.

Or, for that matter, the Philosopher's Stone of alchemy.

There it was again—the Grail legend, still afflicting him. Was it possible that he'd accidentally embodied a higher truth in this fabricated tale, some spiritual insight which the rest of the world had quickly recognized, but which it had taken him another nine hundred years to perceive?

Corwyn thrust the geode down an arm's length away, then stared at it unhappily. It annoyed him that Oliver, in his foolish innocence, had stumbled upon something closer to both the true Stone and the Grail—at least symbolically—than Corwyn had ever been able to find. After all, he asked himself, what vessel of comparable worth had he ever discovered or devised—the bottles used for the breath of demons test?

Corwyn snorted with disgust at this thought. Yet he was too thirsty to ignore the water in the geode, and at length he drained the suddenly bitter contents of the cup.

Unfortunately, Oliver's geode also underscored the similarities between the Philosopher's Stone and the Holy Grail, thereby lending credence to the other claims Cid Hamete made in his book. And this Corwyn resented more than anything else.

Frowning into the jeweled depths of the vessel, Corwyn was struck by sudden insight. A grail might be made of stone, as this vessel of Oliver's was, but it still wouldn't be the true Stone he sought. He himself had made the distinction yesterday, when he realized that his particular version of the Philosopher's Stone would be a liquid, and not a stone at all. *Aqua mysterium*: water of mystery.

But then what nature of substance would this *aqua mysterium* be? A martyr's blood? The piss of a saint? Milk from a virgin's breast? And in what kind of vessel, or "grail," would it be found?

Corwyn began scribbling in the sand with a stick, working through the convoluted symbolic logic of alchemy to solve the riddle of *aqua mysterium*. After a while, he noticed Oliver watching wistfully from a nearby rock, and discovered that the broom had replenished the water in the makeshift cup. But Corwyn was too distracted to spend time with the broom at the moment. He drained the cup a second time and went on with his work, writing feverishly. Later, he would give Oliver all the attention he craved.

Corwyn hadn't felt this close to his goal in centuries.

That afternoon in Pomme de Terre, Sebastian assembled the remaining students in Corwyn's laboratory and shouted to be heard above the confusion. Like chaos ignoring the first call to creation, the boys went on, yelling and punching and chasing one another around the room. Although only a dozen students were still enrolled in the school, they seemed like more, and the five days since Corwyn's disappearance had been the longest in Sebastian's life. He studied the tumult through bleary eyes and wondered if these last few students might withdraw as well. Perhaps if he encouraged their parents to reclaim them . . .

Yet even as he thought it, that hope died. The parents of this lot would keep their sons at the school as long as possible, regardless of any scandal involving Corwyn. They weren't boys at all, Sebastian decided—they were devils, sent here to punish him. If only he knew what he'd done so he could repent and be free of them!

A momentary lull gave the illusion of order. Quickly, Sebastian spoke into the hush. "Today, I'm going to introduce you to the greatest achievement in aquatic alchemy—the breath of demons test."

Jean-Claude, the oldest of the boys and their obvious ringleader, winked broadly to his companions. "Oh, we're already familiar with that test, *monsieur*. Cid Hamete described it in great detail."

The other boys grinned.

"Yes, well, I'm sure you think you understand the test from his description," Sebastian said, "but let me assure you—"

A clap of flatulent thunder erupted from Henri—the short, pudgy bagpipes player—interrupting Sebastian and sending the other students into fits of laughter. "There's a demon's breath for you to measure," Henri crowed.

Around him, the other students wrinkled their noses and fanned the air. "That's no demon's breath," Jean-Claude gasped. "That's a dragon fart."

Sebastian struggled for composure, then gave up as the smell reached him. Grabbing a lighted candle (and hoping the polluted air wouldn't ignite), he led a hasty retreat to the incubatorium, making a mental note to ask Gwen about Henri's diet. Obviously, something the boy had eaten didn't agree with him.

He ushered the students into the incubatorium, counting heads to be sure none of his charges were left outside where they could damage the main laboratory. Satisfied, he closed the door and motioned them around the heavy wooden worktable that stood at one end of the room. Across the room, the water in the stone trough gurgled and sighed on its way to join the Ale.

Sebastian set the candle on the table. "Now," he began, "if there are no more interruptions—"

A knocking, as of knuckles on wood, sounded before he could finish. "I'll get it," Jean-Claude said, moving toward the door.

Sebastian pursed his lips. It had sounded as if the knocking had come from one of the boys—possibly Jean-Claude himself—rapping on the underside of the table.

Jean-Claude opened the door and peered out. "Just as I thought," he said, closing the door again.

"What?" Sebastian asked before he could think better of it.

Jean-Claude grinned. "Another interruption."

Sebastian glowered, cursing himself for falling into another of Jean-Claude's traps. Jean-Claude swaggered back to the table like a conquering hero, where he was greeted with snickering and elbowing from his companions.

Jaw clenched, Sebastian crossed the room to retrieve the bottles Corwyn had placed in the trough five days earlier. He clunked them down on the table more forcefully than necessary, then went back to the trough for a bucket of minnows.

"Tiens!" one of the younger boys exclaimed behind Sebastian's back, his voice quavering. "Are there really demons in there?"

"Mais oui," another replied. "They'll try to escape when we open the bottles, so watch out. And don't breathe!"

As Sebastian returned with the bucket, the smaller boys edged away from the table, their wide eyes glittering in the candlelight.

Jean-Claude waved his arms over one of the bottles, repeating whatever scraps of Latin he'd picked up in his studies. *"Ars magna solve et coagula lapis philosophorum prima materia descensus ad inferos opus alchymicum,"* he intoned in a deep, dramatic voice. Then he leaned forward to peer into the bottle. "Why, I see a demon in there now. It's assuming some hideous shape with which to torment me. It looks like . . . like . . . Oh no, it's the face of *Monsieur* Sebastian!"

With a sigh, Sebastian heaved the bucket onto the table, sloshing water. *"Sacré chou!* You can't see a demon when it's dispersed in a bottle of water. They're only visible when they leave the water and float in the air. Then they can take on the appearance of your worst fear or your strongest desire, whichever will hold you long enough for the demon to possess you."

"You talk as though you've really seen such a thing," Jean-Claude scoffed. "Admit it, *monsieur*—Cid Hamete just made that up. And it's *sacré bleu*, not *sacré chou*."

Sebastian stared at him, waiting until the other boys fell silent. "I'm the master here now, and it's *sacré chou* if I say it is." He raised a hand to ward off Jean-Claude's protest. "And I assure you, I have faced demons. Several times. But don't be afraid. There probably aren't any in these bottles strong enough to harm you."

Jean-Claude huffed indignantly. "You insult me, *monsieur*. I'm not afraid of anything." He glared at Sebastian. "Or anyone."

"Really?" Sebastian replied. "Perhaps you should be."

Jean-Claude sniffed and tried to dismiss Sebastian with a toss of his head. Only his hands betrayed his agitation as he picked at the wax that sealed the bottle.

"And don't break that seal," Sebastian admonished, pleased at having finally got in the last word with the boy. "I haven't told you yet what to do with the bottle."

"Oh, I know what to do with it, *monsieur*," Jean-Claude muttered. "Cid Hamete hinted at as much."

Sebastian, sensing he was being outmaneuvered again, groped for a response. Suddenly, out of the corner of his eye, he spotted an arm pulling away from the minnow bucket. He turned to see Henri at the other end of the table dangling a minnow over his upturned mouth, as if about to swallow it. Around him, the other boys wrinkled their noses in disgust.

"Go ahead, Henri," Sebastian said. "I'm sure we'll have enough minnows left to finish the test."

Henri's round face turned red as he lowered the tiny, squirming fish. "Ah, I wasn't really going to eat it."

"Are you sure?" Sebastian asked. "I wouldn't want you going hungry."

"*Exactement,*" another boy added, whacking Henri on the side of the head. "You're always bragging about how you'll eat anything. Here's your chance to prove it."

Henri's face darkened. The hand in which he held the minnow shot to the collarless opening of the other boy's *bliaut* and the fish disappeared inside the latter's clothing. Quickly, Henri began pounding the boy on the back. A slight squishing sound confirmed the fate of the unfortunate minnow. The boy whose back had become the anvil for Henri's blows grimaced as if he were about to take offense.

Sebastian pulled the two apart, carefully avoiding the damp smear where the former minnow was now seeping through the back of the boy's *bliaut*. He opened his mouth to scold them both, when a gasp from Jean-Claude distracted him. "*Monsieur*, look!" Jean-Claude cried. "*Les poissons*, they're dying!"

For a moment, Sebastian's heart stopped as he beheld the glass bottle which Jean-Claude had opened despite Sebastian's warning and in which two minnows now convulsed. Their tiny spasms crescendoed, then died away, until at last the two fish drifted peacefully, belly up inside the bottle.

The only time Sebastian had ever witnessed such a violent conclusion to this test was when malevolent demons had contaminated the sample in the bottle. "What did you do?" he demanded in a hoarse croak.

"Nothing," Jean-Claude said. "All I did was open the bottle and drop the minnows in. They started thrashing right away. By St. Denys, *monsieur*, I swear it!"

Sebastian hurriedly checked the identifying number on the bottle against a parchment sheet which listed the sample locations represented by each bottle in the test. As he feared, the sample in Jean-Claude's bottle had been drawn from one of the streams that fed the Ale, high above the town. That stream also flowed near the Goblin Mines where Corwyn and Sebastian had trapped a horde of vicious demons two years before, thereby preventing them from possessing any more citizens of Pomme de Terre.

Could those demons now be seeping out of the mines and once more making their way into the water that supplied the duchy? Remote though the possibility was, it was why Corwyn had so closely monitored the water in the mountain streams above Pomme de Terre for the past two years. Perhaps this was what the note Corwyn had left him had been about, the note that was destroyed by acid in the laboratory before Sebastian could read it.

Then Sebastian's jaw tightened. "I don't know what you put in the bottle to poison the minnows like that, but whatever you did, it ruined the test."

"But I swear, *monsieur*, on my life—"

Sebastian waved the boy to silence, feeling grim resolution settle over his face. "Since you've seen fit to ruin the test," he went on, "thereby squandering the hard work Master Corwyn put into setting it up, we shall make an expedition of our own into the mountains to resample the stream this bottle represented." He grinned, thinking how difficult such a trek would be. The outing would teach these young upstarts to show more respect for aquatic alchemy. "We'll leave first thing tomorrow morning."

Jean-Claude looked thoughtful as he weighed this. "Does that mean we'll be staying in the mountains overnight?"

"Of course. We'll come back the following day."

A smirk spread over Jean-Claude's face. "*Trés bien, monsieur*," he said.

Sebastian felt his own smile fade under Jean-Claude's renewed cockiness. For a moment, he considered changing his mind about leading this pack of hellions into the wilderness. Then anger flared in him anew, strengthening his resolve. After all, he was the master, and they the students. It was time they learned the difference. Besides, what could possibly go wrong on such a short trip?

"Tomorrow morning," he repeated. "First thing."

Entremés

SCARCELY HAD DON CORWYN AND SEBASTIAN TRAVELED *half a day from their village when they reached a low line of hills. "Good fortune is with us," Don Corwyn cried, urging Rociandante to a faster pace, "for already we have arrived at the Pyrenees, and soon we shall be in France."*

"Master, I don't know about any Pyrenees, but I do know that's not what these hills are called," Sebastian replied, dodging the puddles left as a result of Don Corwyn's prodding of Rociandante. "We've hardly gone more than a league or two, as I should know, for I've been in these hills many times before."

"There you are wrong," Don Corwyn proclaimed, "for in alchemy, all is enchantment, and nothing is as it seems. Although we have traveled but a short time, our progress has been aided by the invisible forces at my command, and each step we have taken has counted for more than a hundred ordinary strides. And to prove this is true, if you were to take an astrolabe and determine our position by the stars, you would learn that we are indeed in the Pyrenees, as I have said."

"What good would an ass-in-the-glade, or whatever you called it, be in telling our position from the stars, unless the ass knows more than we? Besides which, I don't need an ass or the stars to tell me what my position is, for I am upright and walking behind you—and a good deal of effort it requires, too!"

"An 'astrolabe,' you imbecile," Don Corwyn cor-

rected. "Truly, you must be the most ignorant of all the apprentices that ever any master has been burdened with!"

By this time, they had crossed the hills and reached the edge of a broad plain, where three or four windmills stood in a cluster around a miller's house, their sails turning lazily in the breeze.

Now, Don Corwyn's mind was filled with the accounts he had read of Jabir ibn Hayyan, Al-Razi, and the other alchemists his books spoke of so glowingly, so as soon as he saw the windmills, he said to his apprentice, "Look, Sebastian, those demons are scaling the walls of that French castle. I must use my alchemy to stop them."

"Demons?" Sebastian asked, hoping he had misunderstood. "I don't see any demons, master, nor a French castle. Only windmills, which grind wheat into flour."

"It is quite clear," replied Don Corwyn, "that you are not used to this business of alchemical endeavors. There is indeed a French castle yonder, the towers of which are being attacked by great whirling demons, undoubtedly summoned by my rival, Hydro Phobius. If you are afraid, go say your prayers while I subject them to the purifying rigors of my ars magna."

"You don't appear to have such a 'great arse' as that," Sebastian grumbled, looking over his master from behind to assure himself of the fact. "But you're the alchemist. What do I know about the differences between arses?"

Don Corwyn scowled at him. "How did I ever find so stupid an apprentice? Ars magna is Latin for the Great Art of alchemy."

Just then, the miller and his wife emerged from one of the windmills to get some air, for the day had grown quite hot. Don Corwyn, in his madness, took the pair for a duke and a duchess, and as their faces and hands were covered with flour dust which turned them white, he thought this proof that they had been possessed by demons. He therefore grabbed up his staff Al-Aver and, with a shout commending himself to his beloved Hypatia *del Alexandria, and invoking her aid, he charged the windmill. The miller and his wife, seeing him approach, fled inside, pursued by Don Corwyn. When Sebastian caught up with his master, Don Corwyn was inside the windmill, attacking the structure.*

At this point in the narrative, a curious discrepancy occurs in the archives of Argamasilla, for these otherwise infallible records assure us that although the building was a windmill from the outside, on the inside it seems to have been powered (or otherwise serviced) by water. For when Don Corwyn repeatedly raised Al-Aver aloft and brought it down on the inner workings of the mill, he did so with such violence that at last a conduit of some kind burst, spewing forth water like a severed limb yielding up its vital fluids. The archives further tell us that the force of the spray knocked off Don Corwyn's conical hat and bowled the alchemist over backwards, where he lay stunned in a deepening pool of water.

"¡Madre de dios!" Sebastian cried when he saw what Don Corwyn had done. "Master, didn't I tell you to watch what you were doing, that your so-called demons and French castle were only windmills? And now you've ruined your hat."

"Silence, Sebastian," Don Corwyn groaned. "Matters of alchemy are more subject than most to continual change. You must learn to see beneath surface appearances to the underlying reality. I think—and it is true— that the evil enchanter Hydro Phobius who seeks to destroy my good name has transmuted these demons and this castle into windmills in order to foil me again. Such is the enmity he bears me; but in the end his black arts shall avail him little against my alchemical skills. However, all is not lost, for I have discovered here a treasure that almost rivals the Holy Grail—the hat of that greatest of all alchemists, Jabir ibn Hayyan, which has been missing for all these centuries."

At this, Don Corwyn produced a blackened and tarnished funnel, which the miller had used for filling sacks with the flour he ground. Don Corwyn placed the funnel atop his head as if it really were a pointed hat, where-

upon Sebastian, fearing that the miller and his wife (who had fled the building during the fight) might return at any moment, quickly led his master away.

After this, further adventures descended upon them as abundantly as anyone could wish, all of which are related hereafter . . .

—Cid Hamete Benengeli,
　El Ingenioso Alquimista
　Don Corwyn de La Mancha, Part I

Chapter 6

Which deals with the mysteries of thaumaturgy, alchemy, and publishing.

WHEN SEBASTIAN FINALLY GOT HIS CHARGES SAFELY off to bed that evening, he went looking for Gwen in the school kitchen, feeling guilty that she was having to work so hard during her pregnancy. Although he hadn't told Gwen for fear of alarming her, Corwyn had warned him some weeks before that she was likely carrying twins, and that her pregnancy and delivery could be difficult. The alchemist and the midwife, who had never before agreed on anything, both strongly advised her to spend as much time as possible in bed. So it was to Sebastian's relief that he found she had left the kitchen early, despite pots and pans that still needed cleaning. He finished these quickly and hurried to their room.

He carried the candle in, shielding the light with his hand in case Gwen was asleep. But she was sitting up in bed, reading more of that dreadful *El Ingenioso Alquimista Don Corwyn de La Mancha*. As he entered, she choked back her laughter and hastily shut the book, her cheeks turning red.

Sebastian refused to acknowledge the book. Instead, he told her, albeit a little coldly, about his planned trip into the mountains the following day with the students. She nodded, still looking chagrined. "Sebastian," she began, "are you sure that's wise? After all, you know how—"

His look cut her off. He didn't want advice from anyone who actually liked the Moor's wretched book.

Gwen fiddled with the blankets while he pulled off his boots and hose and readied himself for bed. She groaned a little once, and tried to shift her bulk into a more comfortable position. Immediately, Sebastian's heart softened. He stopped unlacing his doublet and started toward her, anxious to comfort her.

"The book really is quite funny," she said abruptly, sounding defensive. Sebastian halted in his tracks. "I'm sorry you don't agree with me—and with most of the rest of the world—on that, but I do think you're wrong to begrudge my reading it."

"That's easy for you to say," he muttered. "Corwyn and I are the ones the author turned into laughingstocks."

"Oh, Sebastian, is that what you think? But it's not really you he makes fun of, my husband, or I shouldn't be able to read the book at all. Rather, it's some caricature the writer's mind has dreamed up, having little more in common with you than the name."

Sebastian relaxed and inhaled slowly. Then Gwen added under her breath, "Besides, people laughed at you even before the book came out."

"I wonder whether you'd still enjoy reading it if he'd included you in it as well," Sebastian grumbled.

"But I wish he had," Gwen said with a sigh. "I think it would be fun to see what inventions he came up with for me. In fact, I'm a little hurt that he didn't, for then I might have been immortalized. You know, some of the books I've been reading were written long ago, and although the writers and the people they wrote about are long dead, still their ghosts live on in the pages of these books. I'm vain enough to want that for myself, and I'm surprised you don't appreciate having benefited from it yourself."

"Benefited!" Sebastian roared. "What benefit is there in being looked upon as a—?"

But whatever it was that Sebastian believed the world saw him as was drowned out by the whining blare of bagpipes overhead. Sebastian groaned, knowing that even if he hurried upstairs, he wouldn't catch the mysterious player in the act, for the boys had taken to setting sentinels along the stairwell to warn their companions of his approach. And he certainly wouldn't catch Henri in possession of the forbidden pipes, nor Jean-Claude orchestrating the impromptu concert; both boys were much too wily for that.

A smile settled over Gwen's face and she closed her eyes as she settled back to listen. "How lovely. Don't you just love the pipes?"

Sebastian jerked the laces tight again on his doublet. "I'm going over to Corwyn's laboratory," he growled, grabbing up his candle. "There must be something I forgot to do there before we leave in the morning."

He left the room without looking back or bothering about his boots and was soon crossing the courtyard to the laboratory. Once inside, the thick walls muted the dreadful screeching from the school. He paced restlessly in his bare feet, seeking some way of occupying himself, but in truth there was nothing that needed doing in the laboratory. After a while, he mounted the steps to the library on the second floor, still not ready to return to the school.

In the library, he strolled past the volumes ranked on their shelves, idly perusing them all, not looking for anything in particular. Perhaps it was the flickering, uncertain light of the candle that caused him to overlook one slim text, or perhaps it was because this book lay on the floor rather than in its proper place on the shelves, but whatever the reason Sebastian suddenly stubbed a bare toe against the sharp corner of the book's binding. He yelped and hopped on his other foot, almost putting out the candle. Finally, feeling really sorry for himself after this latest indignity, he bent down and retrieved the book, intending to return it to the shelves. Gwen must have inadvertently knocked it off while gathering up her latest selection of chivalric romances. Sebastian decided to be charitable and put the book back for her despite her literary tastes. He glanced at the title to see where it belonged. *Summa Theologica*, he read. Evidently the book by St. Thomas Aquinas. Then he looked again, for the author listed on the cover wasn't Aquinas; instead, it was someone named Simon Magus. Sebastian reread the title.

Summa Thaumaturgica.

Suddenly, Sebastian's knees felt wobbly and the hand in which he held the book began to tremble. Surely Corwyn must be unaware this book was in his library, for the old alchemist disdained anything to do with magic. Sebastian reached up hurriedly to the highest shelf, anxious to put the book out of sight until his master could be alerted to its presence. Corwyn could decide for himself what to do about the offensive text.

Yet Sebastian couldn't manage to let the book go. It frightened him, for he had adopted Corwyn's attitude toward magic, and in this respect the pupil had bettered the master. But the little volume, seemingly so innocent, also intrigued him. He vacillated a moment, then rationalized that it would be best to remove the book from the library altogether lest any of the students accidentally come across it. After all, they were still young and must be protected from the potentially dangerous influences of a work such as this. It was his responsibility to keep the book in his personal care until Corwyn returned.

It was still too early for Sebastian to go back to the school and the apartment where he and Gwen lived; better to wait a little longer and be sure the bagpipe concert was over for the night. In the meantime, he thought, there wouldn't be any harm in taking a peek at this book whose contents were deemed so terrible, particularly if he merely thumbed through its pages to familiarize himself with the nature of its fabrications.

He sat down and began to read.

Gwen had watched in silence as Sebastian stalked out of their room. She'd wanted to call him back, to comfort him, but lately she didn't know what to say— not to Sebastian, not to anyone.

Part of this was due, of course, to the strange feelings which surged through her these days, and the awareness that her body was not her own. Sometimes this was exhilarating, sometimes frightening, and sometimes it produced a sense of peace she found astonishing, of being released into the care of something—a force, perhaps, or a state of being—far greater than her normal self. She, who had always possessed such a strong need to control her own life and destiny, found the surrender of this oddly comforting. But it wasn't anything she could explain, especially not to Sebastian.

And when her pregnancy frightened her, she couldn't share that with Sebastian, either. Not only didn't he understand (what man could?), but also there was the fact that Corwyn had advised her she might be carrying twins, and she didn't want Sebastian to worry about the delivery or the added responsibility twins would entail later. If she actually bore twins, the time when it happened would be soon enough for him to find out.

Yet there was also something else flooding through Gwen in strange and shifting tides, and it was something she didn't fully understand herself. It had to do with the books she'd been reading, and the new worlds Corwyn had opened for her by exposing her to his library and the languages in which many of the books were written. Although Gwen had been able to read a little before she'd met the alchemist, Corwyn had vastly sharpened this skill, and under his tutelage she had discovered her eagerness to learn and the facility with which she mastered languages.

So the quickening of new life within her was of two kinds: one the child (or children) of her body, the other the flowering of her mind.

Gwen tried once again to find a comfortable position, then sighed with resignation and began looking for her place in *Don Corwyn*. She wished Sebastian—and Corwyn, too, for that matter—could see what she saw in the book. But both men were too personally affronted by it to ever appreciate Cid Hamete's humor. They seemed to expect some grand, eternal truth in the books they read, whereas she expected something else—a kind of truth, yes, but not necessarily of an obvious or immutable kind; a more fragile truth that could only be revealed by distorting and rearranging the external, seemingly unchangeable world.

If only she had known earlier that Sebastian would be leaving town for a couple of days, taking the students into the mountains (oh, the poor, foolish man had so much to learn about handling boys!), she would have waited to read *Don Corwyn* until he'd gone. In the meantime, she could have started the *Tristan and Yseult* just recently published. But perhaps that wouldn't have been any better after all. Corwyn had an inexplicable aversion to romances of chivalry, and to Arthurian romances in particular, which Sebastian, ever his master's eager pupil, had been quick to adopt. So although reading *Tristan and Yseult* might have spared her husband's feelings, it also would probably have resulted in another lecture on what manner of books she should be reading instead. And Gwen was quite satisfied with her own literary tastes.

She found the page she'd been reading, and soon the room was filled again with the sound of chuckling as her worries about Sebastian and Corwyn and her fears about the upcoming delivery were forgotten, dispelled for the moment by Cid Hamete's wondrous gift of mirth.

Earlier that same evening, Corwyn had finally settled back on his heels and eyed the results of his work. The surface of the sand all about him was covered with marks and symbols made with his stick. In his hand he held a flat sheet of slate on which he had intended to scratch the ultimate laws governing aquatic alchemy and the nature of *aqua mysterium*.

Yet for all his enthusiasm on starting out, his efforts had quickly fallen into circular arguments and unsound reasoning. He still didn't know what manner of substance this *aqua mysterium* would be, nor was he any closer to discovering the kind of vessel in which it might be found.

He had, however, come up with a promising idea for an elixir to cure seasickness, an affliction which had plagued him repeatedly through the centuries. Not that he expected to need such an elixir anytime soon, but at least it was something.

Other than that, all he had to show for his day's work was a great number of calculations proving to himself just how rich Cid Hamete Benengeli must have become through publication of his cursed book. As the day had progressed and Corwyn seemed no closer than ever to his goal, he had become obsessed with figuring out how much the story of his life was worth to that lying dog of a Moor. Working from a number of assumptions, ranging from ones Corwyn considered quite conservative up through some he admitted were at the extreme end of possibility, he had concluded that Cid Hamete was now or soon should be very rich—perhaps even wealthy beyond imagining! In fact, if twelve hundred copies of the book had actually been printed so far, as Sebastian claimed, and the book was just now being translated into various foreign languages, then by estimating the average price of the book and the portion of that price which went to Cid Hamete, Corwyn found it likely that his speculations erred—if at all—only by falling far short of the actual sum the Moor had already earned.

Earned! What was he thinking? Stolen, he should say. For everything the Moor said in his book was either an outright fabrication by the author, or else it was based in some way on Corwyn's real life story, in which case the profits should by rights go to Corwyn and Corwyn alone.

Furthermore, the constant feeling of being watched throughout the day had not improved his outlook, and he felt irritated with Oliver for spying on him this way. If the broom was so curious about what he was doing, why didn't he just come out of hiding and ask?

Corwyn was transferring a few final, desultory marks from the sand onto the tablet (he might as well keep a record of just how much the Moor owed him, he told himself) when Oliver did sidle over and stood waiting quietly, anxious for Corwyn's attention but reluctant to interrupt. Corwyn scowled, unsettled by the fact that Oliver had approached from the direction opposite from where the alchemist had thought the broom was watching. Corwyn set aside his stick and looked up. "All right, Oliver, what is it?"

Hesitantly, Oliver held out his little leather bag of rocks.

"Yes, you showed them to me, remember? They're very nice rocks." Despite his frustration, Corwyn softened his voice for the little creature.

Oliver laid the bag in Corwyn's hand. Corwyn grunted, surprised by its heaviness. "You want me to look at them again?" he asked.

Oliver nodded.

Corwyn loosened the thong on the bag, then poured the stones into his hand, ready to praise them a second time. But to his amazement, instead of rocks he was holding coins of silver and gold. He looked at Oliver in silent question.

Oliver acted out the scene from the inn yard two nights before, his pantomime making it clear that he hadn't stolen the money, since Corwyn had forbidden this, but instead had secretly traded his precious collection of stones for the coins.

Corwyn imagined the innkeeper's reaction on discovering his money gone, replaced by rocks. Yet even though the image gave him a certain angry satisfaction, he couldn't really rejoice in Oliver's accomplishment. By exchanging common rocks for noble metals, the broom had again in a sense achieved the goal Corwyn had spent his life pursuing. At least it was as close as Corwyn had ever come to a real transmutation.

Corwyn scolded Oliver for what he had done. The broom, obviously startled, turned and ran, covering the two unmatched wooden knots that were his eyes with a stick arm as if crying. Corwyn watched with a deep sense of guilt, dismayed by the broom's hurt feelings. Never before had Corwyn seen Oliver mimic crying, and he wondered whether it was anything more than outward show.

He started to call Oliver back, then hesitated, unable to offer his creation even that. Corwyn knew he was suffering from the anguish of being only what he was, of not managing somehow to be something more. What he sought was forgiveness for this guilt—the assurance of grace—from himself as well as from the universe as a whole. But because the former was so hard for him to grant, the latter was impossible to accept.

And what Corwyn couldn't give to himself, he couldn't give to Oliver either, regardless how much the innocent little broom deserved his understanding. Because Corwyn didn't know how to forgive himself, he also didn't know how to forgive others; he only knew how to inflict his own brooding on those unlucky enough to be around him.

He picked up the stick and started to write again, then angrily lashed out at the surface of the sand, obliterating the marks he'd made. Not satisfied, he picked up the stone tablet and hurled it to the ground, intending for it to land harmlessly in the sand.

Instead, it smashed against the geode Oliver had left that morning, shattering both vessel and tablet in the impact. Water flowed onto the sand, then quickly sank into the grains, leaving only a faint dampness to mark where it had been.

Corwyn sat down heavily, staring at the fading wetness, the shattered stones, and the scattered bits of gold and silver, wondering which of his acts of destructiveness was the worst, certain that he knew the answer.

There we shall leave him for the night, hoping once more that we (as well as Oliver, and even Corwyn himself) will find more pleasure in his company come morning.

Chapter 7

Corwyn asks for a sign and is granted several, whereupon he promptly dismisses them and flees to Barcelona, while Sebastian meets the prophet Toxemiah.

CORWYN AWOKE ON HIS THIRD MORNING IN THE WILDERNESS cold, hungry, thirsty, virtually naked, and alone. Oliver hadn't returned. The fire, untended during the night, had gone out. Corwyn still had no idea where *Roche-naissante* was tethered.

Feeling guilty and thoroughly miserable (from which we may assume our hopes of the previous night are to be dashed), he climbed a rise just east of the dry wash where he had made his camp. There he sat beside a lone, scrubby juniper (more a bush than a tree) that grew on the crest, warming himself in the morning sun.

As the day advanced and the heat increased, he remained atop the rise, staring moodily at the sky and moving just enough to keep the juniper between himself and the burning sun.

Later that day, Sebastian tramped warily up the mountainside into the Pyrenees, his skin crawling from the knowledge that he was being watched.

The year before, Corwyn had shown him how a curved mirror could be used to concentrate the sun's rays on a waterdrop with such intensity that the water would hiss and spit. Today, Sebastian's back had become that drop, and the eyes of his students were like a dozen pairs of mirrors, each insignificant in itself, but together bringing such brilliance to bear on him that it seared through his blouse and into his flesh.

Occasionally, lest he forget, the students whispered and snickered among themselves, as if to remind him that he was still the focus of their attention.

Earlier in the day, feeling too vulnerable at the head of the column, Sebastian had sought a more secure position at the rear. From there, he shouted instructions to Jean-Claude, who was then in the lead. But Jean-Claude invariably veered off in the wrong direction, claiming he couldn't hear Sebastian. As if that weren't enough, Jean-Claude led the entourage beneath every pine and fir tree he encountered. Henri, who was in line ahead of Sebastian, would brush the branches aside as he passed, releasing them just in time to catch Sebastian in the face. Or the scree over which the boys clambered would be kicked loose by Henri's feet and come tumbling down upon Sebastian.

Besides, whatever had disrupted Henri's digestion the day before in the laboratory was still troubling him. Sebastian would have died of asphyxiation had he remained where he was.

Now in the lead again, Sebastian paused, wiped the sweat from his face with his sleeve, and glanced at the sun where it was dropping toward the peaks to the west. Soon, Sebastian assured himself, they would reach the intended campsite near the headwaters of the Ale, just before evening enveloped them. The boys would unpack the loads Sebastian had divided among them, and Jean-Claude would find that his consisted of nothing but rocks. Sebastian chuckled to himself as he thought of Jean-Claude's indignation.

After a brief dinner, the exhausted boys would fall asleep and Sebastian could finally relax. Perhaps he could even read some more of *Summa Thaumaturgica*, which he had hidden inside his tunic. In the morning, he would oversee the boys as they took their water samples, then return as quickly as possible to Pomme de Terre. And never again, he vowed silently, would he ever be fool enough to lead a pack of savages into the wilderness single-handed.

Next time, he'd bring an armed escort.

All of that third day in the wilderness, Corwyn sulked in the scant shade of the stunted juniper, faint with heat, thirst, and hunger. Around him, the sun-drenched landscape shimmered as though a thousand unseen devils danced upon the burning air. Corwyn stared at a rounded rock off to one side, a rock that in this light—and when seen under the influence of an empty belly—looked amazingly like a loaf of freshly baked bread. Corwyn's mouth did its best to water, although the results were nothing more than a slight increase in stickiness.

If he were a competent alchemist, he chided himself, he'd be able to turn that stone into bread. As it was, he couldn't even feed himself.

Of course, Oliver could feed him. Oliver was only a broom, but Oliver could find sustenance in the wilderness. Oliver could provide Corwyn with food and water and start a fire using nothing but sticks. He could turn common rocks into silver and gold better than any alchemist, then locate a grail that didn't even exist. Oliver could do anything—the world was his for the taking.

But if all the things of the earth could be Oliver's, Corwyn wondered, couldn't they thereby be his as well? Surely the broom had demonstrated his eagerness to provide Corwyn with whatever the alchemist wished.

Corwyn snorted and pushed the thought away, angry that it tempted him. He could feel Oliver watching him again, and the alchemist's heat-numbed brain wondered what would happen if he were to stumble from the crest. Would Oliver be able to prevent him from coming to harm on the rocks below? But Corwyn realized he wouldn't be in a position to gloat if Oliver couldn't save him, and if by some chance the broom kept him from being hurt, that might only make Corwyn feel worse.

So he sat there, brooding, steeped in the bitterness of his own limitations, questioning whether he had misspent his life.

"What should I do?" he demanded at last of the gathering stars. "Things used to be so clear; now I just don't know any more. I wish someone would give me a sign."

Undoubtedly, many readers would like to reach into the pages of this history and give the old alchemist a sign, perhaps by shaking him to his senses. And had Corwyn himself reflected first on how his cry for help two evenings before had been answered, and how distressing he'd found that response, he might not have uttered a similar plea just now. But before he could think better of it, the deed was done, the words spoken, their last reverberations spreading like ripples through the dark, infinite reaches of night.

We can only hope that whatever answer he receives will dislodge him from his continued petulance.

Despite his expectations to the contrary, Corwyn did sleep that night, and his fourth morning in the wilderness began with a troubling dream. He was on a journey—he couldn't remember to where—when the road he was following ended at a body of water. Some distance from the bank, a richly dressed man in a boat was fishing. Corwyn shouted to him for directions. At first, the man appeared not to have heard, for he didn't answer right away. Corwyn waited a moment, then tried again. But as he did, the fisherman called back to him, his reply swallowed up by Corwyn's repeated question. Frustrated, Corwyn yelled to him a third time, only to drown out the response again. So it went for the rest of the dream, with Corwyn shouting his appeals over the fisherman's replies, invariably deafening Corwyn to the very answer he sought.

At last he woke, shivering with cold and unsettled by the dream. Around him, the broken landscape lay shrouded in mist, sparsely illumined by the predawn glow to the east. Corwyn started to groan, then broke off when the sound emerged muffled in stillness, as lifeless and heavy as the rocks. He stood, flailing his arms and stamping his feet in the eerie silence, then started up the hill toward the light, eager for certitude as much as warmth.

The sun rose to meet him, topping the hill just as Corwyn reached the crest. The scrawny juniper at the summit loomed starkly in the mist, then seemed to burst into flame as sunlight struck it from the other side. Corwyn watched in awe. The juniper burned, unconsumed, feeding upon the mist, devouring it. Suddenly, a shaft of light pierced the branches and smote Corwyn in the face. He squinted at the sudden brilliance and turned away, feeling uneasy. But then he beheld his shadow behind him, stretched upon the ground like a dark, spectral being pointing the way.

Corwyn shuddered. A lot his shadow knew, guiding him west, he told himself. He snorted and hurried down the hill, anxious to get Oliver's campfire blazing again.

About the time Corwyn was seeking warmth from the Spanish sunrise, Sebastian was awakening on the French mountainside above Pomme de Terre. Birds warbled in the trees, welcoming the morning that was beginning to show her countenance at the doors and windows of the east, shaking from her locks a profusion of liquid pearls.

It must have been this liquid, pearly profusion that brought Sebastian awake, although it felt more like ice water flung in his face. At any rate, thus bathed in a refreshing shower of moisture (whatever the source), Sebastian leaped up, spluttering and swearing, in his excitement falling back upon his native Anglo-Saxon for words adequate to express the depth of his feeling.

In his haste, he failed to notice that someone had bound his ankles together while he slept, and no sooner had he pulled his feet under him and leaped upright than he pitched forward again onto the ground. Around him, trees tittered, given voice by the wood sprites taking refuge behind their trunks.

Sebastian tried to push himself into a sitting position and discovered that his hands were also tied. "You boys come back here and let me loose!" he bellowed.

The laughter haunting the campsite increased.

"I'm warning you!"

One of the sprites came out from behind a tree, as impeccably dressed as if he belonged to the court of Titania, the fairy queen, and carrying himself like one whose authority has never been questioned. Sebastian looked up and groaned. "Jean-Claude, I might have known you were behind this."

Jean-Claude put his hands on his hips and cocked his head while he pondered the figure sprawled before him. "Ah, it was just a harmless prank, *monsieur*. Surely you wouldn't punish us for it."

"Oh, wouldn't I?" Sebastian roared. "Untie me and we'll see about that!"

The youth squinted at the growing light beyond the trees. "Well, now, that presents something of a problem, doesn't it? Why should I let you loose if you're going to punish me for it?" He appeared to give the matter some thought, then shook his head and looked back down at Sebastian. "No, *monsieur*, you'll have to work free by yourself. That'll give us time to get away before you start after us." He jerked his thumb at the trees and headed from the clearing. At his signal the other boys emerged from hiding and began following him.

"Hey, wait a minute!" Sebastian called, straining at his bonds. "You're not going to abandon me like this, are you?"

Jean-Claude shrugged. "You don't leave me much choice." Again he started from the clearing.

"Wait!" Sebastian cried.

Jean-Claude kept walking.

"All right, no recriminations."

Jean-Claude paused. "On your honor, *monsieur*?"

"Yes, curse you—I give my word as a nobleman."

The youth didn't move. "Forgive me, but you're no longer a nobleman, *monsieur*. You'll have to come up with something else."

"All right, on my honor as an alchemist, then."

Jean-Claude squinted at a hawk soaring high overhead until it vanished behind a nearby peak. "Well, now, it seems you're not really a full-fledged alchemist yet, either. You're just a journeyman."

Sebastian stopped struggling. He tried to keep the apprehension from his voice. "What do you want me to swear on, then?"

"Let's see, what significance do you possess that's worth swearing on?" Jean-Claude scratched his chin while he considered this. Suddenly, he eyed Sebastian. "I know—on your honor as a figment of Cid Hamete's imagination."

"What?" Sebastian kicked at the ropes that held him. "Wait till I get my hands on you!"

Jean-Claude gave another shrug. "Then farewell, *monsieur*, until we meet again. If we do meet again, that is. Wolves and bears might come upon you before you get loose."

"Wolves? Bears?" Sebastian peered at the surrounding trees. "Wait a minute."

Jean-Claude inspected his nails, trimming them with the dirk from his belt. "Your word, *monsieur*?"

"Yes, yes, I give my word, damn you. There'll be no recriminations, upon my word as a . . . a figment of Cid Hamete's imagination."

He ran the final words together in his eagerness to spit them out.

"That's the spirit, *monsieur*." Jean-Claude started across the clearing, shifting the dirk in his hand to cut Sebastian's bonds.

A wailing voice from beyond the trees froze the youth in midstride. The banshee cry soared, fell, then rose again, like a lost soul lamenting its fate.

Sebastian's heart lurched, then began pounding so hard it almost drowned out the terrible cry.

Jean-Claude cursed. "It's that crazy hermit, the one who calls himself Toxemiah." He rocked on his toes as if unsure whether to continue toward Sebastian or to flee down the mountainside.

"Cut me loose!" Sebastian shrieked. He stretched his ankles closer to the youth, encouraging him in his choice. Only a few paces separated Sebastian's bonds from Jean-Claude's knife.

A gaunt specter of a man carrying a gnarled staff strode over a nearby rise, the greasy tangles of his hair and stiff strands of his beard scarcely affected by the morning breeze. Sebastian almost didn't recognize him. Gangly even at his former best, the man's half-starved body was clothed in scraps of uncured animal hides and ornamented with rotting fish heads strung on cords. The mad light of someone possessed still burned in his eyes, though whether it was angels or demons that now afflicted him, Sebastian couldn't be certain.

When Sebastian had first met him, the man had been known as Dr. Tox. Now he lived as a hermit in the mountains, calling himself Toxemiah and making a nuisance of himself among the local shepherds with his stench and his prophecies of doom for the duchy.

When Toxemiah caught sight of Sebastian and the students, he headed toward them. "O citizens of Gardenia, hearken to the voice of one crying in the wilderness," he roared, throwing wide his arms. "Behold, straight have I come unto thee, to tell of the ways of iniquity being prepared for thee in the desert by thine oppressor."

"Go away, you fool," Jean-Claude cried. "We don't want anything to do with you." He waved his arms, his knife catching the morning sun. Sebastian wriggled wormlike over the ground in an effort to reach the flashing blade.

Like wrathful spirits clearing a path for his coming, the smells of decomposing animal skins and fish heads preceded Toxemiah down the slope. When the smells reached Sebastian, he stopped squirming and began to gag. Jean-Claude backed away with a grunt. "Keep silence before me, O villeins, that all may heed my call,"

Toxemiah commanded. "Verily, I say, thine oppressor prepareth himself to sow the wind, even to reap the whirlwind, and the harvest of confusion therefrom shall he cast among you."

"Villeins, is it?" Jean-Claude panted. He stooped and picked up a rock. "*Alors*, heed this!" He flung the rock at Toxemiah.

Toxemiah batted the missile aside with his staff. The rock bounced, striking Sebastian in the foot. "Ow!" he cried, then immediately regretted letting out his breath. When he inhaled again, the stench burned his nose and clawed at his throat.

Toxemiah raised his staff and shook it. "My rod, yea my staff, it comforteth me," he announced. "But you it shall vex most sorely." Wielding the implement in both hands, he bore down on the students, ready to thrash them. The boys ran screaming down the mountain.

Toxemiah halted at the edge of the clearing. "What befell Sodom and Gomorrah shall be visited tenfold upon Pomme de Terre," he bellowed after the retreating figures. "Thorns and nettles shall grow up in the great hall of the duchess's castle; yea, it shall be an habitation for serpents, and a court for owls."

He paused, then slowly shook his head when the boys continued running. "They have shut their eyes, that they cannot see," he muttered, "and their hearts, that they cannot understand."

A groan from Sebastian caused the madman to turn with a start, having apparently forgotten him. His eyebrows rose. "Beware ye men," he intoned, addressing his captive listener as if Sebastian were a throng, "even you whose breath is in your nostrils, for thereby shall ye be vanquished."

That much was true, Sebastian reflected, for the air around Toxemiah was sufficient to bring about anyone's undoing. Sebastian coughed and groaned again.

Toxemiah drew nearer. "Many there be which say of me, 'There is no help for him. *C'est-là!*'" He cackled and squatted at Sebastian's side, dropping his voice to a whisper. "But *c'est-là* what, I ask you? Do they know?"

He waved a bony hand after the departed students. "I tell you, the day of the duchy's oppressor is at hand, and the hour of his coming draweth nigh, when all the duchy will tremble at his presence."

"Who?" Sebastian croaked. "What are you talking about?"

"Haven't you been paying attention?" Toxemiah whacked Sebastian over the head with his staff. "He whom I precede, of course. He whose minion I was and whose boots I was deemed unworthy to lick. I go before him now to make straight the error of my former crooked ways."

Sebastian's brain, already foggy from lack of air, reverberated with the blow. He tried to make sense of the madman's words, but the roaring in his ears muffled them beyond all meaning.

Suddenly, Toxemiah paused, staring closely at Sebastian. "Have we met?"

"*Oui.* Don't you remember me, Dr. Tox?"

"Dr. Tox?" The mad prophet stroked his straggly beard, echoing distant mannerisms. "I seem to recall once knowing someone by that name."

"My master and I freed you from the Goblin Mines, after you'd been possessed."

Toxemiah leaned closer and squinted. The fish heads strung around his neck brushed Sebastian's chest, making the younger man flinch. "So you're Dr. Tox, and it was you who let me out of the Goblin Mines after your master locked me in?"

"No, no," Sebastian cried. "We rescued you together, my master and I."

But the madman didn't seem to have heard. "I do remember being closed up in the mines," he murmured, staring at the sun as it rose above the peaks. "The evil apparitions that abideth in that place flew unto me, and the touch of them was like live coals laid with tongs upon my lips. And when I breathed them in, I became thereby a man of unclean soul, and dwelt in darkness among them." He shuddered, then inhaled deeply as if seeking sustenance from the fumes that enveloped him.

"Though not Legion, their name was Several, and they remained within me for forty weeks of days and nights. And when they were at last cast out, then it was that I received my call."

"Call? What call?" Sebastian gasped. "You don't understand—I'm not Dr. Tox, you are. Would you mind standing downwind?"

Again the prophet appeared not to have heard. "Yet then was I but as a child, for I spake as a child and knew only childish things. I fled the mountains and came out onto the plains where, lo, I beheld in the distance a whirlwind, with a huge giant standing in the midst thereof, his four arms turning in the sun like unto four terrible scythes. As a great reaper he stood, ready to advance upon the inhabitants of Gardenia, to mow them down like wheat, and behind him many others of his kind.

"Since that time has Toxemiah preached unto the city of Pomme de Terre, and even unto the whole duchy of Gardenia, as a prophet to warn the sons and daughters thereof, in repentance for his sins."

"Dr. Tox, I don't know what you're talking about, but would you please untie me and let me go? I can't stand this much longer."

Dr. Tox looked at Sebastian's bonds with evident surprise and stretched out his bony hands to them. Then he stopped. "Yea, we would all be free, yet are we not held prisoners by our ignorance? Time and again have I cried out a warning to the duchy, but their ears are stopped and their eyes are blind. That all may believe what I say, therefore, I have brought unto the duchy another sign, and you shall be the witness thereof."

He stood and unslung a small wineskin from over his shoulder, then held the skin at arm's length as if intending to pour its contents on the ground. Before he could remove the plug from the narrow opening, however, a cry erupted from a cluster of nearby adolescent throats, as from children engaging in mock battle. A reagent flask from Corwyn's laboratory sailed past the startled figure of Dr. Tox and shattered against a stone, liberating its contents to smoke and scorch the earth. Three or four empty sample bottles quickly followed suit. Soon the air was filled with costly glassware hurled at the prophet by a ragtag army of advancing, yelling students. In their lead ran Jean-Claude, his arms laden with the makeshift alchemical weapons.

Sebastian, appalled by the wanton destruction of his master's equipment, sucked in his breath to stop them. The sudden gulp of polluted air made him retch. Tears streamed from his eyes. Ever since coming to Pomme de Terre, he reflected dismally, the stink of rotting fish and other hideous smells had been the bane of his existence—and with no sign of their abating! For a moment, he wondered whether Father Ptomaine might let him return to l'Abbaye de Sainte-Tomate. The relative luxury of religious asceticism was suddenly appealing.

Dr. Tox, meanwhile, retreated from the onslaught. At the top of a rise, he mounted a large rock and pounded on it with the base of his staff, shouting to his enemies. "Awake, awake, and hearken unto me! For I say unto you, the moon shall be confounded, and the sun ashamed, when iniquity dwells in Pomme de Terre."

Jean-Claude issued a retort on behalf of the students— a glass retort that tumbled lazily through the air, catching the morning sun. It smashed against the rock in a burst of glittering fragments. The self-proclaimed prophet snorted in indignation, shielding himself from the shower of glass with his arms, then vanished down the other side of the rise.

Sebastian, able to breathe again at last, looked up with surprise at Jean-Claude standing over him. "You came back for me?"

Jean-Claude scowled as if he found his own actions perplexing. "Well, we just couldn't leave you here, could we? I mean, not without knowing what that crazy old hermit might do." He bent down and cut Sebastian's bonds with his dirk, his mouth twisting into a sly grin. "Besides, if anything happened to you, who would we have to torment?"

Sebastian grunted and rubbed the circulation back into his wrists and ankles. He looked around at the scattered shards of glass. "I don't suppose there are any bottles left for taking water samples back to Pomme de Terre?"

"Non, monsieur." Jean-Claude shrugged apologetically, his grin widening. "They were the first to go, I'm afraid."

"I'm sure it just happened to work out that way," Sebastian grumbled. "Well, I guess we'll have to attribute yesterday's breath of demons result to experimental error." He frowned. "Unless you're ready to confess to having purposely ruined the test?"

Jean-Claude's grin vanished. "I assure you, *monsieur*, I did no such thing."

"Exactement," Sebastian replied dryly. "So you told me before." He stood cautiously, wincing from the injuries inflicted earlier to his foot and head. "Then there's nothing else for us to do but return to the school empty-handed." He glanced behind him in the direction Toxemiah had taken. "I just wonder what Dr. Tox was carrying on about. He sounded like some prophet right out of the Old Testament, warning us of impending doom."

"With such a madman, who can tell his purpose?" Jean-Claude's smirk returned. "But I'm sure you've learned from Cid Hamete the hazards of associating with madmen who are nothing more than characters in a book, eh, *señor*?" He elbowed Sebastian in the ribs.

"Hmph!" Sebastian began limping down the mountain, refusing to grant the boy's gibe any further response.

But the encounter with what remained of Dr. Tox, together with Sebastian's still unanswered doubts about the previous day's test result, cast a pall over his mood which even the morning sunshine and growing heat failed to alleviate.

How he longed now for Corwyn's speedy return from Zaragoza!

On the afternoon of his fourth day in the wilderness, Corwyn dozed in the shade to escape the heat. In the midst of a fitful sleep, he dreamed an angel climbed a ladder that rose from the ground beside him, whereupon the creature began slowly to beat its wings, fanning Corwyn with the breeze. But the breeze soon became a whirlwind, and the voice of the wind a terrible cry, burning with sulfurous fire; and the angel's wings were like the spokes of a wheel whose turning shook the earth, or the blades of a great windmill whose revolutions set other, lesser wheels spinning within.

Uttering a roar (or so he dreamed), Corwyn rose up and threw himself at the apparition, furious that he couldn't avoid this parody Cid Hamete had made of his life even in sleep. Corwyn wrestled the angel down from his perch and the two of them grappled on the ground, rolling over and over in the dirt. Throughout their match, the angel struggled silently. Then, just as Corwyn was about to get the better of his adversary, a sharp pain deep in his thigh crippled him. He cried out and released the angel, flinging himself back upon the sand.

Either the muscle cramp or Corwyn's own cry must have awakened him, for he finally realized he'd been wrestling with Oliver. The broom, looking like a disheveled, fallen angel, sprawled across from him in the sand. Nearby were a pair of olive branches which Oliver had apparently been using to fan Corwyn, lying at the base of the rock upon which the broom had stood.

Corwyn pushed himself upright, favoring his injured leg, and stretched out a hand. "I'm sorry, Oliver. I didn't know it was you."

The broom pushed Corwyn's hand aside, as silent as the opponent in the alchemist's dream. The little creature rose like an ungainly child, lacking grace or comeliness, a creature of wordless suffering, despised and rejected even by his maker. Yet for all this, Corwyn realized with a pang that there was something noble about Oliver, and knew too that he often failed to appreciate this fact. Perhaps because Corwyn was so self-conscious about his own creation, he tended to push it away, attempting to dismiss it.

But now it was Oliver who was dismissing him.

Something glistened near the top of the pole that formed Oliver's body, a little drop of wetness just beneath one of the misaligned knots that were the broom's eyes. Corwyn reached out to him. Oliver flinched and drew away, but not before Corwyn touched the droplet with a fingertip. He rubbed his thumb gently against his finger, frowning at the dampness. It was sap, sticky but moist. It couldn't have come from Oliver, Corwyn told himself, for the wood from which the broom was made was far too old still to be exuding sap. Oliver must have brushed up against the freshly cut bark of a tree, perhaps when he'd been gathering olive branches to use for fans.

Before Corwyn could ask Oliver about it, however, the broom bolted away. Corwyn tried to call him back, but Oliver didn't seem to hear.

Later that evening, the sun set behind a strange pillar of cloud, lighting it from behind to form a fiery column in the west that drew Corwyn toward it. Looking like a cloud by day and fire by night, it promised to lead him . . . where? He shook himself, trying to dispel the illusion. Hunger and isolation, as well as the constant sense of being watched, must have affected his senses.

Something grew out of the base of the fiery cloud and approached him. Corwyn blinked, uneasy that anything could emerge unscathed from such an inferno, then saw it was only Oliver leading *Roche-naissante* over the hill toward him. A trick of light—nothing more—had made it seem as if Oliver were walking from the midst of flames.

Nevertheless, the vision left Corwyn shaken. He felt an ominous force urging him to turn westward, to retrace his steps toward the town of Barbastro and its line of cursed windmills. Corwyn gritted his teeth in defiance and accepted *Roche-naissante's* reins. Hurriedly, he gathered up the silver and gold pieces from the inn that Oliver had offered him. He tied the coins in the hem of his undergown, mounted the ass, then looked around for Oliver.

The broom had disappeared. Corwyn called for him, but there was no response. The alchemist pulled *Roche-naissante's* head around to the east and prodded the beast lightly with his heels, his eyes searching the gloom for Oliver. *Roche-naissante* didn't budge. Corwyn kicked her again, harder. She plodded through a half circle and headed west instead, pinching Corwyn's foot against a rock ledge as she turned. Frightened now, Corwyn jerked back on the reins till she was headed east again, then slapped her flank with his open hand. The donkey dropped to her knees beneath him. Corwyn, trembling with fear and anger, grabbed a discarded olive branch, determined to thrash the animal into obedience if necessary. But *Roche-naissante* swung her head around to gaze at him in wide-eyed reproach, and the branch fell from Corwyn's upraised hand.

Roche-naissante snuffled and shook her mane, then snaked her neck around again and stared ahead as if waiting for something. Corwyn, too, peered into the growing darkness, gradually discerning a small figure standing so as to block their way to the east. It was only Oliver, Corwyn realized with a start, yet the broom held himself with unaccustomed confidence. In his twig hands he carried a long staff that—in the faint light—looked more like a weapon than a walking stick. Oliver signaled to *Roche-naissante*, whereupon the animal promptly got to her feet and ambled forward, much to the annoyance of Corwyn. The alchemist held his tongue, however, feeling unsettled by all that was happening.

Roche-naissante halted next to Oliver, and Corwyn reached down to lift the little creature into the saddle. The broom swiveled his trunk to indicate "no," then stood aside and pointed toward Barcelona, as if to say that since Corwyn insisted on going in the wrong direction, he would have to do it alone. Or perhaps the broom was simply fed up with the alchemist and was dismissing him. Corwyn shivered despite the fact that he did want to go to Barcelona—and now more than ever, although anywhere would have been all right as long as it was in a direction other than where the signs that day had been pointing. *Roche-naissante* started to take a step, but Corwyn held her back with the reins. "Aren't you coming?"

Oliver rotated his body back and forth again, then jabbed his finger more emphatically toward Barcelona.

"You want me to go on without you?" Corwyn asked.

The broom bobbed "yes."

"But I don't know when I'm coming back this way. Oliver, I can't just go off and leave you."

Silent as a specter, the broom raised his arm and pointed for a third time. *Roche-naissante* started forward, and this time Corwyn couldn't restrain her. He rode east, watching over his shoulder helplessly as Oliver was swallowed up by the dark.

With luck, he told himself, his business would be concluded quickly in Barcelona and he'd soon be back for Oliver. Even if there were delays, it shouldn't take him more than two or three days.

He prodded *Roche-naissante* into a trot, anxious to hasten his return. At last, his normal compassion was beginning to reassert itself and he could again feel concern for more than just himself.

Entremés

CONVINCED BY NOW THAT THE WHOLE OF SOUTHERN *France (for there the alchemist-errant truly believed himself to be) was infested with demons, Don Corwyn set out to find their source. So it was that he and Sebastian came upon a mine set in the side of a hill. As they watched, a crew of miners rolled an ore cart full of tailings out of the mine and dumped it down the side of the hill, raising a great cloud of dust.*

"Do you see yonder monstrous fiend rising in the air, capable of possessing a dozen individuals simultaneously?" Don Corwyn said, pointing to the cloud. "Doubt not that it is the biggest demon any alchemist has ever encountered, for it is none other than Beelzebub himself, the personal minion of Hydro Phobius. And the miserable wretches with the ore cart are Phobius's slaves, forced to labor deep in the bowels of the earth amid many other frightful demons."

"This will be worse than the windmills," grumbled Sebastian, "for in truth, master, I don't see any demons. All I see is dust raised by the miners."

Don Corwyn whacked his apprentice with his staff, Al-Aver. "Don't contradict your master, whose knowledge extends far beyond your limited grasp."

"Ow!" Sebastian rubbed his head. "Just because your grace's lessons are slow to lodge in my brain is no excuse for you to pound them in."

"Quiet," ordered Don Corwyn. "I have come well

prepared for this situation. Now we shall disperse the demons from the mines and free the prisoners from their toil."

So saying, he guided Rociandante *to the mine entrance, which was once again unattended. He and Sebastian began filling an ore cart with casks unloaded from the donkey.*

"*What's in the casks?*" Sebastian asked.

"*The most powerful force known to alchemy, the secret of which I myself just recently discovered,*" Don Corwyn said, lighting the wicks that protruded from the bung-holes. "*An alchemical form of the gaseous effluvium of dragons.*"

Sebastian scratched his head. "*You mean dragon farts?*"

"*I object to the use of such a crude, vernacular term for so notable an achievement,*" Don Corwyn replied. "*That said, however, unless you wish to be subjected to the aforementioned gaseous by-products yourself, help me push this cart inside.*"

Together, they sent the cart rolling down the main shaft into the mines. Moments later, enraged miners began pouring out of the hill, their eyes streaming tears from the stench, their mouths agape. Once clear of the mines, they set upon Don Corwyn with pick handles and staves, thrashing him like wheat in a mill.

When the miners finished and went their way, Don Corwyn moaned to Sebastian in a feeble, plaintive voice, asking for help in mounting Rociandante *so they could return home to their village.* "*And once you have me in the saddle,*" *he added,* "*if you would be so kind as to apply to my lips a couple of drops of that elixir which I showed you (for in truth, I haven't the use of my arms to reach it), I will soon be well again, for perhaps it is as good for mending broken bones as for curing wounds and diseases.*"

So amid numerous groans, twice as many sighs, and four times that number of oaths and curses, Sebastian raised the alchemist to his feet, whereupon he was forced to stop with Don Corwyn bent in half like a Turkish bow,

*unable to stand any straighter. Sebastian slung Don
Corwyn over* Rociandante's *back like a sack of dung,
then gathered up* Al-Aver *and the funnel and tied them
onto the donkey behind his master. He administered two
drops of the elixir to Don Corwyn as requested, then led*
Rociandante *by the halter toward Argamasilla, with the
donkey expressing her dissatisfaction at having to move
by marking her trail in her usual fashion.*

*For his part, no sooner had Don Corwyn swallowed
the potion than he suffered so many twinges and pangs,
so many sweats and swoons, that he thought his last hour
had come. After a while, he began discharging violently
from both ends at once, and even though Sebastian
waited until darkness to continue their journey so no one
would see the alchemist so grievously afflicted, between*
Rociandante's *urinating and Don Corwyn's purgings,
their path could easily have been detected by anyone
so inclined.*

*And on that unprecedented note did Don Corwyn, the
noblest of alchemist-errants, conclude his first sally.*

—Cid Hamete Benengeli,
   *El Ingenioso Alquimista
   Don Corwyn de La Mancha*, Part I

Chapter 8

Which reveals the sinister purpose behind the windmills being constructed near Zaragoza and introduces a boy destined for advancement in the Inquisition, then tells of Corwyn's visit to Cid Hamete's printer.

THROUGHOUT THE NIGHT, A MUCH-CHASTENED CORWYN rode east toward Barcelona. The terrain rose into the line of mountains that runs along the coast at the city's back and cuts Barcelona off from the interior. The scrubby, arid vegetation of the *meseta* gradually changed to pines and firs, beeches and cork oak. By the pale light of myriad stars and a waning moon, Corwyn glimpsed the jagged spires of naked rock that gave Montserrat its name.

But the old alchemist paid scant attention to his surroundings, for he was deeply troubled by Oliver's recent actions and by a pervading sense that he himself was going the wrong way. His only consolation came from knowing—somehow—that at least he wasn't being watched or followed.

Dawn broke as he crested the mountains and came into view of the coast. He had veered a little south during the night, and Barcelona lay to his left. Ahead and below, sunlight sparkled off a brilliant sea and waves lapped at the tawny sand. Naval galleys glided over the calm water offshore in a mock skirmish, while on the beach a regiment of mounted, armored men kicked up the sand in a dashing display of military exercises. Even at this distance, Corwyn could hear the muted cadence of drums and blaring trumpets that guided horses, ships, and men through their maneuvers.

Corwyn grunted to himself, reluctant to be impressed. He guided *Roche-naissante* onto a narrow path that wound among the trees in a steep descent to the shore.

About midmorning, when Corwyn finally emerged from the palms lining the beach and *Roche-naissante*'s hooves at last stepped onto the golden strand, Friar Carlos Ramon Francisco Vasquez de Diego con Queso sat in the shade of an olive tree many leagues to the west, brushing a fly from his nose. The fly made another halfhearted pass at Friar Carlos, then droned away to a parched clump of grass, succumbing to the torpor that enveloped Spain. Even the most ardent pests were no match for the midday sun.

Except, perhaps, one.

Friar Carlos glanced around furtively, but that wretched boy from Valladolid was nowhere to be seen. The only signs of life were the convict workmen and their guards, all of whom were in Friar Carlos's charge. Nothing else moved on the open, desolate landscape that stretched away in every direction. To the northeast, clouds were forming over the Pyrenees, promising rain that never reached south beyond the mountains. Friar Carlos watched the white masses longingly. At least the boy was gone, he told himself, finding consolation in the thought. He wiped the sweat from his face. Apparently that miserable devil's-spawn had tired of nosing around camp, sniffing out other people's sins, and had returned to Zaragoza where misdoers were more plentiful.

Friar Carlos sighed, the weight of the book hidden under his scapular resting easier on his conscience now that the boy wasn't around. Like the fly, Friar Carlos too surrendered to the season, pulling off his coarse, black woolen outer mantle and settling against the tree trunk. This was the life, he thought; this was the Inquisition the way it ought to be.

He was about to take the book from its hiding place when a slight rustle behind him, secretive as a rat, warned him of someone's approach. Friar Carlos jerked his mantle back on, knowing who it would be: that young nuisance, Tomás de Torquemada, sneaking around again, spying on everyone.

Torquemada rounded the tree trunk and eyed Friar Carlos impassively, as if taking the measure of the man's every fault. Friar Carlos shivered beneath that pious, pitiless gaze and pulled his elbow tighter against the book under his scapular. Torquemada studied the friar for a moment, then turned his attention to the ground at his feet. He advanced cautiously, a hunter stalking his prey. Suddenly, he sprang. Friar Carlos, startled, banged his head against the tree as the boy snatched something from among the dry blades of grass and popped it into a wooden box.

"The Evil One has been at work in this field," Torquemada explained, again holding Friar Carlos with his frosty gaze. "Earlier, several crickets started chirping in the middle of mass, trying to drown out the words of our salvation. Fortunately, I'm here to stop their heresy. I'll put the denizens of this field to the question until all offenders have been brought to justice and purified."

With that, Torquemada stooped to search out more miscreants, letting not even the midday sun dissuade him from his toil.

Friar Carlos repressed a shudder, feeling as though the snow-fed waters of the Pyrenees were coursing down his spine. Torquemada frightened him almost as much as the demons Friar Carlos and his holy brethren were supposed to be shipping out of Spain.

Freeing tormented souls from demonic possession represented a small but highly dangerous aspect of the Inquisition, and in turn imposed responsibility for getting rid of the demons after they were exorcised. Friar

Carlos and his fellow Dominicans certainly didn't want these spirits from hell lingering about the countryside, preying upon unwary citizens. Secretly transporting the demons over the Pyrenees and disposing of them inside France eliminated this problem.

Of course, there was always a chance that, once released on the other side, the demons would find their way into the French watershed and pose a threat to the local population. It was a possibility which had become a reality two years before, when Friar Carlos (then only a novitiate) first arrived at the processing station outside Zaragoza. That incident might have disturbed him had the danger been to his fellow Spaniards. The fact that only the French were involved saved Friar Carlos from any moral difficulty, however; southern France had been such a hotbed of heresy over the centuries that an influx of demons could scarcely add to the dangers already facing their souls. Besides, although Friar Carlos fervently believed in the Holy Mother Church, he was a Spanish Catholic first, and the citizens of other countries could look out for their own. Friar Carlos knew where his Christian duty lay.

The incident two years earlier had raised some practical concerns, however. At that time, demons exorcised throughout Spain were brought to the processing station near Zaragoza, where they were mixed with holy water to stabilize them for the journey out of Spain. The resulting slurries were then placed in barrels and carried by mule train over the Pyrenees. When the French learned of this, the Spanish had of course denied it. Unfortunately, the Spanish had also been forced to stop the shipments out of the country for a time. Since then, the processing station near Zaragoza had been stockpiling the demonic slurries until barrels and wineskins took up most of the available space. Even the addition of an underground warehouse the previous year had only temporarily relieved the problem. Moreover, many batches of slurry were reaching the limits on how long they could safely be stored. Something had to be done to rid the country of these wastes, and soon.

Which was why Friar Carlos was out in this wilderness, overseeing convict laborers, in the first place.

He let his eyes drift over the partially completed evidence of their work: a line of thirty or forty windmills stretching beyond the southern horizon, all the way to the processing station in the valley of the Ebro River. Circular, stone structures capped with conical roofs, their whitewashed plaster walls gleaming in the sun, they stood like a row of snow giants, each with four huge arms. As Friar Carlos watched, a breeze swirled across the ground, picking up dust and setting the giants' arms in motion. The great vanes turned lazily, relentlessly on the high upland plain. Soon, the completed line of windmills would march like an army all the way into the Pyrenees and over to the French side. Connected by a pipeline, they would pump a continuous slurry of exorcised demons out of Spain, their disposal no longer limited to the infrequent passage of mule teams.

Friar Carlos felt a thrill of pride at the thought of what he and his fellows were achieving. Then Torquemada wandered back again, his cold, dark eyes searing into the soul of everything about him, missing nothing. Friar Carlos shivered again. Only his grandmother, her own eyes equally pitiless, could hope to match Torquemada's gaze judgment for judgment.

Squatting on the ground, Torquemada sharpened points on the ends of a half dozen small sticks and stuck them in the dirt, forming a small circle. Then he piled dry grass and twigs around the bases of the upright sticks. Finally, he withdrew something from the box he carried and spoke to it, holding it between his thumb and forefinger. He paused, apparently waiting for an answer, then spoke again. The object in his fingers wriggled. Friar Carlos watched out of the corners of his eyes, pretending he was studying the nearest windmill instead. As he suspected, young Torquemada was talking to one of the crickets he had collected.

After several more questions, Torquemada tied the cricket to one of the upright stakes with a bit of thread, then took another of the creatures from his box and began questioning it. The first squirmed to free itself from the thread that bound it to the stake.

Solemnly, Torquemada filled all six stakes with the insects, looking sad at their recalcitrance in refusing to repent of their sins and receive absolution. He crossed himself and lighted the pyre, then folded his hands in prayer as the advancing flames purified his victims. Friar Carlos stared openmouthed, too dumbfounded to pretend otherwise.

When the little *auto-da-fé* had died and the last wisp of smoke had vanished in the still, hot air, Torquemada got to his feet and walked back down the slight slope, passing near Carlos. "I return for now to Zaragoza," the boy said, his voice reverent, his expression beatific. "When I come again, I'll see if today's heresy has spread. More rigorous measures may be necessary in order to eradicate it."

Friar Carlos fingered the garlic clove that hung inside his habit next to his crucifix, wishing that the herb which had helped protect him from demonic possession for the past two years could save him from the presence of Torquemada as well. He watched until the boy vanished from sight down the trail. Finally, Friar Carlos turned, feeling relieved, only to be greeted by the ashen evidence of the boy's activities. A faint wisp of smoke rose from one of the tiny mounds.

Anxiously, Friar Carlos fumbled under his scapular for the dog-eared copy of *El Ingenioso Alquimista Don Corwyn de La Mancha* smuggled to him from Barcelona several weeks earlier by one of the guards. Friar Carlos had carefully delayed reading the last few pages for fear he would have nothing with which to distract himself once the book was finished. But this morning, the same guard had brought a new crew of convicts to the site, along with rumors that a wineskin full of demons had been opened at an inn near Lérida, causing several demonic possessions. In private, the guard also told Friar Carlos that on his next trip from Barcelona he would bring the friar a new source of diversion, said to be even funnier than the first.

Feeling that he needed a little levity after a visit from Tomás de Torquemada, Friar Carlos opened the book and began reading the final pages.

Meanwhile, Corwyn entered the gates of Barcelona, trailing behind the cavaliers from the beach, who had now finished their maneuvers. The horsemen, accompanied by flying pennants and the martial fanfare of pipes and hautbois, quickly attracted a crowd, which remained to stare at Corwyn as he straggled along at the rear. The alchemist felt painfully self-conscious, his undergown rumpled and dirty, his hair and beard matted and tangled. Nevertheless, he carried himself stiffly erect, as if the cavaliers had ridden out expressly to escort him into the city.

The people on the street stared at Corwyn with a mixture of curiosity and hostility, many mouths turning downward in disapproving frowns. Even so, Corwyn, who was on the lookout for the first tailor's shop he came to, might have emerged unscathed had it not been that the father of all mischief, the Devil himself, induced a couple of boys to shove a handful of briers under *Roche-naissante*'s tail. That gentle beast, ordinarily so tractable, clapped her tail tight in an attempt to avoid these rude and unusual spurs, thereby increasing her discomfort. She began to buck and kick, flinging Corwyn to the ground. Nettled by the indignity, he quickly removed the briers from his long-suffering steed and led her away, turning down an alley to escape the crowd.

He found a ragwoman pushing a barrow of used clothing through the streets. With some of the money from Oliver he purchased a dark, hooded robe which, although shapeless and worn, seemed durable enough to last until he returned to Pomme de Terre. Then he asked directions and set forth without ceremony and on foot (for he feared more boys might persecute *Roche-naissante* unless he stayed beside her) for the shop of Juan de la Cuesta, the printer of Cid Hamete Benengeli's book.

At last he came to a shop bearing the sign of a hooded falcon, and around it the motto *Post tenebras spero lucem*. Over the shop door were inscribed the words "Juan de la Cuesta—Printer of Books." On entering, Corwyn saw men drawing off printed sheets from the press in one area, correcting proofs in another, setting type in yet a third area—in short, performing all the tasks necessary to a printing firm.

Corwyn started toward the press, for he had never seen a book being printed in this manner and longed to see how it was done, but a large man with huge, drooping mustaches moved to block his way. The man examined Corwyn suspiciously. "I'm Juan de la Cuesta. What can I do for you, *señor*?"

"I've come to complain about one of your books," Corwyn announced, drawing himself up to his full five-foot-two-inch height.

The printer shook his massive head. "We don't give refunds."

"I don't want a refund," Corwyn snapped. "I want justice. I want restitution!"

One of the man's eyebrows rose. "And you are . . . ?"

"My name is Corwyn. I'm an alchemist, from Pomme de Terre."

"Oh, Don Corwyn. Of course," the big man exclaimed with a barking laugh. "Well, *Señor* Don Corwyn, I've made you famous. What could you possibly have to complain about?"

"But the book misrepresents me! People think I'm a fool and a madman wherever I go."

Juan de la Cuesta looked Corwyn over, his nose wrinkling. "And you believe such opinions are . . . incorrect?"

"Of course!"

"Ah. Well, I've heard your complaint and you may rest assured that I'll give the matter all the attention it deserves." He turned and whispered to a boy who was sweeping the floor. The boy put down his broom and, casting a sideways glance at Corwyn, hurried from the shop. "Meanwhile, since you're already here," the printer continued, motioning to a man who was packing finished books in crates, "perhaps you'd help us. After all, anyone can get a book autographed by its author, but how often do people get the chance to have a book signed by the story's central character? So if you'd consent to stay in Barcelona a few days and help promote—"

"Help you promote it!" Corwyn roared. "Help you promote the very book I've come to complain about? You must think me mad indeed!"

"Ah, well, I just thought I'd ask, *señor*," Juan de la Cuesta said, evading the issue of Corwyn's sanity. He stepped aside as the man he had signaled brought a crate of books to the front of the shop. "No harm in that. Now, if you will excuse me, I have a business to attend to." He tried to usher Corwyn to the door, where a crowd was gathering outside the shop.

Corwyn ducked under the bigger man's arm, tripping over the crate. "I want your word that you won't print any more copies of that defamatory book Cid Hamete wrote about me. I'm a businessman, too, and it's ruining my reputation."

A guarded look came over Juan de la Cuesta's face. He glanced at the workman, who was dragging a second crate from the back of the shop. "The book Cid Hamete wrote . . . you mean the one where he talks of your becoming an alchemist-errant and your first sally into what you mistakenly thought of as France?"

"Exactly."

Juan de la Cuesta's face brightened. "Then you may be assured, *señor*, that I won't be printing any more copies of that book." He stepped in front of the first crate, as if to block Corwyn's view. "Pirated editions have already made it uneconomical."

Corwyn harrumphed a couple of times, thrown off by having got his way so easily. Of course, the book would still be out there, and in many editions. But Corwyn felt he had won a moral victory. "All right," he said at last, eager to leave the city and return to Oliver. "*Gracias*."

"*De nada*," the man replied, smiling as if at some private joke. "Here, let me get the door for you on your way out."

Just then, the boy staggered back into the shop, gasping for breath. "I did it, *Señor de la Cuesta*," he panted. "I've gathered a crowd outside, as you said."

The printer frowned at the boy and motioned him to silence, but the boy was too winded to notice. He slumped onto the nearby crate, just as the workman came up with the second crate and heaved it off his shoulders to stack it on the first. The workman slewed the crate around to avoid smashing the boy, while the boy leaped aside in the last instant and accidentally jabbed the workman in the stomach with an elbow. The workman doubled over, letting go of the crate. Juan de la Cuesta lunged for it and missed. The crate sailed through the air for a moment, then fell to the floor with a crash. Wood shattered, spilling books everywhere.

Corwyn stared in horror at the cover of one which landed near his feet. *El Ingenioso Alquimista Don Corwyn de La Mancha*, the title read. "What's the meaning of this?" Corwyn demanded. "You said you wouldn't print any more copies of this book."

Juan de la Cuesta shrugged evasively. "No, *señor*, I promised I wouldn't print any more copies of the other book, the one which introduces you and records the adventures of your first sally."

"My *first* sally?" Corwyn glowered. Grabbing up the copy from the floor, he peered more closely at the title. *El Ingenioso Alquimista Don Corwyn de La Mancha*, it still, however, read in large, bold letters. Beneath that, in smaller type, appeared the words:

Part II.

THE
SECOND SALLY

Entremés

AFTER HIS ILLUSTRIOUS FIRST SALLY, DON CORWYN SPENT the long winter months at home, recuperating from his wounds. The barber and the curate from his village tended him throughout this time, the first healing his body while the second tried less successfully to cure his mind.

Finally, a day came when the sun shone hot once more on the plains of La Mancha, and Don Corwyn again grew eager to sally forth in search of adventure and profit and the greater glory of his beloved Hypatia del Alexandria.

"Fool!" the curate shouted when he heard this. He waved his arms. "There is no Hypatia del Alexandria. Your so-called Alexandria is nothing more than the neighboring village of El Toboso, which hasn't any library at all, let alone a great one. And your beloved Hypatia is a common wench of that town, working in the fields and smelling of garlic."

When they were alone, Sebastian turned to his master and demanded, "What did the curate mean about Alexandria and Hypatia not being real? I don't know how I shall ever be granted noble status if everything you've told me is false."

"Haven't I also told you many times," Don Corwyn said, "that I am pursued relentlessly by my nemesis, Hydro Phobius, whose envy of me drives him to turn all my achievements to naught? Clearly this is proof that he has been at work once again, for to confound me further

he has now transformed Alexandria into the village of El Toboso which the curate spoke of, and spirited away the real city's library to some distant land. It is up to us, therefore, to find where Hydro Phobius has hidden the library which properly belongs in Alexandria, and by so doing free both that great city and my beloved Hypatia—whom he has undoubtedly made to look like a common wench—from their evil enchantment. Come, we must begin our search at once."

"But where are we going to look?" Sebastian asked.

"Italy," Don Corwyn, that incomparable flower of Manchegan alchemy, replied. "There has been much talk about the wonders being accomplished there, and I must attribute it to my own shortsightedness that I did not realize before that such works are possible only through access to the vast store of learning which the library of Alexandria alone provides. For know, Sebastian, that the library of Alexandria is the only true receptacle which may rightfully be called the Holy Grail."

"But, master," Sebastian objected, "you said before that the Holy Grail was a vessel containing the elixir sought by all alchemists and known as the Philosopher's Stone (which I gather must be a kind of kidney stone, may it please God that only philosophers can get)."

"So I did, and therefore you may believe that also is true," Don Corwyn responded. "But the Holy Grail is as capable of transmutations and permutations as anything in alchemy, appearing in one place and time as a sacred vessel filled with that life-giving balm which is the elixir, and in another instance taking the form of the library of Alexandria—the one eternal fountain of all wisdom and knowledge."

To which Sebastian replied, "In God's name, master, I can't bear to listen to some of the things you say. This nonsense about grails and libraries and evil enchantments makes me think that everything you've told me about alchemy must be nothing but lies. You resort to appearances and illusions to explain yourself as often as Hydro Phobius and all those other enchanters who ever opposed you combined. A man who persists in saying

*the things you do has to be out of his head. I'm tempted
to stay home and live here simply, as God intended."*

*"Sebastian, you have fewer brains than any apprentice
in the world," Don Corwyn said. "Is it possible that while
you've been with me you haven't learned that everything
to do with alchemy appears to be illusions and folly? Why,
if it were otherwise, and the true worth of what I tell you
were to be seen by all, the whole world would persecute
me in order to extract the secrets that I know."*

*With these and similar admonishments, Don Corwyn
convinced his apprentice to remain in his service, so
eager was the simple rustic for the rewards the alchemist
promised.*

*"Besides," Sebastian grumbled to himself, "I'll be
satisfied with even the illusion of being made a nobleman,
provided the truth remains hidden from my neighbors."*

*So Don Corwyn and Sebastian ventured forth a second
time, the alchemist-errant mounted on* Rociandante *while
his apprentice followed along behind. And it can only be
attributed to* Rociandante's *fine manners and excellent
breeding that, whenever Don Corwyn's heels touched
her flanks, she watered the trail in front of Sebastian,
thereby keeping down the dust where he stepped . . .*

—Cid Hamete Benengeli,
   *El Ingenioso Alquimista
   Don Corwyn de La Mancha*, Part II

Chapter 9

In which Corwyn's discovery in Barcelona sends him forth on a new adventure, and including other such matters as the reader will see or the listener hear in the proper course of this true history.

"A SECOND PART!" CORWYN ROARED. "WHAT'S THE meaning of this?"

Again, Juan de la Cuesta gave an ambiguous shrug. "Exactly as you see, *señor*. The first book was so successful that we have issued a sequel."

Corwyn thumbed through the book in horror. He caught references to Venice and realized this second volume covered his exploits from the previous summer when he'd journeyed with Sebastian and Gwen to Italy. But this book too—like the first—undoubtedly twisted everything that had happened into a parody of the real events.

Corwyn threw the book down and grabbed the end of the unbroken crate, intending to hurl it aside as well. But though he heaved and strained, the crate was too heavy for him to budge. Panting, he raced to where men were setting type in the back of the shop. "Books should be sources of truth," he cried, knocking trays of type onto the floor, "but you have turned them into havens for lies."

"Stop!" Juan de la Cuesta chased after him. "By what authority do you disrupt my business?" He seized the alchemist and dragged him away as the latter began rocking one of the presses, trying to topple it onto its side.

Corwyn sagged in his captor's arms and gasped for breath. "By what authority do you publish these lies?" he countered.

"Authority?" Juan de la Cuesta snorted. "Why, the authority of the king. I pay good *reales* for the licenses to print these books, *señor*."

"But you're making a fortune by ruining me."

"Do you think so?" Juan de la Cuesta responded. "Look around you, *señor*. Does this look like the shop of a wealthy man?"

Corwyn did so, noting for the first time that although the shop was busy and reasonably well-off, it was hardly a fountain of limitless wealth. The walls were plain and unadorned, and some of the equipment seemed in need of repair. Even the printer himself had a frayed and harried appearance, as of a man trying to rise in the world through his own efforts.

"But you've already published so many copies of the first book about me," Corwyn said. "Where did all that money go?"

Juan de la Cuesta's eyebrows raised. "Surely you don't think these men here in my shop work for free," he said, waving an arm. "There are typesetters and proofreaders and press operators to pay, not to mention equipment upkeep and the many businesses upon which I depend for supplies. Then the printed books have to be shipped all over the world, often suffering considerable loss or damage along the way. Once the books arrive at their destinations, arrangements must be made with local booksellers to handle them, as well as agreements on how to return or dispose of unsold copies. And finally, what little profit there is to be made despite all of this is frequently eaten away by unscrupulous competitors who issue pirated editions of books I have paid for the right to publish. I tell you, *señor*, if anyone is making money from my hard work, it is that lazy, undeserving dog of a Moor, Cid Hamete Benengeli, who writes when and how it pleases him, then expects me to pay from my own purse for his manuscripts, leaving me to endure the risks of publishing his books and recouping my expenses."

"Cid Hamete." Corwyn nodded tersely. "Where is he?"

Juan de la Cuesta let go of the alchemist and turned away, suddenly evasive. "Oh, off wherever he lives, I suppose. Somewhere in La Mancha."

Corwyn stared at the printer, realizing angrily that the man either would not or could not tell him where to find Cid Hamete. At last, he grunted and started to leave.

"*Señor*," the printer called to him. Corwyn paused at the door. "If you do find him," the printer went on, "please remind him that he is to have something for me, and very soon. I expect him to deliver on time."

Corwyn waited. "What is he supposed to deliver?"

"Oh, nothing of importance." Juan de la Cuesta turned away again. "Just a little business matter."

Corwyn reached for the door handle.

"One more thing before you go," Juan de la Cuesta said. "Are you sure you won't sign books while you're here? I really think it would spur sales of the second volume and increase your fame in the world."

Corwyn left without replying.

Outside, a crowd had gathered—evidently roused by the boy from the printing shop in the hope of selling a few extra copies of the second part of *Don Corwyn*. The crowd greeted the alchemist with laughter and howls of derision. A decrepit crone sidled up to him. "I'm a poor woman, *señor alquimista*," she cooed with a toothless smirk. "Use your elixir to make me some gold so I can buy bread."

A man who looked as ancient as Methuselah pushed her aside. "Don't listen to her, *señor*," he demanded. "Listen to me. I'm old, and soon I will die. Use your elixir to give me eternal life."

"No, me," a voice cried from behind the poor woman and the old man. They glanced around, then stepped back reluctantly, making way for a leprous looking youth. "Heal me, Don Corwyn," the young man challenged. "If you're the great alchemist you claim to be, then surely your elixir can cure my disease."

Corwyn stared into the mixture of arrogance and hope that burned in the depths of the young man's eyes, feeling helpless.

"You fool, Julio," someone shouted to the young man from the crowd. A burly man, evidently the one who'd spoken, pushed his way through the throng. "He's not just any kind of an alchemist, but an aquatic one. If you need to be cured, be sure the disease affects your waterworks—like this!" He reached inside his breeches and produced a syphilitic member, which he displayed to the crowd. The people nearest him shrank away in pity and terror. "Now if you're really an aquatic alchemist, as you claim, heal me instead. The women of Barcelona will be forever in your debt."

"There are too many of you," Corwyn shouted, frustrated by his own limitations. "Would you have me heal the world? Heal yourselves!"

He took *Roche-naissante's* reins and attempted to flee down the street. The crowd followed him, lacking better entertainment, but gradually they began to drift away as Corwyn stoically refused to acknowledge their catcalls further. Eventually, he found himself alone, or nearly so, in a small side street, where he considered what to do.

He'd intended to plead his case before Juan de la Cuesta (assuming all along that the printer would be swayed by the fairness and justice of his case), and then to return to the mountains where he could find Oliver and return to Pomme de Terre. He was beginning to worry about the broom, as well as about his school and his alchemical practice which he'd abandoned so precipitously. Sebastian might not be capable of managing these enterprises for an extended period of time, and Corwyn really should return to look after his interests. But he felt utterly defeated, and knew that to go back to Pomme de

Terre now would be not a return, but a retreat.

Somehow, he had to restore his reputation, if not his purse.

He headed for the port and searched among the docks until he found a Moorish vessel which was to sail later that day for Andalusia. Corwyn arranged passage for himself and *Roche-naissante* as far as Valencia, where he and the donkey would go ashore and begin the trek inland to La Mancha. There, he would find this Cid Hamete and confront him personally. The Moor would regret the day he had written a second lying book about him.

Contented with his preparations, Corwyn saw to the loading of *Roche-naissante*, then spent the remaining hours before the ship was to sail in an apothecary's shop (the borrowing of which was a privilege he paid for handsomely), concocting the potion whose formula he'd devised while in the wilderness a few days before. All his life, Corwyn had suffered seasickness whenever he ventured onto water, and this professional embarrassment had proved to be a true liability the previous summer in Italy. Besides, an aquatic alchemist whose stomach revolted every time he sailed upon the very element over which he professed dominion didn't inspire confidence in those who might hire him.

When Corwyn was done, he, too, boarded the ship, using his anger at Cid Hamete to keep at bay any lingering doubts as to the effectiveness of his potion. With luck, the voyage to Valencia would be a calm, uneventful one.

Meanwhile, in the mountains west of Barcelona, Oliver waited patiently. He wasn't certain who—or what—he was waiting for; he knew only that he and Corwyn had been followed and observed most of the time since they'd crossed the Pyrenees from Pomme de Terre. At first, this realization had alarmed the little broom, who was skittish by nature. But gradually he'd come to accept the omnipresent Watcher, as Oliver called this presence that followed them, and he even began to look forward to meeting whatever it was face to face.

So he waited, retrieving seeds from the pine cones scattered here and there and feeding them to the birds and other creatures that inhabited this wilderness.

With all the patience he showed while waiting for a timid field mouse to come and take a seed from his stick fingers, so Oliver waited for the arrival of the equally cautious Watcher.

Meanwhile, in Pomme de Terre, Sebastian hid, studying *Summa Thaumaturgica* as a means of escaping the gibes of the students.

Earlier that day, a peddler had arrived from Barcelona selling books. Not just any books, but a sequel to the first adventures of the infamous Don Corwyn. The success of the first book was spurring anyone with an eye for money into a frenzied attempt to print and distribute this second volume as quickly as possible, while people still chuckled over the first. And from all indications, the second book promised to be as good (or bad, depending on one's point of view) as the first.

Which, of course, only fueled the taunts the students made about Sebastian and his master. Ever since the disastrous trip into the mountains, Jean-Claude had been particularly hard to control, and now this new book only made the problem worse.

Beneath the humor with which this latest installment of *Don Corwyn de La Mancha* was being greeted by the citizens of Pomme de Terre, meanwhile, an undercurrent of anger was also making itself felt. Some of the townspeople felt that one book of such derision and foolishness was enough—not that they minded Corwyn's being ridiculed, but they objected to Pomme de Terre and the duchy being dragged into it, even if only indirectly. Word in the streets had it that the duchess and the bishop were particularly upset, and were meeting even now in the duchess's castle to discuss what should be done about the town's wayward alchemist.

Sebastian forced his attention back to the book, avoiding the concerns that flowed like surging tides around him, retreating even further into the obscure intricacies of thaumaturgy. While he read, an idea took shape as to how, at long last, he could exert control over the students, especially Jean-Claude.

Sebastian laughed. To anyone else, however, it might have sounded like a crazed cackle.

Corwyn set sail that same day aboard the caravel *Al-Joppa*, whose wily Morisco captain regularly converted to Catholicism whenever business took him into northern waters, then relapsed to the faith of Islam as soon as the vessel turned south again.

At first, Corwyn was apprehensive about setting foot on a ship of any kind. This time, however, the potion he'd prepared in Barcelona seemed to be working. Of course, calm seas and sunshine undoubtedly helped, but still Corwyn was amazed by how good he felt. Never before had the salty air and sparkling water of a sea voyage so invigorated him.

He took to whistling and strolling around the deck, eating heartily and being so overwhelmingly jovial that it grated on the crew. "This certainly disproves the words of that liar, Cid Hamete," he told everyone who would listen. "I must be a pretty fair aquatic alchemist after all, and a true master of every kind of water."

Soon, the crew began muttering whenever Corwyn approached, and they complained to the captain that the alchemist's incessant chattering interfered with their work. The captain, in turn, realized that Corwyn had gone from an asset to a liability, and he wished the old alchemist would occupy himself in a manner befitting a common passenger—by hanging over the ship's rails, too seasick to get in anyone's way.

Besides, the captain considered it bad luck to exclaim so boisterously about good weather, especially when the person also seemed to hold himself personally responsible for this state (and what other interpretation could Corwyn's claim about being an aquatic alchemist mean?). To the captain's way of thinking, the alchemist had practically challenged the elements to change. He wasn't surprised, therefore, when the weather suddenly

turned one night while they were still several leagues
north of Valencia, with a furious wind and high seas
that pummeled the boat. During the fourth watch, the
captain summoned the ship's mate, and together they
went below to where Corwyn was quartered.

The old alchemist was still sound asleep, which irritated the captain all the more. Like many another fine
mariner before and after him, the captain's own stomach
was none too stable in rough weather, and he resented
Corwyn's newfound ability to sleep through such a
storm. Besides, he'd already figured out who Corwyn
was after rummaging through the ship's cargo, part of
which had been consigned to him by a printer named
Juan de la Cuesta. As a sometimes-Moor himself, the
captain trusted the words of Cid Hamete over the claims
of any infidel.

"What do you mean by sleeping at a time like this?" he
bellowed, encouraging Corwyn to wake up with a boot to
the ribs. "Get up, and call upon your god for help before
we perish."

"Huh?" Corwyn grunted, rubbing the sleep from his
eyes. "What's wrong?"

"What's wrong?" the captain repeated. "Don't you
care that we're about to sink? What manner of man are
you? But perhaps I show too little faith; perhaps the wind
and sea will obey an alchemist. Or perhaps Don Corwyn
de La Mancha can walk on water." He shrugged. "We'll
soon find out."

Corwyn was barely listening as he squinted around the
dark, stifling hold. He swallowed hard. "The ship seems
to be rolling rather heavily, don't you think?"

"And we know whose fault it is that this evil's befallen
us," the captain said. "In fact, we've already cast lots to
see whose absence would lighten the ship most. Guess
whose number came up?"

"Mmmmm?" Corwyn responded, his attention on the
creaking planks of the hull. He licked dry lips and swallowed again.

The captain nodded to the mate. "Take him up and
throw him overboard. With luck, he'll drown right away

and then the sea will calm itself. It's all his fault this tempest is upon us, and I for one don't wish to perish on his account."

So the mate dragged Corwyn onto deck, where the winds had blown great clouds down from the north. Rain and waves lashed the ship. At the railings, crew members were unburdening the vessel by tossing part of the cargo overboard. Near-constant flashes of lightning lighted up the scene as the captain broke open a cargo crate that was to be abandoned and tore the title page from one of the familiar looking books inside. He wadded up the page and stuffed it into the alchemist's mouth. "Here, fill your belly with this, Don Corwyn de La Mancha," he shouted above the thunder's roar, "for we've certainly had a bellyful of you."

"Wait," Corwyn mumbled around the mouthful of paper. "What about *Roche-naissante*?"

The captain stopped the mate, who had begun to drag Corwyn to the railing. "Your donkey? We'll sell her in Valencia to repay ourselves for the trouble of putting up with you this long." He withdrew his hand from the mate's arm, and the mate threw Corwyn into the water. Soon after that, the ship did indeed sail beyond the reach of the storm and safely into harbor, as the captain had hoped.

Corwyn, however, remained within the tempest's grip, clinging to one of the crates from Juan de la Cuesta's shop and rapidly losing his battle against nausea. The title page from *Don Corwyn*, Part II, tasted like ashes in his mouth. He spat the paper out, although doing so almost brought the contents of his stomach up with it.

"Woe is me," he spluttered, "a man ridiculed and scorned throughout the world. Each day, someone new comes upon that wretched book and mocks me. All who read Cid Hamete delight in my confusion." A huge wave enveloped the crate and silenced him for a moment. He came up gasping. "Not only am I troubled at heart, but it seems my bowels are also churning within me. In fact—"

He broke off again, this time to heave his recent and quite substantial meal into the water at his chin. "At least things can't get any worse," he muttered when the purging was over.

Just then, he heard an ominous booming above the roar of the storm. He peered in the direction of the sound and, in the glare of the next lightning flash, made out a rocky coastline toward which he was being swept. Corwyn groaned. With so many leagues of gentle, sandy beach between Barcelona and Valencia, why did he have to get thrown overboard along one of the few rugged parts? He let go of the crate and struck out against the current, swimming toward deeper ocean, pausing occasionally to retch anew.

Despite his flailing, the booming sound grew closer. Finally, too tired to continue the struggle, Corwyn glanced around and saw a high, stone bluff looming behind him, where an endless succession of waves smashed themselves into oblivion. Periodically, the sea drew back in its assault, lowering the water surface enough to reveal a submerged cavern in the face of the cliff, waiting like the open mouth of some giant undersea creature. Then another wave would hurl itself against the bluff, flooding the dark, ferocious maw with a boom that reverberated above the noise of the storm. To Corwyn, it looked as if the cave itself were gulping down vast quantities of seawater in its eagerness to swallow him.

His energy suddenly renewed, Corwyn kicked and thrashed harder. All he did was slow his approach. Finally, one of the swells caught him up like so much flotsam, sucking him into its vortex and flinging him against the cliff. Corwyn's much abused stomach flip-flopped and tried to empty itself of the dinner he'd long ago regurgitated. For a moment, the old alchemist was airborne, and he started to scream, but then water surged around him again, drowning the scream in a gurgle. Darkness engulfed him as the sea poured back into the cave, carrying Corwyn with the flow down a long, submerged tunnel. Corwyn held his breath until his lungs threatened to burst. At last, choking on his own bile mixed with ocean brine, he felt himself being rolled onto a sandy shelf. The wave retreated, stranding him inside the cavern's belly like a beached whale. Corwyn lay in the darkness, gasping for air. The next surge lifted him higher onto the sand. The distant boom of the cavern entrance being submerged echoed around him, making his ears ring. Evidently, he was in a small, underwater chamber, with enough air trapped inside to breathe for now.

Too exhausted to be concerned about any needs beyond the moment, Corwyn fell asleep, lulled by the water sloshing gently on the sand.

Chapter 10

Which recounts Corwyn's predicament in the cave and Sebastian's equally benighted experience with thaumaturgy.

CORWYN AWOKE AND OPENED HIS EYES, ONLY TO DIScover he'd gone blind.

In panic, he closed his eyes, squeezed them tight, then opened them a second time.

Nothing. His sight had been taken from him, replaced by the deepest blackness Corwyn had ever experienced in his overly long life.

He closed his eyes again and sighed. So he was indeed blind, that was the bitter truth of it. But where was he? How had this terrible thing happened?

Resisting the impulse to open his eyes yet another time, he reached out to his surroundings with his remaining senses. He had the impression that he was lying on his back in the midst of some vast and indefinable space, feet together, arms outflung, staring (were he to open his eyes again) up into nothingness. Whatever surface lay beneath him conformed to his shape, supporting him everywhere equally, so that his sense of being held up at all disappeared, as if he were floating in a void.

Then perhaps he wasn't blind after all, he thought. Perhaps he was dead.

Nearby, water murmured softly against an embankment. The River Styx, Corwyn decided. So he really was dead, and his soul was lying on the bank of the river, waiting for Charon to ferry him over to Hades, the dwelling place for spirits.

Corwyn shivered.

It was this that made him reconsider, and for the first time Corwyn became aware of a slight draft from somewhere, blowing over his wet robes and raising goose bumps on his flesh.

Wet robes? Cool flesh?

Memories of the storm and his near-drowning returned, along with a host of other sensations unlikely to be felt by a disembodied spirit—hunger, thirst, aching muscles, and a very full bladder. From these, Corwyn concluded that he was neither dead nor blind. He was trapped in an underwater cave, somewhere between Barcelona and Valencia.

Corwyn grunted. Almost instantaneous echoes from the sound assured him of nearby walls rather than the infinite space he'd first imagined, and he fought for breath in the sudden closeness. He pictured a great stone roof suspended just above him, ready to fall and crush him. His eyes flew open again, as if by seeing the danger he could thereby prevent it. But peering into the darkness only pulled his surroundings closer.

How ironic, he thought, that he who, in the wilderness, had spurned the gift of Oliver's "grail," a stone vessel filled with water, now found himself confined within a stone chamber of a more menacing sort, encompassed about by water. Or perhaps it was like another vessel of his own designing—the kind in which he ran his breath of demons test. If so, then Maritornes, the Asturian wench at the inn, had been more prophetic than she knew with her talk about performing a "breath of alchemist" test, for soon he would use up all the air trapped with him in this cavern.

Corwyn shivered again at this thought. Better to have drowned after all, perhaps, than to end his days by suffocation, a prisoner in such a place.

Another puff of air blew over Corwyn, gently rebuking him for having surrendered so quickly to despair. It was as if the chamber itself were a living thing, breathing in and out around him. In this way, the air was constantly refreshed. Reassured by this, Corwyn sat up, feeling his way cautiously in case the roof were really as low as he'd feared. Though small, the chamber proved big enough to stand in, and he began seeking the source of the breeze.

If air could come in from outside, Corwyn reasoned, then the same route might also provide him with a means of escape.

After much stumbling about in the dark, punctuated by bellows and curses, he finally located a narrow crevice high up on the back wall. He felt around until he located a flat-topped rock near the wall and clambered onto it, then stood on tiptoe to peer into the crevice, hoping for a glimpse of daylight. But though he felt fresh air blowing in his face, inside the hole was only more blackness. Corwyn forced a hand into the crevice and began dislodging rocks to widen the opening.

He had worked his arm in up to the elbow when part of the wall collapsed, pinning his wrist inside the crevice. He panicked and yanked on his arm, almost toppling himself from the rock on which he stood.

Then Corwyn cried out as if from the very belly of hell, in a voice that might have been heard as far away as Barcelona. Yet there was no deliverance from his affliction, and he had to stand extremely still for fear of losing his footing, which would have jerked his arm in its socket like a man put to the torture of the strappado.

So it was that he spent that day and the following night (though he was unable to tell how much time had passed), ever vigilant against falling asleep lest he awaken to find himself dangling by his hand from the crevice.

Sebastian looked up from his work when he heard Gwen calling his name. "Shhh!" he whispered tersely. "In here. But don't let anyone know."

Just then, the knife he was using to carve the sides of a small branch slipped, gashing his thumb. He cried out, more from surprise than pain, and sucked the wound.

Gwen entered the dark stable, breathing hard and moving slowly, a hand on the back of one hip to stabilize her unaccustomed bulk. She took his thumb and examined the injury, clucking to herself. Apparently satisfied, she let go of his hand. "Why don't you want your students to find you? You might try keeping your voice down, you know—they're out looking for you. With you yelping as though you'd hurt yourself, they may have already heard."

Sebastian shuddered, then glanced at the branch on the table. "I don't want to see them yet," he muttered. "Especially not Jean-Claude. But soon." He studied the unfinished tracery of lines cut into the wood, a sequence of delicate symbols written in the thaumaturgical language of CABAL. He retrieved the knife and began carving the last of the symbols.

"Sebastian, when are you going to get the boys to fill the cistern in the kitchen like you promised? It's almost time for dinner and they'll be getting hungry."

"Oh, so the boys are hungry, are they?" Sebastian cackled. "And the cistern needs filling?" Ordinarily, it irritated him that Corwyn—who designed modern water systems for other people—had never got around to providing one for his own school. Today, however, Sebastian intended to put that oversight to good use. "Why, we must take care of the poor little things. And I'll be ready for them soon. Very, very soon."

"Your voice sounds odd." Gwen leaned forward awkwardly. "What're you up to?"

"Nothing, nothing at all. Except that, since Jean-Claude won't listen to reason, I'm forced to deal with him by other means." The lettering finished, he set the knife down and picked up a roll of silver wire that had cost him most of his savings. Silver wasn't as thaumaturgically active as gold, but it was less expensive and would be sufficient for his purpose. Carefully, he began cutting lengths of wire and inlaying the strands in the grooves carved in the wood.

Gwen drew back. "That's not what I think it is, is it?"

"Depends." He lifted up the section of branch, holding it reverently across his palms like a royal scepter. "You know what they say: 'Spare the rod and spoil the child.' Except in this case, the rod is a wand," he said. "A wand of obedience. Jean-Claude will finally do what I tell him, and all the rest of his cohorts will be there to see."

Sebastian uttered these last words with an emphatic hiss that startled even him with its vehemence.

A slight rustle, like the tittering of a ghost, sounded from the corridor beyond the stable door, which Gwen had left open. Sebastian paused, afraid his students might have discovered him before he was ready. He listened, but heard nothing more. It must have been mice chittering in the walls, he told himself. Nonetheless, he motioned for Gwen to close the door.

Gwen lumbered over and shut it, then turned, her expression doubtful. "You know Corwyn doesn't approve of thaumaturgy. What would he say if he knew about this?"

Sebastian's mouth pulled tight. "It's Corwyn's own fault I'm having to do this, after he abandoned me with his demon pupils. And it's the fault of Jean-Claude! He won't acknowledge my authority any other way. I think Corwyn would understand, under the circumstances."

"I'm not so sure," Gwen muttered. She pointed to the wand. "Besides, what if—?"

Sebastian cut her off with an upraised hand. "Gwen, I know what I'm doing."

She snorted, but said nothing, then crossed the room to perch precariously on a stool.

"Do you need to rest?" Sebastian asked, solicitous about her condition. "Maybe you should go lie down."

She shook her head. "I wouldn't dream of missing this."

Sebastian scowled and bent over his work, unwilling to ask what she meant.

Someone pounded on the door. Startled, Sebastian almost cut himself again with the knife. "*Monsieur* Sebastian," came Jean-Claude's voice, muffled by the wood, "are you in there?"

Sebastian cursed under his breath and returned to his work. "I'll be out in just a minute," he called. He thought he heard other voices giggling outside the door, then they fell silent.

"What are you doing, *monsieur*?" Jean-Claude persisted. "We've been looking for you."

Sebastian finished the last symbol and gripped the wand, feeling raw thaumaturgical power surge through it. "What am I doing?" Again he laughed. "Come in, all of you, and see for yourself."

The door burst open and in strode Jean-Claude, followed by the other students. Halfway across the room, Jean-Claude froze, his eyes on the branch in Sebastian's hand. "*Monsieur*, what is that?"

"Jean-Claude," Sebastian said, brandishing the wand, "meet your new taskmaster."

Jean-Claude seemed to study Sebastian's mouth as if watching for his cue to speak. "No, it can't be," he said. His face twisted in horror. "*Monsieur*, you wouldn't—"

Sebastian waved the wand. "Silence!"

The boy fell quiet as if abruptly deprived of the ability to speak.

"That's better." Sebastian drew himself up to full height, aware of the power that was his to wield. "Stand here in front of me, and the rest of you get where you can see. I don't want you to miss any of this." He scowled at Jean-Claude. "Stand up straight!" Again he accompanied his words with a sweep of the wand, jerking erect himself to set an example.

Jean-Claude stiffened, his eyes still on Sebastian's face as if for signs. The only sounds were the scraping of the boys' shoes as they ranged themselves at the back of the stable. A muffled cough sounded from Gwen. Sebastian glanced at her and she seemed to be choking. He started toward her, anxious about her welfare again, but she waved him away and struggled for composure.

Sebastian returned to Jean-Claude, swaggering up to him and holding his attention with a cold stare. "From now on, you will do as I say," he told the boy, striding to the center of the room where he could be seen by all. "You will obey my every command, quickly and quietly."

A short, barking laugh escaped Gwen before she could stifle it. Sebastian glared. She tried to look apologetic, but her face betrayed her mirth.

Sebastian groped for his scattered thoughts. "There will be no more arguing with me—"

Jean-Claude trembled as the thaumaturgical force gripped him.

"You will stop your foolish pranks—"

Jean-Claude's face reddened and his breathing broke into hiccups. Sebastian felt a wave of apprehension; perhaps he had made the spell too strong. But he couldn't back down now, not with the students watching. He pointed to a pair of wooden buckets. "Take those and fill the kitchen cistern." He glanced around at the debris littering the stable, most of it a result of his work. "After that, I think you should do some cleaning. In fact, for the rest of the day you'll do nothing but haul water and clean the school."

A tidal wave of laughter burst the dike of Jean-Claude's resistance, and he collapsed in a flood of guffaws. Sebastian stared, uncomprehending.

"Oh, Sebastian," Gwen gasped, laughing as well, "did you really think it would be as simple as that?"

Sebastian's gaze dropped to the wand dangling from his hand. "But the spell . . ."

Tears of laughter trickled down Gwen's cheeks. "Apparently, it didn't work."

"*Merde!*" Sebastian cursed.

Gwen frowned. "Oh, Sebastian, don't be like that. They're just boys."

Sebastian glared at Gwen's pregnant form. "Then I hope we have a girl!" He slammed the wand onto the work table and drew his short sword from the scabbard at his waist.

Jean-Claude, who had been watching their faces intently, pulled a wad of lint from each ear. "What are you two saying?"

"Sebastian, no!" Gwen shrieked, her eyes darting from Jean-Claude to her husband. "Maybe the spell would have worked—he just couldn't hear."

Too late, Sebastian realized his mistake. Once started, the sword continued on a downward arc, the cold iron of its blade biting deep into the swirling silver letters inscribed in the wood. There was a flash, and a jolt as the spell intended for Jean-Claude flowed backward through Sebastian's arm.

Suddenly, Sebastian found himself jerked upright like a marionette controlled by unseen hands. He tried to cry out, but no words would pass his lips. Without a sound, he scurried across the room to grab the buckets.

The boys made way for him, staring wide-eyed. "What's the matter with him?" Henri asked in a hushed voice.

Jean-Claude shrugged and looked at Gwen.

"He seems to be carrying out the orders he gave you," she said.

A slow grin spread over Jean-Claude's face. "The iron of the sword must have displaced the thaumaturgical flux from the wand, forcing the spell into him. It's making him obey his own commands."

With some distant part of his awareness, Sebastian heard their conversation, but was incapable of either altering his actions or caring what they said.

"Fantastique!" Henri shouted, running after him. "Let's go watch."

Sebastian, meanwhile, raced for the stable door with the buckets. Without interest, he saw Gwen hold up her hand. "Now, boys . . ."

"Ah, just for a little while," Henri protested.

Gwen hesitated. "All right," she agreed at last. "But only till the cistern's full."

Sebastian was dimly aware of the boys spilling from the stable behind him and following him from the school to the public water trough up the street. But even the sight of two matrons gossiping by the trough—one of them a particularly nosy woman who lived near the school—didn't concern him. The neighbor woman stood back, looking down her hawklike beak at him with evident disapproval. The students crowded around, laughing and shouting while Sebastian filled the buckets and hurried back. His movements were jerky, mechanical, and he worked with haste.

There was so much to do before the day was out!

In the wilderness between Lérida and Barcelona, Oliver faced a dilemma. He had met the Watcher after careful waiting, and felt well rewarded for his patience. The two of them had spent the past couple of days conversing (to the extent that Oliver "conversed" with anyone, limited as he was to signs and gestures) about a great many things, but especially about Corwyn. This subject in particular delighted Oliver, for despite his recent anger toward his maker (anger which he had since almost forgotten), he was devoted to the alchemist, as he was to each and every one of his treasured friends, few in number though they were.

But now the Watcher had imposed a terrible decision on the shy little broom, for Oliver had promised Corwyn (in his mind if not exactly in gesture) that he would wait here for the alchemist's return. About that return, Oliver held absolutely no doubt, for he was sure his maker would eventually come to his senses and realize that not only had he treated Oliver badly, but he was also going off in the wrong direction. Oliver didn't know how he knew the latter point, and indeed may not have even been conscious of his knowledge of it; but ever since they had seen the windmills against the horizon and had altered their course to avoid them, Oliver had known something was wrong and that eventually they would have to retrace their steps.

But if Oliver accepted the Watcher's invitation, how would Corwyn find him?

This was the dilemma the broom now faced, and it troubled him as no other decision that had ever confronted

him. He loved his maker, although he had been unhappy
lately in Corwyn's company, and he found himself quite
drawn to the strange Watcher who was almost as silent
as Oliver himself. Yet if Oliver left with this new companion, would he thereby be betraying Corwyn?

So Oliver agonized through the night while the Watcher
snored softly a few feet away, and though the broom never
required sleep, he felt unusually exhausted by the time the
sun rose the next morning.

Several times, Corwyn started to fall, only to catch
himself with a start, dismayed at finding that his attention
had once again wandered. Yet so disorienting was his
plight—balanced in the darkness upon a rock, his hand
trapped inside the cave wall—and so demanding was his
need for concentration, that existence took on an illusory
quality, and he could no longer tell what was real and
what was not, nor whether he was awake or dreaming.

This became especially true on the second day of his
captivity, when bright sunlight again sparkled on the sea
outside and a portion of this light filtered through the
blue-green depths to his chamber. It was an eerie light by
the time it reached him, pale and fragmented by water, and
it played upon the glistening stone walls like candlelight
refracted through precious gems of beryl and emerald.
Then the chamber turned indeed into a kind of grail, a
crystal-encrusted geode such as Oliver had brought him
in the wilderness, with Corwyn its prisoner. He began to
fantasize that he was an imaginary character, trapped not
within a submarine cave, but written onto the pages of Cid
Hamete's books, caught in the Holy Grail of fiction.

Once, the memory of Hypatia rose in his mind, but in
his bewilderment, the real person he'd loved centuries
earlier became confused with the mythical Hypatia del
Alexandria about whom Cid Hamete wrote. Thus the two
images blended into one, and he fancied the resulting
person was in the cave with him, holding his hand.

"Your ladyship seems to be grating my wrist rather
more than fondling it," he chided, even adopting the
fictional Don Corwyn's manner of speaking. "Please

don't mistreat it so. My hand is not to blame for any unhappiness I may have caused you, nor is it right that you should vent your displeasure on so small a part of me."

But as no one was listening to his speech, the rough grip continued unabated.

At other times, he believed he was under an enchantment, and he cursed Hydro Phobius, whom he held responsible for this evil, and he thought with bitterness upon the corruption which the waters of the world must be suffering in his absence while he remained ensorcelled, unable to come to their aid and purify them. Indeed, sometimes the very air within the chamber seemed infected with demons, introduced into the cave by Hydro Phobius for the sole purpose of possessing him.

"A curse upon the day of my birth," he moaned when he became aware once more of where he was, and the true nature of his captivity. "And upon the man who brought tidings of that birth to my father." Yet even then, he wondered whether he should be cursing instead the day on which he'd first been published, and the Moor who had written him.

Outside, night fell, and the strange half-light in the cave vanished. Corwyn was again plunged into blackness. He longed silently then for Oliver, although he felt too betrayed by the broom to admit his loneliness aloud. Instead, he resolved nevermore to voice Oliver's name, even though the unspoken sound of it was like a fire that smoldered in his bones, and the effort of continued forbearance consumed him.

"Enough," he cried at last into the dark. "Cid Hamete, if you're truly my inventor, then scratch out the lines by which you conceived me, for I've lived too long already."

Perhaps it's just that this request was unfounded, or it may be that the published word can no more be recalled than a spoken one. In any case, Corwyn's plea received no answer.

So we leave him for a time, having so briefly regained his composure a few days before only to stumble once more into a labyrinth of self-pity and unable to find a way out again. But in this case, perhaps his outlook can be forgiven—if not for the emotional abyss which seemed to have engulfed his life as a whole, then at least for the physical captivity now confining him.

Entremés

AT LENGTH, DON CORWYN AND SEBASTIAN REACHED
the edge of a shallow lake where an old rowboat
was moored among the reeds that lined the shore.
Don Corwyn, seeing in this as he did all things
evidence to prove his follies, immediately climbed into
the boat.

"See how fortune favors us," he told his apprentice,
"for we have already reached the Mediterranean Sea,
and this boat has been provided for the explicit purpose
of carrying us to Italy."

Sebastian scratched his head. "I think the owner of
this boat will be very angry when he comes looking
for it and finds it missing. Besides which, I'm reluctant to entrust my life to a boat that's already leak-
ing."

Don Corwyn lifted the hem of his robes and studied the
puddle swirling about his ankles. "It is nothing, merely
some rainwater that has collected here from the boat's
being left exposed and open. Bring Rociandante on board
so we may cast off."

Sebastian considered mentioning that it hadn't
rained for several weeks, but let the matter pass.
He pushed Rociandante from behind while Don
Corwyn pulled on her halter, and between them

they got the donkey aboard, straddling the only
seat other than Don Corwyn's. "Where shall I
sit?" Sebastian asked, eyeing the way the alchemist's portly frame completely filled the seat he
occupied.

Don Corwyn also peered about the craft, so heavily
laden that it rode very low in the water. "Why, you shall
stay in the water and follow along behind."

"But I can't swim," Sebastian protested.

"No matter," Don Corwyn said. "Just hang onto the
stern of the boat and it will keep you afloat in perfect
safety." He looked around again. "Besides, I think you
shall have to propel the boat by kicking, for I don't see
any oars."

Reluctantly, Sebastian pushed the boat out onto the
lake, clinging fearfully to the stern. The water rose to his
shoulders. After a while, however, Sebastian noticed that
the depth of the lake was not so great but what he could
still touch the bottom with his feet. He began walking
across the lake floor, pushing the boat ahead of him.

"Look, Sebastian, you don't even have to kick in
order to propel us," Don Corwyn cried. "The boat is
definitely enchanted, for it moves of its own voli-
tion."

"Why, so it does," Sebastian replied, continuing his
slow trek across the slippery floor. "And, indeed, we
must already be far out at sea, as I'm sure you could
tell with one of your rusty blades, for I just felt three
or four of those fierce leviathans and behemoths which
inhabit the deep nibbling at my toes."

"You must be right about our having sailed so far, for
in truth I'm feeling rather seasick," Don Corwyn said.
"And as the very word itself assures us, that cannot
happen anywhere but at sea. However, I must warn you,
Sebastian, not to let any of those ferocious creatures
gobble up too much of you—certainly not more than a
joint or so from one of your legs—or else you might be
unable to keep up with me in my travels."

"Don't worry, master, I'll kick at them to drive them
away," Sebastian answered. He made a show of thrashing

around in the water. "There, I've frightened them off, and I didn't allow them even the smallest bite from any part of me."

"Good. But now, please tell me what you meant about using one of my 'rusty blades,' for I must admit, I didn't understand you. I don't carry a blade, rusty or otherwise."

"By that, I meant one of those things you use to measure your position by the stars."

"Oh, an astrolabe."

"Yes, I suppose. Although whatever it is, we won't need one now, for we've reached the other side." So it was, and a good thing too, for the boat had continued taking on water until the gunwales scarcely rose above the surface. With a final push, Sebastian shoved the little craft into the reeds of the opposite bank.

"So we have," Don Corwyn cried, stepping from the boat. "And that we have truly arrived in Italy, as I have said, the whole world may now know with utter certainty, for you yourself can testify to our safe passage over the perilous depths of the Mediterranean Sea. Although even this proof might perhaps be more readily believed by hardened skeptics if it had been our good fortune for one of those behemoths or leviathans you felt to have eaten off a few of your toes."

"What? I won't have them doing any such thing!" Sebastian sprang from the water and turned to glare back at it lest anything tried to follow him. Suddenly, he frowned, realizing he could still see the other shore. "Is it a long way to Italy?"

"Very far," Don Corwyn grunted, coaxing Rociandante from the craft. "Why do you ask?"

"Oh, no reason," Sebastian replied, reluctant to say anything which could cast doubt on the courage he had displayed in handling the creatures of the deep. The esteem in which his exploit was held might suffer were anyone to learn that his feet had stayed in contact with the seafloor the entire voyage.

Thus they went on, Don Corwyn assured that they were now in Italy, and Sebastian puzzling over the insanities of

*his master. If it hadn't been that Sebastian wanted so bad-
ly to be made a nobleman, he might have abandoned the
alchemist and returned to Spain then and there. . . .*

—Cid Hamete Benengeli,
  *El Ingenioso Alquimista
  Don Corwyn de La Mancha,* Part II

Chapter 11

Wherein Sebastian receives a surprise visit from Toxemiah, and Friar Carlos ponders his future on earth as well as in the hereafter.

THE NEXT DAY, AN EXHAUSTED AND VERY DEJECTED Sebastian leaned against the trunk of a fir on a mountainside overlooking Pomme de Terre. He breathed in the pine-scented air, wishing it would relieve his misery. Bad enough that Jean-Claude had so blatantly abused him the day before, he thought, without Gwen's making things worse by standing aside and allowing it to happen. In fact, she even took advantage of the situation herself! And the whole neighborhood had seemed to be watching. The memory of it was more than he could bear. He glanced again at his chapped and reddened hands, worn raw by the previous day's bout of carrying water and cleaning. Sebastian groaned, unaware that his outlook now matched his master's. So many bucketfuls it had taken to fill the cistern. And after that, so many dirty pots and pans he had cleaned, so many floors he'd scrubbed.

So much laughter Jean-Claude and the students had enjoyed at his expense!

Despite Gwen's initial statement that Sebastian should

carry out only the first part of his self-imposed commands—filling the cistern—when that was done, neither Gwen nor the students had known how to keep him from continuing. At last, Gwen had decided his compulsion to clean might as well be put to good use, so she had him scrub the whole kitchen. Then, since the spell still wasn't used up, she let Jean-Claude and the boys take Sebastian to their quarters, where he did yet more cleaning. The boys' rooms had never been so spotless!

When the spell finally wore off, instead of going to bed for a much-needed rest, Sebastian had left the shop and wandered aimlessly, eventually leaving town (where everyone seemed to be snickering and whispering about him) and ambling all the way up here. Now he could look down on Pomme de Terre and try to put the experience into perspective.

Except that the only perspective he could see, even from here, was one of utter humiliation. And all because he had tried to exercise his rightful authority over Jean-Claude and the rest of those wild, undisciplined boys who refused to heed him any other way.

All in all, Sebastian had a serious quarrel to take up with Corwyn, once he returned. After all, this whole thing was the alchemist's fault in the first place—if he hadn't gone off and left the school in Sebastian's care, none of this would have happened. What could possibly have caused the old alchemist to do anything so irresponsible?

Slowly, daylight waned, giving birth to a shadow forest that stretched across the ground from the roots of solid trees and draped its spectral boughs over the darkening land. The air, stiflingly hot a short time earlier, began to cool. Still Sebastian's mind picked at the events of the previous day, like a dog unwilling to abandon a well-gnawed bone. He couldn't get beyond the image of himself, on hands and knees before his students, scrubbing the floors like a scullery maid. A mindless automaton carrying out his own commands.

And all while Jean-Claude had looked on, gloating!

That was the worst of it, of course. It galled Sebastian that Jean-Claude should emerge from this not only unscathed, but actually the victor. Sebastian knew exactly how Jean-Claude had viewed the entire affair, knew the boy would swagger around the school more arrogantly than ever after this. If Jean-Claude had been difficult before, now he would be impossible.

Sebastian knew this and more because he understood Jean-Claude himself so well. Would-be master and should-be pupil, the two of them had wrestled from the beginning over who was to be in control. Sebastian could almost have hated the boy for this, had it not been that the two of them were so much alike.

So much alike. The thought haunted him—an endless refrain played upon Henri's bagpipes, jangling Sebastian's nerves.

After a while, a peculiar spasm began to twitch along one side of Sebastian's face. He fought to repress it, but the image of himself forced to dance to a tune of his own composing wouldn't fade. The tic returned, accompanied by a quiet rumbling in his chest. The supposed master of the school, he told himself, undone by his own attempt at discipline. Sebastian chuckled, stopped himself, then burst into laughter. The deep-throated sound of it cascaded down the mountainside.

Jean-Claude had been right to laugh—Sebastian must have looked ridiculous!

Eventually, he brought his guffaws under control sufficiently to head back down the mountain toward town. He paused occasionally to let out another chuckle, content that he at last knew how to deal with Jean-Claude and anxious to put his newfound awareness into practice.

On the other side of the Pyrenees, Oliver felt elated. After considerable agonizing, he had decided to explain his dilemma to his new friend. It took a while for the broom to express his concerns in gestures, but at last he succeeded. The Watcher had then explained where the two of them would be going (if Oliver chose to come along) and why. Oliver was doubtful at first, thinking his friend was making the whole thing up just to impress him. But the Watcher offered proof which convinced the broom. It would be like a game, the Watcher emphasized, and in order to work they had to be very careful not to be seen. That, of course, intrigued the broom, who always delighted in any new game. But best of all was the Watcher's purpose. Oliver was beside himself with excitement when he finally accepted what he was being told. Corwyn would be so pleased with this surprise!

Without further hesitation, therefore, Oliver agreed to the Watcher's invitation and was lifted onto the latter's mount, where he rode behind his friend. Oliver never even looked back as they left the sandy wash which had been Corwyn's camp in the wilderness, so certain was the broom of the importance of their journey and its eventual outcome.

Back in Pomme de Terre, Sebastian followed the labyrinthine twists and turns of narrow side streets that led to Corwyn's shop and the school. He whistled happily, walking with a brisk step through the darkness that had enveloped the town. At the end of a particularly disreputable-looking alley, he arrived at the door of the quarters he and Gwen occupied on the ground floor of the school. He put his hand to the latch, then flinched as the skirling of Henri's bagpipes cut momentarily through the evening air. Sebastian shook his head. Short as Henri's concert had been, it had undoubtedly put an end to any rest Gwen might have been taking.

Suddenly, the heavy, oily stench of rotting fish assaulted Sebastian from behind, causing him to stumble. Bony fingers plucked at his sleeve and spun him around. Sebastian gasped for breath, intending to cry out in fear and revulsion, but choked on the foul air instead. He squeezed his eyes shut against the burning, although tears still seeped from beneath his eyelids. Slowly, his knees buckled and he sprawled upon the cobblestones.

A voice made hoarse with madness hissed in his ear. "Dr. Tox," it said, as if that were his name, "Dr. Tox, hearken unto me."

Sebastian groaned, certain now to whom the voice belonged. He forced his eyes open. Through a blur of tears, he saw the shadowy figure of Toxemiah lean over him, brushing him with a necklace of putrid fish heads. With the dignity of a bishop crowning a king, Toxemiah draped an uncured animal hide over him.

Sebastian turned his head to vomit.

"With the mantle of Toxemiah do I clothe thee," the figure intoned. "Yea, even my own robe do I lay upon your shoulders."

Sebastian tried to decline the honor and to ask Toxemiah what he was talking about, but his voice failed him. Again, he retched.

"Soon, thine oppressor will come," the madman went on. "In that day sing ye dirges, O Gardenia, and drink the dregs of a bitter wine." He stood, his scrawny frame strangely ceremonious in the uncertain light. "Hear, therefore, the words that Toxemiah speaks concerning the coming of thine oppressor. For though I now anoint the ground wherein I stand with the contents of but a single vessel, there follows after me one who will pour out corruption upon the whole of the land."

With the gravity of one who bore the responsibilities of the world on his skinny shoulders, Toxemiah raised a small wineskin and poured its contents onto the ground near Sebastian. But no wine splashed upon the cobblestones. Indeed, no earthly substance of any sort spilled from the upturned skin. Instead, a greasy yellow haze flowed with slow deliberation from the opening, an immaterial smoke that swelled upon itself in a ghastly burlesque of mortal pregnancy.

It was a demon!

Finally, the entire creature floated in the evening air, fully birthed from its wineskin prison. Sebastian's stomach, already abused by the smell of decaying fish, recoiled at the sight, but his eyes never left the hideous apparition. He stared, mesmerized, panic-stricken, recalling previous encounters with such phantoms. Always before their presence had set off an avalanche of painful memories, and Sebastian braced himself for another of these.

This time, however, was different. This time, the thing before him, having assumed roughly human form, bored into his soul with dead, empty eyes and flung him forward into a future he dreaded might one day come about. Once there, the specter drew in upon itself, becoming solid even as it grew smaller, until it was Sebastian's anticipated son who stood before him, eyes downcast and sullen, cowed by the vengeful presence of the father Sebastian feared he himself might become. In his mind, the boy cringed as Sebastian had once cringed before his own father, and the stinging words Sebastian hurled at his son echoed the scorn his own father had rained upon him some twenty years earlier.

Tears trickled down the boy's abject face, a face that loomed ever larger in Sebastian's mind. Yet Sebastian also knew it wasn't really the boy who was drawing closer, filling his field of vision, but the demon approaching him, immobilizing him with guilt. Sebastian struggled to free himself from the demon's mental grip, wondering why Toxemiah had exposed him to possession.

Then, just as Sebastian was sure the creature would claim him, the vision wavered. Sebastian's "son" dissolved into a formlessness that expanded rapidly until it was once again the demon from the wineskin, a sickly yellow presence hovering above the ground, horrible still, yet no longer personally damning. The apparition flailed the air in an effort to pull away from the mad prophet, and Sebastian realized through the fog enveloping his brain that the demon was recoiling from the stench of rotting animal skins and decaying fish. Toxemiah, by hovering close to Sebastian and draping him with his cloak, had protected him from demonic possession.

Sebastian's relief was short-lived, however, for the demon's retreat quickly brought it up against the heavy wooden door to Sebastian and Gwen's quarters, with access from there to the school and Corwyn's laboratory beyond. Like an angry cloud, the demon bumped against the iron grille which allowed visitors to be inspected from inside the door. Quickly, the creature began flowing through the grille, into the corridor which led to the room where Gwen was possibly sleeping. Sebastian drew breath to scream a warning, heedless of the smell that burned his throat and lungs.

Just then, the shriek of Henri's bagpipes again ripped through the evening air. Sebastian cringed. He thought he recognized the remnants of a tune amid the noise, a laud Sebastian had been fond of at the monastery. After this, the song would never again sound the same.

Apparently, the demon shared Sebastian's aversion to bagpipes, for the creature suddenly boiled back through the grille in the door and churned its way up the alley.

At the head of the alley, a sow being driven home by a boy turned the wrong way and trotted happily toward the smells of corruption and decay. The boy ran after the sow with his switch, cursing the beast for its stupidity. Then he saw the advancing demon and froze.

The demon, willing to take advantage of any living host in its eagerness to escape the bagpipes, insinuated itself into the sow through the creature's nostrils. The sow jerked to a stop and trembled briefly as the demon gained control, then bolted back along the alley and down the street beyond. Sebastian lurched to his feet and staggered after the beast, fearful for the safety of the town's inhabitants. Behind him ran the boy, crying over his lost sow.

Sebastian slowed as he neared the trough that supplied this part of town with water, the same trough where he had filled endless buckets for the cistern the previous day. Several people had gathered around it, talking excitedly and pointing into the trough. But Sebastian couldn't make out what they were pointing at until someone brought a torch from a nearby house. In its flickering light, he saw the drowned sow floating in the water.

When the boy whose sow it was realized what had

happened, he wailed all the louder. "This is your fault, *monsieur*," he shrieked at Sebastian. "You and those students of yours were conjuring demons, and now one of them has killed my pig."

The townspeople gasped and backed away from Sebastian, staring. He tried to explain about Toxemiah and the demon, but no one listened, so readily did they believe the accusations of a boy against this man who was already known for behaving strangely. "You should have seen this one yesterday," Sebastian's nosy, matronly neighbor cried, poking at him with a fat finger. "He carried on at this very trough as if he was ensorcelled."

Sebastian gave up attempting to explain and headed back to the alley. By morning, this incident would be forgotten, he told himself. In the meantime, he was deeply puzzled. Like Toxemiah with his fish heads, Sebastian and Corwyn had once used smells to control a horde of demons that had infected the duchy. Now Sebastian realized that music (if the jarring noise of bagpipes could be considered as such) would do the same.

But why had Toxemiah brought the thing here in the first place? Evidently, he wanted Sebastian to see it without being possessed—but to what purpose?

He hurried on, anxious to ask the mad prophet about this. But when he turned into the alley, Sebastian found himself alone. Toxemiah had vanished into the night as soundlessly as any demonic vision. Only a lingering odor of spoiled fish attested to his having been there at all.

Slowly, Sebastian entered the school building, lost in thought.

Many leagues away, in the almost-finished windmill where he made his bed, Friar Carlos strove for the blissful release of sleep which only a clear conscience can bring.

At the moment, too many doubts afflicted his conscience for sleep.

Earlier in the day, he had heard rumors about a series of incidents which disturbed his superiors back at the processing station near Zaragoza. None of the incidents was necessarily a problem in itself, but together they were cause for concern.

First, there had been a crazy French hermit who had been seen some weeks before lurking around the processing station and the first windmills constructed there. It was even suspected that this madman had entered the Cave of Montesinos, where demons exorcised by the Inquisition were being stored.

This had been followed by a more recent occasion when a couple of hog-gelders staying at an inn near Lérida had opened a "wineskin" destined for that same processing station. Both men had been demonically possessed, of course—which was no great loss in itself, but had raised fears among other people at the inn.

Then, just a few days ago, the French madman was said to have returned, and this time he had indeed managed to slip into the Cave of Montesinos and escape again, for he had ruptured one of the skins stored in the cave, causing the demonic possession of three Dominican friars.

Friar Carlos shuddered as he contemplated this last incident. While he felt unconcerned about what might happen in France as a result of this project, and little more concerned over the fate of a pair of itinerant hog-gelders, the fact that three of his brethren had been possessed concerned him greatly. The habit and crucifix they all wore in common were supposed to protect them from such a fate.

Anxiously, Friar Carlos clutched the clove of garlic he wore beneath his habit, aware of the sacrilege in reaching for it rather than the cross. It was this which plagued his conscience tonight, although on the whole he felt motivated to take the risk. Damnation in the next world might be probable for what he did, but damnation in this life was a certainty if he didn't.

Tomorrow, he assured himself, he would move the construction camp farther north and east, farther away from the processing station near Zaragoza and all it held. The current series of windmills was virtually complete, and it was time to begin the next.

Yet comforting as it was to move farther from

Zaragoza, Friar Carlos also knew this meant that the time was inevitably drawing nearer when all the windmills would be finished, and he would have to return to the processing station for a new assignment—an assignment which might take him into the very bowels of hell.

In all, Corwyn spent three days and three nights (although he didn't know how much time had passed, and would have believed it had been all eternity) standing on a rock in the dark, his arm stuck in the wall of the cave. At the end of that time, he became aware of water lapping at his ankles.

It took an hour or more for Corwyn's beleaguered brain to register this latest development, his plight having rendered him almost incapable of distinguishing between fantasy and reality. He thought for a while that he felt water rising around his feet, but by this time many things seemed to be so which were not, and a little wetness was a small thing to be concerned about considering the other misfortunes he sometimes thought he was experiencing. However, when a particularly strong surge of water swept his feet out from under him and left him dangling from the crevice by his hand, he finally became convinced of his altered situation.

For a moment, he debated whether his wrist were being cut off or his arm torn from its socket. In the end, he concluded that the difference was academic and began to howl as he would for either condition.

Between bellows, he also cast a little thought (albeit very little) on this rise in the water level. He could only surmise that an unusually high tide, combined perhaps with heavy seas, had contributed to it. Then an event happened which cut short both his shouting and his thinking, for his hand, evidently somewhat reduced in size after his three days of fasting, suddenly slipped free of the crevice, plunging Corwyn into the water. He scarcely had time to flail his way to the surface and gulp in a breath of air before another surge dragged him back into the tunnel through which he'd arrived, vomiting him at last into the world outside.

Chapter 12

Which tells of the impromptu inquisition held over Corwyn's library and how most of his books were consigned to the flames.

SEBASTIAN WAS ROUSED EARLY THE NEXT MORNING BY violent pounding on the main door of the Academy of Alchemical and Renaissance Arts. He grumbled and rubbed the sleep from his eyes, then rolled over to look for Gwen. She was already gone, this being her regular day to visit her parents' tavern. Sebastian snorted; he suspected she made these visits as much to read her books without his criticism as to see her parents.

The pounding continued. Sebastian stumbled to the entryway, grousing at the intrusion.

Outside the door stood several members of the city guard. Their leather jerkins creaked as the men shifted restlessly, pikes in hand. "Are you Sebastian, apprentice to Corwyn the alchemist?" their captain asked.

Sebastian stared in disbelief, for the captain saw him almost every day and frequently greeted him by name. "You know I am."

The captain motioned to a pair of his men, who grabbed Sebastian by the elbows and hustled him down the street.

"Alors!" Sebastian cried. "What's the meaning of this? Where are you taking me?"

"To the duchess," the captain replied. "She will hear the charges brought against you."

The captain refused to say anything further, and the men at Sebastian's elbows kept him marching along too swiftly for conversation. His mind, however, swirled with questions: What charges? Brought by whom? With what evidence? And, of course, what would be the penalty if he were found guilty?

It wasn't until they neared the duchess's castle on a hill at the edge of town that Sebastian remembered he wasn't actually Corwyn's apprentice any more, but a journeyman alchemist. By this time, though, he was panting hard and decided to conserve his breath rather than press the issue.

They crossed the bridge over the Ale River and passed through the castle gate. Halfway across the inner compound, Sebastian stopped abruptly, staring at the great hall ahead of them. Near the back of the building, overlooking the Ale where the river curved around the fortress, the twisted, blackened remains of three windmills dangled precariously from the side of a turret.

The guards flanking Sebastian tugged on his arms to keep him moving, but he resisted. "What happened?" he asked, jerking his chin to indicate the windmills.

"Seems some of the townsfolk are having doubts about our local alchemist," the guard captain drawled. "Since he wasn't around to be burned himself, they decided to make do with one of his projects. Now, get moving."

A shiver coursed through Sebastian as he realized for the first time the gravity of his situation.

Inside the great hall, the duchess waited on her throne in regal splendor, next to the vacant throne of the former duke. Before her stood the bishop of Pomme de Terre, also in full apparel, along with an itinerant friar and the neighbor woman who had witnessed the death of the demonically possessed sow the night before. Behind these three were ranked various nobles and servants of the court.

Evidently, this was to be a formal proceeding, Sebastian thought, the chill he had felt outside the hall now pooling in his stomach.

The guards escorted Sebastian to the throne, stationing him on the duchess's left. The bishop and his entourage, apparently Sebastian's accusers, waited on her right. Sebastian wondered whether there was any significance to their placement.

The duchess, a pale young woman whose extreme beauty was offset by utter ruthlessness, nodded to the bishop. "You may proceed."

The bishop had apparently kept himself at a low boil, waiting for this opportunity. He waved a pair of books which Sebastian recognized as the two volumes of *El Ingenioso Alquimista Don Corwyn de La Mancha* by Cid Hamete Benengeli. "This is what Master Corwyn's alchemy has brought us to!" the bishop roared. "Disgrace and infamy! Pomme de Terre held up to ridicule throughout the world! And now this good woman with me assures us that Corwyn's apprentice and students are practicing sorcery and conjuring demons."

"Journeyman," Sebastian corrected, determined not to allow this error to go unchallenged a second time.

"What?"

"I'm a journeyman alchemist now." Sebastian straightened. "I'm not just Corwyn's apprentice anymore."

"All the worse for you," the bishop replied, "for you must share the blame. Now we shall root out the cause of your ruin before it destroys yet more innocent souls. A curse, *oui*, a thousand curses on those books of alchemy which have conspired to bring about this evil! By the sign of the cross, I swear we'll burn them all by nightfall."

Behind him, the matron nodded vigorously, eyeing Sebastian as if he were an evil apparition himself.

"You forget yourself, your grace," the duchess cautioned. "After all, you're here for our approval to this scheme. We haven't given it yet."

The bishop bowed gravely to the duchess. "*Pardon, madame.* I speak, of course, conditionally, anticipating that you will see the reason in what I propose and will concede to its execution." He glared at Sebastian as if the duchess's reprimand had been his fault, while the neighborhood gossip continued to peer fearfully at the young alchemist from behind the bishop's robes. On the other side of the bishop stood the friar, whose timid glance also lighted briefly on Sebastian before returning to the floor at his feet.

"What do you propose?" Sebastian asked his accuser, the word 'execution' still ringing in his ears.

The bishop puffed himself up to full stature. "Why, an inquisition, of course. First over your master's books, which he has made a considerable point of bringing into the duchy over these past two years. Then, if necessary, over you and the students of this so-called Academy of Alchemical and Renaissance Arts."

"What!" Sebastian leaped at the bishop, but the two guards held him. "You can't do this. You don't have the authority."

The bishop studied Sebastian with ponderous dignity. "Authority? I'll have you know that it is on behalf of the Holy Office of the Inquisition that we are here. I intend to put that library of your master's to the question."

"But you're not allowed to conduct an inquisition," Sebastian objected. "Not of a library, not even of a single book. You don't belong to a mendicant order."

"No," the bishop agreed, "but he does." He pointed to the friar, who squirmed as if trying to disappear through the floor. "I will merely assist him."

Sebastian shook his head at the incongruity of a bishop assisting a lowly friar. Not only were they separated by great differences in rank, but the established clergy had long resented the mendicant orders, which claimed independence from the church hierarchy by answering directly to the pope. The fact that the papacy had also invested the mendicant orders with authority for carrying out the Inquisition only added to the bitterness between the two factions.

"Why would a friar need anyone's help?" mumbled Sebastian, whose brief career in a monastery had put him, too, at professional odds with the mendicants.

"Because he's illiterate," the bishop replied haughtily, as if the question had been directed at him. "Since he can't read, I must help him carry out judgment against these heretical books."

The friar shrugged at Sebastian apologetically.

"Again, you forget yourself, your grace," the duchess reminded the bishop. "If you were certain of your ecclesiastical authority in this, you wouldn't be asking for the support of our civil authority as well."

The bishop reddened and nodded stiffly as the matron edged around him to address the duchess. "It's true, your ladyship, what the bishop says. I saw this young man summon Satan himself last night and make a pact with the fiend for his soul in exchange for earthly power. Why, he conjured up all kinds of demons, then killed an entire herd of pigs with a flick of his finger. Might have killed me, too, if I hadn't scared him off with the sign of the cross!"

The duchess looked at Sebastian. "*Tiens!* What do you have to say for yourself, journeyman alchemist?"

Sebastian realized his mouth was hanging open and closed it. He shrugged. "What can I say against such a charge? It's preposterous!"

The duchess turned away. "Fine. The accused says nothing in his defense."

"Wait," Sebastian cried, "that's not what I meant!"

One of the guards silenced him with an elbow to the stomach. Sebastian doubled over, gasping for breath.

"Personally, we do not find much evidence against this young man," the duchess told the bishop. "Nevertheless, we do not wish to oppose our esteemed representative of the church. Therefore, do as you will." She frowned and added under her breath, "I'd wash my hands of the matter, if the stupid peasants hadn't ruined the windmills that provided the water for it."

She stood and swept out of the great hall, ending the audience. The bishop smiled menacingly at Sebastian. "Bring him along to the alchemist's library," he said, striding from the hall to lead the way. The matron and the friar took up places behind the bishop, while the guards dragged Sebastian after them.

At the alchemist's shop, the bishop paused long enough for a guard to open the door, then barged on ahead. The matron hesitated at the threshold, looking indignant and frightened at the thought of entering into the midst of so much wickedness. The friar smiled self-consciously at Sebastian again and scurried after them.

As he was shoved inside by the guards, Sebastian wondered at the strange silence pervading the vicinity of the school. This wouldn't be a good time for the students to pull one of their tricks.

The entourage mounted the stairs to the second floor, where the bishop flung open the library door as if storming the gates of hell, revealing a room which housed more than a thousand books, large and small. As soon as the neighbor woman saw them, she shrieked and ran from the building, returning a few minutes later with a bowl of holy water and a bunch of hyssop. "Take these, your grace," she said, thrusting the bowl and herbs at the bishop with a curtsy, "and sprinkle the room with them in case one of the enchanters in these books tries to cast a spell over us, punishing us for our intent to banish him from the world."

The simplicity of this made the bishop laugh. The friar, however, glanced at the books uneasily, and the guards holding Sebastian took a step back.

The bishop motioned the friar to the books. "Hand them to me one by one, that I may examine them individually and see if some deserve to spared from the flames."

"No," the matron pleaded, "there's no reason to pardon any of them, your grace, for they're all offenders in this crime. Throw them into the courtyard and set fire to the lot." So eager was she for the slaughter of these innocents that she yanked open a window overlooking the small, cobbled yard, bordered on three sides by the building which housed the school and Corwyn's laboratory, and bounded on the fourth side by the stable.

The friar, a load of books already in hand, edged toward the window with a questioning look in the bishop's direction. The bishop sent two of the guards down to light a fire, but insisted on at least reading the titles of the books before throwing them to the courtyard below.

The friar handed the bishop a slim but elaborately bound volume of obvious antiquity. "*The Emerald Tablet*," the bishop read, "by Hermes Trismegistus. I've heard of it. They say this was the first alchemical text, and that all the rest owe their origin to it."

"No!" Sebastian wailed. "Don't destroy that one!" He wrenched at his arms to free himself, but his captors held him firmly.

The friar glanced at Sebastian, then at the bishop, and cleared his throat with a squeak. "If it's the first of its kind, your grace, and as much imitated as you say, then perhaps it's also the best of the lot and therefore worthy of our clemency."

"No," the bishop replied. "We must not weaken. For the very reason you have stated I am of the opinion that we ought to condemn it without mercy to the flames. That is its proper sentence for having fathered so heretical a breed." He handed the book to the neighbor woman, along with the two books by Cid Hamete. "Take them, good mistress, and throw them into the courtyard. Since the first book sired the others, let it light the fire by which they shall burn as well." Without another look at the condemned volumes, he turned to the friar for the next book. "Ah, another ancient work, this one by Mary the Prophetess, also known as Mary the Jewess, who was rumored to be Miriam, the sister of Moses."

Appalled by the prospect of a second such loss, Sebastian again struggled to get free. Again, his captors held him.

"Well, her brother shall not save her from the bonfire," the bishop went on, "for if Hermes Trismegistus is the father of all these alchemical books, then his fate must descend upon his daughter as well. Toss it into the courtyard with the others."

The matron did so with great alacrity, and thus Mary, or Miriam, took flight and—with pages flapping like the wings of a phoenix—landed on her own funeral pyre.

Sebastian groaned.

The bishop glanced at several more titles in quick succession. "Here are three—*The Book of Amulets, The Great and Small Books of the Scroll*, and *The Paradise of Wisdom*—by Prince Khalid ibn Yazid. And a pair of comic alchemical romances by someone who from his name appears to be an English clerk, yet who seems to write under the patronage of the Spanish duke of Alburquerque." The bishop looked closer and grunted. "Even worse than his subject perhaps is that the writer of these last two books shows himself thankless of the debt he's under, for he misspells his patron's name by leaving out an *r*." He handed the stack of books to the matron. "Obviously all descendants of the same line as the others. I should burn my own father if I caught him reading such books. Into the courtyard with them."

"Me, too," the friar mumbled.

"Hmmm?" The bishop turned, having apparently forgotten him. "What's that? You wish to be thrown into the courtyard too?"

"No, I mean I'd burn him, too, your grace."

The bishop drew himself up. "You'd presume to pass judgment on my father?"

"No, *my* father. I'd burn my father if I found him reading such books." The friar frowned. "If he could read."

The bishop eyed the friar dubiously and accepted the next volume. It was large and old, well bound with a brass cover engraved in a strange script. The bishop opened the book and felt the pages. "Not paper or parchment," he said. "Maybe papyrus. And the text is in Latin. This must be the infamous book of Abraham the Jew, claimed to have been recovered by Nicholas Flamel. Into the yard with him, for he cannot be anything but a braggart."

"With all my heart, your grace," the matron replied, and did as she was bidden. Through the window, smoke could now be seen rising from the courtyard, and Sebastian thought he heard the crackling of flames.

"Here are two by Solomon Trismosin," the bishop said, taking the next books. "*Splendor Solis* and *Aureum Vellus*, the latter also called *The Golden Fleece*. But the only things splendid or golden about either of these books are the titles. Let them join their brothers."

So it went with the rest of the volumes—from a copy of *Tsan-tung-chi* brought back from Cathay, to the Italian *Summa Perfectionis*—until at last the friar grew tired and suggested they throw them all, large and small, into the courtyard. The bishop, weary from reading so many titles, nodded his agreement and ordered the matron to proceed. His command didn't fall on deaf ears, for she'd rather have burned those books than been privy to the best gossip in the world. Seizing a number of volumes at once, therefore, she hurled them out the window and turned for others, pausing between armloads only when one of the books chanced to fall at the bishop's feet.

"Bless my soul!" he cried, peering down at the book. "Is Garroc Grimwulf's son here? Give him to me, good woman, for this *Sceadu Seofonth Mona* is a veritable treasury of wisdom and poetic wonder. Despite his being a heathen, this saga ranks among the best in the world. Take it home and read it," he told the friar, offering the book, "and you'll see what I've said of it is true."

The friar's eyes were downcast as he worried the hem of his robe. "I can't read, remember?"

"What?" The bishop looked disdainful. "Oh, yes. I forgot." He frowned, then took another volume from the ones in the matron's arms—which happened to be a stack of Gwen's chivalric romances—and opened it. "Well, what shall we do with these other books? They appear to be not of alchemy, but chivalry. Perhaps they should be spared the fate of the others because they cannot work the mischief that the books of alchemy have. These are books of considerable entertainment and diversion, without danger to anyone."

"Oh, your grace," cried the matron, "you should have them burned like the rest. I wouldn't be surprised if

Master Corwyn, once cured of the disease of alchemy, didn't start reading these books instead. He's liable to take it into his head to lead these young students of his through woods and fields in military revels, jousting and fighting, and what is worse, turning knight, for they say that disease is catching and incurable."

"The good woman is right," said the bishop, avariciously eyeing the romances she held. "It would be wise to spare Master Corwyn such a stumbling block in the future. I am, therefore, of the opinion that those books of chivalry in your arms should not be burned, but be removed to the bishopric, and there placed under my protective custody." Eagerly, he relieved the matron of her load. "Now, what about the others in the room? Should they be examined as well, or shall they be turned over to the secular arm for punishment with the rest?"

At this point, the inquisition was interrupted by the horrible din of bagpipes, fifes, and drums all playing in concert in the alley outside the laboratory. The bishop blanched at the noise and the friar covered his ears. "*Bon dieu!*" the matron shrieked. "That's how they conjured that demon last night!"

Instinctively, the guards loosened their grip on Sebastian and edged away, their eyes on the corners of the room. Sebastian bolted from the library and dashed down the stairs, bowling over another guard who stood watch inside the laboratory door, sword drawn against the unseen enemy. "To me, boys, to me!" he cried as he burst through the door and into the midst of the students gathered outside. The gleeful look on Jean-Claude's face evaporated at this unexpected reaction from Sebastian. Clearly, the youth had anticipated a different response to the students' newly formed band.

"The bishop's forces have won the day," Sebastian explained, continuing up the alley. "We must find Corwyn."

The boys, too bewildered to understand what he was saying, followed his lead blindly. Jean-Claude scowled and stood his ground until two of the guards erupted from the laboratory door, at which point the youth made a hasty decision to rejoin his fellows and hurried after them.

The guards chased Sebastian and the boys through the town, followed at a considerable distance by the bishop. The matron, however, remained in the library, anxious to finish her task and taking the bishop's absence as permission to do so. "Although I think a better remedy would be to seal up the whole building," she muttered as she finished flinging the books out the window and onto the pyre below, "with boys and books and master and all inside, and let the devil himself come and take them!"

The friar, meanwhile, also stayed behind, and he fidgeted indecisively, unable to make up his mind what to do or whom to help, and as a result doing nothing. The scrutiny of the library thus proceeded no further before the remaining books were destroyed, and it is believed that St. Augustine's *City of God* and Thomas à Kempis's *Imitation of Christ*, along with rare copies of many another venerable book, were consigned to the flames by the matron, unseen and unjudged. Had the bishop been aware of these remaining treasures, undoubtedly he would have spared them from so harsh a sentence; but as it was, these and perhaps others equally worthy never received the pardons they deserved, thereby proving the old saying that sometimes the saint must pay for the sinner.

Sebastian, meanwhile, fled from Pomme de Terre, accompanied by his twelve young disciples. For his part, the bishop seemed content to let them leave, and barred the city gates behind them.

About this time, Corwyn was nearing Valencia, sharing the back of a peasant's cart with a goat and several chickens and feeling the chagrin of a condemned man being carried in a tumbril to his hanging. Only weakness from his captivity in the cave, combined with having fasted in the wilderness on his way to Barcelona, forced Corwyn to accept the disgrace of such a ride. To make matters worse, he had lost the new conical alchemist's hat he'd purchased for the trip in Barcelona. The hat was yet another victim of that storm which had deprived him of everything save the bedraggled black robes covering his body—robes now so shapeless that he looked more like a wandering friar, begging for a living, than a successful alchemist.

The cart ambled through a hilly strip of fertile coast pinched between the sea on Corwyn's left and the gray mountains that rose to the *meseta* on his right. Wide, sunny beaches alternated between pebbles and fine sand, broken occasionally by rock promontories. But most distinctive was the lush, dark green of the citrus orchards that abounded everywhere, sometimes stretching to within a few yards of the sea. Although the region received little rain, the Romans had built an elaborate system of irrigation, later improved upon by the Moors, and from this the area derived its name, *La Huerta*.

Interested though Corwyn usually was in anything to do with water, all this meant at the moment was that after three days of fasting he could stuff himself silly on the many vegetables and fruits (especially oranges!) grown in the region. He thus felt somewhat comforted by the time the cart actually reached Valencia, entering through *Los Torres de Serranos*, a pair of massive towers that guarded the northern gate to the city.

The farmer carried him all the way through the newer, outer city to the walls of the oldest part of town, where the architecture revealed the curious blend of Iberian, Phoenician, Carthaginian, Roman, Visigoth, and Moorish influences that had shaped the entire Levant throughout its tempestuous history. At the *mercado* near the church of San Juan, the farmer stopped to sell his wares. For a while, Corwyn wandered around the old city, gawking like a peasant at sites ranging from the *Palacio de la Generalidad* where the general tax was collected (and for which the building was named), to the *Lonja* built by the local silk merchants in a flamboyant attempt to outdo the commercial centers of rival cities.

This wasn't strictly idleness on Corwyn's part, for the whole time he was aware of being alone and destitute in a foreign city. Before anything else, he needed money. While he walked, therefore, he also considered how to put his talents to use.

Outside the cathedral, just recently finished, he stopped to watch members of the local water tribunal hear a dispute involving irrigation rights in the *huerta*. This intrigued Corwyn, and he learned from a fellow bystander that the tribunal met here, outside the Apostle Door of the cathedral, each week to settle such disputes, with the hearing, judgment, and sentencing (usually a fine or, in severe cases, suspension of water privileges) taking place all at one time. Corwyn nodded approvingly at the swiftness of the system, at the same time thinking that perhaps he would do some sleight of hand back in the *mercado* to earn a few *maravedis* from the passersby. He was even tempted to revive his old fortune-telling routine, although that might attract unwanted attention from the Inquisition.

The need for money made Corwyn appreciate Oliver's company more than ever—and not just to cure his poverty. If only the broom were with him now.

He started to leave before he realized the man who had explained about the water tribunal had spoken to him again. Corwyn turned. *"¿Qué?"*

The man jerked his head to indicate the cathedral behind him, telling Corwyn that as a visitor to Valencia, perhaps he would be interested in seeing the chapel where one of the most sacred relics in Christendom was kept.

Corwyn listened, first out of politeness, then in outraged disbelief. Finally, he stormed into the cathedral to see this abomination for himself, not bothering to thank the man for his suggestion. There, behind the altar in the special chapel set aside to house it, half-surrounded by twelve alabaster reliefs, stood a magnificent little cup of purple agate. Corwyn ground his teeth and snorted through his nostrils like a horse, wondering whether he could escape this legend even by traveling to the ends of the earth.

The cup was said to be the Holy Grail.

Abandoning all thought of earning money or remaining in the city for any reason, Corwyn stalked out of the chapel. The sooner he found *Roche-naissante* and returned to Pomme de Terre, leaving Valencia and its misbegotten Grail behind, the better.

However, before pursuing Corwyn in his hurried trek to the port (where he will undoubtedly encounter yet further adventures), we must first catch up on other aspects of this history.

Entremés

AFTER SEVERAL DAYS OF UNEVENTFUL TRAVEL, DON Corwyn and Sebastian climbed to the crest of a low hill, where they perceived a city some distance ahead.

As has been related, Don Corwyn's madness was such that in his imagination he transformed all ordinary things into matters of alchemy as described in the books he read, and the city before him now was not spared this fate. He therefore turned to his apprentice and said, "This is the day, Sebastian, on which shall be clearly seen the good that fate has in store for us; this is the day, I say, on which I shall prove the true worth of aquatic alchemy by performing such deeds as shall be written about in the books of fame for succeeding ages. Do you see that city ahead? Know that it is none other than the Venetian state, the Pearl of the Adriatic, and beyond it the sea. It is here, you may be assured, that we shall find what we seek."

Sebastian squinted into the distance. "I do see a city, and the sea beyond," he said. "But it looks more like Barcelona than this venison steak you're talking about, which—if you'll pardon me for saying so, master— doesn't sound like a city or a pearl, but more like a side of meat."

The hill, meanwhile, ended in a small bluff, and there Don Corwyn and Sebastian stopped. Don Corwyn, seeing in his imagination what did not exist, pointed to the plain that extended from the base of the hill all the way to the city and said, "That you are wrong may be *clearly seen by this lagoon below us, upon whose shore we stand and whose waters envelop Venice in a loving embrace. As further proof of this (as if any more were needed) you can see sailing upon the lagoon a fleet of Venetian fishing boats with their brightly colored sails, and beyond them a gondola or two, nearer the canals of the city.*

"As for the city itself," he went on, sighing like a smitten lover, "what other vision in all the world could equal this view of Venice? There lies the Piazza San Marco, with its Doges' Palace of pink marble, its golden Basilica, and its red brick Campanile. By the Molo stand two granite columns, the gray one topped by St. Mark's lion, the red one by St. Theodore."

So he went on, naming buildings and monuments as his fancy dictated and giving to each its special attributes. By God! How many of them did he name! How many wonders did he enumerate, so absorbed was he in all he had read in his lying books!

Sebastian, meanwhile, hung on his words without uttering one. At last he said, "Master, I'll commend to the devil any canal, building, or monument of all those you mentioned that is actually there. At least I do not see them, for all I see of your boats and lagoon is a mule train stirring up the dusty plain on its way from the city, and a pair of travelers plodding wearily on foot to the gates of what still looks to me like Barcelona, but which you insist is actually Venice. But perhaps this, too, is enchanted, as has happened so often in the past."

"What, do you not see the wonders of Venice?" Don Corwyn exclaimed. "Do you not smell the fragrance of the lagoon?"

"I see nothing," answered Sebastian, "except what I have already told you. And as for the smell"—he wrinkled his nose and checked the back of the alchemist's clothes—"what I think it is would best remain unsaid."

"The fear you are in," said Don Corwyn, "allows you neither to see nor to smell correctly, for one of the effects of fear is to disturb the senses and make things seem different from what they are. If you are so afraid,

wait here with Rociandante *upon the shore while I swim the lagoon to Venice, for I alone am sufficient to recover the Holy Grail which is the stolen library of Alexandria and to break the evil enchantments of Hydro Phobius.''* With these words he dismounted and stood at the edge of the bluff, preparing to dive into what he believed was water.

"No, master, don't!" Sebastian shouted at him. "I swear to God that you'll be leaping into solid ground. Look! There are no canals, nor doges' palaces, nor libraries of Alexandria, nor Holy Grails."

Don Corwyn, however, paid no heed, but dived gracefully from the top of the escarpment to the plain a few feet below. When he hit, the harder parts of him cracked and crunched while the softer parts made squishing sounds. A flurry of dust rose around his crumpled form. Sebastian, who was tearing his hair and cursing the hour they had met, saw the alchemist-errant lying in a motionless heap and slid down the short incline to his master's side. He found Don Corwyn injured but conscious, and said, "Did I not tell you, sir, to stop, for that lagoon you were trying to swim wasn't water, but hard ground?"

"That rascal of an enchanter, Hydro Phobius, can make things vanish," Don Corwyn said, lisping through a mouthful of broken teeth. "It is a very easy matter for such a man to make us see whatever he pleases, and this malignant persecutor of mine, envious of the glory I was to reap in this endeavor, has changed the lagoon into an ordinary plain. Either that, or the water is shallower than I remember. For my sake, Sebastian, do one thing to undeceive yourself and see the truth of what I'm telling you. Follow this seeming plain around its edge, and you will see that when you have gone a little distance away, it will return to its original form, and ceasing to be dry land, will become water again as when I first described it to you. But do not go now, for I need your assistance. Look and see how many of my teeth are missing, for I fear I do not have a single one left in my mouth."

This fear proved incorrect, although the discovery of Don Corwyn's few remaining teeth was in part offset upon finding other pieces of him broken, specifically his nose, several fingers, and a couple of ribs. But the worst loss, Don Corwyn claimed, was when he saw his bottle of elixir had shattered, for he counted on its curative powers to heal him. However, Sebastian maintained (though he never said so out loud) that this last was the only fortunate outcome from the entire incident, for he firmly believed his master would never have survived the combined effects of both the fall and the elixir.

So the apprentice loaded Don Corwyn onto Rociandante, *and together they crossed the lagoon to the city, stirring up dust as they walked. . . .*

—Cid Hamete Benengeli,
 El Ingenioso Alquimista
 Don Corwyn de La Mancha, Part II

Chapter 13

In which we hear briefly of Sebastian and the students before returning to Corwyn for his unprecedented, never-to-be-forgotten ride on that most famous of wooden steeds, *Clavileño*.

SEBASTIAN KEPT THE BOYS MOVING AT A RAPID PACE until they were well away from Pomme de Terre, leading them into the mountains along roughly the same route they had taken on their sampling expedition several days earlier. When some of the younger boys began lagging behind, however, Sebastian was forced to announce a rest. Most of the boys flopped on the ground, still clutching the musical instruments they had been playing before their flight. Only Sebastian remained on his feet, pacing the area and watching for signs of pursuit.

These boys were his responsibility, he told himself, and vigilance was necessary to keep them from being caught. For Sebastian had no doubt that the bishop's forces—and perhaps the duchess's as well—would be after them.

If only he could find Corwyn. The alchemist would know what to do, how to keep them safe.

He heard snickering behind him and turned, caught Jean-Claude whispering something to one of the other boys. Evidently, the laughter had been directed at Sebastian, for the second boy stopped when he saw Sebastian watching. Suddenly uncomfortable, the boy got up and edged away, pretending interest in a nearby pile of rocks. Jean-Claude glowered at Sebastian.

With effort, Sebastian kept his anger in check. He reminded himself of his decision the previous day about how to deal with the youth, and summoned the resolve to try it now. Feigning an assurance he didn't feel, he motioned Jean-Claude over.

The youth swaggered toward him, chin out, eyes narrowed. "What's the matter, *monsieur le caractère imaginaire*, didn't you like our music? Was it so bad we had to flee from Pomme de Terre?"

"What?" Sebastian asked, having forgotten their concert for more pressing concerns. "Oh, that." He grinned as he realized the boys' playing may have saved his life. "For once, I loved every awful note."

Jean-Claude looked startled and some of the swagger went out of his step. "You did? Then why the hurry to leave, and why have we come here?"

Sebastian motioned him farther from the rest of the boys where they wouldn't be overheard. Briefly, he explained what had happened and the need to find Corwyn in Zaragoza.

"So?" Jean-Claude demanded when Sebastian paused for breath. "It's your problem the bishop is after you. What has that to do with me?"

"The boys are in danger, too," Sebastian said, "and I need your help in keeping them safe."

Jean-Claude's chin lifted a trifle, but his face betrayed interest.

"They look up to you," Sebastian went on. "They'll do what you say. I need someone I can rely on to watch out for them, to help keep them in order while we make our escape."

"And you think I'll do it?"

"No one else can. Oh, if you don't, I'll try, of course," Sebastian said. "But we both know what will happen. Either we'll be caught or the boys will get lost in the mountains or something else terrible will occur—few if any of them will ever reach the safety of Zaragoza." Casually, Sebastian walked away. "It's up to you. Let me know what you decide."

Sebastian walked several paces from the group, then forced himself to stand still, his attention on the forest around him, not daring to look back even when he heard the rustling and grumbling of the boys getting to their feet. At last, there was a tap on his shoulder, and he turned to face Jean-Claude. "They're ready," the youth said. He smiled self-consciously. "You lead the way. I'll see that they follow."

Sebastian nodded and resumed the trek over the mountains into Spain, resisting the urge to check behind him at every step, determined to show complete confidence in Jean-Claude.

Like most major cities in the Levant, Valencia was built a league or so inland as protection against pirates, rather than right on the coast. The actual port was therefore in the smaller town of El Grao east of the city.

Once in El Grao, Corwyn went straight to the docks in search of *Al-Joppa*. From the agent who had handled the ship's transactions, he learned that the captain of the ship had sailed for Malaga two days before, after apparently selling *Roche-naissante* and the rest of Corwyn's goods. According to the agent, an ass matching *Roche-naissante*'s description had been purchased by a Master Pedro, an itinerant puppeteer who needed the animal to pull his wagon. From here, Master Pedro had mentioned that he would head west, hoping the audiences of La Mancha would prove receptive to the new set of tales he had adapted for his show.

Corwyn thanked the agent and started back up the street, wondering what to do. He was anxious about Oliver, who by this time must have grown quite worried by Corwyn's delay, and he was eager to return to Pomme de Terre and relieve Sebastian of the now-desirable task of running the school. But Corwyn was also angry over the theft of *Roche-naissante* (one of the finest asses he had ever owned) and determined to bring Cid Hamete to account for his sins.

Corwyn was mulling all this over when someone called to him. Turning, Corwyn saw a well-dressed man in green (evidently a nobleman from his dress and demeanor) who had entered the agent's shop shortly after Corwyn. "Excuse me, *señor*," the stranger said, waving a book at the alchemist, "but I couldn't help overhearing the last part of your conversation back there. Did I understand correctly that you are missing your donkey, and that her name is *Rociandante*?"

"Yes," Corwyn said, still distracted. "That is, I am missing my donkey, but her real name is *Roche-naissante*. In the books, they got it wrong."

"Then do I truly have the honor of addressing Don Corwyn de La Mancha, the cream of alchemist-errantry?"

Corwyn paused, wondering if the man's eagerness held a touch of derision. "It's just 'Corwyn,' though I am an alchemist."

"Oh, no need to be so modest, *señor*. It is my good fortune to meet the most famous Manchegan and the most celebrated alchemist-errant in the world." He thumped the book for emphasis. "In fact, I hold your stories in such high esteem that I feel personally obligated to see that you are reunited with your missing animal. Come, there is no time to waste. We start at once!"

Corwyn tried to refuse, but the man in green proved an insistent host and, holding his book in one hand and taking the alchemist's arm firmly with the other, led Corwyn to a nearby plaza. The square was bordered on three sides by warehouses and busy streets, and on the fourth side by docks and the open sea beyond. Around the square, wagonloads of wine and grain, of wool and olive oil were being stowed aboard ships bound for foreign ports, then the empty wagons were quickly reloaded with cloth and tools and finished goods destined for the Spanish interior.

The man in green signaled to a group of liveried servants and retainers who were lounging by an elegant

carriage. "This is none other than Don Corwyn de La
Mancha, the famous alchemist-errant all the world has
read about," he told the servants when they approached.
"Don Corwyn has lost his ass, and I have promised to
help him find it again."

One of the servants peered around at Corwyn's back-
side. "Why, there it is, Don Antonio, right where he left
it. It's a real fool who can't find his ass with his own
two hands, I'd say."

"Well, that certainly describes Don Corwyn!" another
replied.

Corwyn tensed, but the man in green (whose name
apparently was Don Antonio) had a firm grip on his
arm. The nobleman finished whispering something to
another of his servants, then rejoined the conversation
while the person he had spoken to hurried away. "Now,
now," Don Antonio chided, "we must show Don Corwyn
due respect. An alchemist-errant who loses his ass is in
sorry straits, indeed."

Corwyn peered at his host, trying to discern whether
there had been mockery in his words. But the man's
expression told nothing.

"What do you know of *Rociandante*'s fate?" Don
Antonio went on, speaking now to Corwyn. "Did the
agent tell you anything?"

Corwyn considered correcting his host again as to
Roche-naissante's name, then decided against it. "She
was sold to a Master Pedro—"

"Ah, that's it, then!" Don Antonio interrupted. "All
we have to do is find this Master Pedro." With that, he
led Corwyn and the others around the square, calling at
the top of his voice for Master Pedro. His servants joined
in the shouting, and soon they attracted a considerable
crowd. But although several of those present answered to
Pedro, none of them had recently purchased a donkey.

About that time, a local wine merchant who recognized a business opportunity when one presented itself,
brought a couple of serving wenches with their pitchers
over from his shop and began selling drinks to the crowd.
Thereafter, a constant flow of wine was maintained by

a scullery boy whose job it was to keep the pitchers replenished.

Corwyn, meanwhile—increasingly uncomfortable with the mood of the crowd as well as his host's insistent attention—tried to free his arm. One of Don Antonio's servants closed in on him from the opposite side. "It's not polite to refuse a gentleman's hospitality," he growled at Corwyn, grabbing the alchemist's other arm. "My master might take offense if he thought you unappreciative."

Corwyn winced at the servant's grip, then made an effort to relax. He surveyed the crowd and realized that everyone was laughing at him. He would find no allies here; there was nothing to do but go along for now with whatever game Don Antonio was playing.

Just then, the servant who had run off earlier after receiving whispered instructions reappeared. He ran up to his master, huffing for breath and carrying a dented tin funnel and an old, dilapidated broom.

"Why, here's your alchemist's hat," Don Antonio cried, taking the funnel and clapping it on Corwyn's head. "As is related in your history"—again he thumped the book—"this is the selfsame hat once worn by Jabir ibn Hayyan, the greatest of all alchemists . . . until now, of course! And your enchanted staff, *El Aver*." He thrust the broom into Corwyn's reluctant hands. "Or is it *Al-Aver*? I have been curious about the answer to that."

Corwyn bit his lip, refusing to respond, although the hooting and laughter from the crowd made a reply unnecessary.

"But we still haven't found *Rociandante*, have we?" Don Antonio continued. "Well, I have a solution. If we could not find her by calling for her new master, then we must call for the ass herself." He looked inquiringly at the crowd around him and was met with eager nods. "So, Don Corwyn de La Mancha," he went on, "can you demonstrate for us just how this ass of yours sounds?"

When Corwyn again failed to respond, the servant at his side snarled, "Give me a minute alone with him, *señor*, and I'll see that he cooperates."

"No, no," Don Antonio said, after whispering new orders to the servant who had fetched the broom and funnel. "It wouldn't be right to treat our guest that way. Undoubtedly, learning of his fame has left the good Don Corwyn tongue-tied. We must overcome his reticence with gentle encouragement. In the meantime, we shall assume that *Rociandante* sounds much like any other donkey, and proceed with calling for her as best we can. Don Corwyn and I will go one way, while the rest of you split up in other directions."

With that, Don Antonio began braying loudly, pulling Corwyn and the servant accompanying them along one of the adjacent streets. The excited crowd quickly dispersed in all directions, each man trying to outdo his companions at sounding like an ass.

For the next while, Don Antonio dragged Corwyn up one street and down another, constantly insisting that he heard *Rociandante* around the next corner, only to encounter other brayers from the crowd instead. And whenever any of these brayers met, there was laughter all around at Corwyn's expense, followed by further drinking.

Corwyn gritted his teeth and waited.

It was getting dark when Don Antonio at last led Corwyn back to the plaza from which they had started. The mood of the crowd had become festive. "I'm afraid it's hopeless," Corwyn's host announced loudly. "The noble *Rociandante*, who pisses streams more copious than those of any other donkey, is lost. But don't despair, Don Corwyn de La Mancha, for we have for you another steed, almost as famous as the first. And, indeed, this one possesses the additional virtue of flying, for it is none other than the wooden horse, *Clavileño*, which can traverse more than a thousand leagues in a single night."

At this point, Corwyn saw a wooden barrel suspended on ropes between two trees on the plaza. At first he assumed it was a cask of wine. A stick head had been nailed to one end of the cask, with straw for a mane and a pair of drooping leather ears. From the bunghole at the other end protruded a bit of rope for a tail.

Don Antonio and his servant swung Corwyn onto the wooden beast and held him astride while another man, his movements made awkward with wine, tied Corwyn's hands about the stick neck of the horse. Corwyn, knowing he couldn't overpower all three of them, appeared to submit while cautiously tensing his muscles enough to create some slackness in his bonds. When the three were satisfied that Corwyn's hands had been tightly tied, Don Antonio placed the broom across the alchemist's lap and stood back. Four men pulled on the ropes by which *Clavileño* was suspended, lifting the barrel off the ground. The crowd cheered drunkenly. As soon as Corwyn was high enough for his hands to be concealed in the deepening gloom, he began working at the knots that held him.

"Unfortunately, *Clavileño* has never allowed himself to be saddled," Don Antonio called after silencing the cheers, "so you must endure unprotected the hardness of his flanks. Of course, that isn't much of a concern, unless the route he takes is stormy."

As if on command, the men with the ropes began yanking them back and forth, so that Corwyn bounced and swayed high above the ground, his backsides connecting heavily with the wooden body of the horse at each jounce. The funnel flew off his head in one direction, the broom slid from his lap in another. The cheering and scoffing grew louder. Corwyn concentrated on the knots, working by touch alone.

"Ah, it is most regrettable that you have lost your hat and staff," Don Antonio cried, "for there is a unique hazard in flying among the clouds which are home to Pegasus and others of his breed. The hat would have protected your head, and with *El Aver* you could perhaps have deflected away from the rest of you those noxious excretions which even flying horses are prone to emit."

With that, the crowd began gathering clods of manure from the street and hurling them at the alchemist, trying to pelt him from all directions as if he were really riding directly beneath an entire herd of flying steeds.

It was at this point that Don Antonio's plans began to go awry. For one thing, he had not anticipated the difficulty the drunken revelers encountered in hitting a moving target. Few of the missiles released by the crowd succeeded in reaching Corwyn, falling back to the ground on every side instead. This in turn created a second problem when the returning dung clods began raining down upon the participants themselves, ranged as they were in a circle around their intended victim. Startled men bellowed accusations across the ring at one another, then quickly followed up their words with fists. Even Don Antonio stood rooted in astonishment when his green velvet coat was spattered.

Corwyn, meanwhile, ignored the tumult below as he picked at the knots, working one of the strands loose at last.

In the plaza below, Don Antonio held up a lighted torch and shouted to be heard over the noise. "Now that we have given Don Corwyn de La Mancha this horse to replace his lost *Rociandante*," he yelled, "and having warned him as well of the pitfalls of riding such a steed, we must bid him farewell and send him on his way."

The men with the ropes stopped the barrel from bouncing while Don Antonio raised his torch aloft on a long pole. Corwyn twisted around and saw the torch hover near his mount's tail. He redoubled his efforts to free his hands, yanking free of the last loop of cord just as the sulfurous smell of burning black powder reached his nostrils. He glanced over his shoulder again. The rope tail had ignited. It sputtered, seemed to go out, then flared anew as the hissing flame crept toward the bunghole.

In the confusion below, someone collided with Don Antonio, knocking him down and putting out the torch. The plaza was plunged into darkness. Feeling suddenly more nimble than he had in years, Corwyn scrambled up a guy rope into one of the trees and hid among the branches.

The tail burned down to the barrel and the flame disappeared inside. For a moment, nothing happened.

Then *Clavileño* erupted, pissing smoke and sparks from the bunghole in such profusion that even *Rociandante*'s legendary streams were put to shame. The plaza shook with thunder and the upturned, squinting faces of the crowd stood out in the glaring light. The wooden horse lunged and bucked. Suddenly, the bottom of the barrel blew off and *Clavileño* took to the skies in a rush of flame. The men tending the guy ropes were dragged several feet into the air before they had sense enough to let go. They dropped to the ground and the barrel shot on, its ropes dangling uselessly.

From his perch in the tree, Corwyn watched the wooden horse hurtle past the docks and out over the water, where *Clavileño*'s course aimed it at an arriving ship. Startled sailors jumped into the sea from the rigging. Then *Clavileño*'s wooden staves, unable to withstand the enormous pressure any longer, collapsed and the steed flew apart in midair. The remaining black powder lit up the sky in a harmless flash.

For a while, there was silence in the plaza as everyone stared at the spot where *Clavileño* had ceased to exist. "We killed Don Corwyn," someone murmured at length in a voice tinged with awe.

In the harbor, meanwhile, the ship's captain was unaware that the danger had passed and thought he was being fired upon from shore. He swung his vessel broadside and ordered the cannons rolled out. Observing this, the equally alarmed port commander ordered the shore batteries readied. Only the greatest of luck and diplomacy prevented the incident from touching off a war, and both sides vowed to bring those responsible to justice.

Even so, Don Antonio and his fellow pranksters might have escaped, had it not been for earlier complaints from some nearby residents which brought the civil guard to the plaza to investigate. To Corwyn's delight, the captain of the guard heard that someone had been tied to the barrel, and the captain confronted Don Antonio about it.

"Well, yes," Don Antonio admitted, "I suppose there was a man on it."

"And what is his name?"

"Don Corwyn de La Mancha."

The captain stared at the nobleman. "*Señor*, do you take me for a fool?"

"No, of course not."

"Yet you say it was Don Corwyn de La Mancha who was tied to the barrel."

"*Sí.*"

"But there is no Don Corwyn de La Mancha. He's just a fictional invention, and created by a Moor at that."

"Exactly," Don Antonio said, brightening. "He doesn't exist, therefore we couldn't really have killed him."

"Yet you admit you tied someone to the barrel?"

"Well, it *looked* like someone, although that might have been just an impression conjured up in our minds. . . ."

"Conjuring? You mean this incident might have been caused by witchcraft or spirits?"

"That's it!" Don Antonio agreed.

There was a long silence while the captain stared at him. "If that is so, then this is a matter for the Holy Inquisition."

"Oh, no!" Don Antonio replied. "No, it wasn't spirits or witchcraft, I'm sure of that now."

"Then it was a man?"

"*Sí.*"

"And what was this poor unfortunate's name?"

"Don Corwyn de La Mancha."

The captain sighed loudly enough for Corwyn to hear from his hiding place in the tree, then ordered his men to bring the entire crowd to the guardhouse until the matter could be resolved. So it was (though Corwyn wouldn't learn of it until later) that Don Antonio and his fellow pranksters were still in the custody of the civil guard when the ship's captain and the port commander came looking for the culprits who had nearly set off a war. Furthermore, the penalty for this second offense was far harsher than for the relatively minor crime of murdering a man whose existence couldn't be proved, and Don Antonio soon had reason to rue the day he had ever heard of Don Corwyn de La Mancha.

Corwyn, meanwhile, waited until the plaza had been cleared, then climbed down from the tree. He moved stiffly, wincing, for the ride on *Clavileño* had bruised him more than any journey on *Roche-naissante*.

Near the base of the tree, Corwyn came upon the book Don Antonio had been carrying, apparently dropped when the crowd was taken into custody. Corwyn picked up the volume gingerly and read the title in the faint light. When he saw it was the second part of *Don Corwyn de La Mancha* by Cid Hamete Benengeli, he almost hurled the book away. But he resolved to take it with him, deciding it would be better to read it now and know the worst than to be constantly at the mercy of those who had. Then he began making his way westward out of town. Not only was he anxious to catch up with Master Pedro and *Roche-naissante*, but he also wanted to avoid being found—real and alive—while Don Antonio was being charged with either madness or murder. Knowing that the Inquisition might be brought into the case against Don Antonio made the situation even more satisfying. For once, being thought of as an imaginary character had its benefits.

Nevertheless, there was even more Cid Hamete had to answer for now than ever.

Chapter 14

Which relates several episodes as essential to this history as they are entertaining, culminating with an account of Corwyn's friendly reception by the citizens of Argamasilla.

PASSING THROUGH THE FERTILE HILLS ALONG THE COAST, Corwyn soon came to a steep ascent—a region cut by deep ravines and gorges where the land rose to a plateau, the *meseta* of central Spain. He struggled to the top and emerged at last upon the great, barren expanse of Castile.

Thereafter, Corwyn trudged across a harsh, monotonous landscape of blazing sun and dense shadows, a vast tableland of withered foliage scattered over an earth bleached colorless like old, dead bones. Centuries of sun and wind and infrequent torrential rains had scoured away the soil, so that little remained but sand and rock. Only the sky held any color, and that of the deepest blue—a dazzling bowl stretching overhead which, in its brilliance, somehow intensified the sad and lonely silence of the world below.

Unfortunately, thinking of the sky as a bowl only reminded Corwyn of that other vessel, the Holy Grail, which seemed destined to haunt him forever. He tried thinking of the world as a giant breath of demons test instead, and the sky as the bottle in which the test was performed, but even this didn't help. It only further confused the distinction between fiction and reality, between sacred vessel and ordinary bottle.

For food, Corwyn accepted what manna was offered to him, usually wild medlars and the sweet acorns of the region. Once, he came upon some shepherds, who, although taciturn to the point of wordlessness, shared their simple meal of bread and cheese and goat stew, all served with fiery hot condiments.

Sometimes, Corwyn passed through isolated villages, the houses of sunbaked brick huddled around the inevitable church as if seeking protection from the severity of the elements. Here, the women worked and visited around the village's equally inevitable sun-drenched arcade, passing the monotonous procession of hours that marked each day. During this time, the men left the villages for distant fields—small plots of land wrested from desolation and coerced into producing scant harvests of grain, which was then ground into flour at one of the scattered windmills that dot- ted the land. At dusk, the men returned home on their mules, singing plaintive, haunting tunes in the brief twilight.

Most of the time, however, Corwyn was alone—so alone that at times he almost imagined he was again being followed, and he wondered occasionally whether Dr. Tox might have pursued him all the way to La Mancha. But then he reminded himself that he was being absurd, that the idea of his being followed was only the invention of a mind desperate for human contact.

So Corwyn trudged on, discovering for himself the truth of the Manchegan saying about the cycle of seasons on this high, desert plain: nine months of winter and three months of hell. The whole time, he carried Cid Hamete's second book as if it were a cross, and he on his way to some personal Calvary, waiting until he found the right spot to sit down and read the cursed thing.

*   *   *

As the boys grew more tired and the terrain increasingly rugged, Sebastian had to stop oftener than he liked while they rested. But he knew Jean-Claude was right in insisting on frequent breaks if the smaller boys were to make it all the way through the mountains and on to Zaragoza.

Still, he felt compelled to find some way of encouraging them on. At last, he asked Henri to play something brisk and lively on his bagpipes while they walked.

Henri stared, openmouthed. *"Monsieur?"*

"You know, a tune," Sebastian said. "Something to lift our spirits."

Henri glanced at Jean-Claude, who nodded. Henri shrugged, took the mouthpiece between his lips, and tucked the bag under his arm. He began playing another religious melody, an offertory this time, and Sebastian winced. "Don't you know anything livelier?"

Henri shook his head. "As an altar boy, all I ever learned to play were church songs."

"You mean you never learned songs like 'Mistresse Mary'? "

Henri gave him a quizzical look, although perhaps, Sebastian thought, it was the fact the he had used the song's title in English. "How's it go?" the boy asked.

Sebastian hesitated, aware of having blundered into a potentially difficult area. At last he cleared his voice and began to sing, again keeping to his native tongue:

> *Comme, goode laddes, and lette us plumbe*
> *The qyunt of Mistresse Mary.*
> *Though shee be balde atop hyr heade,*
> *The parte we seeke is hairy.*

Again, Henri shook his head. *"Je ne comprends pas.* What does it mean in French?"

"If you don't understand it, I'm not going to translate," Sebastian said, feeling his face turn red. "Go ahead and play the tunes you know. I'm sure they'll do just fine."

*   *   *

Corwyn finished the last page of *Don Corwyn de La Mancha*, Part II, and closed the book, conscious of each nuance in his movements, the slightest contraction of every muscle. So great was his fury that had he not controlled himself, he feared he might burst into a thousand pieces, disintegrating in midcourse like the ill-fated *Clavileño*. Instead, he lay back upon the dirt where he had been sitting and flung out his arms, yielding himself up to the universe.

"Take me," he groaned to no one in particular, yielding once more to his sense of theatrics. "Isn't it enough that I suffered this persecution while still at home in Pomme de Terre? Certainly I didn't travel hundreds of leagues just to endure more. But things are what they are, and it seems I cannot change them. Take me, therefore; I don't wish to grow any older."

At first, it seemed the universe's only response was to send a fly to plague him further. The fly droned around Corwyn's face a few times before settling on his nose, where it began to preen itself. Corwyn's eyes strained to bring it into focus. He considered swatting it away, but closed his eyes instead. Anything else required too much effort, and might distract him from his self-absorption.

Corwyn had picked this place as one where he could read the book in private and then give himself up to whatever dramatics might follow. With a keen sense of irony, he had even chosen to sit in the shadow of an abandoned windmill, telling himself that although he expected to suffer anguish and deprivation in his exile, he might at least be shaded from the sun. In fact, he felt lucky to have found the derelict structure, for it offered protection amid the wasteland, yet without the danger of attracting anyone who might interrupt his isolation.

If Corwyn was to endure hardship, he wanted it tempered with a few amenities.

But what Corwyn wanted and what the universe was willing to provide were apparently different things, for during the afternoon a wind sprang up—a wind of such fierceness as may only be experienced in vast, unbroken terrains. The wind stripped the sparse soil from the ground and lifted it into the air, depositing it at length several leagues away; it battered the ancient windmill so relentlessly that at last the building—once given life by the wind—now collapsed under its onslaught.

Corwyn clambered through the rubble, shielding his eyes from flying dirt as he searched for shelter. Eventually he found a small hollow formed by the fallen stones and he climbed inside. Throughout the rest of that day and the following night, he listened to the howling wind and swore at whatever fates were in charge of his destiny. Even here, it seemed, as in Pomme de Terre and on the route to Zaragoza, windmills were to be used to torment him. He wondered if this might be a sign, like the strange visions he'd experienced near Barcelona. Then he shuddered; if they were signs, they seemed to call him toward Zaragoza, and that was the last place he wanted to be.

On the other hand, perhaps they were signs that he should continue pursuing Cid Hamete Benengeli and avenge himself upon the Moor by wringing his worthless neck. Corwyn grinned, being careful not to open his lips to any blowing grit. That was the convenient thing about signs—if you didn't like one interpretation of them, their meanings could always be construed another way.

It wasn't until the next morning, when the wind had calmed and the day dawned bright and clear, that Corwyn for the first time gave serious consideration to the windmills he had seen near Zaragoza. Here in La Mancha, at least some grain was grown that needed milling into flour. But there, outside Zaragoza, the land had been rockier and, if anything, even more barren.

Then what would be the purpose of windmills, he wondered, where there was nothing to grind?

Silence pervaded the school now that Sebastian and the students were gone. At first, Gwen had found it unsettling, and she had considered moving in with her parents at the tavern to await their return. But she quickly adapted to the slow, quiet currents that carried her through the days, her senses turning ever more inward to focus on the new life growing inside. Sometimes she worried about Sebastian and the boys, although she knew they had escaped capture by the bishop. She reassured herself with the thought that by now they were undoubtedly with Corwyn, and he would take care of them until they could safely return to Pomme de Terre. Meanwhile, there was little for her to do except eat and rest.

And read.

The only problem was that, once she finished *Tristan and Yseult*, she wouldn't have anything else to read. Now that Corwyn's library had been destroyed, she lacked a way of replenishing her supply of books.

Aware of this limitation, therefore, she picked up her copy of *Tristan and Yseult* again, reading slowly to prolong the pleasure of its ending.

"*Monsieur* Sebastian," cried one of the boys, "can't we stop for a rest?"

"Come on, everybody," Sebastian said, ignoring the request. "Keep up the pace."

Jean-Claude slipped up beside him. "*Monsieur*, they really are tired."

"Just keep putting one *chou* in front of the other," Sebastian called out gaily.

"What's that mean?" whined Henri.

"It's a joke." Sebastian drew Jean-Claude aside. "We have to keep them moving," he whispered to the youth, his eyes on the slope the students had just descended.

"What? *Monsieur*, they can't travel any faster. Some of the little ones are having trouble as it is."

"Then the bigger boys must carry them," Sebastian insisted. "You and I can help. But we must move faster."

"Why?"

"Because," Sebastian said, still eyeing the terrain behind them, "I think we're being followed."

Two days later, Corwyn arrived at last at the village of Argamasilla de Alba, considered by many to be Don Corwyn's home. Cid Hamete never revealed exactly where his character was supposed to live, but occasional references in the books to an Academy of Argamasilla and its archives suggested this as the most likely candidate.

As a result, Corwyn thought this was also where he might find Cid Hamete.

From the outskirts, however, the village didn't look promising. It consisted of a few dusty, whitewashed huts, a handful of tiny gardens wilting for want of shade, a church, and a dilapidated inn—nothing to suggest an academy or archives worthy of merit.

At that point, Corwyn's ruminations were interrupted by two boys pummeling each other on the communal threshing floor at the edge of the village. "Don't upset yourself, Periquillo," one said to the other, "for you'll never see her again in your life."

On overhearing this, a wave of despondency washed over Corwyn, for he thought these words were a sign that he would never find *Roche-naissante*.

Corwyn walked on past the threshing floor and the two boys stopped, suddenly aware of a stranger. They followed from a distance, whispering excitedly.

Just then, a couple of mangy mongrels loped in Corwyn's direction, chasing a hare. The hare, hard pressed by their pursuit, darted between the alchemist's legs and squatted for cover. The dogs yipped and snapped at her, barely missing Corwyn's ankles. The hare bolted and the dogs took off again, plunging between Corwyn's legs and almost knocking him over. *"Malum signum!"* he muttered, regaining his balance. "A hare runs away, hounds pursue her, and *Roche-naissante* is nowhere to be seen. Bad signs, indeed!" Not that he believed in signs, he reminded himself. Still, his reception here was most unsettling.

He approached the inn, keenly aware of hunger and thirst, aware as well that he had no money. He hesitated at a withered fig tree, his hopes rising only to be quickly dashed. Angrily, he cursed the barren tree, as if his words could prevent it from ever again bearing fruit. Behind him, the boys snickered. It wasn't his curse, Corwyn knew, but the fact that the tree was already dead which ensured that no one else would receive from it what he had not.

Inside the inn, Corwyn smacked his dry lips and hoped the innkeeper would take the hint. The innkeeper paused from butchering a side of mutton and studied Corwyn balefully, a meat cleaver in one hand.

"I've, uh, heard great things about your village and its academy," Corwyn said, eyeing a pitcher of wine. "So much so that I decided to see your renowned archives for myself."

The innkeeper glared, saying nothing. His knuckles whitened around the handle of the cleaver.

"I'm a scholar myself, you see . . ." Corwyn, faced with utter silence, let his voice trail off. "Actually, I'm looking for someone," he said after a while, mustering himself for the effort. "Perhaps you know where I might find him. His name is Cid Hamete Benen—"

"Cid Hamete!" the innkeeper roared, becoming animated at last. "So you're looking for Cid Hamete Benengeli. Why? Are you a friend of his?"

The innkeeper's tone suggested that friendship with the Moor would not be an appropriate response.

"No," Corwyn replied cautiously, "no, I'm not a friend. Anything but. The fact is, Cid Hamete owes me, and I'm here to collect. You might say it's a matter of revenge."

"Revenge." The innkeeper nodded, apparently understanding that word. He hefted the cleaver, brought it down viciously on the mutton. The blade bit deep into the meat. "Revenge," the innkeeper repeated, a bitter gleam in his eye. "Against Cid Hamete." His lip curled with satisfaction at the thought.

Corwyn cleared his throat. "Yes, well, if you could tell me where he is—"

"Tell you where he is?" the innkeeper said, his gaze returning to the alchemist. "Oh, *señor*, if only I could." The cleaver rose again, then came down on the mutton, hitting bone with a resounding *thunk*. "If only I could. He used to live here, you know, with his niece and housekeeper. Then the first of his books was published, and we haven't seen him since."

"You mean he became rich and famous from the book and moved away?"

"Rich? No, *señor*, I don't think so. I mean he had the good sense to leave town quickly, during the night." Abruptly, the innkeeper turned away. "So you've heard about the Academy of Argamasilla, have you? Would you like to see its famous archives for yourself?"

"Well," Corwyn began, "actually I'd rather just—"

"Here," the innkeeper said, ignoring the protest. He thrust a couple of parchment sheets into Corwyn's hand. "Read these."

Corwyn looked at the top sheet. It was a poem addressed to him—or rather, to his fictionalized alter ego—and it read as follows:

Ode from the Curate to Don Corwyn de La Mancha

> O mysterious man from La Mancha
>   Of whom we never had heard,
> Please take your insanities elsewhere—
>   You're making "Manchegan" a bad word.
>
> Thou flower and mirror of alchemy
>   Made famous by the Moor's foolish tract,
> The petals of your flower are shriveled,
>   The glass of your mirror is cracked.
>
> You claim to be from La Mancha
>   Although you and I've never met;
> I'd rather you chose for your birthplace
>   Somewhere I could sooner forget.

Corwyn reached the end and glanced at the innkeeper with raised eyebrows.

"Go on," the innkeeper said. "Read the other one."

Corwyn turned to the second page. He wasn't surprised that this sheet contained a poem as well. It read:

Poem by the Barber of Argamasilla

They say I set your bones and healed your wounds—
  Perhaps then I shaved you as well.
Fool that I was not to have known at the time
  The madman whose face I beheld,
For by shaving your beard a bit closer to home
  I could have sent your soul off to hell!

Corwyn came to the end and turned over the page, expecting another one. There weren't any. He looked again at the innkeeper. "These two poems . . . ?"

"Those two poems are all there is of the Academy of Argamasilla and its archives," the innkeeper finished. "And even they didn't exist until the first part of that wretched book appeared. Suddenly, there was the name of Argamasilla for the whole world to see, published by our neighbor and supposed friend, and we knew nothing of any academy or archives which were said to reside here. In desperation, the barber and the curate composed these poems, so we might at least have that much to show for ourselves. Only later did we realize the book was all a joke that put our good town and its citizens to shame." The innkeeper turned and spat. "A curse upon Don Corwyn and that lying Moor!" The cleaver rose and fell with the regularity of hammers in a fulling mill. Flecks of meat and bone flew.

"So you don't know where I could find Cid Hamete?" Corwyn asked. He eyed the cleaver nervously and took a step back.

The innkeeper shook his head, then stopped abruptly and looked again at Corwyn. "But you said you, too, wanted revenge on the Moor. Tell me, stranger, what is your name?"

"I'm, uh . . ." Corwyn thought fast. "Dante. My name is Dante Alighieri."

"Dante Alighieri," the innkeeper repeated. He furrowed his brow. "Haven't I heard that name before?"

"No," Corwyn said, "I'm sure you haven't."

"Well, Dante Alighieri, you look like a man who

could use something to eat and drink." He filled a mug
from the pitcher, then brought a roast capon—or the
fly-covered remains of one—from under the counter.

Corwyn's gaze flicked to the cleaver, still sunk in the
mutton carcass a few inches from the innkeeper's hand.
"I have no money."

The innkeeper shrugged. "Any enemy of Cid Hamete's
is certainly a friend of mine. Eat heartily, *Señor* Alighieri.
It's on the house."

Corwyn needed no further urging. He brushed the
flies away and stuffed himself, while the innkeeper
droned on about the many attractions to be found
there in Argamasilla—a ewe that he claimed produced
more milk than any other in La Mancha, a pair of
magnificent fighting cocks owned by a Gypsy on the
edge of town, and of course the house once lived in
by Cid Hamete, whose housekeeper and niece still
remained there, stoically enduring the shame. Finally,
Corwyn belched, wiped his mouth with the back of a
hand, and thanked his host.

"But you're not leaving, are you?" the innkeeper protested. "You haven't seen anything of our town."

"I'm sorry," Corwyn said, backing toward the door.
"Perhaps another time. Meanwhile, I must redeem my
honor by finding this Cid Hamete."

"Ah, so it's a matter of honor." The innkeeper nodded.
"Go then, *señor*, and may the saints protect you."

Corwyn hurried from the inn. Only when he was well
away from town did he slow his steps.

Despite the innkeeper's hospitality, all Corwyn could
think about was what that cleaver would have done to
him had anyone in Argamasilla learned his real name.

Entremés

AT THIS POINT IN THE CHRONICLES, SO SCRUPULOUSLY preserved in most regards by the archives of the Academy of Argamasilla, there arises another of the few and therefore all the more perplexing uncertainties which occasionally shroud critical details in this otherwise faultless history. For the records disagree as to whether Don Corwyn's staff, Al-Aver, first began to reveal its acquisitive nature once they had arrived in Barcelona (which Don Corwyn took for Venice), or while still en route to that city.

At any rate, by the time Don Corwyn and Sebastian began their search for the exact location of the abducted library of Alexandria—that holiest of all grails—this new aspect of Al-Aver had become manifest, and the staff began drawing other people's possessions to it like a lodestone attracting spilled pins. Perhaps this was due to the staff's peculiar shape, which was quite twisted and bent and might therefore be prone to snag on the irregularities projecting from many items. Such an explanation would also explain why this trait had not been evident earlier (if indeed it had not) while in the desolate expanses of La Mancha, for crowded city streets offered many more opportunities for the staff to brush against things that belonged to others. Yet such reasoning fails to account for the undeniable fact that many of the items acquired by Al-Aver during this time had no projections or irregularities whatsoever, and

therefore could not have become ensnared in the staff's
angles and bends. This latter objection, however, cannot
be taken seriously since it would tend to implicate Don
Corwyn as an active participant in the affair and would
thus discredit his reputation as an alchemist-errant.

So it can be seen that the outcome of these questions
is of considerable importance to this history. Yet without
conclusive evidence from the archives, the matter must
be left in doubt for the individual reader to decide.
The only fact which can be stated unequivocally is that
this new tendency on the part of Al-Aver *caused Don*
Corwyn considerable embarrassment while he remained
in the city, as will be seen hereafter. . . .

—Cid Hamete Benengeli,
  El Ingenioso Alquimista
  Don Corwyn de La Mancha, Part II

Chapter 15

Which follows Chapter 14 and precedes Chapter 16, and which concentrates exclusively on Corwyn.

CORWYN REACHED EL TOBOSO AT DUSK, COMING FIRST upon a potter who was working clay on a wheel outside his shop. So intent was the potter on his task that he didn't seem to notice Corwyn. The alchemist paused to watch while the potter smoothed a vessel into shape. Then, just as the potter began slowing the wheel so he could remove the finished pot, his hand slipped. A deep depression in the clay marred the vessel's side. With scarcely a sigh to acknowledge his mistake, the potter sped up the wheel again, then gathered the clay into a ball and started to shape another pot.

Corwyn went on, oddly troubled by the incident. He tried to dismiss the potter as just another craftsman plagued by a faulty grail. Corwyn chuckled at this thought, but his irritation remained even after his laughter faded on the air. He sensed that the potter's vessel had symbolized his own reputation as an alchemist, and this had been badly married, indeed. But Corwyn's hand hadn't done the damage; rather it had been that of Cid Hamete. Nonetheless, there seemed little Corwyn could do other than begin over, like the potter, resolutely giving form once more to what was lost.

Unlike the potter, Corwyn did more than sigh at the prospect—he groaned aloud, then clenched his fists and tipped his face to the sky. He was much too old for starting over again, he told the first stars twinkling overhead. He'd started over many times in his life already. For once, he didn't want simply to restore his lost reputation by beginning yet another time, not after all he had endured these past few weeks. He wanted more than mere justice.

He wanted revenge.

Corwyn stalked on into town, transformed by rage into more than just a man—a giant in the service of righteousness. All he lacked was someone on whom to unleash his holy anger. Of course, Cid Hamete was the proper target, but in lieu of the Moor, he might find another outlet. So let the villagers of El Toboso be warned, he thought to himself, not to bother with Corwyn the alchemist tonight. Anyone who tried would get more than he bargained for.

With evening had come a slight breeze that rustled the dusty leaves of the stunted poplars scattered about the village. Locusts, roused from their daytime stupor, formed a chorus of high-pitched whines. Crickets chirped as if welcoming night.

The noise of the insects accentuated the strangely deserted feel of the village, and Corwyn realized he had not seen any inhabitants other than the potter. Yet he thought he heard a commotion somewhere ahead. He walked toward it, his fists balled, and the sound of voices grew louder. At last Corwyn rounded a corner and, coming upon the village plaza, discovered the commotion's source.

A miniature theater had been set up on one side of the plaza, next to a wagon that announced Master Pedro's traveling puppet show. Lighted wax tapers illuminated the front of the theater and cast a festive glow over the villagers clustered about the plaza. A stout man clad in chamois leather, hose, breeches, and doublet—his left

eye and cheek covered with green taffeta as a sign that
disease or accident had afflicted this side of his face—
stood before the crowd, his arms upraised.

"Enough talk," a man called to him from the crowd.
"Get on with it, and let's pray there's a bit of novelty
in your show to amuse us for a while."

"A *bit* of novelty?" the stout man (evidently Master
Pedro) repeated, sounding hurt. "*Señor*, this show of
mine has sixty thousand novelties in it. Let me tell
you that it is one of the things most worth seeing in
the whole world, and for your pleasure I have brought
it to your very doorsteps. But *operibus credite et non
verbis*, as they say. 'Let deeds speak, not words.' And
so, to work, for it's growing late, and we have much to
do and say and show tonight."

Master Pedro bowed as though expecting applause,
but if so, he was disappointed. He closed himself up in a
tiny closet at the back of the theater to work the puppets.
A small boy, apparently Master Pedro's servant, stood
outside to act as interpreter and explain the mysteries of
the show. At the end of the show, he would probably
also canvass the crowd for money.

An expectant hush settled over the plaza. Suddenly,
from inside the theater came a fanfare played on a cheap
trumpet and a drum. On stage, a small black-powder
charge ignited with a flash—its brilliance magnified by
the surrounding darkness—and smoke billowed from the
theater. The audience gasped and drew back. Inside Master Pedro's closet, the trumpet's tinny notes gave way to
a fit of coughing. When the smoke cleared, two puppets
occupied the stage: one a tall, angular man dressed as a
clown; the other short and round, dressed in black robes
and wearing a dented funnel for a hat. This second figure
also held a tiny broom, all bent and twisted like *El Aver*.
Corwyn groaned.

Master Pedro's assistant pointed at the puppets with a
stick painted to resemble a wand and announced, "This
true story that is here represented before you is taken
word for word from the chronicles in which it is published, and from the mouths of the multitudes who repeat

these stories daily upon the streets of cities throughout Spain. For this is none other than one of the many true tales told about that illustrious alchemist-errant and Spanish Ovid, Don Corwyn de La Mancha, together with his apprentice Sebastian, which stories have been dutifully recorded for the world's entertainment and edification by that most truthful and renowned of historians, Cid Hamete Benengeli."

The boy, winded by this speech, paused for breath. Corwyn shifted his weight from foot to foot and forced himself to remain quiet. He wanted to object loudly, to force this puppet master and his audience to acknowledge the truth about him, but after his previous experiences he was wary of letting his identity be known. Too many sweaty, hulking peasants stood massed around him, their bodies coarse and strong from endless toil. Although Corwyn felt emboldened by the justice of his cause, he was also aware of being a mere five-foot-two-inch, eleven-hundred-year-old avenger surrounded by men bigger and stronger by far. One puny David could never stand against so many Goliaths.

"Having arrived in what Don Corwyn insisted was Venice (but which Sebastian still thought looked more like Barcelona)," the boy continued, "the two split up to search separately for the stolen library of Alexandria, which Don Corwyn claimed was in fact the Holy Grail."

A snort escaped Corwyn, and he coughed into his fist to cover it. He told himself that equating the library of Alexandria with the Holy Grail was only an absurd invention of Cid Hamete's, yet the association echoed deep within him, demanding to be heard.

Meanwhile, Master Pedro whisked the puppet figure of Sebastian away, leaving only Don Corwyn on stage.

"Now, Don Corwyn," the boy went on, "having injured his face when he dived into the waterless lagoon that surrounded the city (and indeed, until it healed his face looked even worse than my master's without his taffeta patch—)"

"Enough about my face!" Master Pedro roared, causing the theater to tremble. "Get on with the story."

"As I was saying," the boy continued, unruffled, "Don Corwyn found it necessary to disguise himself, for word of his attempt to swim across hard ground and the damage this caused to his face had already spread throughout the city. Therefore, in order that his injuries not be recognized, he adopted the likeness of a wealthy heiress from the mainland, veiling himself from view."

The puppet figure tried to sweep the funnel-hat from its head, although the funnel was so well stuck on with flour paste that Master Pedro had to make the figure beat itself about the head soundly with the broom before finally dislodging the obstinate funnel. The crowd laughed. Corwyn scowled and chewed his mustache to keep silent. Once free of its makeshift hat, the puppet raised its other hand, to which was stitched the corner of a black scarf. The figure draped the scarf over its head and face, transforming itself into something that vaguely resembled an old woman in mourning.

"In this guise," the boy said, "Don Corwyn proceeded to search the city, seeking that lost library I already told you about."

The puppet hobbled across the stage, against a fantastic backdrop which Corwyn supposed was an attempt at representing Venice.

"Meanwhile"—the puppet of Don Corwyn was jerked offstage and replaced by the clown—"Sebastian, too, assumed a disguise, although for very different reasons."

The clown danced and frolicked, flinging one hand up to its head with an elaborate jeweled turban and holding it in place, while with the other hand donning a gold-trimmed, scarlet cloak.

"Loving fine food and expensive clothes as he did, Sebastian chose to pass himself off as a wealthy Venetian merchant, borrowing against assets he didn't possess in order to support this appearance. He then spent his days in the company of loose men and women who, recognizing him for what he was, entertained themselves at his expense by encouraging his foolishness."

A painted hussy and a sneering young man joined the clown on stage and began dancing with him, spinning him round and round until the clown staggered drunkenly, either from dizziness or tangled strings.

Corwyn snickered. He couldn't help himself; the caricature depicted Sebastian's weaknesses so accurately.

"In the course of these revelries, however," said the boy, "Sebastian began experiencing some guilt as he recalled what he and his master were really here to do. And so, when he heard about someone masquerading as an heiress and causing expensive personal possessions to disappear (although the latter was actually the fault of *El Aver*), Sebastian decided this must be that enchanter who persecuted Don Corwyn at every turn. He further vowed to challenge this evildoer on his master's behalf, should their paths ever happen to cross."

The clown drew a stubby sword—scarcely more than a short dagger—from the overly long scabbard at his hip and brandished the weapon overhead.

"Don Corwyn, meanwhile," the boy continued as the puppets were again exchanged, "had also been hearing tales spread from lip to ear among the citizens. What he heard, however, was of a ridiculous imposter who pretended to be a wealthy merchant, running up debts with moneylenders and legitimate businessmen. Don Corwyn, too, assumed this was his nemesis come to plague him further and he set out to confront his adversary."

The old woman–Don Corwyn puppet challenged invisible foes with its miniature *El Aver* and strode across the stage. Purloined jewelry dangled from every fork and bend in the broom. In the audience, the real Corwyn huffed indignantly and edged his way from the crowd. While he had to admit that the clown bore a certain likeness to Sebastian, and even *El Aver* to the real Oliver, the figure of Don Corwyn showed absolutely no resemblance to Corwyn himself, and any suggestion that it did offended him. The rage and frustration he had felt on entering the town came back redoubled, and he decided to use the distraction offered by the show while he searched for *Roche-naissante*.

"At last, Don Corwyn and Sebastian met," the boy announced, "each disguised and thinking the other was his enemy."

A titter of expectation rippled through the audience. Despite himself, Corwyn glanced back at the theater, rooted by perverse curiosity. The clown puppet, dressed as gaudily as some Oriental potentate, and the Don Corwyn puppet, still looking like an old woman veiled in black, stared across the stage at one another without moving. Then the Don Corwyn puppet charged, thrashing its opponent with the broom. Stolen jewelry flew. The Sebastian puppet, abandoning its sword, fought back with the empty, but much longer, scabbard.

"Both fought valiantly, suffering many blows and clubbings," the boy said, speaking loudly now to be heard above the laughter of the crowd. The hilarity increased when the Don Corwyn puppet knocked the turban from the Sebastian puppet's head, just as the Sebastian puppet flung away the Don Corwyn puppet's scarf.

In the audience, the real Corwyn shook his head with dismay at the sight of such foolishness. But he couldn't bring himself to start moving again. Not yet.

"In the end, however," the boy announced, "Sebastian's scabbard—"

"Hold on," called the man in the crowd who had interrupted Master Pedro earlier. "Do you mean to say these two didn't recognize each other, even after losing their headgear?"

"No, they didn't, *señor*," the boy assured him, "for in fact both were still disguised."

As if to underscore this point, Master Pedro's hand made an unscheduled appearance on stage and he hurriedly restored the puppets' turban and scarf. In the audience, Corwyn chuckled grimly, more amused by the show's technical blunders than by the story.

"But for a moment there they weren't disguised," the man in the crowd insisted. "Besides, wouldn't Don Corwyn recognize his own apprentice, even if he was wearing a turban and strange clothes? And surely Sebastian would recognize *El Aver*."

"I assure you this is a true story," the boy said, glaring at the heckler. "You may believe, therefore, that the facts are as I tell you, and not as you may perceive them to be."

And that, Corwyn thought, was the heart of the problem: People were willing to discount their own senses, preferring instead to place their belief in someone like Cid Hamete, whose words gained authority for having appeared in print. Once, when Corwyn was young, books had been worthy of such reverence, but since then their contents had grown trivial even as printing techniques had vastly increased the number of published works. With greater availability, something essential had been lost, and the effects of that loss were being seen here tonight in the remote village of El Toboso, where, although few could read, all were anxious to be read to or told stories from the most outrageous and sensational of books.

The boy, meanwhile, had paused in his narration from just such a book. When there was no further interruption from the heckler, he went on. "In the end, as I said, Sebastian's scabbard was no match for *El Aver*, and Don Corwyn overcame his opponent."

The Sebastian puppet, reeling under *El Aver*'s assault, sprawled backward into a bookseller's handcart. The handcart toppled, spilling a load of freshly printed books in the street.

"Don Corwyn," the boy recited, "recognizing his apprentice at last—"

"Wait a minute," the man in the crowd interrupted again. "Why did Don Corwyn recognize his apprentice now and not before?"

"Because when Sebastian fell into the cart, his turban fell off," the boy explained.

"No it didn't." The man pointed at the theater. "See for yourself; Sebastian's still wearing his turban."

The boy sighed and rolled his eyes while Master Pedro's hand made an encore appearance to dislodge the turban. Then the Don Corwyn puppet stood, frozen in amazement while the Sebastian puppet struggled to its feet, prepared to continue the fight. Seeing this, the Don Corwyn puppet snatched the shawl from its own head, revealing itself to its opponent. Alchemist and apprentice stared at each other in surprise, while Master Pedro exaggerated the effect by leaning the puppets into one another. At last, the Don Corwyn puppet swung its head ponderously from side to side, surveying the scattered books.

"Although the books were merely a cheaply printed edition of the latest chivalric romance," the boy said, underlining Corwyn's sad reflections, "and all copies of the same story at that, upon seeing them, Don Corwyn immediately concluded that they were the stolen library of Alexandria which he sought."

The Don Corwyn puppet eagerly gathered up the fallen books, littering the stage with pages that had torn loose from their bindings in the accident, while the real Corwyn grieved over ancient losses and wondered how anyone could equate the chivalric romances of the day with the glory that once had been the library of Alexandria.

"So Don Corwyn bought the lot, damaged books and all, thereby appeasing the bookseller who had been prepared to have the alchemist-errant and his apprentice arrested for ruining an entire shipment of merchandise." The boy's words began to pick up speed, like a horse catching sight of its stable after a long and tiring ride. "Don Corwyn and Sebastian then returned home triumphantly with their library, proclaiming the greater glory of Hypatia del Alexandria, who, as is well known, is really Aldonza Loren—"

"No, no, no!" screeched a girl from the crowd.

The boy's face settled into weary resignation, as if realizing he wouldn't ever reach the stable at this rate. "Now what?"

A plump peasant girl of about sixteen elbowed her way through the audience, shaking her head and crying. "It's not fair," she wailed when she reached the theater. "I'm not this Hypatia del Alexandria, whoever she is. I never claimed to be. People can't keep calling me that."

The boy peered at her. "Who are you?"

"I'm Aldonza Lorenzo," she sobbed.

The name startled Corwyn, for he remembered having read it in Cid Hamete's books and sympathized with the ill-treatment she had been subjected to there. Immediately, he began pushing through to the front of the crowd, anxious to console this unfortunate child.

"Oh, so you're the one Don Corwyn's always trying to impress," the boy exclaimed.

"No, I'm not!" the girl shrieked. "I've never met him, never seen the man. I don't even know that he exists." She looked around frantically, then grabbed the wand from the boy and lunged at the stage. "It's all his fault," she cried, slashing the wand crosswise like a sword and cutting the pasteboard figure of Don Corwyn in half. "He made it all up." The wand caught Sebastian on the backstroke, beheading him. Indeed, had Master Pedro not ducked inside his compartment, the same blow might have sliced off his ear as easily as if it had been made of almond paste.

Corwyn paused to give his intention of consoling the girl further thought.

"Stop!" Master Pedro shouted from where he huddled inside the theater. "Look and you'll see it's not the real Don Corwyn and his apprentice you're destroying, but only little pasteboard figures! Sinner that I am, you're wrecking my livelihood."

Aldonza, however, did not stop raining downstrokes, cross-strokes, backstrokes, and slashes until, in less time than is required to recite two credos, she knocked the entire stage to the ground, its backdrop cut to pieces and all the puppets dead or wounded.

The villagers milled about in confusion. Some murmured in protest or called upon others to stop the girl, but no one dared approach her. The boy who had narrated the story crouched in fear next to the ruined theater. Near the front of the crowd, Corwyn vacillated, still debating whether to step forward.

The complete destruction of the show being accomplished, Aldonza became somewhat calmer. "I wish I had here before me now all those who've had any part in inventing this book of lies," she said, "but most especially Don Corwyn himself, who mocks me and ruins my life by claiming he loves me. I'd see how much he loved me without his *huevos*." She brought her left hand up as if grabbing something, then with her other hand sliced the wand through the air just above her fingers, gelding an imaginary Don Corwyn. The real Corwyn winced and clutched his groin. Still hunched in this protective position, he retreated to the rear of the crowd, more eager than ever to find *Roche-naissante* and leave.

"Then let Don Corwyn discover love without his *huevos*, and may you keep them pickled in a jar," Master Pedro groaned. "Only let me die, I'm so unfortunate. Moments ago, I was wealthy beyond belief, with all the kingdoms, empires, and estates of fiction to my name. Now, I'm the basest of poor beggars, having lost everything to Don Corwyn's madness and the passions he arouses in those who claim to be sane."

A timid man emerged from the crowd, his nervousness increasing the closer he got to Aldonza. "I'm Lorenzo Corchuelo, Aldonza's father," he told Master Pedro in a whisper. "Whatever mischief she has done, I'll pay for it."

Master Pedro brightened and the two men began negotiating prices for the damaged puppets and theater. The villagers clustered around, offering advice on the worth of each item Master Pedro presented and seeming to enjoy the dickering as much as they had the puppet show.

Corwyn, meanwhile, located *Roche-naissante*, who was tethered nearby. The donkey parted her lips to bray at seeing her master, but Corwyn quieted her. Soon he was mounted and riding into the night, fleeing El Toboso and the fury of Aldonza Lorenzo's scorn.

For the past eleven hundred years, Corwyn had known exactly who he was; now, he wasn't sure. The only thing he knew for certain was that he'd been wrong in his interpretation of the potter and the damaged pot: It wasn't just Corwyn's reputation that was being reshaped like clay in Cid Hamete's hand, but Corwyn himself, for the Moor seemed able to mold the alchemist into whatever shape he pleased.

Even that might not be so bad, Corwyn thought, if Cid Hamete hadn't chosen to be fruitful and to remake the alchemist who had been Corwyn in the Moor's own demented image, perpetuating himself like a worm that multiplies in a rotten apple, or a serpent that crawls from its old, dead skin to creep anew upon the earth.

Chapter 16

In which several momentous meetings and reunions take place, as will be revealed herein.

TOMÁS DE TORQUEMADA WAS BACK!

Friar Carlos repressed a groan as the pale, pinched-face boy came striding into the new construction camp with an air of devout purpose, clutching his wooden box under one arm. Friar Carlos shook his head in disbelief. The boy was actually *striding*. Nobody in his right mind strode anywhere in Spain during the heat of the day. Not in the middle of summer.

Nevertheless, Tomás did just that, entering the camp like a boy invested with a sacred mission—which was, of course, exactly how he saw himself.

He marched up to Friar Carlos and gave a curt nod. "As I feared," he said, getting right to the point, "the heresy I uncovered several days ago has spread."

"Heresy?" Friar Carlos responded, too dazed by the heat to think. Even the convict laborers were being granted a *siesta* today. "What heresy is that?"

Tomás peered at him, eyes burning with eager suspicion. "Can you have forgotten? Or is there, perhaps, some other motive for this curious lapse of memory?"

As so often when confronted by the boy, Friar Carlos

219

felt a chill that would have done justice to wind off a Pyrenean glacier. "Oh, that heresy," he said quickly. Now that he thought about it, he did recall the boy having burned a number of insects in a miniature *auto-da-fé* at the previous construction camp. He shuddered. "Of course. How stupid of me."

"Stupid?" Tomás replied. "Perhaps. Or maybe a sign of something infinitely more serious."

Friar Carlos cleared his throat and quickly changed the subject, trying to match the boy's serious manner. "What will you do about the heresy now?"

"Adopt more rigorous measures." Tomás's voice hissed with religious ecstasy. "I will do whatever is necessary to eradicate all heresy from the face of the earth."

Friar Carlos said nothing, not trusting himself to reply.

Still in the thrall of his inner vision, Tomás carried his box to a small, withered field a little way off, where he proceeded to catch grasshoppers and crickets. When he had accumulated several, he opened the box and took out a set of finely crafted, tiny instruments, each a working replica from the torturer's profession. He set them up and built a small fire, then alternately prayed over and pleaded with his captured victims, urging them to renounce their heretical ways. Yet each apparently refused this chance to regain salvation, for in the end Tomás was compelled to subject them all to the vicissitudes of the rack, the wheel, and red-hot pincers. All the while, his face glowed brighter than any fire with the zealous light of fanaticism.

After a while, Friar Carlos, unable at first to stop himself from staring, felt his stomach lurch in rebellion. He gathered his wits and hurried off to start the convicts working. Although the sun still burned fiercely overhead, Friar Carlos preferred its heat to the holy flames of Tomás's spiritual fervor. Besides, the sooner he got the labor crews working again, the sooner they could move closer yet to the Pyrenees.

Friar Carlos hoped that eventually the construction camp would be too far away from Zaragoza for Tomás de Torquemada to visit him.

*   *   *

That day the sun did indeed burn more fiercely than usual, and Corwyn halted during the heat of it to rest at the mouth of a scorched and barren gorge. *El Valle del Huesos Secos,* it was called—the Valley of Dry Bones—for millennia of frequent winds and occasional rains had eroded the steep walls, exposing innumerable fossilized bones that protruded from the multihued layers of rock and sand. More of these petrified remains littered the valley floor, making it look like some vast and ancient charnel house where a race of gods or giants had once disposed of whole herds of dead animals.

Corwyn had often seen such fossils in his travels, and had entertained some extraordinary thoughts as to their origins, particularly since many of the bones were from animals he'd never seen. Moreover, the bones tended to be unusually large, suggesting bodies the size of behemoths that would have shaken the earth when they walked. As Corwyn sat now in the sun, half-stupefied with heat, it seemed to him that he could almost envision the bones coming back together, rising from their makeshift graves deep inside the earth and reassembling themselves into complete skeletons once more. Then flesh re-formed upon these bones, and skins to cover them, and a hot, dry wind blew the length of the valley to animate forms that had long lain dead, restoring the breath of life within them. Strange and mighty creatures they were, dominating the earth and inspiring Corwyn's awe as he beheld them.

But when he tried to visualize them with the freedom once more to move about at will, the illusion wavered. Flesh vanished, once more revealing the naked skeletons beneath. This time, however, it wasn't bones that remained, but books—brittle, dusty relics from the bygone library of Alexandria. Lost for centuries and presumed destroyed, these volumes now took shape again, if only in Corwyn's mind. His longing for them was a blade piercing his side, so greatly did he revere these forgotten tomes.

Yet the books, like the ancient creatures whose fate

they shared, were but a mirage born of heat and fantasy, and their pages fell away like sand, becoming dust that drifted in the air, whipped about by the merest breeze. Books or bones—all flew asunder, dead and scattered as before, and the place returned to being that Valley of Dry Bones Corwyn had entered.

Dry bones or dry tomes, Corwyn thought in despair; what was the difference? Either way, they were gone from the face of the earth. He felt somehow chastened for having dared to imagine bringing forth such mighty hosts from out of their graves and presuming to make them live again.

The vision troubled him as he mounted *Roche-naissante*, intending to resume his journey. But when he glanced over his shoulder in the direction from which he'd come, he saw a speck approaching from the distant horizon. For a moment, he thought it might be another illusion conjured up by his fevered brain. He rubbed his eyes. The image remained. A horse and rider, it seemed at first; then, on drawing closer, Corwyn realized two riders sat astride a single, hackneyed mount. The larger of the two was a tall, gaunt, swarthy man in well-worn traveling clothes. The smaller figure—so thin the other looked heavy by comparison—was brightly arrayed in Moorish style, with colorful flowing robes and a turban that seemed to envelop his tiny head.

Corwyn stared at the second figure. He blinked, stared again.

It was Oliver.

That same day, Sebastian led his twelve disciples to the top of a hill north of Barbastro. He had brought them over the Pyrenees and down into Spain, taking a more erratic, torturous route than Corwyn's had been in an effort to escape whoever was pursuing them. But though they had managed to stay in the lead, they couldn't outdistance their follower. The boys had begun to tramp along with the broken air of desperate refugees, clutching the instruments they had been playing in Pomme de Terre as if these were treasured relics that still connected them to their earlier lives. The forced march and hard conditions wore at their rebelliousness until little remained of the students Sebastian had known at the school. To his surprise, he missed their former mischief, perhaps because he could see the exhaustion that had replaced it written on their faces. He hoped their lost spirits would be restored once they reached the safety of Zaragoza and Corwyn's protection.

At the crest of the hill, they crossed Corwyn's trail again, as they had unknowingly done many times, and here they came upon an unusual sight. A line of newly constructed windmills (now extending considerably beyond the ones Corwyn had seen) stretched toward them from the Spanish interior as if aimed at the mountains and the duchy of Gardenia on the other side.

Sebastian halted the boys and stared at the structures, more of which were being built even as he watched. He felt strangely uneasy about them, for they reminded him of something, though he couldn't recall exactly what. Whatever it was, the association seemed to be one he preferred to forget.

Just as he was about to start the boys moving again, heading toward the windmills with the intention of following them to Zaragoza (or however close to that city they came), Jean-Claude called to him from behind. "I think I've discovered who our pursuer is," the youth told Sebastian as the latter drew near. He pointed in the direction from which they had come. In the distance, a spindly man with unkempt hair and beard walked toward the group like a prophet out of the distant past.

Sebastian groaned. "You mean we've been half-killing ourselves trying to escape from Dr. Tox . . . er, Toxemiah? I thought we were being chased by at least a dozen civil guards."

Jean-Claude shook his head. "From a glimpse or two I've had in the past couple of days, I think he may be all there is."

"Merde!" Sebastian sat down heavily, disgusted with himself. "Some leader I turn out to be."

Meanwhile, Toxemiah was approaching rapidly, his

arms flapping like a windmill gone mad, swinging his staff through the air. Words spewed from his mouth with the unchecked force of a flowing river long before they could hear. At last, Sebastian made out what the man was saying.

"Yea, verily do you now see for yourselves what an abomination they are upon the land. For I tell you, here is thine oppressor's army being raised, to march in terrible judgment on Pomme de Terre."

Sebastian turned toward the windmills again, suddenly completing the connection he'd been unable to make before. They looked like the race of giants Toxemiah was always warning everyone about. So there really was a measure of sense to the madman's claims after all. But Sebastian was sure the truth of it ended there.

What harm, he asked himself, could a line of windmills possibly cause?

Despite the self-discipline Gwen showed in drawing out her reading, at last she reached the exquisite, tearful ending of *Tristan and Yseult*. There was nothing left in the school for her to read. The horror she had felt on coming home to find the library burned now flooded her again like a returning tide, and she discovered on a personal, intimate level how the loss of a book could rank with the loss of a close and valued friend. It was senseless of the bishop to try putting a stop to the river of stories being published in books, she told herself, especially the stories relating to Arthur. They were too popular.

Gwen sighed and imagined Guinevere and Lancelot in the room with her, locked in a tragic embrace that could be neither defended nor denied. She could almost see them, almost taste their kisses mixed with tears—

Abruptly, Gwen sat up, startling the child (or children) within her into kicking. She rubbed her belly absently, calming the tiny fists and feet, her thoughts elsewhere.

By now, she knew almost every aspect of the Arthurian stories; indeed, there had seemed little left for newer writers to invent with which to amaze her. Yet still she hadn't encountered the story in all its fullness, as she knew in her heart it should be told. She envisioned that story now, hearing the sonorous flow of its words in her mind. Hurriedly, she took quill and ink from the chest beside the bed, then located a sheet of parchment and began to write:

It befell in the days of Uther Pendragon, when he was king of all England and so reigned, that there was a mighty duke in Cornwall that held war against him long time, and the duke was called the duke of Tintagil . . .

She scribbled furiously far into the night, unaware of the passing time, determined to commit her words to paper while they still rang clear and true in her head.

Corwyn jumped from *Roche-naissante*'s back and ran toward Oliver, ignoring the heat, oblivious of his own breathlessness. Then he stopped.

What was Oliver doing here, dressed like that? And who was he with?

The broom, however, showed none of the alchemist's hesitancy, but leaped to the ground as well and quickly crossed the remaining distance. His stick fingers plucked joyously at his maker's gnarled, ancient hands, drawing the alchemist into a frenzied dance. For a few moments, Corwyn relaxed his wariness and allowed himself to be swept along in the creature's revelry. But after a while, he pulled back, breathing hard, and eyed Oliver's turban critically. "What's this you're wearing?" He turned toward the gaunt stranger, still mounted on his scarecrow of a horse. When the alchemist spoke again, his voice had acquired a chilly tone. "And who's your friend?"

Oliver ran back to the horse and excitedly motioned the stranger down. The man dismounted with grave and bony dignity, hampered by a crippled left hand. He approached Corwyn slowly while the broom tried with gestures to introduce them. "*Señor* Corwyn," the stranger said, executing a formal bow.

"You know me?" Corwyn asked, startled.

"*Sí*, I know you well. I have studied your work from a distance for some time."

"I'm not that 'Don Corwyn' character you may have read about," the alchemist explained hastily. "I don't know what you expected, but I'm not him."

"Oh, I realize that."

Something about the man puzzled Corwyn. "Then you didn't learn about me from that dog of a Moor, Cid Hamete Benengeli, and his books?"

"No." The reply came more slowly this time. "No, I knew of you before they were published."

Oliver, meanwhile, was hopping around them excitedly, obviously delighted to have his two friends meet. After a moment, he darted back to the horse, grabbed something from a saddlebag, and hurried over to Corwyn. In his outstretched hands he held an open notebook, which he offered to the alchemist.

When the stranger saw this, he tried to block the broom. "No, *Al-Aver*, not that," he said. "Not yet."

But Corwyn had already accepted the notebook, and more curious than ever now he glanced at it. The book was almost filled with neat, flowing script. He flipped to the first page. *El Ingenioso Alquimista Don Corwyn de La Mancha*, it read, *Part III*. Beneath that, in the same hand as the writing in the rest of the book, was the signature, "Cid Hamete Benengeli."

Corwyn dropped the notebook and lunged for his persecutor's throat.

THE
THIRD SALLY

Entremés

SO DON CORWYN DEPARTED AGAIN FROM HIS HOME IN LA Mancha and ventured forth on yet a third sally, reaching at length an inn which in his madness he mistook for a castle. To him, moreover, this was no ordinary castle, but the legendary Grail Castle wherein the vessel he sought is said to reside. There, he came upon an Asturian serving wench who was removing a chamber pot from one of the rooms. In Don Corwyn's fevered brain, however, the pot was transmuted into the Grail itself, and the wench (whose personal services could be had each night for a fee) he transformed into that fair maiden who is said to present the Grail to those worthy of achieving it.

A brief struggle for the vessel ensued. In the end, it was not the strength of Don Corwyn's arm which determined the outcome (for the serving wench, though bent and deformed, was much stronger than he), but rather the fact that the contents of the pot slopped onto the maid in the tussle. While she left to clean herself from the spill, Don Corwyn carried off the prize.

Fearing that he might not, in fact, be a true alchemist-errant after all (for he had never been properly initiated into the mysteries of that art), Don Corwyn took his grail to the innkeeper and persuaded the fellow to remedy this unfortunate situation. The innkeeper, always one to appreciate a good jest, gathered his guests in the inn yard to enjoy the entertainment, then anointed Don

Corwyn with the contents of the pot, proclaiming him an alchemist-errant as Don Corwyn desired.

There is only one aspect of this joyous occasion which remains unexplained, and that is the curious malady which afflicted a pair of hog-gelders during the subsequent celebration. For it seems these two, upon sampling a new skin of their host's wine, were immediately rendered senseless—not that temporary condition common to those who indulge in excess drink, but a permanent kind which left them deranged, like men possessed. However, since these two were sampling a skin that hadn't actually been offered to them by their host, it is possible that the latter caught them in the act, and that their behavior afterward was caused not by the wine itself, but by whatever penalty the innkeeper saw fit to exact from them as repayment for their theft . . .

—Cid Hamete Benengeli,
   El Ingenioso Alquimista
   Don Corwyn de La Mancha, Part III (manuscript)

Chapter 17

In which the meetings and reunions of the previous chapter are continued, much to the delight of everyone involved.

CORWYN LET OLIVER PULL HIM OFF CID HAMETE WHEN it became obvious the Moor—even with a maimed hand—would overpower him if he didn't. Nevertheless, the alchemist made a show of protest.

The Moor straightened his worn doublet with an air of injured dignity.

"What are you doing here?" Corwyn demanded. He tried to growl the words, but found he was panting too hard. If Oliver hadn't dragged him off Cid Hamete, heatstroke might have stopped him even quicker than the Moor. As it was, he had to sit down, despite the fact that this gave his opponent an advantage.

"*Al-Aver* insisted," Cid Hamete replied. Gaunt and tattered though he appeared, his words conveyed the lofty manner of a nobleman as he frowned down at Corwyn. "*Al-Aver* couldn't stand following you and observing you from a distance all the time, interviewing everyone you had spoken to, without being able to travel with you himself. For some reason, he's quite devoted to you."

Corwyn grunted, glancing guiltily at the broom. If Cid Hamete was questioning Corwyn's right to such devotion, that was no worse than the accusations the alchemist had already inflicted on himself. "His name is Oliver, not *Al-Aver*," he said.

Cid Hamete gave a noncommittal shrug.

"Why have you been watching me?" Corwyn asked, annoyed by his own defensiveness as much as by the Moor's response.

"Because, *señor*, I owe Juan de la Cuesta another book." Cid Hamete gestured toward the notebook Oliver had shown Corwyn, then sighed heavily and sat in the dirt opposite the alchemist. "With the first two books, the events had already happened; I knew what the stories were before starting to write. But with this one, I'm placed in an awkward situation. Juan de la Cuesta wants the next book printed while there's still interest in the previous two."

"Well, I'm sorry to make things so difficult for you." Corwyn's apology dripped with syrup. "Next time, I'll try to be more considerate."

"That's all right." Cid Hamete brushed the matter aside, apparently unaware of the alchemist's sarcasm. "It's not your fault. Although it would help if you'd stay where I could see you, and be around people I could talk to afterward. When you went into Juan de la Cuesta's shop, for instance, I couldn't very well go in later and ask him what the two of you had talked about."

"Why not? He's the one who wants your next book."

"*Sí, señor*. That's the problem. I've been hiding from him for the past couple of months, trying to finish it. If he sees me, he'll want to know how the book is coming."

"At least you have enough sense to be ashamed of the things you write," Corwyn grumbled. "You must feel pretty guilty, if you don't want your own publisher to see this latest manuscript. I suppose that's some consolation."

"No, no, *señor*, that's not it at all. I'm proud of what I write. It's just that until recently, I wasn't able to start this book at all. I had nothing to show him. That's why I've been following you around, writing the book as I go. But I need to be able to see you when you're around other people, to watch you embark on new adventures and get into new predicaments. When you wander off alone in the wilderness for days, it leaves me with very little to write about."

Corwyn grunted, too startled for a stronger response.

"And then there was that unexplained gap between the day you set sail from Barcelona and the day you finally straggled into Valencia on foot. Where were you? What happened during that time?"

"What's the matter, does it leave a blank page in your book?"

"Well, yes, it does. Several, in fact. Besides, *Al-Aver* was worried."

"Oliver, not *Al-Aver*!" Corwyn snapped. "And whose life is this, anyway—yours or mine?"

"Yours. But I'm trying to write a story based on it. So what did happen during those missing days?" Cid Hamete retrieved the notebook and found a quill in one of his pockets. "Tell me everything."

"Why, so you can change it all around? Even if I tell you what happened, all you'll do is distort the facts. You go to all the trouble to research your books— and you have done your research, I admit that—but then you stray from the truth whenever it pleases you. You manipulate facts to create elaborate lies instead of telling what really happened."

"But, *señor*, what's the point of using facts to simply tell the truth, when it is a far more notable achievement to use the same information to fabricate a great untruth?"

"Are you saying that those who write works of fiction are not obliged to rack their brains over finer points of truth?" Corwyn asked, aghast. "My answer to that is, the more truthful a work appears, the better it is as fiction, and the more probable and possible it is, the more it captivates. Works of fiction must match the understanding of those who read them, and they must be written in such a way that, by toning down the impossibilities, moderating the excesses, and keeping their readers in suspense, they may astonish, stimulate, and entertain so that admiration and pleasure go hand in hand." His voice rose until he was shouting. "But no writer will achieve this who shuns verisimilitude and imitation of facts, in which the highest qualities of literature are found!"

"Any fool can reconstruct the truth, given a sufficient number of facts to guide him." Cid Hamete sat erect and brushed his frayed doublet and hose. "Only a true artist can take these same grains of truth and gently redirect them away from their natural course to create the edifice of a grand and fantastic half-truth, or even an outright lie, all while giving the appearance of sound construction upon a solid foundation of what actually happened. That is the real art of a storyteller, *señor*, as opposed to a mere scribe or historian."

"And that's what you are—a storyteller, a weaver of lies?"

Cid Hamete nodded modestly.

"Then why do you claim to be reporting the truth about my life?" Corwyn demanded, again feeling faint from the heat and exertion. "Why not just make a character up, instead of subjecting me to this?"

Cid Hamete looked askance at him. "Didn't you do the same thing when you invented the Holy Grail? That was a complex blend of fiction and truth. And I must tell you, it has been a great inspiration to me."

"Ah." Corwyn felt himself flush and turned away. "So you know about the Grail, do you?"

"Of course. As we've both acknowledged, I do my research. Which returns me to my complaint. I can't do that research when you're off in the wilderness, *señor*, nor when you go into towns such as Argamasilla and El Toboso where I'm not welcome. I would appreciate it if you could avoid such places in the future."

"I noticed your former neighbors don't seem very happy about your success," Corwyn said dryly.

"No." Cid Hamete looked pained. "It bothers me deeply. I only wanted to bring my own village to the attention of the world. I thought my friends and neighbors there would applaud my effort. Instead, they condemn me. It's a sad world, my friend."

"I'm not your friend," Corwyn snarled. "Personally, I'm on their side. Except, unfortunately, they don't understand that and would like to hang me from the same tree as you."

Cid Hamete spread his hands. "I am sorry. What can I say?"

"What can you say?" Corwyn snapped, warming to the argument again. "Oh, it's easy for you to be so complacent, so smug. After all, you're the one who got rich with all the money you've made from the first two books. And when this next one's printed, I'm sure you'll make even more."

"Money!" Cid Hamete's voice rose. "All what money? I work like a slave to write these books—and make no mistake, *señor*, writing them is very hard work—then Juan de la Cuesta pays me a few *maravedis* for the right to print them and he keeps all the profits. I tell you, *señor*, my labor has made him a wealthy man."

"He didn't seem all that wealthy to me," Corwyn muttered, more puzzled than ever by the mysteries of finances and publishing. "But then, neither do you. I thought all of you were making a fortune from me."

Cid Hamete indicated his threadbare cloak, his worn boots, and the places where his green hose had been mended with threads of different colors. "For myself, my state is as you see."

"Hmmmm." Corwyn, reluctant to concede anything to his opponent, made no further comment. "Well, you have returned Oliver to me, and I thank you for that. Now we'll bid you farewell and return home, hopefully never to see your face or your name again." He got to his feet and signaled to Oliver, who had wandered off while the two men argued.

"Oh, but *señor*," Cid Hamete said, rising as well, "I will accompany you. After all, I have a book to finish, a deadline to meet."

"What? You're certainly not coming with us!"

Cid Hamete shrugged again, further irritating Corwyn. "Very well. Then I shall follow along behind, as I have done so far. However, it would be much easier if I joined you. Besides, then we'd have the pleasure of sharing one another's company."

Corwyn swore under his breath but made no further response until he had remounted *Roche-naissante* and pulled Oliver up behind him. Then he turned to Cid Hamete. "I can't prevent you from following. But you'd better stay far enough back to keep out of my sight!"

Without waiting for a reply, he used his heels to goad the ass into moving, perhaps kicking her a little harder than was necessary in his eagerness to leave the Moor behind.

"Waste and destruction shall herald his coming; yea, corruption will mark the path of his feet." Toxemiah, heedless of the effect his presence had on others, continued his insane prophecies as he approached Sebastian and the students. "The eggs of the cockatrice he hatches with his schemes, and the plans he weaves are the webs of spiders."

Sebastian groaned where he sat on the ground, then blanched as the smell of the madman reached him.

"Who's he talking about?" Jean-Claude asked, edging away from the stench.

Sebastian shook his head, unwilling to waste precious air on an answer. He wouldn't be able to breathe again until Toxemiah left.

"He shall come as sulfurous smoke unto your noses, as a fire that stings your eyes!"

The hair on the nape of Sebastian's neck prickled at this. The statement could well be applied to Toxemiah himself, but it was also true of Sebastian's encounters with another kind of entity.

Demons!

His mind—reeling though it was from Toxemiah's proximity—flashed back to a few nights earlier when the prophet had unleashed a demon for him to see in Pomme de Terre, and the fiend had killed the sow.

With everything that had happened since, Sebastian had overlooked the incident, as well as the question it inevitably raised: Where had Toxemiah got a demon in the first place?

Sebastian turned to mention this to Jean-Claude. The fumes from Toxemiah made his head spin worse than any strong drink. When his vision settled, Sebastian discovered he was alone with the madman, Jean-Claude and the rest of the students having retreated upwind. "Who're you talking about?" he croaked.

Toxemiah whacked him with his staff. "Your oppressor, of course. Haven't you been listening? Incline thine ears, you fool, and hear; open thine eyes, imbecile, and see."

By now, Sebastian's eyes were streaming so many tears he couldn't see anything; and as for his ears, they were filled with the sounds of his own groaning and retching.

"Thine oppressor shall pour forth upon Pomme de Terre the corruption he hath gathered from Aragon and Castile," Toxemiah went on. "From throughout Iberia hath he assembled the unholy waters with which to vex the duchy. Even the inhabitants from out of the bowels of the earth shall he send among you, and thereby cast the whole of Gardenia into utter confusion."

The sick feeling in Sebastian's stomach worsened, but now it was from fear as much as the stench. That certainly sounded like demons. "Who?" His voice was a hoarse whisper. "Who will do this?"

"Hydro Phobius, you idiot!" Toxemiah accompanied his answer with another whack from his staff.

"Ow!" Sebastian gasped instinctively for breath, immediately regretting it. "That's impossible. Hydro Phobius is dead."

"No." The single syllable fell from Toxemiah's lips, the word sounding as dead as the fish heads around the madman's neck. Through a fog of tears, Sebastian saw Toxemiah point his staff at the windmills. "Behold, his host comes against you in a destroying wind, carried upon a flood of mighty waters to drown the duchy in cursedness and damnation. And the waters thereof stinketh, and offendeth the nose of heaven."

It wasn't just the waters Toxemiah spoke of that stank, Sebastian thought, nor only the nose of heaven that was offended. He wrinkled his own, trying to escape the smell. "How . . . how do you know this?"

He expected another blow from Toxemiah's staff, but the prophet squatted by Sebastian instead as if preparing for a long explanation. "That's a good question," he said with a nod. "You're not as stupid as I thought."

Sebastian clutched his stomach and writhed, wishing he could withdraw the question.

"During the time that I was in league with Hydro Phobius," Toxemiah began, "I beheld a vision of great wheels turning in the wilderness, and lesser wheels turning within these wheels, such that the work of many over a long time might much more quickly be accomplished by a very few. In my foolishness, I spake this vision to my master, and he rebuked me for it; yet he did not forget what I had revealed to him.

"Then came a time wherein my master grew wroth with me, inasmuch as I had stolen from him. And he flung me into outer darkness, closing me up in a vault with many unclean spirits; yea, with great gnashing of teeth was I confined therein. And the apparitions of that place flew unto me, and the touch of them against my lips was like live coals laid with tongs upon my mouth—"

"Yes, yes," Sebastian said. "You told me this part before."

Toxemiah scowled and again brought his staff down on Sebastian's shoulders. "Don't interrupt!" Then he hurried through his next words as if to finish his speech before Sebastian cut him off again. "And when I breathed the creatures in, I became a man of unclean soul, and I dwelt in the midst of unclean souls and knew the wrath of Hydro Phobius."

The prophet paused, seeming to watch Sebastian for further protest. When the young alchemist offered no more objections (being much too busy throwing up),

Toxemiah went on. "After I at last was freed and the demons were made to depart from me, I chanced in my wanderings to journey over the mountains and saw how my former master had remembered the vision I had spoken to him, and the race of giants he had raised against the duchy as a result of my words. Then I heard my voice saying, 'Who shall go unto Gardenia, and warn the people thereof? For, lo, Hydro Phobius gathereth an even mightier host than that with which he afflicted the duchy previously.' And I answered myself, saying, 'Here I am; send me.' Wherefore as Hydro Phobius's former servant do I now go before him, making straight the errors of my crooked ways."

Sebastian tried to stand, hoping to get away. Instead, he pitched forward onto the ground and rolled helplessly. "You're crazy!" he choked.

He braced himself, expecting the full weight of Toxemiah's staff between his shoulder blades for this remark. But when the blow came, it was desultory, scarcely bruising the skin or knocking Sebastian's bones out of place. The prophet sighed. "You're none too sane yourself, getting mixed up with that alchemist and becoming a mother hen for his students." He jerked his head at the boys, flailing his matted hair and beard. "Still, who am I to talk? I once envied your master and tried first to surpass him, then when that failed, to destroy him in any way I could. Look where it's got me."

Sebastian did look (as well as he could through a constant haze of tears), startled that words this sensible should come from the mouth of a madman. Yet when Toxemiah spoke again, it was to return to the insanity for which he was known. "Thorns shall spring up in the castle of the duchess," he mumbled sadly, his eyes on something distant and possibly long past. "Nettles and brambles shall grow in the great hall thereof, and it shall become an habitation for dragons, yea, and a court for owls."

It seemed to Sebastian that Toxemiah had said this before, too, back in the mountains above Pomme de Terre. Until he repeated this foolishness, Sebastian was considering whether to look into the prophet's warnings about the windmills. Now, that thought evaporated. Sebastian groaned, rolled onto hands and knees, then forced himself to his feet. "*Alors!* That may be, but I haven't seen any signs of dragons or owls taking over the duchess's castle yet—unless you include the bishop."

He lurched far enough away to breathe, then signaled to the students. "We'll follow this line of windmills toward Zaragoza," he said. "With luck, they'll take us close to the city. There, we'll find Corwyn."

"They neither know nor understand," he heard Toxemiah mutter behind him. "They have shut their eyes that they cannot see, and their hearts that they cannot perceive." In a louder voice he added, "The alchemist didn't go to Zaragoza. I watched him get this far, then turn toward Barcelona. Like you, the fool couldn't understand the truth even when it presented itself right before his eyes."

Sebastian paused to counter this charge against his master. But midway through turning his head, the madman bolted past him and ran toward the distant windmills, waving his arms as wildly as before and uttering a constant stream of absurdities. Sebastian stood rooted, too startled to proceed. As Toxemiah neared the windmills, armed guards leaped forward to encircle him, pressing in upon him as closely as they dared and escorting him down the slope.

Sebastian hesitated, wondering at what he had just witnessed. It could be that Toxemiah had made a nuisance of himself around the windmills before, and that this was why the guards had been so quick to capture him. Yet he couldn't shake the thought of Toxemiah's warnings. Besides, Toxemiah had also assured him that Corwyn never went to Zaragoza. If that was true, then there wasn't any point in Sebastian's taking the students there.

In the end, it was the responsibility he felt for the students that decided him. Armed guards implied some form of hostility, and regardless of how ridiculous Toxemiah's claims might be, Sebastian couldn't lead the boys into the midst of whatever conflict might lie ahead.

He turned left, thankful that Henri hadn't announced their presence to whoever was at the windmills by playing his bagpipes as they arrived. Ignoring the questioning looks from Jean-Claude and the boys, he led them east, following an unseen path to an uncertain destination.

At the windmills, Friar Carlos roused the guards to their jobs again despite the heat, seeking to distract himself from Tomás de Torquemada's entomological chamber of horrors. The guards grumbled and cursed as they got to their feet, then resorted to that universal balm available to those in their position—taking their frustrations out on their prisoners. Several men bore stripes from the whip that afternoon in the name of Friar Carlos, but the man who received the most was a newly convicted prisoner from Valencia named Don Antonio. He had arrived the previous day clothed in the remnants of a green suit that might once have marked him as a nobleman, and it was said that at his trial the judge had offered him a choice of either working on the windmills or rowing in the galleys. With a disdainful air (it was said), Don Antonio had picked the first, believing it to be the lighter sentence.

Undoubtedly, he regretted that decision now.

Be that as it may, Friar Carlos no sooner precipitated this series of events than all work again came to a halt, this time because of a disturbance that erupted onto the construction site from the north.

The disturbance was Toxemiah, and he arrived shrieking like a banshee. Even Henri's bagpipes would have been hard pressed to rival the din he made.

Friar Carlos, however, had neither met Henri nor heard his bagpipes, and so had nothing worthy of comparison to the noise assaulting him. He assumed that the legions of hell were being unleashed upon him (or more accurately, upon the construction site) for contriving to rid Spain of the demons infesting the land. Friar Carlos grabbed the hem of his habit and ran in the opposite direction, mumbling every prayer he could think of and clutching his garlic clove for good measure. He might have fled all the way to Zaragoza, had he not collided with Tomás de Torquemada first.

By the time Friar Carlos separated his limbs from those of Tomás and picked himself up off the ground, the disturbance was over and several guards were leading Toxemiah toward him. He brushed the dirt from his habit and struggled for composure while Tomás de Torquemada glared at him sourly.

"You killed it," the boy told him.

"Killed what?" Friar Carlos looked down at his feet and found he was standing on the splintered wreckage of what had been Torquemada's rack for insects. Friar Carlos moved aside hastily, but the damage was already done; the rack still lay in splinters. A smear of yellow ichor and a black carapace were all that remained of its most recent victim.

"What a coincidence that you should step on this particular one just as it was about to reveal the source of its heresy," Torquemada hissed.

"But it was an accident," Friar Carlos protested. He told himself it was ridiculous for a grown man of his authority to be put on the defensive by a child. Nevertheless, his blood ran cold.

"An accident," Torquemada echoed. "How convenient for anyone at risk from what this creature might have disclosed."

Friar Carlos was saved from having to answer by the approaching guards, who were loosely clustered around a lone man dressed in tattered rags and animal skins. With an air of grave dignity, Friar Carlos motioned two of the guards aside and stepped into the circle to question the captive. Then the clinging, oily smell of decaying fish and the putrid stench of uncured hides struck him, dropping him to his knees, and Friar Carlos realized why the guards had kept their distance from the prisoner.

One of the guards grabbed Friar Carlos's arm and dragged him to fresher air. When the friar could stand again, he spoke to the prisoner, this time remaining outside the ring of guards.

"Who are you? What are you doing here?"

The man answered in a torrent of French. "Howl, ye multitudes, for the day of Hydro Phobius is at hand; yea, it shall come as destruction from the south, for verily I tell you, the hour of his vengeance draweth nigh, full of cruel wrath and fierce anger, to lay the land desolate."

Friar Carlos was puzzling over this when Tomás de Torquemada came up and whispered in his ear, "He's that crazy Frenchman who's been causing problems back at the processing station. Your superiors will surely smile on the man who hands this heretic over to them."

Friar Carlos straightened, already basking in the glow of his superiors' favor. He commanded several of the guards to take the man immediately to Zaragoza, unwilling to delay his reward a moment longer.

Then he noticed the look of calculating malevolence with which Tomás de Torquemada studied the stranger, as if measuring him for the instruments of torture which would accompany his questioning. Without a word, the boy fell into step with the guards making the journey to Zaragoza.

Suddenly, Friar Carlos felt nothing but compassion for this poor madman he had unwittingly delivered into the hands of such voracious cruelty. Falling back upon his own guards' remedy for dealing with frustration, he angrily ordered everyone remaining at the construction site back to work.

Chapter 18

Wherein is related, among other things, several thoughts on books and writing which are separately considered by various participants in this history.

"W‍HERE ARE WE GOING NOW, *M‍ONSIEUR*?"

Although Jean-Claude kept his voice low so the rest of the students wouldn't hear, Sebastian was aware of an edge of criticism underlying the youth's words.

"This is the direction Toxemiah said Corwyn took," Sebastian replied.

Even to him, it sounded inadequate.

"You believe something that old fool told you?" Jean-Claude's voice was becoming belligerent.

Sebastian stopped, held the youth with a steady gaze. At last, he said, "I told you I needed your help keeping the rest of the boys in line, and that's more true now than ever. But I didn't ask for your suggestions as to where we should go or for your comments on how I go about getting us there. Unless you're asked, keep your opinions to yourself."

He turned and strode off, not looking to see whether Jean-Claude followed. But although he could make a show of rejecting the youth's judgments, it was harder to dismiss the doubts he had about himself.

Corwyn, too, was refusing to look behind him, although he could feel Oliver swiveling around to do so almost constantly. It irritated Corwyn that the little creature showed so much concern about Cid Hamete Benengeli.

The alchemist rode north, the sun hot on his back, pushing the donkey to a swifter pace than she preferred in such heat. Corwyn sympathized with the beast, but he was determined to reach Pomme de Terre as soon as possible. Once back, he intended to retreat into his laboratory for a long vacation.

Let Cid Hamete write what he would, but he'd have to do it without cooperation from Corwyn!

Yet the writer's words kept coming back to disturb him, and he thought about all the Cid Hametes and all the Juan de la Cuestas there must be in the world. The Cid Hametes were busy writing—scribbling constantly, hurriedly, as if their words were something fleeting that might escape them if they hesitated too long. The Juan de la Cuestas were equally industrious, printing whatever the writers turned out—or at least those parts that they thought would sell. What with all this writing, the great numbers of pens covering endless stacks of parchment sheets with words, and all the printing, the presses rising and falling like fulling hammers day and night, so many books were now being produced that they quickly surpassed the combined holdings of the greatest libraries of the ancient world.

Yet what knowledge or wisdom filled these books, Corwyn wondered? What vast wealth of lofty thoughts and divine inspiration deserved to be recorded and handed down throughout the generations in such abundance?

The answer, he told himself, rode behind him in the form of Cid Hamete on his bony horse.

In his mind, Corwyn pictured the great books of antiquity—the ones that had made Alexandria famous for its library—piled atop one another like mud bricks, fired for strength and mortared together to form a tower upon an open plain. Though modest in stature, Corwyn knew this edifice was sturdy and would withstand the passing centuries, for the bricks with which it was built were as solid as any stones.

Then he imagined another tower beside the first, a tower far larger and infinitely more grand. The bricks from which this second tower was built were the books being printed today, and the tower they made rose into the sky, challenging the very gods for dominion. Yet though the tower looked impressive, Corwyn suspected it was constructed from unfired, inferior bricks, and in his mind the structure toppled and fell, the flawed books from which it was made strewn like seeds of folly over the face of the earth.

They did not promote real understanding or learning, these newer books, Corwyn told himself. Rather they multiplied confusion, a babbling as of many tongues speaking at once, uttering nonsense.

Behind him, he felt Oliver turn to gaze wistfully once more at the writer of such works who followed in the distance, a constant presence haunting Corwyn's thoughts as surely as did the world itself that was changing so swiftly around him.

It was late when Sebastian and the students came upon the inn outside Lérida. Exhausted and famished, they stared at the building with ravenous longing. At one time, it had obviously been a castle, and a single, dilapidated turret of *Mudejar* design (a style combining Christian and Moorish influences) still stood some distance from the part that was now the inn. Sebastian studied the crumbling turret uneasily, wondering how it had stood so long.

"Now what?" Jean-Claude growled behind him, forcing him back to the present.

"Now we go to the inn, have some dinner, and spend the night," Sebastian replied.

"And when they find out tomorrow that we haven't any money to pay for our food and lodging?"

Sebastian turned, looking not at Jean-Claude, but at the straggling column of boys, still clutching their musical instruments as if these might deliver them from their present troubles. Sebastian couldn't resist a smile. "Maybe we'll play for our supper."

Jean-Claude snorted. "How can you joke at a time like this?"

"Tiens!" Sebastian spun on him. "What would you have me do? The boys desperately need food and rest. They can't travel any farther tonight. So tell me, Jean-Claude, what would you do in my place?"

Jean-Claude, too, examined the boys. "You're right, *monsieur,*" he said softly. "I'm sorry. Please forgive me."

Sebastian shuffled, not quite comfortable at being treated with respect. He nodded brusquely and started toward the inn.

In Pomme de Terre, Gwen arranged pages into a neat stack on the chest by the bed, amazed by how much she had written. Yet she'd barely begun telling the whole story!

She paused, waiting out a brief spasm that rippled through her womb. It wasn't time yet, but soon, soon. . . . If Sebastian didn't return in the next few days, she would move in with her parents until the babies arrived.

She smiled to herself, having accepted the thought that she was carrying not one child, but two. She patted her belly and spoke softly to them, comforting them against the time soon to come.

In the meantime, she would keep writing. Not that she expected to finish the story before the births—she had no illusions of getting that much done!—but she wanted to be as far along as possible. After the babies were born, her time would become much more fragmented, and it would probably take years to finish what she had set out to accomplish. But in time, she would tell the whole story as she knew it should be told.

Maybe it would even be published!

Only one thing disturbed her about this—none of the books she had read were written by women. Oh, Corwyn had assured her that women were often respected scholars in antiquity, and he encouraged schooling for both sexes. Still, Gwen knew the reality of her own time, and a woman author wasn't likely to be accepted.

Unless people didn't know she was a woman.

She pulled the first page of her manuscript from the stack and studied it absently, thinking about names and the images they create. This wouldn't be the first time she had made the best of necessity by pretending to be someone she wasn't—even a man.

After a while, she took up her quill, dipped it in the ink pot and wiped away the excess, then with a flourish she signed the first page *Thomas Malory*. It was a good English name, she thought; Sebastian would appreciate that. She smiled to herself and added *Sir* before the name. He would like that touch even more.

She sighed, knowing she was stalling, and pulled a clean sheet to her. It was time to get back to the story. She began writing, slowly at first as she thought her way through the next few passages, then faster as the work gained momentum. Soon she was adding new sheets to the stack of pages on the chest.

The innkeeper, a man named Juan Palomeque (though he was now often referred to as "the left-handed baptist" by those who knew him well), eyed Sebastian and his entourage suspiciously before admitting them to his establishment. Sebastian let go of his breath, which he found he'd been holding, and followed the larger man into the inn's common room. There, he asked what the innkeeper had to offer the boys for supper, to which Juan Palomeque replied that "the boys' mouths would be the measure," for they had only to ask for what they wanted and it would be provided.

"This inn," he said, "is well stocked with the birds of the air, the beasts of the earth, and the fish of the sea."

"There's no need for all of that," Sebastian said, his mouth watering. "If they'll roast us half a dozen chickens we'll be satisfied."

Juan Palomeque replied he had no chickens, because hawks had stolen them.

"Well, then," said Sebastian, "let *señor* innkeeper tell them to roast several pullets, as long as they are tender ones."

"Pullets! ¡*Madre de dios*!" said the innkeeper. "Indeed and in truth, only yesterday I sent over fifty to the city to sell. Aside from pullets, ask what you will."

"In that case," said Sebastian, "you must have veal or kid."

"Just now," said the innkeeper, "there's none in the house, because it's all gone; but next week there will be plenty."

"Much good that does us," muttered Sebastian. "I'll bet that all these shortcomings are going to end up in plenty of bacon and eggs."

"¡*Sangre de cristo*!" Juan Palomeque said. "My guest must be joking! I tell him I have neither pullets nor hens, and he expects me to have eggs! Think of some other fancy dish, if you please, and don't ask for hens again."

"*Merde!*" Sebastian glanced at the boys, several of whom looked faint with hunger. "Let's settle the matter; tell me what you have, and we'll cut short the discussion."

"Really and truly, *señor* guest," said the innkeeper, "all I have is a few cow's feet that look like calves' feet, or several calves' feet that look like cow's feet—in truth, I'm not sure which they are. They are boiled with chickpeas, onions, and bacon, and at this moment they are saying, 'Eat me, eat me.' "

"We'll take them! Don't let anybody else claim them and we'll pay better for them than anyone. Although normally I wouldn't touch such things, tonight we're all so hungry that I doubt any of the boys will care whether they are calves' feet or cow's feet, so fast will they be eaten."

"Nobody else shall claim them," said the innkeeper, "for the other guests I have, being persons of high quality, bring their own cooks and provisions with them." Chuckling, he returned to the kitchen.

Sebastian and the boys seated themselves around a large trestle table and waited for their dinner. Without particular interest, Sebastian studied the large common room, including what looked like recent frescoes covering two walls. Shoddily executed in bold, exaggerated forms and colors, they nevertheless drew his eye. Suddenly, Sebastian sat bolt upright.

"What's the matter, *monsieur*?" Jean-Claude asked at his side.

Sebastian pointed at the frescoes. "Look! They're of Corwyn!"

Indeed, the pictures did represent the alchemist—or rather, his alchemist-errant alter ego made famous in fiction, committing the great acts of folly recorded in the two books by Cid Hamete. In a scene from the first book, he was mistaking an aged, sickly ibex for a unicorn; in one from the second, he was holding aloft a small glass sphere which he claimed was the crystal ball that gave his rival, Hydro Phobius, the power to threaten Venice.

But there were also other scenes—scenes that included Sebastian! One in particular troubled him, for it showed him engaged in a furious sword fight with an empty suit of armor, an event which was nearer to reality than he cared to admit.

"I'll wager that before long, there won't be an inn or tavern in the whole of Spain that doesn't have our supposed 'adventures' painted on its walls," he grumbled under his breath. "Just the same, I wish our present host had hired a better painter than the novice who daubed these."

A third wall held a partially finished scene which Sebastian didn't recognize, for it wasn't taken from either of Cid Hamete's books. Although it was hard to tell what the finished picture would be, it appeared to show Corwyn (or Don Corwyn) at this very inn, casting a magic spell over a wineskin which had assumed a curiously humanlike form and which Corwyn was using to chase two very frightened looking men.

A platter of calves' feet (or cow's feet, as was more likely) was brought to the table by a short, flat-headed, hunchbacked woman named Maritornes. While the boys—the ones who hadn't fallen asleep on the table— began gobbling down this delicate fare, Sebastian asked Maritornes about the unfinished fresco.

"¡Madre de diablos!" Maritornes responded in a hiss, crossing herself hurriedly. Her eyes, which tended to wander one from the other anyway, stared into different corners of the room. She looked askance at Sebastian with her good eye while the other darted freely. "It was right here, *señor*," she said, "in this inn, that the enchanter Don Corwyn de La Mancha conjured up the fiends of hell. He used them to possess a pair of innocent hog-gelders before my very eyes, all because Don Corwyn took offense at my master's sense of humor."

Sebastian shook his head, amazed at how readily works of fiction could be accepted by simple people as if the deeds they recorded were true. "It's just an imaginary story," he told the Asturian. "None of it really happened, or at least"—he glanced at the scene of himself with the suit of armor—"not as it's told in the books. Besides, Corwyn or Don Corwyn isn't an enchanter anyway; the enchanter is his enemy, Hydro Phobius."

Maritornes peered at him with her one unnerving eye. "Think what you will, *señor*," she said in a low voice. "I know what happened. I was here. I saw for myself."

With that, she turned and stalked off to the kitchen, her good eye glancing hastily at the unfinished fresco while she crossed herself again.

Most of the boys—especially Henri—gobbled down the bovine feet of undetermined origin. Sebastian nibbled one distastefully and wondered what had really transpired when Corwyn had passed that way. While he didn't believe what Maritornes had told him, it nonetheless disturbed him to hear more about demons so soon after his encounter with the one brought to Pomme de

Terre by Toxemiah. Like a nightmare that wouldn't stop, demons seemed to be haunting his every waking hour these days.

Such nonsense people dreamed up after reading Cid Hamete's books!

One thing reassured him, however; at least he could be certain Corwyn had preceded them to this inn, and that they had stumbled upon his trail.

Chapter 19

In which is recorded, after certain other incidents, the extraordinary event that might pass for an adventure which befell Corwyn and Cid Hamete.

TOWARD DAYBREAK, SEBASTIAN LAY AWAKE IN THE inn's common room where he and the boys had spent the night. They hadn't taken individual rooms because Sebastian didn't want to add to a debt they were already unable to repay, and so had remained in the common room with the other travelers who had chosen this over more expensive lodging.

Around him, Sebastian heard the snores of those who slept, and he envied them for it. Something had been troubling him for much of the night and he couldn't sleep.

It was that cursed unfinished fresco!

However mad or foolish Toxemiah might be (and he was certainly both!), the man had captured a demon from somewhere to unleash in Pomme de Terre. And he had been crying out for months now about windmills and doom and damnation about to befall the duchy. Of course, he had also spoken to Sebastian of Hydro Phobius, and Sebastian knew Phobius was dead.

At least, he was pretty sure of it.

Suddenly, the hair on Sebastian's neck prickled, and he remembered the breath of demons test Jean-Claude had sabotaged in Corwyn's laboratory. So much had happened since then that Sebastian had almost forgotten the incident. Now he peered at the youth in the half-light, watching him sleep on one of the inn's long wooden benches. What if Jean-Claude had been telling the truth, and he hadn't ruined the breath of demons test after all?

In that case, the test would have been indicating the presence of a particularly malignant presence in the water, a demon like the one Toxemiah had brought to Pomme de Terre. But where could two such demons have come from?

Where else but the Inquisition?

He glanced uneasily at the fresco, unable to make out its details in this light, while Maritornes's words came back to him. Demons had possessed the two hog-gelders, she claimed. Not demons conjured up by Corwyn, as she had said, but perhaps released by him, even if inadvertently. But where had they been before he released them?

The wineskin!

Sebastian shuddered, wondering what chamber of supernatural horrors awaited him in the storeroom where Juan Palomeque kept his wine. Quietly, he awakened the boys and began whispering instructions.

Corwyn woke early, stiff and sore from sleeping on the ground, shivering with cold. It was surprising how cold the desert could get at night, after long daylight hours of the fiercest heat. He stirred the embers of the previous night's fire and added more sticks, wishing he still had some of the money Oliver had given him on the way to Barcelona. Then they'd be able to stay at inns instead of going hungry and sleeping outdoors. Maybe the broom could acquire more money somehow for tonight.

But no sooner had this idea occurred to him than Corwyn snorted in disgust. Talented at petty theft though Oliver was, not even he could make money appear in the middle of the *meseta* when no one else was around. He had to steal the money from somebody!

On the heels of this thought came the realization of how avaricious he himself had become, envying the wealth he'd believed Cid Hamete and Juan de la Cuesta were making and now wanting Oliver to steal for him. Suddenly embarrassed, Corwyn turned his attention overhead in an effort to distract his thoughts. The stars still burned brightly, cold little flecks of light suspended in the vast bowl of darkness that was the night sky.

There it was, that bowl image again, he reflected with a sigh. Everything seemed to come around to one form of it or another, whether as a bowl, a bottle, or a grail.

Always, he seemed to be encountering some form of vessel.

This time, however, the thought didn't discourage him as it had previously. Instead, he found it strangely heartening, and he recalled a related idea he had considered once before, on the way to Argamasilla. The whole world really was one huge vessel, he decided now—a container in which a great breath of demons test was being carried out on a cosmic scale. When this thought had first occurred to him, he had considered it nonsense, an oversimplification of the real alchemical procedure. But now he saw that it had been his own perspective that was distorted, for he had been too close to the laboratory test he himself had devised to recognize all that it symbolized.

Alchemy had always been a subject in which everything revolved around metaphors and symbols, yet in its midst Corwyn had fallen into the error of perceiving the world too literally. He had developed a test in which the world within a glass bottle symbolized the larger world outside, but when he had tried to turn the symbols around and see the world as another bottle, a larger reflection of his test, his rational mind had balked.

But if that were true, then what greater implications for himself might be contained within the concept of the grail, another vessel which he had devised and therefore perhaps had never truly understood?

Increasingly uncomfortable with the direction his thoughts were taking, Corwyn looked for Oliver and saw the broom staring off into the dark, his gaze on the glow of another campfire being rekindled in the distance. Corwyn frowned. Oliver wasn't about to forget Cid Hamete, nor to forgive Corwyn for banishing him.

Suddenly, Corwyn had an idea. He had reluctantly let go of his belief that Cid Hamete had accumulated a fortune from his books; nevertheless, he must have made some money from them. It was only fair that he use part of that money now for Corwyn's benefit, after ruining the alchemist's reputation with those same books.

"*Trés bien*, Oliver," he said. "Go get your friend and tell him he can accompany us."

The broom jumped up and began hurrying across the ground, his brushy base stirring up dust as he ran.

"But only if he pays for us to stay in an inn tonight," Corwyn called after him.

The broom scarcely took time to bob an acknowledgment before rushing off again, certain Cid Hamete would consent to this condition.

The noise of bagpipes skirling and drums beating brought everyone in the inn instantly awake.

Juan Palomeque crashed and stumbled around in his darkened room until he found a lamp and managed to light it, then hurried toward the storeroom from which the noise seemed to be coming. Along the way, he passed guests and members of his staff cowering in the halls and wondering at the commotion. He pushed past them all, yelling for them to accompany him, and finally reached the storeroom, where he was greeted by a curious sight.

His newest guests, the boys with the French accents, were grouped at one end of the room, playing upon their musical instruments, each apparently playing a different tune and keeping time to a different rhythm. Meanwhile, the tall blond young man who led them was standing in the middle of the floor, wielding the short sword he wore at his waist.

He seemed to be attacking Juan Palomeque's supply of wineskins!

"Stand back," the young man shouted at him. "I have them in my power!"

"Who?" Juan Palomeque cried in dismay as the young man lunged at the first skin, piercing it with his sword over and over until red wine ran like blood across the floor. "Who do you have in your power?"

But the young man was too busy to answer, going from skin to skin and dealing each the same violence as he had the first. At last, Juan Palomeque's entire stock of wine lay pooled upon the floor. The young man stared down at the flood, looking perplexed. His companions gradually ceased their discordant playing and peered at the wine as well.

"I could have sworn there'd be demons in at least one of those skins," the young man muttered.

"Demons!" Juan Palomeque roared, pushing through the boys to advance upon the young man despite the latter's sword. "You sound as crazy as that alchemist-errant Don Corwyn, may we all live long enough to forget the day he came to this inn. If it's demons you want, I'll send you where there are plenty of them—for you're about to make your way to hell!"

In his eagerness, however, he slipped in one of the puddles. He hit hard, splashing wine everywhere. For a few moments, he thrashed about, cursing and bellowing. By the time he regained his feet, the young man with the sword had circled around him and made his escape from the storeroom, yelling to the boys to flee as well.

Juan Palomeque caught up with them in the inn yard. The young man brandished his sword at the innkeeper and motioned the boys behind him. Then he began backing toward the gate. "I'm sorry about the wine, *monsieur*," he said, "truly I am. But it was an accident. We will return and pay you for it as soon as we can."

"I'll take my payment now," Juan Palomeque growled. "Your hides will be my new wineskins." He moved in on the young man, his eyes on the sword. Despite the apparent disadvantage, Juan Palomeque knew a thing or two about fighting that this young fool obviously didn't.

The young man seemed to sense his opponent's confidence. "Boys," he said, "I think it's time to play another tune."

With that, they began blowing and beating upon their instruments again with such vigor that Juan Palomeque was forced to cover his ears. "For the love of God," he yelled, "stop this din at once!"

Just then, the old tower in the corner of the former castle—perhaps disturbed from its gradual collapse by the noise of the instruments, or perhaps having simply reached the end of its allotted years—fell with a roar and a great billowing of dust.

When the stones had settled at last and peace reigned over the inn once more, Juan Palomeque, who had been staring at the tower in disbelief, discovered he was now alone in the quiet yard.

His unwelcome guests had escaped without paying while the tower crashed to the earth.

Sebastian and the boys were some distance from the inn before they stopped running, and then it was only because a couple of the smaller boys were stumbling and falling behind. One little boy fell on his lute and smashed it, which started him crying.

At that point, Sebastian agreed to a brief rest before they resumed moving again.

"This is just like our flight over the mountains all over again," Jean-Claude grumbled.

Sebastian, who felt the same way, said nothing.

"*Monsieur*," Jean-Claude went on, apparently determined to get a response, "where are we going now?"

Sebastian halted, looking around in surprise. The sun was rising behind him, devouring shadows and bathing the land in the warm glow of its light. Soon it would be hot. Everything seemed normal for a sunrise in Spain.

Except that the sun shouldn't be at Sebastian's back—not when they were supposed to be traveling east to find Corwyn.

"I guess I just started running toward the only place around here that I knew," he admitted sheepishly. He jerked his chin to indicate the direction of the windmills, beyond the horizon ahead.

Jean-Claude snorted in derision and stalked away. Sebastian, feeling embarrassed and resentful both at once, watched the youth climb a slight rise off to one side. At the top, Jean-Claude looked east toward the rising sun—in the direction they should be going—and shook his head as if despairing of Sebastian's leadership. Then, with a smirk to emphasize his point, he looked northwest where they were actually headed.

Sebastian, now greatly annoyed, started to turn away when suddenly Jean-Claude motioned to him. "*Monsieur*, come here," he cried, staring into the distance. "Quick!"

Reluctantly, Sebastian climbed the rise, suspecting another of Jean-Claude's traps. He sighed, already missing the brief interval of respect he had enjoyed from the oldest student.

When Sebastian reached the top, Jean-Claude pointed to a broad, shallow depression half a league or so ahead. There the land, slightly sunken, lay filled with the remaining shadows of night. As he watched, Sebastian could see the sharp, western edge of shadow draw back across the ground as sunlight encroached on night's former domain. "So?" he asked with a shrug, wondering what Jean-Claude wanted him to see in this.

"Wait." The youth's voice was tense. "They've gone into the hollow. You can't see them in the dark. They'll come out the other side in a few minutes."

Sebastian watched, increasingly doubtful, certain he was being duped. Then, just as he was about to leave, a pair of mules emerged from the pooled darkness into the light. Behind them came another pair, then another, and yet another. Evidently, it was a mule train that had departed from the inn well before daybreak. After a while, the whole train could be seen, guided by three mule skinners with long whips. This in itself wasn't surprising, for mule trains were the most common way of freighting goods overland in Spain, and it was reasonable that the mule skinners would want an early start, before the day grew too hot. What was surprising was the cargo this particular train carried.

Each pair of mules was laden with a large skin of wine!

"I don't think the fresco is meant to depict the wine in Juan Palomeque's personal storeroom," Jean-Claude whispered. "I think it has to do instead with skins of wine that were merely passing through."

Although Corwyn had agreed to let Cid Hamete travel with him, the alchemist refused to talk with the Moor, and so they rode through the day in silence. That evening, they reached an inn which Corwyn remembered with some discomfort as the one he had stayed at before, the one where he had been "initiated" into alchemisthood.

Nevertheless, he chose to stay there a second time rather than spend another night on the open ground. In order not to be recognized, however, he pulled the cowl of his robe well over his head and let Cid Hamete make the arrangements for their stay. The inn was buzzing with talk about a tower that had toppled earlier that day, and indeed, the turret Corwyn remembered from his previous visit was now a heap of rubble in a distant corner of the inn yard. But Corwyn was little interested in the plight of outdated architecture and paid scant attention to the tales of how the tower had collapsed. Nor did he take time to notice the frescoes on the walls of the inn's common room.

To further avoid discovery, Corwyn decided they should eat in their room instead of downstairs, and he immediately withdrew there with Cid Hamete and Oliver (the latter of whom was still dressed as a tiny Moor, while the former didn't much look like one at all). Corwyn kept his head and face covered while Juan

Palomeque, who seemed more sullen today than when Corwyn had been here before, brought in a pot of goat stew and set it on the table.

The innkeeper was on his way out the door when Cid Hamete called to him. "Can we get some wine?"

Juan Palomeque turned slowly, glowering. "*Señor*, you may have all the wine you want," he replied, "so long as you're willing to lap it off the storeroom floor." Then he stormed out of the room, the floor trembling at every heavy step.

Corwyn and Cid Hamete were just helping themselves to the contents of the pot when they overheard part of a discussion from the other side of the wall, for the rooms of the inn were separated by the thinnest of partitions.

"As you live, *Señor* Don Jeronimo," they heard someone say, "it's a good thing we brought our own supply of wine. So while the innkeeper is bringing our supper, let's read another chapter of the third part of *El Ingenioso Alquimista Don Corwyn de La Mancha*."

The man who had been addressed as Don Jeronimo replied, "Why would you have us read that absurd stuff, Don Juan, when it is impossible for anyone who has read the first two parts of the history of Don Corwyn de La Mancha to take any pleasure in reading this third part?"

"Nevertheless," said the one addressed as Don Juan, "we may as well read it, for there is no book so bad that there is not something good in it. Besides, what else can we do here to pass the time except read and drink?"

Corwyn turned to Cid Hamete. "Third part?" he demanded, his anger rising. "You've already written the third part? You told me you hadn't finished it yet."

But the Moor was already on his feet, scowling in fury at the wall.

Entremés

Don Corwyn de La Mancha, being as foolish as he was mad, became concerned after his first two sallies that the world might think better of his opponent, Hydro Phobius, than of him, for never in their confrontations had fortune favored the alchemist-errant over his elusive rival. Nor was his fear alleviated by the fact that some people questioned the very existence of this Hydro Phobius, for without him Don Corwyn would have no one to blame for his failures.

He thus set out on a third sally to prove his preeminence over the much maligned and grievously persecuted enchanter, coming at length upon a melon patch on the outskirts of a village. In his folly, he mistook the melons for the heads of the village's residents and assumed they had congregated in this field for a town meeting. He further determined to put the issue of who was better, Hydro Phobius or himself, before them for a vote. Dismounting from Rociandante, *therefore, he addressed them as follows:*

"Inasmuch as many have dared to doubt my unquestionable superiority over my opponent, I hereby place

the matter in your hands (if this worthy council of disso-
ciated heads even has hands with which to take up such
a weighty issue) for a final, absolute, and irrevocable
testament to my unparalleled excellence in all areas of
alchemy."

He then paused, expecting a chorus of affirmative
replies granting him that favored status which he
so desired. When his request was greeted only with
silence, however, he became furious at the villagers' recalcitrance, and he began striding through
the melon patch, flailing so violently at the melons
with El Aver that he knocked many of them loose
from their vines and damaged or bruised many
others.

The owner of the melons, meanwhile, had been
standing guard at the far end of the field, for
numerous pilgrims and wanderers passed this way,
stealing his fruit. Seeing the destruction that Don
Corwyn was causing to his livelihood, therefore, he
picked up a rock the size of his fist and placed
it in his sling. He whirled it overhead several
times, then let fly the stone, which struck Don
Corwyn squarely between the eyes. Don Corwyn
crumpled to the ground, blood flowing copiously
from his wound, while the melon owner, fearing he had killed the intruder, ran off to his
village.

When the alchemist-errant regained consciousness,
his insanity had increased thirtyfold, either as a result
of the blow to his head or the damage done to his
self-esteem. Thus determined to gain vengeance for
the wrongs done to him, he retrieved El Aver and
laid about him more furiously than ever, until he had
slaughtered every melon in the patch as an example to
all others who presumed to defy the will of Don
Corwyn.

Believing he had depopulated the village by decapitat-
ing its citizens, Don Corwyn again mounted Rociandante
and rode off, vowing to continue his campaign
of retribution until all question of his supremacy

over his unsuspecting opponent was forever laid to rest....

—Alonso Fernández de Avellaneda,
  El Ingenioso Alquimista
  Don Corwyn de La Mancha,
  Part III (the "false" *Don Corwyn*)

Chapter 20

Which deals with further matters pertaining to this history and not to any other.

"WHAT DISPLEASES ME MOST ABOUT THIS THIRD PART," continued the man who had been called Don Juan, "is that it was not written by the original writer, Cid Hamete Benengeli, but rather by this imposter, Alonso Fernández de Avellaneda, whoever he may be. I only hope the Moor hasn't abandoned his character to the care of lesser writers."

On hearing this Cid Hamete, full of wrath and indignation, raised his voice and said; "Whoever dares to claim that Cid Hamete Benengeli has or ever could abandon the character of Don Corwyn to another writer lies, and I will personally teach him the truth of that fact if the person who makes this claim will but face me like a man."

"Who answers us?" asked the voices from the next room.

"Who else," cried Cid Hamete, shaking off Corwyn's restraining hand, "but that Moor whom you disparage with your words, and who will make good all that I have said."

Cid Hamete had hardly uttered these words when two gentlemen, for such they seemed by their dress and manner to be, flung open the door and entered the room. One of them, on spying Corwyn, threw his arms around the alchemist's neck as if he recognized him and said, "Your appearance cannot leave any question as to your name, nor can your name fail to identify your appearance; unquestionably, *señor*, you are the real Don Corwyn de La Mancha, north pole and morning star of alchemist-errantry."

"And you," Corwyn replied, turning his face from the man's wine-laden breath, "are drunk."

"If what you say is true, Don Jeronimo," the second gentleman cried, greeting Cid Hamete in similar fashion, "and certainly I must believe it to be so, then this must be the Moor who invented Don Corwyn and has recorded his worthy exploits, despite the false writer who has sought to usurp the alchemist's good name and annihilate his author's achievements, as the writer of this book which I here present to you has done."

With that, he took the book which Don Jeronimo carried and gave it into the hands of Cid Hamete, who accepted it without replying and began to leaf through it.

"Here," Corwyn snapped, grabbing for the book, "it claims to be about me. Let me see it."

But Cid Hamete refused to relinquish the book. "A fine historian this Alonso Fernández de Avellaneda is, may he contract the pox!" the Moor snarled after a moment. "In the little I have seen I've discovered several things this author relates that deserve to be censured, and when a man errs on as many points as he has, there is good reason to fear that he is in error on every other aspect of his so-called history." He thrust the offending volume back at Don Juan. "Take the book again, *señor*, for I want nothing to do with it."

"Well, I do," Corwyn insisted, grabbing the book before Don Juan could take it.

"I believe every word you say," Don Juan replied to Cid Hamete, spreading alcohol fumes on the air as thickly as his companion. "And if it were possible, an order should be issued that no one should have the presumption to deal with anything relating to Don Corwyn except you, his original author Cid Hamete. But won't you read some more of the book, for I would like to hear what you have to say about it."

"Consider it read," Cid Hamete snapped, "for it is utterly worthless and should not be glorified with further attention. We should keep our thoughts, and still more our eyes, away from whatever is obscene and filthy— and that includes this wretched, lying, deceitful book!"

Corwyn meanwhile, continued studying the volume in question, noting first the inferior quality of the printing and the paper—worse even than most books being produced these days. Obviously, it had been written hurriedly and rushed into print with tremendous haste in order to capitalize on the current popularity of anything to do with Don Corwyn.

But more than that, Corwyn was startled by the vicious way in which this new book portrayed his fictional self, and by the sympathetic tone it took toward Hydro Phobius. In fact, it almost seemed that the book—

"Phobius!" he hissed, breaking off in the middle of his own thought.

"Hmmm," responded Don Jeronimo, drinking deeply from a bottle he took from his coat. "What's that?"

"Hydro Phobius wrote this book," Corwyn explained, speaking to Cid Hamete rather than the two newcomers. "He did it as a personal challenge to me, and to shift the blame for his misdeeds onto my head."

Don Jeronimo laughed drunkenly and passed the bottle to Don Juan. Corwyn ignored them. "This was published in Zaragoza," he said, leafing to the front of the book, "and that's where it reports me to be." He slammed the volume shut, but didn't give it back when Don Juan stretched out his hand for it. "That's where he's waiting for me. Hydro Phobius wants me to come after him." He stopped abruptly, puzzled. "I thought he was dead." Then he shook his head. "That's what I get for not making sure at the time. Somehow, he escaped the waters of the Adriatic."

The two gentlemen, meanwhile, were falling all over one another with laughter. "This is better than the books,"

Don Jeronimo gasped, wiping the tears from his eyes, "even the first two books by Cid Hamete!" Suddenly, he froze. "What's that?"

"What's what?" Don Juan asked, peering in the direction his companion pointed. Then he crossed himself and moaned. "*¡Maldito sea!* What is it?"

Oliver—no longer dressed as a Moor, or indeed as anything at all—emerged timidly from the shadows of the room and skittered over to Corwyn.

After watching what clearly was a broom that moved about on its own, the two gentlemen stumbled over one another in their hurry to leave, each of them promising heaven that he would never again drink to excess if only he'd be allowed to escape unharmed from this hideous monster.

Oliver looked around nervously, wondering what monster they had seen. But when he didn't find anything to be frightened of, he decided the two men were simply imagining things.

Corwyn, too, started to leave the room as soon as the men were gone.

"*¡Oye!*" Cid Hamete said, "where are you going?"

"Zaragoza." Corwyn paused only long enough to motion for Oliver. "Hydro Phobius is up to something and I've got to stop him."

"Wait for me," Cid Hamete called. "This is great—what a break for my book!" He quickly slipped his boots back on and hurried after the alchemist and Oliver.

Sebastian paused from scratching symbols in the sand and examined the lute which the youngest student had fallen on and broken during their escape from the inn. Sebastian shook his head. Evidently, the boy had been too young to understand when he chose the instrument that the intention was to create as much noise as possible in order to annoy the acting schoolmaster. If the boy had understood, he would have picked a louder, more dissonant instrument—like the bagpipes or drums most of the students had chosen.

What attracted Sebastian's interest now, however, was not the instrument—what little was left of it—but its strings. They were gut, of course, not metal. After all, who had ever heard of a musical instrument with metal strings! Nor had he ever heard of any substance other than metals, especially silver and gold, being thaumaturgically active. Nonetheless, since thaumaturgy affected living things, Sebastian figured that gut strings, coming from something that had once been alive, might have retained some tiny portion of thaumaturgical activity.

He only needed them to possess the slightest amount.

Sebastian wondered again whether the boys' music (if it could be called that) had had anything to do with the tower's collapsing back at the inn. He made a few revisions to the marks he'd scribbled in the sand, trying to recall everything Simon Magus had said in *Summa Thaumaturgica*. Had Sebastian remembered the symbols correctly? At last he shrugged. There was only one way to find out. He called to Henri.

The boy straggled over. Despite his weariness, he looked more trim than he ever had in Pomme de Terre. *"Oui, monsieur?"*

"Henri, since you're the one who initiated this musical interest among the students—"

"What, me, *monsieur*?" The boy managed a look of shocked surprise. "Why, I had nothing to do with that."

Sebastian snorted softly and went on. "For your part in that, you get to volunteer your bagpipes for an experiment."

This time, Henri's shocked look was genuine, especially when Sebastian withdrew a dirk from his belt with one hand and held out the other for the boy's bagpipes. Henri stepped back, clutching the instrument with both hands. "What are you going to do?"

"Amplify its effect," Sebastian replied. "I hope."

Looking very doubtful, Henri handed over the pipes. Sebastian lightly touched the finger holes of the chanter pipe as if playing a melody, then examined the two drone pipes, each of which would emit a bass note of constant pitch while the instrument was in use. This instrument was more like the large pipes Sebastian had used in England than were the smaller French *musettes* owned by the other boys, and it was because of this familiarity that he had chosen it to be first. With the dirk, he began carefully carving symbols into the chanter, checking his progress against the marks he had drawn in the sand. He did his best to ignore Henri's histrionics every time the blade scored a new groove in the wood, and was relieved when Jean-Claude finally led the distraught boy away, leaving Sebastian to his work.

Sebastian finished the chanter, then had Jean-Claude organize the boys into scavenging parties, scouring the area for traces of sticky resin. By the time Sebastian had carved another, simpler set of symbols into the drone pipes, the boys had collected enough resin for him to coat one of the strings from the lute. Then he cut the sticky cord into segments and laid them into the grooves in the wood, just as he had done with silver wire when he made the wand in Pomme de Terre. He tamped the strings into place, making sure they would stay, and stood.

He had a couple of the boys pile rocks atop one another to make a small, crude cairn, then motioned everyone back. The boys watched with wide-eyed interest, not daring to make a sound.

Sebastian tucked the bag under his arm the way he had been taught. It felt awkward, and Sebastian flushed with embarrassment. But he couldn't ask one of the students to do this in case something went wrong. He called Jean-Claude over and whispered for him to guide the boys back to Pomme de Terre if anything happened to him during the test. Jean-Claude nodded, swallowing hard, and rejoined the others. Sebastian took the mouthpiece between his lips, put his fingers to the chanter. He filled the bag and squeezed with his arm. His fingers stumbled over the unfamiliar holes, playing what was supposed to be the tune to "Mistresse Mary." The instrument's response was a hideous noise, not all of which could be blamed on thaumaturgy. The boys covered their ears and backed away. Sebastian watched the cairn.

After a moment, the piled stones began to tremble, then shake. Finally, they rattled together so violently that the cairn fell apart—a miniature reenactment of the tower collapsing at the inn.

Sebastian stopped playing and grinned, while the students stared at him as if he were crazy. "Boys," he said, "we're going back to the windmills."

If he expected this announcement to be greeted with cheers, he was mistaken, for their groans sighed across the bleak landscape like the sounds of a disapproving wind.

Later that day, while Sebastian and the students angled northwest from the inn toward the upper end of the line of windmills, Corwyn and Cid Hamete rode out from the same inn with a similar destination. But because Corwyn was seeking Hydro Phobius, whom he placed in the neighborhood of Zaragoza, the alchemist and the Moor headed due west, thus failing to overtake the much slower students.

They did, however, come upon a different party.

But this anticipates an event that happens later in this history, for Corwyn and Cid Hamete (and, of course, Oliver) traveled at first without encountering anyone. For a time, they rode in silence. Even Oliver seemed unusually restrained. Eventually, after much inner struggle, Corwyn burst out, "I don't know why you had to make your stories about me comedies. You might at least have dignified them, and me, by relating the events of my life as tragedies, which would certainly be more true to the nature of the difficulties I've endured."

Cid Hamete looked shocked. "But, *señor*, to do that would be to uphold the values of alchemy."

"And you don't want to do that?" Corwyn asked after some hesitation.

"That is the very thing I set out to discredit."

Corwyn winced, then growled, "What do you have against alchemy?"

"*Señor*, as I am a good Christian"—which was news to Corwyn, for he had thought the Moor was Muslim—"you will have to give an account to God for the foolishness you are committing with your pursuits. Who ever put it into your head that you are an alchemist and that there are such things in the world as transmutations, elixirs of life, and Philosopher's Stones?"

Corwyn drew a breath to object, intending to refute this charge, but evidently Cid Hamete didn't expect an answer, for he quickly went on. "If you want my advice, *señor*—which you shall have whether you ask it or not—you should go back to your home and see to your family, if you have one, and give up roaming the world, swallowing wind and making yourself a laughingstock of those who know you as well as those who don't. We are rapidly entering an era when reason and logic shall rule the affairs of men, and when the workings of the world around us will be brought under our control. Where, then, in this new scheme of things is alchemy to find a place? It is an outdated, arcane, and ultimately elitist pursuit which is contrary not only to the broader appeal of our times, but also opposed to that populist, literate society which the development of printing has already begun to bring about."

He stopped, looking very puffed up with himself, then added quickly, "But I do hope you won't follow my advice to abandon alchemy until I've finished writing the third book about you. I still need a few more ridiculous incidents and encounters to round out the ending."

Corwyn gasped and huffed, seeking in vain for an answer strong enough. "And you are a man of reason and logic?" he asked at last.

"*Sí*," Cid Hamete replied proudly. Then his maimed hand fumbled with a little silver vial suspended on a chain around his neck. "Most of the time."

"I thought *I* was," Corwyn muttered. He went on, allowing himself to slip into a measure of self-pitying hyperbole and speaking more to himself than Cid Hamete. "Apparently, I am to be the beginning and the end of alchemy, the first and last practitioner of this noble art. As I was present at its birth"—he hadn't been, but didn't think Cid Hamete would know that—"so then shall I preside in time over its dying."

They rode in silence for another league or more, Corwyn lost in bleak and despairing thoughts, Oliver nestled quietly at his back. Evening began to descend.

"If you despise what I do so much," Corwyn finally asked, "then why do you occupy yourself with writing about me?"

"As I said, I want to discredit alchemy, and comedy does this by taking a set of values—yours, for example—and reducing them to absurdity." Cid Hamete sat erect and gestured grandly with his crippled hand. "Think of it as a kind of dramatic or literary alchemy, a trial by fire in the quest for pure gold. The character of Don Corwyn which I create from you is a crucible or vessel embodying the values you hold dear."

Corwyn scowled. Here was that vessel business again, returning once more to haunt him.

"In the course of telling the story," Cid Hamete went on, "I subject these values to the equivalent of a laboratory furnace or caustic chemical assault. When the crucible (that is, the character) degrades in the course of this, it is because the values upon which the person was based were false and impure, fool's gold." He nodded to Corwyn, emphasizing his point. "Had the crucible withstood the assault, even though the character himself might die in the process, that would be tragedy and the set of values would emerge unscathed as real gold."

"Ah ha!" Corwyn replied, gloating. "You said comedy is a kind of dramatic alchemy. That makes you a kind of alchemist as well."

Cid Hamete frowned as he considered the unfortunate twist he had given his argument. "But that's different," he said. "I'm a verbal alchemist."

"A verbal alchemist?"

"*Sí.*" Cid Hamete sighed, shifting uncomfortably in his saddle. "I had hoped to turn my words into gold, and that my books would then transmute me into a rich and famous author." He glanced pointedly at his threadbare clothes, the gesture barely noticeable in the growing darkness.

"So, *señor*, which of us is the greater fool after all?"

Corwyn said nothing, fearing he had won some point in this discussion which he would prefer instead to have lost.

By this time, the sun had set and the night, lacking a moon, had turned quite black. The route they followed began to descend in a gradual incline. Soon after, they entered an oak forest, which further deepened the darkness. Corwyn and Cid Hamete rode slowly, letting their mounts pick their way among the trees. At one point, Corwyn felt something brush his head and, reaching up a hand, he grasped a man's feet and stockings. Trembling at finding such strange fruit hanging from the tree, he goaded *Roche-naissante* forward, but under the next oak he encountered the same thing. He halted and called to Cid Hamete in a hoarse whisper.

The Moor—or rather, Morisco, since he was Christian—drew alongside him and, guided by the alchemist's hand, felt the forest's bounty. Oliver's stick fingers promptly followed Cid Hamete's, then drew back with a start. Together, the three of them explored several other trees, all of which were filled with human legs and feet.

"It's nothing to worry about," Cid Hamete said, his mouth sounding dry. "These must be the limbs of bandits who have been hanged and left here as warnings to others of their kind. From this and the fact that we have for a while been descending into the valley of the Ebro, I conclude we must be nearing Zaragoza. They hang bandits where they catch them here, often in bands of twenty or thirty. The brethren assigned with carrying out the Inquisition seem particularly determined to stamp out these highwaymen, and indeed, to suppress any form of unauthorized travel in this vicinity."

Corwyn shuddered, for this served to reinforce his growing suspicions about Hydro Phobius's activities in the area, especially if he was working with the Inquisition again and wanted secrecy.

Just then, they noticed flickers of light wending their way through the trees to the right of them, as if a handful of stars had fallen from heaven and taken up residence in this forest. Corwyn swallowed past a knot of fear in his throat. Oliver clung to him more tightly. "Come on," the alchemist whispered. "Let's go see what those are."

"What?" Though Corwyn couldn't see Cid Hamete's face, the Morisco's voice sounded aghast. "They're probably more of these bandits hanging above our heads, except that the ones over there are still alive and therefore more dangerous."

"Would bandits, fearing capture and execution, disclose their presence with torches?" Corwyn asked. "More likely, it's some of those brethren of the Inquisition you mentioned, doing whatever it is that they want to keep unseen."

"All the more reason to avoid them," Cid Hamete grumbled. Nonetheless, Corwyn heard the soft footfalls of the Morisco's nag as he fell in behind *Roche-naissante*.

Slowly, they made their way north, leaving the Ebro somewhere behind them and rising again to that barren plain which stretched from here to Lérida. The oak forest thinned, then disappeared altogether. They could see the lights clearly now as torches held aloft by three mule skinners, who were guiding their mule train through the night, determined to reach their destination. But where, Corwyn wondered, could they be going? They had left the road that would have taken them the remaining distance to Zaragoza.

"You wanted more adventures to fill up your book?" he whispered to Cid Hamete. "Well, I think you shall have them."

Cid Hamete crossed himself with his maimed hand, a gesture dimly revealed by the faint starlight. "If those are phantoms ahead, as they appear, I would just as soon do without. After all, who says this book has to be as long as the others?"

Corwyn shook his head in the dark. "They aren't phantoms, although if what I suspect is true, the cargo those mules carry may be something worse."

They rode on, silent now, staring into the night to make out its dread secrets. At last, the mule train passed through a small olive grove and halted before a modest, mud-brick house covered with cracked and peeling plaster. Corwyn, Cid Hamete, and Oliver remained under the olive trees and watched. The front door of the house was flung open, spilling light from inside onto the ground. Without a word, several figures emerged and helped the three mule skinners unload their beasts, using barrows to carry the bulky wineskins inside. The mule skinners led their animals around to a stable on the other side of the house, then they too went in the house, closing the door behind them.

Corwyn frowned. The building was much smaller than he had expected. He doubted it could possibly contain an operation of the size Hydro Phobius would need if he was again in charge of getting rid of the Inquisition's demonic wastes.

Cid Hamete interrupted his thoughts with a tap on the shoulder. "*Señor*," he whispered, pointing in the faint light, "what is that?"

Corwyn squinted in the direction the Morisco was pointing and saw a large, dark structure standing out against the lighter darkness of the sky about a hundred yards beyond the house. The hair lifted on the back of the alchemist's neck, and a chill far colder than that of the night coursed the length (short though it was) of his spine.

The structure was a windmill, a big one, apparently the first in that chain of windmills he had seen being constructed on his way into Spain from Pomme de Terre.

Entremés

*AFTER THE EPISODE IN THE MELON PATCH AND THE IGNO-
minious blow to the head which Don Corwyn suffered
during that conflict, the old fool grew more convinced
than ever of the need to bring down his foe in the eyes
of the world. Unable to ruin the good name of Hydro
Phobius by legitimate means, he eventually decided to
discredit his nemesis by impersonating him while carrying out some particularly horrific scheme.*

*He therefore stitched flames and devils cut from scar-
let cloth to his black alchemist's robes, making himself
appear like an unrepentant heretic condemned to the
stake. Obsidian moons, black and shiny, he affixed to
his pointed hat, like dark mirrors reflecting the bleakness
of his soul. To disguise his face and hands (those being
the only parts of him that remained visible), he then
donned the skeletal mask and bone-painted gloves worn
by the character of Death each year during Carnival.
At last, he harnessed* Rociandante *to a borrowed oxcart,
turning it into* La Carreta de la Muerte, *the Cart
of Death.*

*Outfitted in this frightful manner and calling himself
Hydro Phobius, he journeyed to Zaragoza, that being
one place where his antics had never before been
witnessed and where he could thus go unrecognized.
Once in that fair city, he began to work his evil plan,
plotting the destruction of an innocent duchy north of
the Pyrenees in France, the blame for which would then*

descend squarely upon the head of his unknowing and guiltless victim, Hydro Phobius. . . .

—Alonso Fernández de Avellaneda,
   El Ingenioso Alquimista
   Don Corwyn de La Mancha,
   Part III (the "false" *Don Corwyn*)

Chapter 21

In which music, although failing to soothe the savage breast, does put an end to the Inquisition's schemes, convincing Friar Carlos to abandon his present career.

ABOUT THE TIME THE HAIR ROSE ON CORWYN'S NECK and he saw the first of the windmills looming against the sky ahead of him, Sebastian sat hunched before a small fire, hidden behind a mound of rocks, a few hundred yards away from the other end of the line of windmills.

Around him, the boys slept fitfully. Once, Henri spoke in his sleep, calling out for a raspberry tart. Only Jean-Claude had stayed awake with Sebastian. Even now, the youth struggled to keep his eyes open while he watched Sebastian carve thaumaturgical symbols into the last of the musical instruments—in this case, a drum. Sebastian, too, fought against sleep, pausing occasionally to rub his eyes. He finished the symbols and held out a hand to Jean-Claude, who placed the last piece of resined lute string in his open palm. Sebastian noticed that Jean-Claude's hand trembled with fatigue but he said nothing, grateful for the youth's company. He laid the string into the grooves he had cut in the drum and tamped it into place, then set the instrument down and sighed.

"We're done," he told Jean-Claude. "Get some sleep."

Jean-Claude cocked an eyebrow. "And you, *monsieur*?"

"*Oui,*" Sebastian answered wearily. "Me too."

He lay down and listened to the scrabbling sounds of Jean-Claude trying to get comfortable on the broken ground. In a few minutes, the youth was asleep, his snores joining the chorus from the other boys. But tired as he was, sleep evaded Sebastian. He lay wide-eyed in the darkness, worrying about the coming day. He was concerned about his own safety, of course, although that was mostly because he would be a father soon and had to consider his new responsibilities. But that wasn't all that disturbed him. He was fretting about the students' welfare as well, and regretting the need to expose them to the same risks he himself had chosen to face.

It was a novel perspective for him, he realized. Before, it would have been Corwyn lying awake, worrying, while Sebastian, like Jean-Claude, slept, trusting in the other's ability to take care of things. Well, the *chou* was on the other foot now, he told himself. He grinned at his own joke, strangely content with the changes that had been taking place somewhere deep within him.

Although he wasn't aware of having the students for neighbors that night, nor did he suspect anything of what their presence would mean to him in the morning, Friar Carlos also lay awake in his bed, worrying. It had become a habit for him of late, and he saw no reason to give up the practice now.

With Tomás de Torquemada away from the camp for a while, and the line of windmills extending ever closer to their destination, he told himself he should feel more at ease. But no amount of rationalizing could alter the news that had reached him late that afternoon: Toxemiah had escaped en route to Zaragoza (he stank so badly, none of the guards were willing to stop him when he simply walked away), and as a result Tomás de Torquemada had decided to remain at the processing station for a while instead of continuing on to the city.

To make matters worse, something odd, even troubling, was going on at the processing station where the windmills originated. Friar Carlos had heard a rumor earlier that day about a stranger who had appeared there recently, and that Hydro Phobius had vanished a few days before. The stranger, it was said, was now in charge of the station.

The whole thing had sounded too unbelievable to be true. Now, however, Friar Carlos wasn't so sure.

By the flickering light of a candle stub, he looked again at the new book that had been smuggled to him that day (along with the news about Toxemiah and Torquemada). It was supposed to be a continuation of the previous two volumes of *Don Corwyn*, although this book was not as well written, having issued from the pen of a different author. Still, that wasn't what troubled Friar Carlos.

What did trouble him was that the description of the stranger who was rumored to have taken over at the processing station matched the description of Don Corwyn given in this book.

Friar Carlos's head swam. It was becoming increasingly difficult to tell where fiction stopped and reality began.

Before dawn the next morning, Sebastian gathered the students and explained his plan. He warned them about the dangers and told them there would be no disgrace for any who chose to remain behind. He wanted only those who volunteered to come with him.

To his surprise, they all did, seeming to regard his plan as just another game, albeit more exciting than most.

Feeling a mixture of pride and apprehension for his young charges, Sebastian helped them ready their instruments. Henri protested when Sebastian appropriated the boy's bagpipes for himself, so Sebastian took him aside and assured him that someone would need to spell the small boys, and that he hoped Henri would undertake that responsibility. After that, Henri was very solicitous about helping the younger boys and even winked knowingly once at Sebastian when he caught the latter's eye.

The last thing Sebastian did was to have the boys plug their ears with scraps of cloth torn from their clothing. Finally, when the first rays of sunlight burst over the eastern horizon, they all trooped out from hiding and marched toward the nearest windmill. The boys didn't play at first, saving their breath until they were within range of their targets. As a result, the guards and laborers in the adjacent camp were caught by surprise when Sebastian and the students suddenly descended upon them, seeming to walk right out of the rising sun at them like a band of avenging angels.

Then Sebastian signaled for the boys to play, setting an example by breaking into a rollicking rendition of the only song he knew, "Mistresse Mary." Thaumaturgical flux flowed along his limbs, crackling and raising his hair like the static charge of a nearby lightning strike. The boys joined in, each playing his favorite tune to the tempo of his choice. The din was horrendous. Guards dropped their pikes and clapped their hands over their ears. Convict laborers tried to do the same, although it was more difficult to reach both ears at once with their shackles.

A young friar, his Dominican habit only half on, rushed out from somewhere into the fray as the first notes shattered the morning calm. He stood in the middle of the camp, staring wildly at the intruders, his white face drained of blood. His hands clutched a book with such fierceness that Sebastian assumed it must be a Bible. Finally, when Sebastian was only a few paces away, the friar shrieked and flung the book in the air, then ran in a wide arc around the students and headed for the northeast horizon, where the Pyrenees rose unseen beyond. He stripped off his habit and threw it aside as he ran. The last Sebastian saw of him, he was dressed only in his undergown, so determined did he seem to leave behind every trace of his involvement here.

The book had fallen near Sebastian's feet, and he glanced at the title as he approached it. Seeing that it was a third volume in the infamous series about

"Don Corwyn," he stepped squarely in the middle of the cover and marched on, trampling the book underfoot.

He led the boys around the base of the nearest windmill, making seven circuits before their playing produced results. Just as Sebastian began to despair, cracks appeared in the newly whitewashed plaster. Puffs of dust spurted from the mortar between the stones, and the stones themselves started to tremble. One stone fell out, then another, until gaps formed in the circular wall and the whole structure eventually crumpled. At last, like the walls of Jericho falling before the trumpets of Joshua and his men, only a pile of stones and plaster dust marked the spot where the windmill had stood, its vanes lying broken and askew amid the rubble. The twisted remnants of strange machinery that had been housed inside could be seen here and there, protruding through the heap of stones.

Sebastian, excited now, led the boys to the next windmill.

A couple of guards made desultory attempts to defend the structures, gritting their teeth against the sound as they shuffled toward the intruders and leveling their pikes before them. But they couldn't tolerate getting close enough to present a real threat. Eventually, all of them threw down their weapons and ran. Even with his ears plugged, Sebastian found the noise daunting. He hoped that as they proceeded down the line of windmills, none of the guards they encountered would turn out to be deaf.

Some of the convicts also tried to run away, although this, too, was more difficult for them, since they had been chained together in columns and each column thus had to agree on a direction and pace before starting to flee. Most of the convicts simply huddled on the ground, still struggling to cover both ears at once.

Sebastian broke into a jig as he guided his entourage toward the third windmill, elated to have at last developed an appreciation for music.

*   *   *

When dawn came, Corwyn, too, watched with apprehension as the windmill he would attack—having had the appearance of a sinister, spectral form throughout the night—became solid and real with daybreak, the stones from which it was made seeming to root themselves with their brethren deep in the earth.

It still looked as sinister as it had by night.

In the growing sunlight, Corwyn saw others of its kind stretching out beyond it in a line that ran straight toward the Pyrenees and the duchy of Gardenia on the other side. But this first windmill was obviously different— larger, more complex, the command center from which the entire operation would be controlled.

Keeping carefully out of sight, Corwyn studied the structure, his mind delighting in the superiority of its technical design, his soul shuddering at its purpose. At first, the alchemist was baffled by the apparent lack of a pipeline or conduit connecting the windmill with the next one in line; then he realized that the ground between the two showed traces of having been disturbed, as if a trench had been dug and then covered over again. He smiled to himself, granting Hydro Phobius his grudging respect. In order to keep suspicions down and make the windmills appear as normal as possible, he had buried the conduit. Anyone seeing the windmills would naturally assume (as Corwyn himself had done) that they were intended for grinding grain, not for pumping demonic wastes over the mountains.

This first windmill was clearly the key to the pumping system, and it would have to be destroyed. But in the meantime, Corwyn was also concerned about the house that seemed too small for its purpose. A couple of guards with pikes stood guard outside the single door, while another pair made constant circuits around its walls. Several figures—too many for the size of the structure— emerged from inside and went about their business. One of them, a thin, pale boy with dark hair and piercing eyes, left the house carrying a wooden box under one arm and began poking among the stones and weeds that made up the yard. Occasionally, he opened the box and popped something inside.

Corwyn figured the house must be a temporary storage site for the demon slurries waiting to be pumped out of Spain, and probably some kind of stabilizing center as well. After all, the demons would have to be incapacitated with holy water or other arcane substances long enough to be handled safely while the slurries were being prepared. That in turn called for specialized equipment and a staff of technicians trained in its use.

All of which, Corwyn reasoned, required a much larger facility to hold everything than the modest house before him.

He was considering this when Cid Hamete tapped him on the shoulder and pointed. To Corwyn's dismay, Oliver—as curious as a cat—had left the olive grove and was trotting toward the dark-haired boy to see what he was doing. The broom had forgotten his clothing at the inn, and now he was naively disregarding both cover and disguise in his eagerness. A guard spotted him and ordered him to halt, the voice sounding hesitant. When Oliver ignored him, the guard called to his companions for help, unwilling to venture closer to so odd a broom without assistance.

At the guard's cry the boy looked up and saw Oliver approaching. His expression was quizzical at first, then took on a look of keen, even malevolent, anticipation. Oliver, self-conscious now at being seen, sidled up to the boy and gestured toward the wooden box. The boy ignored him, poking and prodding at the broom instead with growing excitement. Something about the way the boy studied Oliver made Corwyn shudder. He shook his head in dismay, a sinking feeling in his stomach.

Another guard hurried up to the first, then they both stood there uncertainly, waved back from approaching by the hungry-eyed boy. Oliver, frustrated at not being understood, finally took the box gently from under the boy's arm and opened it, peering inside. The broom froze, then began removing implements of torture— thumbscrews, bands with spikes for piercing eyeballs, and other grisly items. Corwyn groaned. The boy, who seemed indifferent to the box now that Oliver stood before him, made a lunge to grab the broom. Corwyn cried out in warning, but Oliver had already sidestepped, throwing down the box, and turned on the boy in fury, using his broomstick-body to beat the boy about the head and shoulders. Corwyn's mouth sagged. He'd never seen the mild-mannered broom react so violently.

The guards edged forward, still reluctant to confront a broom that acted on its own and beat small boys. Besides, neither of them liked this particular boy very much. The boy, crying and throwing up his arms to protect himself from Oliver's blows, ran blindly into the olive grove. Oliver pursued him. Armed men began spilling from the house (again, far more of them than the tiny house should have contained) and spread out to defend it, their eyes sweeping the area for signs of attack. Two men spotted Corwyn. They signaled to the others, then fanned out in a wide circle, surrounding the alchemist and Cid Hamete. Corwyn swallowed hard; there was no escape.

Just then, a croaking voice bellowed from the top of the main windmill, ordering the guards to stop. They did, showing more fear at the voice than they had with Oliver. Corwyn shivered in recognition, then turned and saw a short, squat figure standing on a narrow walkway that circled the top of the windmill. The figure leaned against the railing, his black robes and black, conical alchemist's hat giving him a faint resemblance to Corwyn. But the similarity ended there, for the figure's robes were brightly ornamented with scarlet flames and devils, and obsidian moons gleamed against the dull cloth of the hat. More startling still, however, were the figure's face and hands, their real features veiled in black and replaced by the stark, white-painted likenesses of a grinning skull and fleshless, bony fingers.

It was Hydro Phobius.

"Corwyn!" he cried, his cracked voice rising to a screech. "I've been waiting for you." His laughter cascaded from the walkway. "The histories the Moor has written about you claim you're experienced at battling windmills. Well, let's see how you do against this one. Come and get me . . . if you can."

Still cackling, Hydro Phobius disappeared inside the structure. Corwyn turned to Cid Hamete, trying to edge away from the windmill. The attempt was countered by the guards with raised pikes. Corwyn stepped tentatively the other way, toward the structure. The silent guards made no move to stop him.

"I want my donkey," he said, refusing to go any farther.

A guard shook his head and prodded Corwyn with the tip of his pike, but Corwyn wouldn't budge. After a moment of this, Hydro Phobius's white skull-face (or rather, the white skull-face painted on Hydro Phobius's mask, for his own face looked more like that of a pop-eyed toad) appeared again at the walkway of the windmill. "What's taking so long?" he demanded.

The guard explained the delay, his voice betraying his nervousness.

"Let him have his donkey," Phobius bellowed. "Lot of good it will do him." He disappeared inside again.

The guard who had spoken ran to the olive grove, seeming to know right where *Roche-naissante* and Cid Hamete's nag were tethered.

Oliver returned just then, without the boy and strutting as if pleased with himself. He stopped when he saw Corwyn and Cid Hamete being held captive.

"And my broom," Corwyn added, nodding to Oliver.

The guards looked uncertain at this, glancing to the windmill for guidance. But Phobius wasn't there to give them direction and, reluctant to disturb him, the guards at last agreed. Corwyn motioned to Oliver, who came over slowly, then hurried through the ring of guards. They parted ranks for him just as hastily, and it was hard to tell which side was more nervous about the other. Oliver squeezed against Corwyn's side.

"*Señor*," Cid Hamete said to the alchemist, "you don't have to do this. They can take us prisoner, they can even beat and torture us, but they can't force you to make a fool of yourself by assaulting what must be a fortified, impregnable windmill."

"No, they can't force me," Corwyn agreed. "I choose to do it. It's an adventure that seems to have been reserved for me ever since I crossed the Pyrenees into Spain, and this time I won't evade its calling." He gave the Morisco a lopsided grin. "Who knows, maybe I'll win. Wouldn't that be a surprise?"

The guard returned with *Roche-naissante* and Corwyn mounted, lifting Oliver up behind him. Before putting his heels to the animal's flanks, however, he once more addressed Cid Hamete. "When this is over, regardless of the outcome, I want you to swear that you will kill off Don Corwyn at the end of Part III and thereby put a stop to his insane adventures."

Cid Hamete considered this, then nodded. "I've been thinking of retiring from being a writer anyway," he said. "I think I'll return home to Argamasilla and make amends to my neighbors. Maybe I'll buy a flock of goats and take up the pastoral life of a shepherd. It should be at least as rewarding financially."

Corwyn acknowledged the Morisco's nod, then prodded his mount to his intended attack against the windmill. But the outcome of the ensuing battle, however futile it might seem, must wait to be told in the next chapter.

Chapter 22

Wherein is recorded Corwyn's most extraordinary and final encounter with a windmill, an event which has since been grossly misrepresented in popular fiction.

CORWYN SET OFF TOWARD THE WINDMILL FEELING THAT he was confronting a giant. He knew Hydro Phobius must have arranged some kind of trap—he just couldn't figure out what it might be.

He studied the windmill again, noticing that the only entrance at ground level was a small door set into the wall directly under the windmill's blades. Undoubtedly, the trap lay inside this door.

But the vanes of the windmill were turning slowly, and this gave Corwyn an idea. If he grabbed one of the arms, it would swing him up to the top of the structure, where he might be able to climb onto the walkway and get inside through the door Hydro Phobius had used when he came out to challenge Corwyn.

Then Corwyn halted *Roche-naissante*, trying to remember whether the blades of the windmill had been turning before. He didn't think they had. He moistened a finger and held it in the air. There wasn't any hint of a breeze.

Proceeding more slowly, Corwyn allowed himself a tight smile. Hydro Phobius had made a mistake. He had shown his hand too early, and now Corwyn knew what the real trap was. The vanes of the windmill had been set in motion through some power source inside the structure, allowing them to turn independently of the wind. Once Phobius had the blades revolving fast enough, they would create their own wind, sucking air toward the building and drawing anything else along that lay in the wind's path. If the wind were strong enough, it would suck Corwyn into the vortex, chopping him up in the swiftly spinning blades and flinging the leftover pieces of him against the windmill's stone wall.

What a gruesome death, Corwyn thought. *Who but Hydro Phobius would devise something like that?*

As Corwyn expected, the vanes began whirling faster the closer he got, and soon he could feel the breeze they made whipping against his face. Corwyn's smile broadened, for he had figured out a way to avoid his intended fate. If he got off *Roche-naissante* and crawled toward the windmill on his belly, he might be able to keep from being sucked up by the wind.

Then a cold knot of fear settled into his bowels. Why was the wind in his face?

He halted *Roche-naissante* again, worried now, realizing that even without his moving forward, the air still blew in his face. But when the windmill's blades were turning, they should be sucking air toward it. Something was wrong. He watched the revolving arms carefully, trying to see them anew.

They were turning in the wrong direction. Hydro Phobius had set up the structure to blow any attackers away from the windmill instead of drawing them into it. But what good would that do? It wouldn't get rid of the attackers permanently; it would merely annoy them. If they did get blown away from the front, they could come at it again from the opposite side, more determined than ever. They would still have to slip around to the front to get through the only door, but with enough determination and a strong enough attacking force, it would certainly be possible.

Had Hydro Phobius committed that grievous an oversight? It didn't sound like him.

The wind was becoming extremely strong now, the arms spinning very fast. Corwyn's hat bent back and the hem of his robe whipped in the wind. Sand stung his eyes. He dismounted from *Roche-naissante* to work his way to one side and then forward on foot. He could still crawl on the ground, going against the wind, if he needed to.

He was swinging his leg over *Roche-naissante*, his attention momentarily diverted, when the donkey brayed and shied violently. Corwyn barely had time to leap free of the stirrup and grab Oliver before the animal bolted away. Corwyn spun back toward the windmill to see what had startled the beast.

A number of shimmering, bloblike, greenish yellow shapes were issuing from vents in the roof of the windmill, then getting sucked into the spinning vanes from behind. The speed of the blades quickly chopped the forms up, blowing the shredded pieces toward Corwyn. But as soon as they were past the initial turbulence of the vanes, the blobs began reforming, drawing their scattered fragments back into themselves.

They were demons, and Hydro Phobius was blowing them directly at Corwyn.

Corwyn shuddered and wondered briefly whether he could outrun the fiends. But even mounted, he wouldn't have been fast enough. As they hurtled toward him on the wind, Corwyn realized that Hydro Phobius's plan left no avenue, not even an alleyway, for escape. The hideous shapes had already begun to violate Corwyn's soul, ripping open his most secret depths and turning them against him. His body felt sluggish, unresponsive, as if he were a boy facing some huge and terrible opponent, all while burdened with an adult's heavy brass armor, unable to move. Corwyn still had a hand on Oliver, and to his afflicted mind the broom seemed a spear, but of such a size and weight that he could not hope to wield it against his giant foe.

How odd, he thought, that the very armor which was supposed to protect him would be instead the cause of his undoing. He had the feeling that there was some greater significance for him in this, if he survived. But that, of course, was an impossibility.

So he stood, facing the Philistine, dragged down by the weight of the very armor he had borrowed for the match from a much larger king, armed not even with so much as a shepherd's sling. In a moment, the apparitions would be upon him, and he would be possessed.

Sebastian hoped they were nearing the end of the windmills. The boys were tired and straggling again. His own arms ached with playing and his head throbbed. He wondered whether his poor, abused ears would ever hear properly again.

He considered calling a rest, but was loath to give the forces of the Inquisition time to regroup. Surprise was the strongest weapon Sebastian had on his side, for if his opponents simply stopped up their ears, they would be immune to the noise. Sebastian had to keep them on the run and continue toppling windmills before they had a chance to come up with this remedy themselves.

A ways ahead, he saw a windmill larger than the rest, beyond which there arose no others. At last, he thought, they were reaching the end of the chain. Then Sebastian noticed that the vanes of this last windmill were turning, and that something repulsive and smokelike was billowing from the roof and blowing away from the structure on the wind created by its revolving arms. His stomach turned as he recognized the vile apparitions. But why were they being released? Had there been some terrible accident up ahead?

For a moment, he thought of leaving whatever Inquisition forces were stationed there to be possessed by the very demons they had sought to pump over the mountains into France. But even for the Inquisition, that seemed too harsh a fate. He motioned the boys to pick up the pace, hurrying toward the scene.

Then he saw Corwyn and broke into a run.

Corwyn gasped for breath and held it, knowing it would be his last but determined to resist being taken by the demons for as long as possible. The fiends were all around him now, and the blades of the windmill stopped turning. A dead calm fell over the land. One of the shapes settled on the air in front of Corwyn to wait, hovering so close to his nose that his sinuses burned. He held the lungful of air until his chest hurt from needing to breathe. Just when he thought he couldn't hold out any longer, certain that he would be possessed, the first strains of a peculiar sound reached him.

Apparently, the same notes reached the apparition in front of him as well, and whatever the thing used for ears picked up the sound, because it suddenly pulled back and convulsed, as in a supernatural version of a sneeze. The appearance of a giant it had assumed, robbing the image from Corwyn's own mind, now wavered and collapsed. For a moment, the demon drew inward upon itself until it was nothing but a smoky, roiling blob, lumpy and without definite form. Then it began corkscrewing backward through the air as rapidly as it could, desperate to escape the noise assaulting it. Its companions did the same. Even when the windmill started up again, the wind the vanes generated couldn't keep the apparitions from fleeing.

Corwyn could understand their determination, for the noise was dreadful. At first, it had sounded vaguely akin to music, but that illusion was quickly dispelled. The closer the sound got, the worse it became, and soon Corwyn's knees buckled, dropping him to the ground where he tried in vain to block out the noise by covering his ears.

Demonic possession began to seem the preferable fate, and he cursed Hydro Phobius for having developed something so hideous with which to torture his victims. He forced his eyes open, expecting to see his nemesis gloating from the railing around the top of the windmill. Instead, to his shock, he looked up in time to see the railing fall away, and great cracks appearing in the wall of the building. The demons had fled, working their way against the wind in their anxiety to escape the noise, and now there was no sight of them.

The cracks in the windmill widened, becoming gaps in the wall. Then the wall wasn't a wall any longer, but a plummeting avalanche of mortar and stone. Inside, complex equipment stood briefly revealed before it, too, was rent asunder by the force of the sound.

Corwyn turned, fighting the noise for control of his body, and saw Sebastian and a dozen students coming toward him, playing on instruments that must have been fashioned in hell. Sebastian waved gaily to the alchemist as he led the boys on past and toward the little house. Corwyn watched dumbly as the existing cracks in the house's plaster penetrated the underlying mud-brick walls as well, thinking there was some reason why he should object. A score or more people began pouring from the house like angry ants from an anthill, screaming and running for their lives as soon as they were outside.

Suddenly, Corwyn remembered the wineskins full of demons. "Stop!" he cried, the warning inaudible amid the din. He forced himself to his feet and lurched to the front of the students, waving his arms. *"Arrêtez!"* he shouted over and over until at last the boys stumbled to a halt and the sound of their playing died away.

The sudden silence roared deafeningly in Corwyn's ears. Scarcely able to hear his own words, he gasped for Sebastian to check the ruined windmill for Hydro Phobius.

"What?" Sebastian asked, pulling wads of cloth from his ears.

Corwyn drew a deep breath and repeated the command, then let his knees give way again and deposit him on the ground.

It was still only morning, but what a day it had been!

"Sebastian!" Corwyn, somewhat recovered, frowned as the younger alchemist returned from the ruined windmill, where he and the boys had captured a dazed and pathetic Hydro Phobius in the debris. Corwyn's frown was startled, however, rather than disapproving. "What are you and my students doing here?"

Sebastian scratched his head. *"Alors!* You know, it's funny but I've started thinking of them as my students now. But to answer your question, I suppose you could say we're here because of a message in a bottle." He grinned, evidently thinking this was some kind of joke.

"A bottle?" Corwyn's frown deepened. "You mean a vessel, like some kind of grail? Sebastian, you're not dragging *my* students all over the countryside on a foolish Grail Quest, are you?"

"Grail Quest? No, I don't think so. Although you could call it a grail, if you wanted to. But we're not looking for it, we're here because it sent us." He wrinkled his nose as if getting lost in his own convolutions. "All I mean is that we're here because of what happened with one of the bottles in the breath of demons test you set up before leaving. When we put minnows in the bottle with the sample you collected up near the headwaters of the Ale—"

"I didn't collect it," Corwyn interrupted, the pieces of the puzzle beginning to fall into place. "Toxemiah gave me that sample!"

"Was that where it came from?" Sebastian said. "That explains a lot."

"But didn't you read my note?" Corwyn asked. "I told you all about that sample."

"The oil of vitriol ate away most of the note before I could read it."

"Oil of vitriol?" Then Corwyn remembered. "Oh, yes. Ummm, go on with your story."

"Well, the minnows died right away, but I thought Jean-Claude had sabotaged the test."

"Reasonable assumption," Corwyn mumbled, eyeing the youth who was listening over Sebastian's shoulder.

"No, not as it turns out," Sebastian said.

"But only because I hadn't thought of it yet," Jean-Claude added, unable to refrain from joining the conversation.

Corwyn scowled at him.

"Anyway," Sebastian continued, "I thought he had purposely ruined the results, so as punishment I took him and the rest of the students into the mountains to collect another sample."

"Whom were you trying to punish," Corwyn asked, "them or you?"

Jean-Claude did his best to look insulted.

"And while we were up there," Sebastian went on patiently, ignoring them both, "we came across Toxemiah. From that encounter the whole thing got started. The bishop thought we were conjuring demons, so he held an inquisition over your library—"

Corwyn started to interrupt, wondering how conjuring demons fit into all of this and why the bishop would hold an inquisition over the library, then thought better of it.

"Anyway, after the library was burned—"

"Burned!"

"—we had to flee from Pomme de Terre so the same thing wouldn't happen to us. And that's how we got here, because of that one bottle."

Corwyn's head was spinning. "I see," he said at last. "You're here because of a bottle—a bottle from my breath of demons test at that—and you claim this bottle is a grail, but only because it sent you on this quest, not because you went looking for it. . . ." He trailed off, confused.

"I didn't *claim* it was a grail," Sebastian muttered. "I just said you could think of it that way."

"If you wanted to," Jean-Claude added.

Corwyn shook his head. "Never mind. I'll take your word for it. Just don't either of you try to explain any more of it to me."

Sebastian shrugged. Jean-Claude grinned, looking pleased with himself.

Corwyn started to walk off, then noticed Cid Hamete laughing a few paces away. He went up to the Morisco. "At least when they talk about a grail, they're referring to a real vessel, not a book or library."

"But a book or library *can* be a grail," Cid Hamete said. "For you, I suspect that's probably the case. The point is that anything can be a grail, as long as it has special meaning for the person seeking it."

"That's ridiculous," Corwyn snapped. "If a grail can be anything, then how does a person know what to look for, or where?"

"That's what the Grail Quest is all about," Cid Hamete replied with an enigmatic smile. "It is the responsibility of each person to seek his own grail, without knowing what it will be or where he will find it." Abruptly, his expression became serious and he gazed at Oliver, who was off chasing butterflies. "For some, the true grail might even be a thing as simple yet profound as a broom." With his maimed hand, he touched the tiny silver vial suspended on a chain around his neck, and Corwyn recalled having seen him make this gesture previously. "Especially when that broom is a vessel of absolute innocence and purity."

Corwyn felt a twinge of uneasiness at this, as if he had been excluded from something, and he wondered again what had transpired between the Morisco and Oliver while they had journeyed together, following him. Oliver had never had a friend who had not been Corwyn's as well, and the newness of the situation troubled him.

"You certainly take liberties in interpreting a legend I created," he said bitterly. "One would think you had invented the Holy Grail."

Cid Hamete shrugged, the gesture as indefinite as Sebastian's had been a few moments earlier, and just as aggravating. "I reinvented it, as everyone does for whom the legend takes on significance," Cid Hamete said. He looked again at Oliver, then spun back to Corwyn as if he had just decided the outcome of some inner struggle. "Did you know *Al-Aver* sheds tears?"

"What?" Corwyn flushed, embarrassed that the Morisco might be telling him something he hadn't known about his own creation. "No he doesn't. And it's Oliver, not *Al-Aver*."

Cid Hamete smiled again, holding up the vial on its chain. "He cried after dismissing you outside Barcelona. I was so moved, I collected the tears in this flask."

"You act as if they were some kind of sacred relic," Corwyn said, angry with himself for having caused the broom such distress, but taking it out on Cid Hamete. "And here I thought you were a good Christian."

"But I am a good Christian." Cid Hamete's words were sharp, his expression stern. "You have no reason to call my faith into question, *señor*, for I have accepted the holy trinity—Allah the father, Hey Zeus, and the Sacred Djinn."

Corwyn eyed the Morisco in disbelief. "It's pronounced '*Hay-soos*,' not 'Hey, Zeus.' "

"That's what I said—Hey Zeus, born of the Urchin Mary."

Corwyn threw back his head and laughed. "I think it would be best if you stayed away from the topic of religion while we're traveling together," he called to the Morisco over his shoulder as he walked away. "I'd hate for the Inquisition to think you and I share the same views."

Yet what Cid Hamete had said about Oliver's crying haunted him, and he remembered having wondered something of that sort before leaving the broom on the way to Barcelona. Corwyn had even touched one of the droplets, finding it sticky and thinking it had been sap from some tree limb Oliver had brushed against. So it had been one of Oliver's tears after all! But it hadn't felt like a normal tear. Which made sense, Corwyn realized now—Oliver's tears wouldn't be the same as anyone else's. They wouldn't be ordinary saltwater. But what would they be?

He jerked to a stop as the answer hit him.

Aqua mysterium.

He shook his head, not liking this answer. But it wouldn't go away. What had Cid Hamete called Oliver— a vessel of absolute innocence and purity? Then what would the contents of such a vessel be?

The answer was still the same—*aqua mysterium*, as if Oliver truly was a kind of grail. Corwyn shivered, feeling a chill slide down his spine. How long had it been since he'd created Oliver, and perhaps in all that time never really known the broom?

It is the responsibility of each person to seek his own grail, Cid Hamete had said, *without knowing what it will be or where he will find it.*

Corwyn strode over to the wreckage of the main windmill, pretending to study it, needing to be alone. He had much to think about, and most of it was very humbling.

Some might say that it was about time he regained a sense of humility, for he had often been difficult to put up with during this journey. Yet perhaps we should not condemn him too hastily. After all, might not he be forgiven this brief interval of self-pity after living for so many hundreds of years? It is an affliction to which even the noblest sometimes succumb.

At any rate, we may be assured that he either is now or soon will be over his Middle Ages malaise, and neither he nor we will need to endure it much longer.

Chapter 23

In which is recorded Corwyn's memorable descent into the Cave of Montesinos, after which he and Oliver retire to a distant realm quaintly known as "the land beyond the forest."

A LITTLE AFTER MIDDAY, A BREEZE DID GUST ACROSS northern Spain, kicking up dust from the piles of rubble that had been windmills. Corwyn, sitting beside the largest of those piles, heaved a sigh, having decided half an hour before what he must do, yet still wanting to put it off. Occasionally, he had heard voices talking softly behind him, and knew Cid Hamete, Sebastian, and the students were being very respectful of his privacy. Only Oliver had wandered over and seated himself beside the alchemist, blithely ignoring Corwyn's efforts to cut himself off from everyone.

Corwyn was grateful to the broom for that.

But now he had work to do. He patted the broom affectionately—a difficult accomplishment when one is patting a broom, but Corwyn had had centuries in which to practice. Then he pushed himself to his feet and walked over to the house.

It had an empty, desolate feel to it now, its inhabitants having fled. Yet it retained an air of unexplained mystery. Corwyn examined the cracked and sagging walls, the door hanging askew from its jamb. Gently, he pushed the door open and went inside.

As he had suspected, the "house" consisted of a single, unused room. The real purpose for the building was to disguise a hole the size of a large well in the dirt floor. Through this hole, the cavern beneath this site could be entered. Over the opening, a windlass had been erected, making the hole look even more like a well, except for the fact that this windlass raised and lowered a small wooden platform rather than a bucket. It was by means of this platform that "wineskins" full of demons had been lowered into the cavern for treatment and storage; and it was the same platform which had raised and lowered the men who worked below.

It was also the platform which would now take Corwyn into the bowels of hell.

He turned resolutely from the opening and went to find Sebastian. It wasn't hard to do; Corwyn almost ran over the young man as he emerged from the house, which led him to suspect that Sebastian had been hovering outside, keeping an eye out for the older alchemist's welfare. Corwyn apologized gruffly for bumping into Sebastian, then he asked to borrow the young man's sword.

Sebastian looked startled. "My sword?"

"Oui," Corwyn said, his hand out. "Just for a while . . . I hope."

Sebastian's hand jumped to the hilt, though whether to draw the sword for Corwyn or to protect it from him wasn't clear. "You know this sword is very important to me—that it was my father's?"

Corwyn nodded. "I know, and I will do my best to take care of it. But right now I need it for dealing with the wineskins full of demons."

Sebastian drew the sword reluctantly and laid it across Corwyn's open hand, his fingers lingering on the hilt as if caressing it. He looked again at Corwyn, and his expression was a plea.

"I'll be careful with it," Corwyn assured him again. "By your own blade"—he rested his other hand on the cold steel—"I swear it."

That seemed to mollify the young man, who glanced at the sword quickly and nodded, then shuffled away. Corwyn drew a deep breath and went looking for Cid Hamete. The request he had to make of the Morisco would be every bit as difficult—at least, it would be for Cid Hamete.

He found the writer sitting in the shade of the olive grove, scribbling in his notebook at a furious pace. "Ah, *señor*," he said, glancing up at Corwyn, "I must thank you for your exploit today. It was most helpful—just what I needed for my book."

"I didn't do it for you," Corwyn growled. Then, remembering his purpose, he added, "But you're welcome . . . I guess."

Cid Hamete had gone back to writing and seemed scarcely aware of Corwyn's reply. Corwyn cleared his throat. The Morisco paused and looked up again, his expression annoyed at this second interruption. "*¿Sí?*"

"I need to perform another, er . . . exploit." The word rose with difficulty to his tongue.

Cid Hamete's face brightened. "That's wonderful of you, *señor*. Very generous. I can't thank you enough."

"But I'll need your help."

Cid Hamete scowled. "It's really much better if I don't get personally involved. There's been too much of that already." He shuddered. "I should remain off to one side, where I can watch and record everything that happens. Otherwise, if I take a more active part, it ruins the objectivity of my writing. You understand, don't you, *señor*?"

"Oh, of course." Corwyn uttered the words through clenched teeth, trying to coat them with honey. "And this won't require you to take part in the exploit at all. I just need the contents of the vial around your neck."

Cid Hamete blanched and grabbed the vial. "*¿Qué?*"

Corwyn squatted. Not sure what to do with the sword, he laid it across his lap. Cid Hamete eyed the blade uneasily. Corwyn rested his hand on the weapon's hilt. "You said Oliver could be a grail, and that he is a vessel of absolute purity and innocence—"

"Innocence and purity," Cid Hamete corrected, eyes still on the blade.

"What?"

"Innocence and purity," the Morisco repeated. "You had the words turned around."

"Very well, innocence and purity," Corwyn said, restraining himself. "At any rate, I need the contents of that grail now to combat the demons stored here underground."

Cid Hamete's glance, even more nervous than before, darted across the ground where he sat, considering the implications of the alchemist's words. "Couldn't we just leave them there?" he asked hopefully. "Seal up the entrance, perhaps?"

Corwyn shook his head. "We don't know how many other cracks or vents there might be through which they could eventually seep out. We can't risk that." He paused, then added, "It might look bad to your readers if these demons escaped, especially if they knew you could have prevented it."

"That's not fair, *señor*."

"No," Corwyn agreed, "it's not."

The Morisco tried to hold the alchemist's stare, but at last he fidgeted and looked away. "All right," he grumbled, lifting the chain from around his neck and handing it to Corwyn. "But I don't like it."

Corwyn made sure he had the vial firmly in his grip, then said, "I don't like being the subject of your books." Without waiting for a reply, he rose and walked back to the small building, Sebastian's sword in one hand, the chain and vial from Cid Hamete in the other.

He explained to Sebastian what he intended to do and what he needed from the younger alchemist and the students. Sebastian started to offer to go in his master's place, but Corwyn cut him off. "You're in charge of these boys now; they need you. And you're going to be a father. You can't risk your life at every whim anymore."

Sebastian rewarded him with a thin smile and Corwyn stepped onto the platform. Just then, Oliver rushed past Sebastian and tried to join Corwyn, but the alchemist wouldn't let him. "You stay here," he said. "Until I get back."

He couldn't voice the words he wanted to say—that he didn't want Oliver trapped down there if anything happened to him.

The broom moved away reluctantly and Corwyn nodded to Sebastian. "*Tiens*, lower me down."

Sebastian and the students slowly let the windlass crank unwind, reeling off rope from the drum. The platform lowered jerkily, and Corwyn grabbed the rope for support. For a while after leaving sight of the room, he was suspended in blackness. Somehow, it hadn't occurred to him to bring a torch. The morning's "exploit" must have affected his senses more than he'd realized.

Eventually, the walls of the shaft opened out and the platform set down on the floor of a small cavern. Corwyn could see something of the place because, fortunately, a few of the torches left behind when the workers abandoned the cavern earlier were still sputtering. Corwyn found a stack of fresh torches and quickly had new ones burning.

The small cavern he was in opened onto another where the demonic wastes had been stabilized, as Corwyn had suspected. He checked to see that none of the wastes were still in the chamber, then hurried on to the next. Finally, after passing through a series of smaller chambers devoted to specialized tasks, he found the one he was after. It was a huge cavern, with rack upon rack of skins, shimmering and pulsing with a faint light of their own. Corwyn's stomach turned at the sight, and he thought he could detect a hint of sulfur in the air. He approached the skins on wobbly legs.

Even through the skins, the demonic presences seemed aware of him and reached out to probe his soul. Corwyn had difficulty remembering where he was and what he had come here to do, for it seemed to him that he stood in the center of hell itself, watching the fiends at their entertainments. Two devils in particular caught his attention. They were playing badminton with rackets of fire, and whenever they hit the shuttlecock it burst into flames and disintegrated, forcing them to start over.

Corwyn shook his head to dispel the vision. He squatted and again laid the sword across his lap, then carefully opened the vial. With trembling hands, he shook a drop or two of the sticky fluid out and smeared it over both sides of the blade. Then he stood, gripped the sword with both hands, and walked to the nearest skin.

The vision of hell returned, stronger this time. Now Corwyn could smell the sulfurous smoke (or was that the demons in the skins he smelled?), and he could feel the heat of the fiery rackets the two badminton players used. They were growling and surly, possibly because they could never return one another's volleys and constantly had to start anew. The heat seemed to singe Corwyn's beard and eyebrows.

He forced himself closer and plunged the sword into the nearest skin. The sword quivered and the hilt burned his hands, but he held it firmly. After a few moments, the quivering and burning stopped. Corwyn withdrew the sword. A trickle of clear water oozed from the cut in the skin. Corwyn watched it for any sign of active demons. When there wasn't any, he slit the skin open and examined the contents.

Water flowed over his feet, leaving only a layer of gritty, insoluble salt in the bottom of the skin—all that was left of the demons. The *aqua mysterium* had precipitated them out in solid form, binding them up for the next millennium as impure crystals.

Corwyn went to the next skin and again drove the sword through the thick hide. This time, however, he didn't bother to cut the skin open afterward, knowing the demons inside had been incapacitated. He hurried on to the next.

Despite his successes, however, the image of the hellish badminton game kept returning. And each time, it got worse. Instead of shuttlecocks, the two fiends began using books, and these too burst into flame and disintegrated when struck with the rackets. It wasn't so bad when the fiends started out using popular chivalric romances, then went on to Cid Hamete's two volumes of *El Ingenioso Alquimista Don Corwyn de La Mancha*. In fact, Corwyn rather enjoyed seeing them ignite and burn, leaving only ashy residues. Yet he felt the intensity of the heat more than before, as if his own being was somehow caught up in those books. Whatever punishment was dealt to them seemed to be inflicted on him as well.

From these, the fiends went on to other, more valuable books, graduating eventually to the volumes once contained in the library of Alexandria. By this time, Corwyn's anguish was excruciating. He reminded himself that the books weren't real, that they were merely illusions conjured up by the demons to torment him. But that didn't help. He still felt the destruction of each ancient, irreplaceable text as a personal loss.

He hurried faster, struggling to control his shaking hands. But he had to be careful not to go too fast, for he couldn't risk letting the contents of a skin leak out before the *aqua mysterium* on the blade had worked its purifying effect.

At last, it was he himself who was being bandied about by the fiends with the flaming rackets, burning up each time he was struck only to reappear again for yet another fiery volley. The distinction between himself and the books he had seen destroyed earlier became vague, uncertain. He wasn't sure any longer whether he was a person or one of those books, nor did he know which of these states—book or person—held the greater reality.

The experience left him emotionally drained as well as physically exhausted, and when at last the final skin had been decontaminated, the remnants of the vision still clung to his mind, refusing to vanish. He stumbled wearily back to the platform and signaled his readiness to be taken back up. But though he left the hellish underworld behind, he knew he also carried part of it within him. He had the uncomfortable feeling that he would be dealing with the questions this encounter raised and the doubts it engendered for years to come.

Two weeks later, Corwyn and Oliver sat in the sunshine outside an abandoned shepherd's hut in the mountains above Pomme de Terre. They were playing a game Oliver had invented which used a number of sticks and small, rounded stones, and although Corwyn had little notion of the rules or object of the game, he was content to go through the motions because it delighted Oliver.

In many ways, Corwyn felt he had just begun to truly know the broom during these past two weeks of idyllic seclusion.

He heard someone scrabbling over the stony ground and looked up to see Sebastian hurrying to greet them. The younger man arrived out of breath and trying to talk anyway, succeeding only in giving himself a case of the hiccups.

"You were right," he said at last, as soon as he was capable of gasping out anything. "She had twins—a boy and a girl. Gwen's doing fine and, oh, they're wonderful!"

Corwyn smiled. A longtime observer of the ebb and flow of life, he nevertheless felt the stirring of renewed hope such news always brought him. "I'm glad," he said. "And the students?"

"*Alors*, they're doing fine, the little rascals." Sebastian grinned. "Actually, I think they've been going easy on me since we've been back, because of the excitement of the births. But that'll wear off in time and things will get back to normal."

"You sound as though you're enjoying being headmaster as well as a full-fledged, master alchemist."

"*Oui*," Sebastian admitted, blushing. "I am. So much so, in fact, that it surprises me."

Corwyn nodded, satisfied. "You'll do fine."

"But are you certain you won't come back to Pomme de Terre?" Sebastian asked, his expression turning serious.

"No," Corwyn said. "My work there is in good hands, and I suspect you'll actually do better for my not being around, watching over your shoulder and criticizing all the time. The bishop seems placated by the idea that I'm dead, and there's nothing to fear from Hydro Phobius now that he's been committed to La Casa del Nuncio for thinking he was me—or rather, that he was Don Corwyn." The alchemist's smile widened as he recalled how they had been able to turn Phobius's plan against him, convincing the king of Aragon that Hydro Phobius had really believed he was who he'd pretended to be. Despite its elegant name, "La Casa del Nuncio" was nothing more than an asylum in Toledo where madmen too dangerous for society were imprisoned.

"It's time I retire," Corwyn went on. "I'm looking forward to relaxing, doing a little reading, and spending more time with Oliver."

The broom glanced up at hearing his name, then turned his attention back to the game.

"Oh, speaking of reading reminds me!" Sebastian reached under his *bliaut* and removed a small, well-worn book. "Here, you'll probably want to start a new library when you get wherever you're going."

Corwyn accepted the book with a puzzled frown. "Is this all that's left of my library here?"

"Oui," Sebastian said, then amended, "Well, almost. There is one other book, *Tristan and Yseult*, but Gwen was hoping you'd be willing to leave it with her."

Corwyn grimaced. "Gladly. May it please her more than it would me."

"It will. You know how she loves romances of chivalry." Sebastian looked hesitant, then blurted out, "She's writing one herself."

"What?"

"She's calling it *Le Morte Darthur*."

Corwyn groaned.

"It's not bad, actually," Sebastian hurried on, still sounding out of breath. "I think she wants to publish it when it's finished. There's a printer in England, a man named Caxton, I suggested she approach. He's shown an interest in books about English history."

"Mmmm." Hoping to change the subject, Corwyn turned the book over in his hand and glanced at the title. He groaned again more loudly. "*Summa Thaumaturgica*? Sebastian, what's this?"

"How did you think I managed to enchant the instruments the boys and I were playing?" Sebastian replied belligerently.

"I thought you just couldn't play them very well," Corwyn mumbled.

"Besides," Sebastian went on, "I found it in *your* library."

"It must have been an accident." Then the old alchemist smiled. "Well, maybe I should look into thaumaturgy. There seems to be more to it than I have acknowledged. Besides, it'll give me something to dabble in during retirement."

Sebastian's expression grew downcast. "But where will you go? Will we ever see you again?"

"You're always welcome to come and visit me," Corwyn replied. "I think I've found just the place in which to retire—a tranquil, little-known realm whose name means 'the land beyond the forest.' "

"The land beyond the forest," Sebastian repeated. "It has a pleasant sound."

He tried to sound interested, but Corwyn caught his glances in the direction of Pomme de Terre and knew he was already anxious to return home.

Corwyn nodded and rose. "If you need me, you can always find me there." He embraced Sebastian fondly, if a little awkwardly, then turned him to face downhill. "Now go on home. That's where your mind is, and where you're needed as well. Oliver and I'll be all right."

Sebastian started down the slope, trying not to act too eager. A few steps away, he stopped and called back over his shoulder, "What's this place called? I mean, its actual name?"

"Transylvania."

Sebastian repeated the word to himself a few times, then waved and hurried off.

"Well, Oliver," Corwyn said when the young man had disappeared from sight. "What do you say? Shall we get started?"

The broom bobbed up excitedly, promptly forgetting his game, and together the two friends started out, each looking forward to the peace and quiet of their new home.

Epilogue

BELIEVING, THEREFORE, THAT THE ARMS OF THE WIND-
mill were causing the wind rather than turning as a
result of it, and further convinced that this vile creature
(as he perceived it to be) was trying to blow him off the
face of the earth, the noble Don Corwyn hurtled toward
the structure at as rapid a gait as Rociandante could
be coaxed into running. He raised Al-Aver aloft as he
had when initiating his adventures with his assault on
a similar windmill in his first sally.

This time, however, the result was much more tragic,
and Don Corwyn impaled himself on his staff even as the
broomstick was driven deep into an arm of the windmill by
the force of the collision. So Don Corwyn died, revolving
on the blades of one of the very machines which marked
both the zenith and the nadir of his famous career.

Such was the end of the Ingenious Alchemist-Errant of
La Mancha. The whole story having been told, therefore,
I now hang my quill to rest upon this wall; may it
and Don Corwyn rest peacefully together, and let no
presumptuous or malignant historians attempt to take
it down once more, profaning both the pen and its
noble subject by bringing the alchemist-errant back to
life falsely and inventing interminable stories about his
achievements.

For me alone was Don Corwyn born, and I for him; it was his to act, mine to write; we two together made but one, in spite of that pretended writer Alonso Fernández de Avellaneda, who dared to venture with his great, coarse, ill-trimmed ostrich quill to write the achievements of my valiant alchemist-errant. Here was no burden fit for Avellaneda's shoulders nor subject for his sluggish wit. If perchance you should come to know him, warn him to leave at rest the weary, moldering bones of Don Corwyn where they lie and not attempt to carry them off, in opposition to all the laws of death, to Zaragoza, making the alchemist-errant rise from the grave where in reality he lies stretched at full length, powerless to make any further expedition or new sally.

And I shall remain satisfied to have been the first who has ever enjoyed the fruit of his writing as fully as he could desire; for my wish has been no other than to cause mankind to abhor the false and foolish books of alchemy, which, thanks to these accounts of the true Don Corwyn, are even now tottering and doomed to fall. Gracias y adiós.

—Cid Hamete Benengeli,
  El Ingenioso Alquimista
  Don Corwyn de La Mancha, Part III

DOUGLAS W. CLARK spent much of his childhood playing at and around the small sewage treatment plant in southern New Mexico where his father worked as a civil engineer—an experience that was to influence him for the rest of his life. He writes, "Water takes on a mystic quality in any desert culture, and so it did for me. Yet in the world I was introduced to at the treatment plant, water was also irrevocably associated with mechanical systems and analytical thinking, with logic and reason and conscious application of the human mind. So it has come to symbolize both aspects for me, maintaining them in an uneasy state of dynamic tension, a constant struggle that somehow straddles the unbridgeable gap between logic and illogic, between reason and intuition, science and art." Later he traveled to Europe with his parents, visiting the usual tourist attractions—and exploring the history of Western civilization as revealed by its legacy of water and sewage works, from ancient Roman aqueducts to modern treatment plants.

Mr. Clark earned his B.S. in biology at the University of New Mexico, but after a brief foray in graduate school, found himself back in the "family business" as a laboratory technician at the local sewage treatment plant. Eventually he began publishing technical articles and founded a newsletter, *The Bench Sheet*, for laboratory analysts involved with water and sewage. It was on the pages of that newsletter that Corwyn, the world's only aquatic alchemist, was born. Though he has since sold the newsletter, Mr. Clark has continued to write about Corwyn's adventures in short stories and novels.

A note of warning, however: Any similarity which the reader might perceive between Cid Hamete Benengeli's accounts of Don Corwyn as quoted in this book, and the stories related about the "real" Corwyn in Mr. Clark's two previous novels, *Alchemy Unlimited* and *Rehearsal for a Renaissance*, must be considered coincidence. After all, what author would ever treat his own works so scandalously?